RE

A KING'S RANSOM

"James Grippando is a very inventive and
ingenious storyteller."
Nelson DeMille

"A well-thought-out thriller. . . . [Nick is an]
engaging character, resourceful and lifelike.
His father . . . captures our interest from
the moment we lay eyes on him. And the
plot . . . is convoluted without being overly
labyrinthine. . . . Readers who appreciate
an intelligent thriller will be well pleased."
Booklist

"Grisham will probably wish he'd thought of it.
Grippando proves he's worthy of this
comparison with fast-paced
A King's Ransom."
Miami Herald

"Grippando's writing is crisp, his characters
sympathetic and well-drawn."
San Antonio Express-News

"Former Florida lawyer James Grippando's
skills as a storyteller have ensured that
he'll never have to worry again
about billable hours."
Milwaukee Journal Sentinel

"Grippando is *really* good."
James Patterson

"[A] fast pace . . . surprising twists. . . .
Nick is an easy hero to root for. . . .
Grippando skillfully weaves together
a chain of unlikely events, creating
a page-turner that will assuredly
be popular."
Library Journal

"Grippando writes with the authenticity
of an insider."
John Douglas, *New York Times*
bestselling author of *Mind Hunter*

"The thriller writer to watch."
Wall Street Journal

"Grippando excels."
St. Paul Pioneer Press

"James Grippando [creates]
hard-to-resist novels."
Ft. Lauderdale Sun-Sentinel

"From Alfred Hitchcock to
Harlan Coben . . . Grippando has a secure
place on that list. . . . [He] just gets
better and better."
Newport News Daily Press

"**G**rippando shows . . . storytelling brilliance."
San Diego Union-Tribune

"**[A** *King's Ransom*] will kidnap your
imagination from the first
heart-pounding scene."
Barbara Parker

"**[G**rippando] writes in the realm of
Harlan Coben with a breakneck pace that
begs for a big screen adaptation."
Jackson Clarion-Ledger

"**G**rippando obviously has a keen eye on
what readers like in a bestselling mystery."
Naples Daily News

"**[G**rippando] hits the bulls-eye. . . . His
punchy plotting builds up a quick and
enjoyable head of steam."
Kirkus Reviews

"**[H**e delivers] exciting and cleverly
plotted novels."
Denver Post

"**I**'m a James Grippando fan.
I've read every book . . . and
I'm waiting for the next."
Phillip Margolin, *New York Times*
bestselling author

By James Grippando

Afraid of the Dark*+
Money to Burn+
Intent to Kill
Born to Run*+
Last Call*+
Lying with Strangers
When Darkness Falls*+
Got the Look*+
Hear No Evil*
Last to Die*
Beyond Suspicion*
A King's Ransom
Under Cover of Darkness+
Found Money
The Abduction
The Informant
The Pardon*

Coming Soon in Hardcover
Need You Now+

And for Young Adults
Leapholes

*A Jack Swyteck Novel
+Also featuring FBI agent Andie Henning

ATTENTION: ORGANIZATIONS AND CORPORATIONS
Most Harper paperbacks are available at special quantity discounts
for bulk purchases for sales promotions, premiums, or fund-raising.
For information, please call or write:

Special Markets Department, HarperCollins Publishers,
10 East 53rd Street, New York, New York 10022-5299.
Telephone: (212) 207-7528.   Fax: (212) 207-7222.

JAMES GRIPPANDO

A king's ran$om

HARPER

An Imprint of HarperCollinsPublishers

This is a work of fiction. Names, characters, places, and incidents are products of the author's imagination or are used fictitiously and are not to be construed as real. Any resemblance to actual events, locales, organizations, or persons, living or dead, is entirely coincidental.

HARPER

An Imprint of HarperCollinsPublishers
10 East 53rd Street
New York, New York 10022-5299

Copyright © 2001 by James Grippando
Excerpt from *Need You Now* copyright © 2012 by James Grippando
Author photo © Monica Hopkins Photography
ISBN 978-0-06-202453-4

All rights reserved. No part of this book may be used or reproduced in any manner whatsoever without written permission, except in the case of brief quotations embodied in critical articles and reviews. For information address Harper paperbacks, an Imprint of HarperCollins Publishers.

First Harper premium printing: December 2011
First Avon Books mass market printing: October 2002
First HarperCollins hardcover printing: May 2001

HarperCollins® and Harper® are registered trademarks of Harper-Collins Publishers.

Printed in the United States of America

Visit Harper paperbacks on the World Wide Web at
www.harpercollins.com

10 9 8 7 6 5 4 3 2

If you purchased this book without a cover, you should be aware that this book is stolen property. It was reported as "unsold and destroyed" to the publisher, and neither the author nor the publisher has received any payment for this "stripped book."

In memory of Artie Pine—onward and upward!

Part One

Some called it a crown jewel. Others said it was a diamond in the rough, with the emphasis on rough. It was a matter of perspective, whether Cartagena stood apart from the violence that besieged Colombia or was shrinking in its shadow.

It was one of the Caribbean's most striking port cities, a special blend of colonial heritage, natural beauty, and *salsa* into the wee hours. The top attraction was the old town, a city within the city, surrounded by nearly six miles of impressive fortress walls that were built under four centuries of Spanish reign. There were smaller marvels too, like *cazuela de mariscos*, a local seafood soup with chunks of cassava instead of potatoes—*deliciosa!* The crowded beaches on the Bocagrande peninsula weren't spectacular, but white sand and turquoise seas were close enough at Playa Blanca or, even better, Islas del Rosario. Throughout the city, colonial mansions painted in pastels and electric blue stood as reminders that the overall feeling here was decidedly tropical, in no small part Afro-Caribbean. Glorified by countless artists and writers over the centuries, Cartagena continued to evoke romantic sentiments as a unique place that, despite the influx of luxury condos, managed to retain the feel of Old San Juan and Havana in its heyday. It was, after all, the official "sister city" to beautiful Coral Gables, Florida.

Yet behind the exotic intrigue, beyond the hopeful hype of tourist agents, lurked an element of danger that was a fact of life in modern-day Colombia. Especially for an American.

Matthew Rey had visited Colombia before and was aware of the tragic headlines. Eleven sport fishermen kidnapped on their boat off Barranquilla. Busloads of children commandeered on their way to school in Ocaña, north of Bogotá. More than a hundred churchgoers taken at gunpoint in the middle of a Catholic mass in Cali. As a businessman, Matthew didn't deny the risks of a country besieged by four decades of civil war. As a fisherman, he savored the natural beauty, albeit from a half mile offshore.

Matthew was in the commercial fishing business, which was big business indeed. He'd started his company in Miami with a rusted but trusted old lobster boat and a mountain of debt. Twenty years later he was part owner of Rey's Seafood Company with forty boats and two processing plants in Nicaragua. With the United States importing more than eighteen million pounds of edible fish *weekly* from Central and South America, he was always looking for new equipment, opportunities for expansion.

It was that kind of thinking that had brought him to Colombia.

"Hector!" he shouted.

He got no reply. He tried again, louder. "Hector!"

Hector Díaz was one of six Nicaraguan crewmen that Matthew had brought to Cartagena to overhaul three old shrimp boats and bring them back to the Mosquito Coast. They were the *Niña*, the *Pinta*, and the *Coco Loco*. It was just a hunch, but something told Matthew they weren't originally a set. All three were anchored side by side in the bay like a pontoon bridge, close enough together for the workers to step from one to the next. A noisy generator on the *Pinta*, the middle boat, powered the working lights and welding tools for all three, making it impossible for Matthew to be heard from one boat to the next.

He switched off the generator. The lights went out, the noise stopped. It was just past sunset, but the afterglow afforded just enough natural light for the men to see each other.

"You done fixing the head yet?" asked Matthew.

Hector had been working on the plumbing all afternoon. "All but the marble tile and Kohler bidet, boss."

He was a habitual wisecracker but worth the trouble, as he and his son Liván could be trusted to sail just about anything from *Punto A* to *Punto B*, even three old shrimp boats. Hector was half Miskito Indian, and in Matthew's book the Miskitos were the greatest fishermen on earth. For centuries their tribe had fished the Caribbean along Nicaragua's Mosquito Coast. Tall and lean, the Miskitos were natural divers, and in his prime Hector had been a top lobster diver. His skills were legendary, like the story of the time he and Matthew got lost in a blinding storm at sea. Hector promptly jumped off the boat and dived down thirty-five feet for a good look around the reef. In a matter of minutes he popped back up and told Matthew to turn the boat around and hold the course steady for about three hours. They sailed into port two hours and forty-five minutes later. Only then did Matthew fully appreciate the way the Miskitos knew their ocean—top and bottom—like their own backyard.

Matthew smiled and shouted back, joking, "You're worthless, you know that?"

"That's why I work for you, boss."

Matthew snarled, but it was just a game they played. In truth, he envied Hector. Fishing had been a long tradition in the Díaz family, passed on from father to son for generations of Miskitos. Matthew had a son too, but not the same bond that Hector and Liván shared.

The sun was gone, the orange and purple afterglow fading. All along the rim of the bay, city lights emerged as twilight turned to darkness. Cartagena was coming to life. The parties would soon begin in earnest. The first time Matthew had visited the city, he'd ended up playing the accordion in some bar that boasted authentic *vallenato* music of the local *costeño* people. He couldn't vouch for the music, but the one-fifty rum had delivered as promised. That was twenty years ago. Cartagena had changed much since then. He'd changed, too. Coke instead of beer and rum, and his bladder wasn't what it used to be. Just one stinking soda and already he had to break the proverbial pee seal.

He started belowdecks, then stopped, startled by the shouting up top.

"*¡Manos arriba!*" Hands up!

It had come from the *Niña*, two boats away. Matthew climbed two rungs of the bridge ladder, just high enough to see over the clutter on the deck of the middle boat. Hector and Liván were face-to-face with five men with guns.

On impulse, Matthew dived for cover behind a huge pile of shrimp nets. From there he could see three of his crew members on the *Pinta* standing on deck with their hands over their heads. The fourth was crouched down in the bridge, hiding, as yet unspotted by the guerrillas. He caught Matthew's eye and silently mouthed the word, "*¡Guerrilleros!*"

Matthew's heart pounded. For all his travels, he'd never actually laid eyes on armed guerrillas before. All wore ski masks, high leather army boots, and black leather gloves. Their green combat fatigues and bright red armbands were typical uniforms. One wore a cowboy hat that was flipped up on one side, Australian-style, and a grenade attached to his belt. Matthew had heard that these bands of rebels were brazen enough to dress as the guerrillas that they were, never blending into the crowd with disguises, thriving on the publicity their group garnered from their very public crimes. They'd probably been watching the boats for hours, waiting for darkness so that they could pull up in silence and take the busy crew by surprise. That was the problem with noisy generators after sunset. If the crew was focused on work, an aircraft carrier could pull alongside them and no one would notice.

From his hiding spot, and with the generator off,

Matthew was close enough to hear Hector arguing with the men in Spanish two boats away.

"Where's the American?"

"No American here," said Hector.

"We know he's here."

"You must have the wrong boats."

"Who's that?"

Matthew peered out from behind the nets. The guy doing the talking, the one wearing the hat, had focused on Liván.

"Julio Iglesias," said Hector.

"You think this is a joke?"

"You don't want the boy. He's Nicaraguan, not American."

"I said, who is he?"

"My son."

The guerrilla delivered a quick blow with the butt of his rifle. Liván's head jerked back, and then he stumbled backward and fell to the deck, his face bloodied.

Hector rushed to him. "Liván!"

The guerrilla stood over them, his tone louder and more threatening. "Once more, where is the American?"

"You broke his nose!"

"And with the next shot I kill him. Where's the American?"

Matthew had to do something, but what? Five men with automatic weapons, and he was unarmed. Just then he caught sight of one of his workers on the *Pinta*, the one the guerrillas had not yet accounted for. He was crawling toward the rail, armed with a shotgun that was kept aboard for emergencies. Quietly, he took aim.

Matthew sensed disaster. If the shotgun discharged, they'd all be killed. He had only one choice: reveal himself. He was sure they'd take the American alive and spare the others.

"It's me you want!" he shouted in English, but it was too late. The shotgun blasted. One of the guerrillas was hit, his chest exploding in red. His body dropped through the open hatch and into the hull. The other four immediately returned fire with fully automatic assault rifles. A barrage of bullets rained down on the *Pinta*, bits and pieces of the wood trim splintering into the air, the windows shattering. Paint cans exploded, ruptured cans of mineral spirits spilled onto the deck. One of the workers was bleeding from the head, his body motionless on the deck. The others leaped off the boat and into the harbor.

It was all happening at once, but in Matthew's mind the sequence seemed to unfold separately, as if in slow motion. His panicked workers diving off the *Pinta* into the bay. The guerrillas scattering and firing wildly. And finally, in one cruel and senseless act, the tough guy in the Australian hat spraying the deck of the *Niña* with a shower of bullets. Dozens of crimson welts exploded across the bodies of Hector and Liván.

"No!"

It crushed Matthew's spirit, as he knew instantly that his friends were dead. The guerrillas turned their guns toward Matthew, two boats away, but they didn't shoot. The three surviving crew members who'd abandoned ship were swimming away in the darkness, but the guerrillas didn't pursue them. They obviously wanted only Matthew—alive. The guy in the hat shouted; then the others shouted, too. All five took aim and commanded him to surrender.

No way, thought Matthew. *Not to these murderers.*

Two guerrillas started toward him, cautiously crossing the middle boat on their way to *Coco Loco*. It was decision time. He could resist and surely end up dead. That wouldn't bring back Hector and his son. He saw only one way to avenge the murder of his friends—live to fight another day.

"*¡Manos arriba!*" their leader shouted.

Matthew took a long look, memorizing those cold black eyes behind the mask. He raised his hands to feign cooperation, then took one slow step back and suddenly tumbled over the rail. He splashed head-first into the warm, black waters below, holding his breath as long as he possibly could, fighting to stay down without air, swimming deeper and farther than ever before, knifing his way beneath the surface with long strokes and powerful kicks.

He was diving like a Miskito, the way his good friend Hector had taught him, thinking only of escape.

2

I was seated at the long, polished mahogany table in the main conference room on the thirty-first floor, ostensibly assisting my supervising partner in a morning settlement conference, in reality staring out the window at the cruise ships in the Port of Miami while thinking about Jenna. More precisely, thinking about the last time I'd seen Jenna.

It was a month ago today. We were engaged at the time. She'd invited me to take a long walk on the beach, said she'd meet me there. Any dolt could have seen what was coming, but I was so wrapped up in my own world and oblivious to our relationship that I'd actually shown up with a Frisbee, a radio, and a bottle of wine. This was going to be one of those talks that wasn't really a talk, more of a speech with a few permissible interruptions. It was so overrehearsed that Jenna had lost all sense that it would hit me like a five-iron between the eyes. The way she looked on that day would never leave my memory, the sad smile, her sandy-blond hair blowing in the gentle breeze, those big eyes that sparkled even in the most dismal of circumstances. I was speechless, the way I was the first time I'd ever laid eyes on her, only this time for far less enchanting reasons. The silence was insufferable once she'd finished, both of us waiting for me to move my lips and say something. Nothing came, and then it started to rain. At least I'd thought it was raining. I felt a drop on my head, and Jenna promptly lost it right before my eyes. She was embarrassed to be laughing, laughing not at me but at the absurdity of the situation, yet laughing nonetheless. It was then that I heard the shrill screech above me, saw the winged culprit swoop down from the sky in one last mocking pass. A seagull had shit squarely on my head.

This, of course, we took as an omen. I got my diamond ring back and hadn't seen her since. It wasn't a bitter breakup, but I surely would have understood a few hard feelings. We'd met five years ago as students at the University of Florida and had been virtually inseparable. She was from Tampa, hated Miami, and agreed to move here for me. I moved here for Coolidge, Harding and Cash. With me working sixty and seventy hours a week in the Miami office of a Wall Street law firm, it was inevitable that someone with whom I was supposed to share the rest of my life would eventually ask, "What life?"

"Can we try a different approach?" Duncan Fitz suggested.

Duncan was my supervising attorney. I was at his side, as usual. Seated to his left was our client, a regional vice president from Med-Fam Pharmaceuticals. On the other side of the table was Teesha Williams, the plaintiff's counsel, along with her client, Gilbert Jones, an overweight former police officer who was now on permanent disability. Two years ago he'd been told to drop thirty pounds or retire from the force. He'd turned to a drug manufactured by Med-Fam. He lost the weight and, in the process, shaved about thirty years off his life. The drug had so damaged his heart that he needed a transplant that would never come, not with the inherent surgical complications presented by his weakened condition and obesity. His remaining time on this earth could be measured in months, perhaps weeks. He wheezed with each breath, walked only with the aid of a cane, and kept a portable tank of oxygen at his side for intermittent moments of extreme difficulty. It was hard not to feel sorry for him—something I didn't dare admit to Duncan.

"Try whatever approach you like," said Teesha, her tone less than amicable. "If this case doesn't settle today, we're going to trial."

Duncan smiled thinly and said, "Let's make a deal."

"I'm listening."

"That is my proposal: Let's make a deal. As in the old television game show from the seventies. You know, Monty Hall, Carol Merrill."

"Are you on drugs?" she said.

I was no longer thinking about Jenna. This was actually getting interesting. For twenty minutes these two lawyers had been trading self-righteous speeches to impress their clients. I'd said nothing, which was exactly my job. Watch and learn. That was the Cool Cash method of training its young lawyers, and Duncan Fitz was regarded as one of its best teachers. Duncan was a seasoned litigator whose two favorite forms of recreation were boxing with men half his age at the gym twice a week and, whenever possible, depriving an unprepared plaintiff's lawyer of a nice, fat contingency fee.

Duncan said, "Clearly we're at an impasse. Med-Fam has very generously offered to settle for fifty thousand dollars. You want ten times that amount."

"Twenty, if we go to trial."

"Which will be a year from now. Then Med-Fam takes an appeal, which tacks on another year. By the time my client forks over a dime, Mr. Jones will be long since dead. The only winner will be his lawyer."

"How dare you," she said. "We're outta here. My client doesn't need to hear this."

"Yes, I do," said Gilbert. He spoke with a hint of a Caribbean accent, as he was Bahamian by birth. Tiny beads of sweat had gathered atop his shaven head, the dark, smooth skin glistening beneath the fluorescent lights. His gaze moved slowly from one person to the next, soulful eyes that bespoke resignation. "Mr. Fitz, you're right, mon. I don't have time to wait for trial. And I'm tired of standin' on the sidelines while you lawyers yakkity-yak-yak my precious time away."

Teesha sank back into her chair. "All right, then. What's the offer?"

"I've been a litigator for thirty years, and I swear, every time I step in front of the jury it's an adventure," said Duncan.

"Nature of the beast. It's a roll of the dice."

"Precisely. So why not roll them now?" Duncan removed three documents from his briefcase and laid them on the table, one after the other, like playing cards dealt face up. "Med-Fam has executed three standard settlement agreements. The legalese in each is identical. Mr. Jones agrees to dismiss his lawsuit and forever release Med-Fam from any liability. In exchange, Med-Fam agrees to pay him a sum of money."

"How much?"

"Excellent question. As you can see, the amount payable is hidden by white adhesive tape."

"You want Gilbert to guess?"

"That's where the game gets interesting. In one document the hidden amount payable is zero. In another it's the amount of Med-Fam's previous offer: fifty thousand dollars. But in the third we pay Gilbert Jones the full amount of his latest demand: five hundred thousand dollars."

"This is preposterous. Let's go, Gilbert."

"Can't go," he said. "My only chance is this."

Reluctantly, she closed her briefcase. "You don't settle a case this way."

"Why not?" asked Duncan.

"Because . . . you just don't. For one thing, my client loses two out of three."

"He *wins* two out of three," said Duncan. "He loses only if he pulls up the zero. Or if he listens to his lawyer and goes to trial."

"There should at least be a fourth choice. The amount Gilbert would win if this case went to a jury."

"It's my game, Counselor. Take it or leave it."

"This be legal?" asked Gilbert.

"Absolutely," said Duncan. "Med-Fam has already signed all three. Whichever one you sign, that's the deal."

"Don't do it," said Teesha.

"Quiet. I'm trying to think."

"Take your time," said Duncan.

Gilbert stared at the choices before him, as if trying to see through the tape that hid the numbers. He licked his lips once, then again. His eyes darted from one document to the next. The thick creases in his brow grew deeper with concentration.

I could tell that Duncan was enjoying himself. He was even starting to sound like a game show host. "What's it going to be, sir? Door number one? Door number two? Or door number three?"

Teesha said, "As your lawyer, I strongly advise you to get up and walk right out of this room. They wouldn't ask you to play this game if they didn't know you were going to win at trial and win big."

"But the man's right. I'll be dead by then. This be my only chance to see my money."

The room was silent. Duncan slid a cartridge pen across the table. Gilbert glanced at it, then locked eyes with Duncan. Finally he looked at me—why, I don't know. Perhaps he misconstrued my silence as impartiality. The expression chilled me, made me feel his desperation. This lawsuit was all this dying man had left in his life.

His right hand shook as he grasped the pen. He stared at the first document and then at the second. The pen started toward the third, then stopped. He went back to the first one, signed on the blank line, and dropped the pen, mentally exhausted.

"Lordy, lordy," Teesha said, groaning.

Without emotion Duncan said, "Number one it is. Let's see what you could have won, had you chosen document number two. Nick," he told me, "pull the tape."

I obliged.

"Fifty thousand," said Duncan. "Whoa, Nelly. That means Mr. Jones has either struck out completely or hit the jackpot. Let's have a look, shall we?"

He nodded at me once more, again delegating the honors. I was beginning to feel like an unwilling accomplice, but I did as I was told and removed the tape.

Gilbert froze. His lawyer was speechless. He'd chosen the zero.

"Ooooooh, I'm so sorry," said Duncan. "If only you had trusted your first instinct and gone with number three." He removed the tape himself this time, as if throwing salt in the wound. It was really there: five hundred thousand dollars.

"This is bullshit!" Teesha shouted.

"Only because you lost."

"What are you hiding, Fitz? If you put a half million on the table, the case must be worth ten times that much."

"Right now it's worth zero."

"It's gambling. The agreement's illegal and unenforceable."

"Maybe it is, maybe it isn't. But I'd truly hate to put your client through the ordeal of getting a court order to enforce a settlement agreement. So tell him there's five grand on the table, and we all walk away happy. The offer's good for twenty-four hours. After that, I move to enforce the deal."

"You're bluffing."

"Try me." Duncan tucked the signed document

into his coat pocket. "Nick will show you the way out." With that, he gathered his papers and walked out the door with a delighted client.

It was an awkward moment, me left behind like the six-foot fly on the wall in the aftermath of one of Duncan's client-pleasing stunts. I stepped away from the table and waited near the door, praying that Gilbert was not a violent man. But he didn't appear to be angry. He was stunned and silent, rocked by the loss of a half-million-dollar settlement.

"Hope you're proud of yourself," said Teesha.

I did a double take, realizing that she was talking to me.

"Tricking a dying man, playing on his desperation. You bastards are unbelievable."

I couldn't disagree, but I couldn't disown my own supervising partner, either. I just wanted to let Mr. Jones know that this hadn't been my idea. "Is he going to be okay?"

"What do you think?" she said sharply.

My question was stupid, admittedly.

"Just leave," said Teesha. "We know our way out."

I left quietly, catching one last glimpse of Gilbert's stunned and pathetic expression. Had I not known what his case was really worth, Duncan's showboat tactics might not have disgusted me so. But I'd sat through the confidential strategy conferences. I'd heard the client privately admit responsibility for Mr. Jones's injuries. Med-Fam would have been getting off cheap even if it had coughed up the half million dollars hidden behind door number three. I'm not so pious as to refuse to represent anyone who shows up in my office wearing a black hat.

But I had to draw the line at toying with a victim, destroying what little was left of his life, and then going back to Duncan's office to celebrate.

"Victories" like this one made me wish I'd listened to my father and literally gone fishing the rest of my life. Dad would have liked that, but only if it had been my choice, only if I'd truly shared my old man's love of the sea, the salty air, the squish-squish of fish guts beneath rubber boots.

I couldn't deal with Duncan right then. I started back toward my office, then heard my name called as I crossed the main lobby.

"Nick Rey, caller holding."

It was a page from the operator, which concerned me. The firm's policy was to refer unanswered calls to the voice-mail system. Pages were only for true emergencies. I took the call at the phone bay off the main lobby. It was my mother, which only heightened my worries. Never did she bother me at work. She sounded awful.

"What's wrong?" I asked.

"It's—" Her voice broke.

I could tell she'd been crying. "Mom, what is it?"

"It's about your father."

My heart leaped to my throat. "Is he okay?"

"We don't know. He's missing."

"What do you mean, missing?"

"He may have been kidnapped."

"When?"

"Last night."

"Where?"

"On one of his boats, in Cartagena."

"Colombia? What was he doing there?"

"No one seems to know anything for sure. It's all so confusing to me, the things I'm hearing."

"Who told you this?"

"I went numb when he called. I'm sorry. Maybe you should call him back and speak to him directly."

"Who, Mom? Who did you talk to?"

"Oh, dear. I'm blanking out. Your father's business partner in Nicaragua."

She was getting more scattered by the minute. "Guillermo," I said.

"Yes, Guillermo. He was trying to be strong, but he sounded so worried."

Guillermo had survived Nicaragua's earthquakes, revolutions, and hurricanes. If he was worried, I was worried. But I didn't dare let Mom pick up on my concern. "Don't be scared. Everything's going to be okay, I'm sure."

"Just come home, please. The FBI will be here any minute."

"Did you call them?"

"No. Guillermo did."

"That's good. Things are moving already."

"I need you here now. I can't do this by myself."

"I'm on my way."

As I hung up, I noticed my hand shaking. A deep breath calmed my nerves. None of that in front of Mom, I told myself. Then I ran back to my office to grab my car keys.

3

Shortcuts shaved about twenty minutes off my trip. I knew all the winding back streets, having logged thousands of miles as a kid on a bicycle in the area known as the golden triangle in Coral Gables. My parents still lived in the same colonial-style house on Toledo Street that the family had moved to when I was eight and my sister was five. It was all so familiar, with one exception: the unmarked vehicle parked in the driveway. It was a reality jolt, my first visual confirmation that Dad was really in trouble and that the FBI was truly involved.

I parked my Jeep on the street and hurried up the sidewalk. Through the front window I saw my mother seated on the edge of the living room couch. A man was seated in the armchair, his back to the window. I entered quickly without a knock, then halted in the foyer. My mother rose, and we locked eyes. She said nothing, but the expression said it all. I went to her and held her. She was heavy in my arms, sobbing. Finally she broke away to dab her eyes with a tissue.

"I'm sorry," she said with a sniffle. "I'm being so rude. Nick, this is Agent Lester Nettles from the FBI."

Nettles rose but didn't smile, almost too somber even for an occasion as serious as this one. He was well groomed, handsome, very professional-looking. He struck me as the African-American version of the quintessential G-man portrayed on those old television shows back when the FBI seemed to be comprised entirely of white ex-Marines. We shook hands, dispensing with the formalities as I got right to the point.

"Is my father okay?"

"We believe he's alive."

"What happened?"

He finished off the last swallow of coffee my mother had brought him, then continued. "It appears that three fishing boats belonging to your father's company were overtaken by force while in port in Colombia. Three crew members were shot and killed. Three others jumped in the harbor and swam for their lives. One is still missing. Two have been recovered, the only witnesses so far."

"Do any of them know what happened to my father?"

"No one's a hundred percent sure. They all say that the gunmen seemed to want to take your father alive. But there was a lot of gunfire exchanged."

"That doesn't mean he was hit. He could have escaped, right?"

Nettles was slow to respond. Too slow. My mother shuddered, realizing that there were only two realistic possibilities, neither of them pretty.

"For now," said Nettles, "we're assuming an abduction."

"Who is this 'we' you keep referring to? Is the FBI doing an investigation?"

"No. The only information the FBI has so far is through intelligence bulletins from the State Department."

"That's not too reassuring. I just called the U.S. embassy in Colombia on my way over here, and they weren't very forthcoming. I'm not sure what to make of that."

Nettles glanced at my mother, then at me. "You didn't hear this from me, okay? But the primary interest of the State Department is foreign policy. Most American families who go through this ordeal are surprised to find that the one government agency that puts the interests of the victim first is the FBI."

"Well, then, thank God you're here," said Mom.

Nettles seemed to enjoy the praise, but if we were going to get all kissy-face, I decided to push for extra information—like the things the embassy had told me were for the government's eyes only. "At least now we have someone who can tell us what's in the State Department's intelligence bulletins."

"What do you want to know?" he asked cautiously.

"For starters, who took my father?"

"That's not clear yet. One of the attackers was killed in the skirmish. According to the local police, he was dressed as one of the guerrilla groups that operate in Colombia. Combat fatigues, the whole getup. But it could also be someone who was trying to make it look like the work of guerrillas. We can't rule out common criminals or even one of the para-military organizations."

"Excuse me," Mom interrupted. "Are you saying my husband may have been kidnapped by the Colombian military?"

"Quite the opposite. The Colombian Army has been at war with both right-wing and left-wing groups for years. The Marxists are the guerrillas. The right wing is paramilitary."

"Why would they want my dad?"

"They don't. They want your money. You should expect a ransom demand to come by mail or international courier service very soon."

I stepped toward the window, not quite believing this. "You're saying that some Marxist group over a thousand miles away killed half my dad's crew, kidnapped my dad, went to all this trouble, just to squeeze a little money out of the Rey family from Coral Gables?"

"First of all, it won't be a little money. They usually have inflated ideas about the wealth of American families."

"How inflated?"

"It's best not to speculate about these things. Whatever the demand is, it's negotiable."

"Negotiable?" I said, almost scoffing. "We're talking about my dad, not a used car."

"Trust me, if you decide you have no choice but to pay a ransom, you still negotiate. It's sad, but kidnapping has turned into a big business worldwide, and in Colombia it's literally out of control. Two hundred a month, at least."

"My God, it's like some kind of a mill."

"A money mill, to be exact. Hundreds of millions of dollars in ransom every year. These groups would like the world to think that they're politically motivated, but they're mostly thugs looking for money to bankroll drug labs and other criminal activity."

That last remark struck me, especially coming from an FBI agent. "So if we pay a ransom, we're dumping cash into some criminal's war chest."

"In a broad sense, yes."

"And the FBI doesn't have a problem with that?"

"We're not thrilled about it. For years we had a no-concessions policy in dealing with international kidnappers. But the more progressive view in the bureau these days is that if the family wants to pay a ransom, we don't stand in their way."

"What if we just can't come up with the money?"

"If you're asking whether the U.S. government will pay the ransom or even lend you the money, the answer is no."

"So then what happens?"

With the subtle arching of an eyebrow he seemed to be signaling that it was best not to answer that question in front of my mother.

"Stupid question," I said, backtracking. "Of course we'll get the money."

Mom asked, "What happens next, Mr. Nettles?"

"There's a lot involved in an international kidnapping," said Nettles. "Not the least of which are jurisdictional issues between Colombia and the U.S., between the FBI and other U.S. agencies, between the Colombian police and the Colombian Army."

"I think my mother and I are in agreement that we don't want to leave this up to anyone but the FBI."

"That's right," said Mom.

"I hate to inject a dirty word like 'politics' into the equation, but certain matters of diplomacy must be resolved before the FBI can officially get involved."

"What does that mean?"

"The bottom line is that the FBI's negotiators can't assist in a case outside the United States until the State Department invites us. As yet, we haven't been formally invited."

"This isn't a wedding. What kind of invitation do you need?"

"It's not just a formality. The State Department has to respect local autonomy, and they have relationships with the host country that have to be maintained long after the resolution of this kidnapping. They don't just send in the FBI every time an American gets into trouble."

"Is there something we can do?" Mom asked.

"Yes," he said. "Make a list of who you know and call them. I hate to say it, but connections matter. The higher up, the better."

"I don't have any connections," said Mom.

"I'll work on that," I said.

"Good," said Nettles.

I thought for a second, then backtracked. "Except, how am I going to be plying for contacts? Shouldn't I go to Colombia?"

"My advice is no. You'll find yourself much more effective here, trying to get your own government moving. You should send someone down to represent the family. Your lawyer, a friend of the family."

"Guillermo," my mother said.

"My father's business partner," I explained.

Mom said, "He's going to be in Cartagena tonight. He has to check on the surviving crew members and make arrangements for the ones who passed away. And he's Nicaraguan. His Spanish is a lot better than yours, Nick."

"That's perfect," said Nettles.

I was a little reluctant. I didn't really know Guillermo, though it was true that he'd been my father's partner for over a decade. I glanced at Mom, however, and it was obvious that she didn't want me to leave her here to deal with the FBI and State Department by herself.

"Okay," I said. "We'll let Guillermo handle things in Colombia."

Nettles seemed to approve of the decision. He glanced toward the door, as if it were time to leave. He'd dumped a ton of information on us, and he seemed experienced enough to know that the family needed time to digest it, time alone to grieve. Mom shook his hand and thanked him profusely. I saw him to the door and followed him outside.

"Level with me," I said as we reached his car in the driveway. "If this is a kidnapping, and the kidnappers are some kind of guerrilla group, what're the chances of my father coming back alive?"

"Too early to say. There's so many variables."

"You must have statistics of some sort."

"Reliable numbers are hard to come by. The

police, the army, the politicians—just about everybody in Colombia has a stake in making the situation seem better than it is."

"All I want is a general idea, not an answer written in stone."

He hesitated, then answered. "The most reliable numbers I have are from our legal attaché in Bogotá. One hundred four kidnap victims murdered from January to June of this year.

"But the violence can go in spurts, depending on how the war is going between the rebels and the Colombian Army. If the guerrillas are trying to make a statement, you may see more kidnapping victims murdered."

"How many more?"

"I don't know."

"Come on. The family deserves to know the truth."

He seemed to be searching for a positive spin. "The truth is, worldwide only about nine or ten percent of kidnapping victims are killed or die in captivity."

"*Only?*" I said.

"The flip side is that there's a ninety percent chance of survival. Pretty good odds."

"Oh, really? Think of the last ten people you said hello to. Now imagine one of them dead. How good do those odds sound to you now?"

His expression fell, as if he'd never thought of it quite that way.

"We need the FBI on this case," I said. "Let's get that State Department invitation."

He said nothing, but I knew what he was thinking. I needed to get to work on my list of connections. It was time for me to call on friends in high places.

Now I just had to figure out who the hell they were.

4
·

Faster than you can say "Who do you know?" I was back in my office—or, more precisely, Duncan Fitz's office.

Working as an associate in one of the largest law firms on earth certainly had its disadvantages. The lawyers who set my salary and measured my progress toward partnership knew me only from written annual review forms completed by the handful of partners in the Miami office. Ninety-eight percent of my colleagues were virtual strangers, whom I would never meet, never even talk to on the telephone. They worked in different states, different countries, different time zones. Many spoke English as a second or even third language. When one of them was fired—or sometimes even when an entire office closed—I usually found out about it weeks after the fact, usually by happenstance, and then only by inference from the fact that an e-mail I'd sent was returned as "undeliverable." Cool Cash could be an overwhelming, impersonal workplace.

At the same time, it had a way of making the world seem very small.

Duncan was in an exceptionally good mood, having just returned from a long celebration lunch at the City Club with his client from Med-Fam Pharmaceuticals. From the looks of his red nose, it appeared as though a few glasses had been raised to the health of the not-so-healthy Gilbert Jones.

"Sorry you didn't join us," said Duncan, seated behind his antique desk. "Where did you run off to?"

"Emergency. I got some distressing news."

His grin completely vanished. "Those bastards didn't call the judge, did they?"

"No. It's not about the Med-Fam case."

"Good."

"It's about my father."

As a rule, Duncan didn't shift easily from work to personal issues, but he listened with concern as I told him everything I knew so far—the phone call from Mom, the meeting with the FBI agent. I didn't come right out and ask for any favors. That wasn't the way to operate with Duncan. I just made it clear that the FBI wouldn't get involved in the case without an invitation from the State Department and that political connections might expedite the process.

"Consider it done," said Duncan.

"You can help?"

"Can camels spit?"

I had to think about that one.

"We have a former undersecretary of state working in our Washington office. I'll call him right now."

"That's fantastic. I can't believe it."

"Believe it," he said proudly. He leaned back in

his leather chair and rested his hand atop the globe on his credenza. It was another antique, a distinctive but ugly piece with the oceans in black. He gave it a spin and asked, "What do you see here?"

"The world?" I said tentatively, sensing a trick question.

"Look closer. It's Coolidge, Harding and Cash. We're everywhere. Which is very good news for your father. This phone call I'm about to make is only the beginning."

"Thank you."

He opened his desk drawer, removed a three-ring notebook, and handed it to me. "Open it."

I thumbed through the first few pages. The book was filled with pictures and bios of influential people—members of Congress, the U.S. attorney general, even the president of Costa Rica. It went on for pages, at least two inches thick. "What is this?"

"It doesn't have an official name, but call it our A-list alumni registry. Everyone in that book has worked at this law firm in one of our offices around the world. If you think any of them might be able to help your father, you just let me know. All I ask is that you let me make the phone calls for you. Nobody is going to jump for a young associate in the Miami office, even if your father is kidnapped."

"Damn, Duncan. Maybe you aren't the heartless son of a bitch everybody says you are."

"Don't be so sure. It doesn't hurt to have the most promising young lawyer in Miami beholden to me for life."

He was half smiling, but I knew Duncan well enough to know he was at least half serious. Sure,

I'd owe him big time if he could pull this off, and that was fine by me. Dad would have sold off his fleet to save me. At least I liked to think so.

I moved to the edge of my seat as Duncan picked up the phone and dialed our Washington office.

An hour later I was at my mother's house, trying to cheer her with a little good news. The wheels were in motion, I assured her, and I tried to put on my best face. I was fooling her no more than she was fooling me, the way she emerged from her bedroom every forty-five minutes, trying to hide her red and puffy eyes, assuring me it was allergies.

We sat down together at the kitchen table and made a list of people we should notify. Mom made the first few calls, but it was emotionally exhausting. I picked up where she left off, and soon the grapevine was in full swing. By midafternoon our phone was ringing off the hook. Dad's friends, Mom's friends, friends of friends, people we hadn't heard from in years—all were offering to help in any way they could. Other than to keep Dad in their prayers, we didn't know what to tell them. This was all foreign to us. The only thing we knew was that, by the end of the day, the one phone call we'd wanted had yet to come.

There was still no word from the FBI or the State Department.

I decided to stay with Mom that night, though my being there only seemed to highlight the fact that my sister wasn't. In a crisis like this, I suppose it was natural for Mom to want both of her children, even if she and her daughter weren't even technically on speaking terms.

My parents had given me the right amount of freedom as a child, but Lindsey they'd strangled. Especially my mother. From preschool on, whatever Lindsey was doing, Mom was right there, as room mother, assistant soccer coach, teacher's aide, you name it. It was all out of love, surely, but Mom just couldn't seem to grasp that taking her eyes off her daughter for more than five consecutive minutes didn't constitute abandonment. A disastrous semester of home schooling in the eighth grade made it almost inevitable that Lindsey would run with the wrong crowd in high school, and by her junior year she was barely speaking to either parent. I became Lindsey's only lifeline to the family. Knowing that she was a bright kid, I talked her into going to college, though it was her own idea to enroll at the University of Puget Sound near Seattle, farther away from home than any other school in the contiguous United States. She earned a degree in journalism, and for the past two years she'd been traveling across the Americas in search of her first byline. Unlike my mother, I didn't see it as the end of the world that she wanted to go out and find herself. She never phoned our folks, and even her calls to me were pretty rare, maybe once every six weeks. I'd find out where she'd been, send her a little money, whatever she needed. For my parents' benefit, I'd subtly try to convince her that finding herself didn't necessarily mean losing her family. She didn't seem to be biting.

Mom and I stayed up talking till after the eleven o'clock news, then said good night. My old room was virtually unchanged since the day I'd moved out to go to college, preserved like a time capsule. The dim light of the moon shone through the window, just bright enough to reveal an outline of my past. The Miami Dolphins team poster I'd worshipped as a teenager was still on the wall, hovering over the old dinosaur of a computer I'd used to explore everything from Super Mario Brothers to—well, dinosaurs. I half expected the door to open at any minute and my father to check on me the way he did when I was in high school. Spot checks were his way of keeping his teenage son from sneaking out at midnight to hang with the cool crowd in Coconut Grove. But as the minutes slowly passed, the house slipped deeper into an eerie silence. It seemed empty without Dad, and it made me ache inside. I wondered where he was sleeping tonight, if he was sleeping, if he was still alive.

The phone rang at half past midnight. My immediate hope was that they'd found Dad. My fear was that they'd found his body. It was FBI Agent Nettles on the line, which put my heart directly into my throat.

"Don't be alarmed," he said.

"What is it?"

"It's sort of an administrative issue."

"At this hour?"

"I've just received confirmation that the Colombians are officially treating this case as an abduction. Which is good news. That means they have reason to believe your father is still alive."

"Have they heard from the kidnappers?"

"No, but their divers have searched the area thoroughly. No body was found."

No corpse. That was good news, I supposed.

"Will the FBI take the lead now that it's officially a kidnapping?"

"It's not legally a kidnapping until there's a demand for ransom. It's an abduction."

"We're still talking about a United States citizen. I'd like to see the FBI assert itself."

"That's the other reason for my call. I'm afraid that the FBI isn't going to intercede in this case."

I'd been pacing across the bedroom with the phone to my ear, but I suddenly stopped cold in my tracks. "Come again?"

He paused, as if measuring his words. "As I explained to you and your mother earlier, the FBI can't get involved in cases of international abductions or kidnappings unless the State Department invites us."

"That's being taken care of. The supervising partner at my law firm assured me that the State Department would extend an invitation within twenty-four hours."

"That much has been done. They've extended an invitation."

"Then what's the problem?"

"The FBI has declined it."

"What?"

"The State Department placed certain conditions on the FBI's involvement that were out of line. It was impossible to accept their invitation."

"What kind of conditions?"

"I'm not at liberty to elaborate."

"Come on. You have to give me something."

"I'm sorry, I can't."

"Look, I'm not trying to put you in a bad spot.

Let's set up a meeting with your supervisor first thing in the morning."

"It won't do any good. This decision wasn't made in the Miami office."

"I'll fly to Washington if I have to. Just give me the name of the person to talk to."

"I don't have any specific names for you."

I didn't understand it, but clearly I was being stonewalled, and it was making me angry. "So that's it? 'Too bad, so sad, see you later?' That's totally unacceptable. At least tell me which door to knock on. Should I start with the FBI or the State Department?"

"I wouldn't go either of those routes, if I were you."

"Is that some kind of threat?"

"No. I'm trying to steer you in the right direction, so listen carefully to what I'm saying. If it was my father who was kidnapped, I wouldn't waste time trying to change the way the FBI and State Department think."

"If *your* father was kidnapped, the FBI and State Department wouldn't be bogged down in political testosterone."

He fell silent, then replied in a noticeably softer tone. "I wish I had better news for you. I mean that sincerely."

"Just what my father needs. Sincerity."

He bade me a hollow "Best of luck," and with the click in my ear, I had the unsettling sense that the whole FBI had just hung up on me.

Me *and* my father.

5
•

It was my job to tell Grandma everything. Or not. Mom left it up to me to decide what a seventy-eight-year-old woman could stand to hear about her only child.

I left the house at 9:00 A.M. It was an hour's drive, so I phoned Duncan on my cellular with an update. He was as baffled as I about the FBI's declination of the State Department's invitation to intervene in the case.

"Those twits," he groused. "Let me make another phone call."

"Who are you going to call this time?"

"Whoever it takes. I've been concentrating only on the State Department so far, but sounds like it's time for a full-court press. I'm sure we know someone who can get right to the FBI director."

I loved it when Duncan was fired up about something I needed done. I thanked him several times before hanging up.

By ten o'clock I was in the Upper Keys, having driven slowly. I wasn't sure how to put a positive

spin on this for Grandma, and part of me kept hoping that the whole conversation would be preempted
by a sudden phone call from Mom, a miraculous
message that Dad had somehow found his way to
the U.S. embassy unharmed. He'd been missing for
almost thirty-six hours, however, and the possibility of his successful escape seemed less likely with
each passing minute. Abduction was the only logical inference.

Unless he was dead.

Not in a million years would Grandma believe
that her son had fallen at the hands of some deadbeat
Colombian guerrillas. Her son was a fighter, a survi-
vor, like her. Grandma was a "Conch," a native of
the Florida Keys. When she was twelve years old,
her house was destroyed by the monster hurricane of
1935 that killed more than four hundred people.
The Upper Keys were ravaged, entire families were
lost, a rescue train was washed into the sea. At least
one fool braved the storm trying to save his fishing
boat. Grandma found her father's body naked in the
mangroves, his clothes ripped away by two-hundred-
mile-per-hour winds. Nine months later she and her
mother moved into one of twenty-nine houses built
by the Red Cross for the survivors who'd insisted on
staying put and rebuilding their shattered lives.
They were built for fishermen and farmers, plain folk
who had lost everything. They were built to last. The
frame, the walls, the roof were all poured concrete,
two hundred fifty tons of it, reinforced by another
hundred and fifty thousand pounds of steel rods—
all for a two-bedroom house that was a mere six
hundred square feet of living space. It was a bunker,

virtually indestructible, symbolic of the Conch spirit. Grandma inherited the house when her mother died and made it her home as a young bride. That was the house my father had grown up in.

It wasn't an easy life. I remembered seeing an old photo of my father as a young boy seated in the kitchen, each leg of the table resting in a tin can of kerosene to keep the cockroaches from climbing up and walking off with the family meal. Not that there was ever much food around the house. At the age of six my father became the man of the house. He loved the ocean, but hunger had really inspired him to fish. He caught them, Grandma cooked them. It was all they had and all they needed, each other and their Red Cross house. Together they'd survived the occasional hurricane and anything else the world could throw at them.

Now it was up to me to tell Grandma that her son was missing.

"Get out!" she shouted.

I was standing just inside the front door, hadn't even set foot inside the living room. It wasn't a case of killing the messenger. It was just one of her bad days. Grandma had Alzheimer's disease.

She was seated on the couch watching *Judge Judy* on the tube, dressed casually in a cotton blouse and plaid Bermuda shorts. Her hair was done the way she'd always worn it, neatly cut with a hint of reddish tint. She looked just fine, and it pained me to see her act this way. For months my parents had been trying to persuade her to move in with them, but she wouldn't budge from her concrete bungalow. A home-care nurse helped her get by from day to day.

"It's okay, it's only me, your—"

"Don't you dare set foot in this house!"

The nurse interceded. "Now, don't be rude, Marion. It's family."

I tried to make eye contact from across the room, hoping to establish a connection. Her expression was cold, though it wasn't an unknowing blank stare. She seemed to know me all right. She just didn't seem to like me very much.

"I stopped by for a visit," I said.

"You pop in once a year, that's supposed to make everything okay?"

"It's okay if you don't remember, but I was here last month."

"Just go!" she shouted, this time flinging an ashtray across the room.

I ducked as it flew over my head, then shattered on the wall behind me. The nurse pulled me into the hall, out of Grandma's line of fire. "It's not a good day for her."

"I didn't mean to bring this on."

"You didn't. Just try again some other time."

"Would it really make a difference?"

"You'd be amazed. The earlier in the day, the better. Before breakfast is best."

"I can come back tomorrow."

"I'll call and let you know how she's doing before you drive all the way down."

I thanked her and started out the door.

"You bastard, Matthew! What kind of a son are you anyway?"

I looked at the nurse, almost speaking to myself. "She thinks I'm my father?"

"She's terribly confused today. But truthfully, you two do look a lot alike. You even sound alike."

It wasn't the first time I'd heard that, but usually it was intended as a compliment. I had my dad's smile, my dad's good heart, whatever. No one—least of all his own mother—had ever mistaken me for my father the bastard.

Again I thanked the home-care nurse, then closed the door on my way out. As I cut across the front lawn to the pebble driveway, I tried to dismiss the outburst as irrational, knowing that the anger expressed by Alzheimer's patients toward loved ones was often baseless and imaginary. But it made me realize how windows to the past could close forever, whether by the slow onset of a disease or a sudden abduction. There were so many questions that I might never have the chance to ask my father now, not just about family matters but about the separate life he'd built for himself in another part of the world—all those trips to Central and South America that had finally gotten him abducted. Or worse.

I got in my Jeep and drove away, fearful that I'd forever feel the weight of conversations we'd never had.

The drive up to Miami ended the same way the drive down had started, with a phone call to Duncan. His secretary said he was meeting with a new client and couldn't be interrupted.

"Do you know if he spoke to anyone at the FBI or State Department this morning?"

"I'm sure he hasn't," she said. "This meeting has been going nonstop since you called."

A more encouraging end to the conversation would have been nice, but at Cool Cash, paying clients always came first. I was sure that Duncan would eventually make a few phone calls to try to break the deadlock that was keeping the FBI out of my father's case, but time was slipping away. I decided to call the embassy myself, my contact person at American citizen services in the consular section, William Ebersoll.

"Anything new?" I asked.

"Nothing I'm aware of."

"I got an interesting call from the FBI last night. They tell me that the State Department invited them to work the case but they declined."

"I'm not in a position to confirm or deny that."

"I was told that the reason they declined was that the State Department had placed unreasonable conditions on their involvement."

I sensed he was fuming. Nettles had evidently related more details to me than the State Department had expected. "Whoever told you that is mistaken," said Ebersoll.

"Are you saying that there were no conditions?"

"No. The conditions were not unreasonable."

"What were they?"

"Very simple. The State Department welcomes the involvement of the FBI, so long as the FBI agrees to refrain from taking any actions that are inconsistent with the U.S. government's long-standing policy on terrorism."

"What policy do you mean?"

"The same policy we have espoused for many years. In cases of international terrorism, American law enforcement personnel cannot play any role in negotiations with kidnappers that lead to the payment of ransom or other concessions in exchange for the release of hostages."

"Are you saying that if the kidnappers promise to kill my father unless we pay them a nickel, the official position of the U.S. government is to tell my family to start making the funeral arrangements?"

"That's not a very realistic example. Nor is it productive for me to debate our policy with you. I can certainly understand how harsh this might seem to you or any other private citizen caught in this terrible situation. But the U.S. government does not give in to terrorists. That would only promote more terrorism."

"The FBI advised my mother and me that if we wanted to pay a ransom, the government would not stand in our way."

"That's true. We won't withhold basic administrative services, such as putting you in contact with local law enforcement agencies. But you will not have the support and approval of the U.S. government. More to the point, the State Department will not invite the bureau to assist in any case abroad if the FBI negotiators intend to actively develop strategies that will facilitate the payment of a ransom."

"I can't believe that the State Department is keeping the FBI out."

"I assure you, we're not."

"If the State Department hadn't insisted on strict compliance with an outdated policy, the FBI would have accepted your invitation to work on the case."

"That may well be the explanation given to you

by a particular FBI agent, but the bureau is fully aware of the U.S. policy against concessions to terrorists. If they're declining to get involved in the case, it's for their own reasons."

"Such as?"

"Reasons other than a disagreement over policy."

"What possible justification could the FBI have for ducking a case involving a kidnapped American citizen?"

"We can't force the FBI to get involved. We can only invite them. Theoretically, any number of things could lessen the bureau's interest in a case abroad. Conflicts with local law enforcement. Special dangers to FBI personnel. The identity of the victim."

It was subtle, but he seemed to place emphasis on the last point.

"Are you suggesting that the FBI's declination has something to do with my father?"

He hesitated, as if he'd said too much. "I was simply talking in hypotheticals."

"Is there something I should know?"

"Perhaps you should ask the FBI."

"Perhaps. But why do I have the sense that you know something you're not telling me?"

Again he paused. "Like I said, ask the FBI."

Pressing for more would only have antagonized him. "Thank you," I said. "I definitely will ask them."

As we hung up, I finally noticed the streams of cars speeding past me on the interstate. I'd been driving like my grandmother, not sure what to make of things. Mom and I had taken a liking to Agent Nettles at our initial meeting, but it seemed impossible to reconcile the excuse he'd given me last night with the explanation offered by the consular agent this morning. The FBI was not taking the case, but why?

One way or the other, my own government was lying to me. It was only a matter of which agency.

My head was pounding as I cut across the expressway and took the fast lane back to Miami.

6

•

Mom and I cooked dinner ourselves, even though her friends had brought over enough casseroles and covered dishes for her to kiss the Cuisinart good-bye forever. Those closest to our family felt as compelled as we did to do *something*, even if it was as simple as keeping our cupboard stocked. For Mom and me, cooking was something to do besides worry, a way to pretend that we could weather the crisis together and maintain a semblance of normalcy.

Dinner was a delicious shrimp creole made with— you guessed it—shrimp from Rey's Seafood Company. They weren't the gigantic ones from deep, cold waters off Venezuela that made such beautiful shrimp cocktails, but they were of good size for the Mosquito Coast. They tasted so fresh, and as the son of a fisherman I knew why. They were fresh-frozen, which sounds like an oxymoron, but Americans eat far more fresh-frozen seafood than they realize. Restaurant patrons in New York, Chicago, or Boston would never guess that when their snooty

ssures them that today's snapper is "fresh,"
means "fresh-frozen"—as in fresh when it
ght, frozen in the boat on its way to the dock,
for processing at the plant, refrozen for ship-
thawed again when it was sold, and therefore
h" when it finally lands on a dinner plate. Unap-
zing as all that sounds, if it weren't frozen at
ious stages of the long journey from Nicaragua to
ur plate, that delicious grilled whitefish drizzled
with mango butter would taste like whale dung and
smell even worse.

Of course, Mom just picked at her dinner, wondering if Dad had anything to eat. Honestly, I hadn't
seen her sit down and eat a real meal in almost a day
and a half.

"Any leads on Lindsey?" she asked.

My sister was still missing, which by itself wasn't
alarming. She traveled with no itinerary in pursuit
of her journalistic pipe dream. With one member of
the family kidnapped, however, it would have been
nice to be able to account for her.

"This afternoon I spent an hour calling people I
thought she might stay in touch with. Some of them
seemed to think she was in Costa Rica, a couple
others said in Guatemala. It's all hearsay. I just can't
find anyone who's talked to her recently."

Mom was about to say something, then slipped
back into her thoughts, pushing her food around.
The plate was still full. Mine was empty.

"You should eat something," I said.

"I can't."

"It won't do any good to starve yourself."

"This tomato sauce is kind of nauseating."

"As co-chef, I take serious exception."

"Sorry. I'm just not hungry. I've been nibbling since five o'clock this morning."

I did seem to recall predawn noises in the kitchen. It was all part of the screwed-up pattern. A little reading at midnight. Letter writing till 2:00 A.M. Housecleaning at three, and organizing the closets at four. Neither of us was sleeping well, but Mom was especially affected. She was accustomed to nights alone while Dad traveled for work. This time was different, however, her lying awake in the lonely king-size bed wondering if that empty space beside her might be permanent.

"Have you talked to Jenna?" she asked.

That seemed out of the blue. Mom and I hadn't talked about her since I'd gotten back my engagement ring and washed a dollop of seagull droppings out of my hair. "No, I haven't."

"I noticed her name wasn't on your list of people to call."

"That's because she's my *ex*-fiancée."

"Don't be like that. She and your father were very fond of one another."

"I know. But I'd rather just not deal with her right now."

"Your father could use all the prayers he can get."

Mom certainly had a way of backing me into a corner. "You're right. I'll drop her a line or something."

The phone rang as we were clearing the table. Mom answered, and her eyes lit up. It was Dad's Nicaraguan business partner, Guillermo, calling from Cartagena. He'd gone down to make funeral arrangements for the dead crewmen, arrange for transportation back to Nicaragua for the two they'd found alive so far, and generally to check on the company's newly acquired boats that were now riddled with bullet holes.

I picked up the phone in the family room. Mom remained on the line in the kitchen.

"Any news?" I asked.

"Yes," he said with excitement. "Police have found one of the missing."

"Could it be Matthew?" Mom shrieked.

My heart was pounding right along with hers.

"No, no. It's Carlos, one of the welders who was missing. The third crewman."

I watched through the open doorway as Mom nearly collapsed in disappointment. I asked, "Is he okay?"

"Tired, but okay. These Miskitos are unbelievable. He swam for hours and finally hid in some mangroves along the coast. He was there for almost two days, afraid to come out. Finally he walked into town and found the police station."

"Does he have any information about Matthew?" Mom asked.

"Yes. It's good news, I think."

"You think?" I asked tentatively.

"He saw the guerrillas pull Matthew from the water."

"Alive?"

"Yes, alive."

I glanced across the room toward Mom. She was sitting down, her elbow on the kitchen table as she dabbed her eyes with a napkin. "That's good," I said. "At least he's alive."

"Yes. That part is good," he said.

I sensed there was bad news to go with it, and I worried whether Mom should hear it. Guillermo forged ahead without my encouragement.

"He says the guerrillas took Matthew away by boat. They were shouting, vowing to avenge the death of their friend with *la mina*."

"What do you mean?"

"You know, the guerrilla who got shot and killed in the exchange of gunfire on the shrimp boat."

"I understood that part. I meant '*la mina*,' what's that?"

"Your father. The gold mine."

My heart sank. Apart from Dad's safety, that was my biggest fear: the kidnappers' inflated expectations.

"Have you talked to the Colombian police yet?" I asked.

"Yes, that's where I am now. They're writing down Carlos's statement as we speak."

"Maybe I should fly down and speak to them myself."

"Probably not a good idea. From what the officer tells me, you will likely receive a communication from the kidnappers in the very near future. It wouldn't seem right to leave Cathy alone to handle that."

I took another glance toward the kitchen. Mom had the phone to her ear. I knew she was listening. But she was now too overcome to respond.

"You're right," I said. "I'll stay put. But let me talk

with one of the officers on the case. I just want to introduce myself."

"How's your Spanish?"

"Pretty good. Not perfect."

"Hold on. Let me try to find someone who can speak to you in English."

I heard muted conversations on the line, the sounds of a busy office in the background, followed by a click. I saw that my mother had hung up. She was walking briskly toward the bedroom, another so-called allergy attack from which she'd emerge with red and puffy eyes. I felt a few pangs of pity for her, but they were mostly crowded out by my anger toward those murderers who'd dubbed my father a gold mine.

A man came on the line, speaking English with a heavy Spanish accent. "Hello, this is Officer Trujillo speaking."

"Thank you for taking the time to speak with me, officer. As you can imagine, my family is very concerned—"

"*Claro,*" he said, then caught himself and continued in English. It was about as good as my Spanish. "I understand complete. Please know that we do everything possibly to bring your father safe. Judicial Police has twell hundred officers working kidnap cases."

"That sounds very good."

"*Sí.* Is very good. We all have much experience."

"Can you tell me anything about my father? Do you know if he is safe?"

"Not for sure. But is *muy importante* to know most kidnaps in Colombia end with victims home safe to families. Ones who are shot are usually ones who try escape. Others are killed if trouble goes wrong when the kidnappers take the victim. *Es muy bueno que* we see no sign of fight at the kidnap of your father, and since he has eighty-six years of age, is very not likely that he would try escape."

"What are you talking about? My father is fifty-one. He did try to escape, and three people were killed during the botched abduction."

There was silence on the line. "You are Mr. Alvarez, no?"

"No. Nick Rey, from Miami."

"My apologies, señor. Please understand, I have so many files."

The statistics from Agent Nettles suddenly flashed in my mind. More than twenty-five hundred abductions a year. Roughly eight a day. One every three hours. No wonder this guy couldn't keep his cases straight. "Forget it," I said.

"I am so sorry. Do not have fear of my words," he said, backpedaling. "Not everyone who tries escape is shot."

"It's all right, really. But please keep my phone number in your file and call me with any news in the case."

I gave him all my phone numbers, and as best I could tell, he was writing them down.

"I promise you will hear from me," he said.

"Thank you," I said, wondering if he would be calling me or the mysterious Mr. Alvarez.

I hung up, with mixed emotions. Dad was alive, or at least he'd been taken alive. But Officer Trujillo wasn't the first person to tell me that the stronger personalities, the people bold enough to try to escape, were the ones singled out for abuse, the ones kidnappers eventually discarded as more trouble than they were worth.

That made me very afraid. My dad didn't have a submissive personality. I knew he'd try to escape at every turn.

Mom knew it, too. That was why she cried so often.

I drew a deep breath, then walked to the bedroom to check on my mother.

7

The dawn of the third day was actually at sunset. Almost exactly forty-eight hours after the abduction, his blindfold finally came off. Matthew Rey shielded his eyes from the sudden burst of light, then staggered out of the back of the van, prodded from behind by the muzzle of an AK-47 assault rifle.

"*Adelante!*" one of the guerrillas shouted. Move it.

Matthew said nothing, simply obeyed and kept walking.

For two days he'd bounced and rolled on the cold metal floor of a speeding truck. Frequent sharp turns had slammed his head against the metal sides at least a dozen times, once nearly knocking him unconscious. Even by South American standards, the driving was breakneck, the roads were merely adequate—and both were deteriorating as the journey wore on. At first he'd tried to keep track of turns in hopes of discerning the direction of their travels, but after a dozen left turns, a half dozen right turns, and two or three trips around traffic circles, that proved impossible. The disorienting effect of the blindfold wasn't helping his sense of direction any. With his ear to the wheel well, he let the tires tell him this much: they'd moved from pavement to gravel to dirt to no roads at all.

The normal sounds of city life had long since vanished. It had been at least two bathroom breaks since he'd heard another vehicle rumble past in either direction. That was quite a while ago. The driver obviously didn't have the bladder of a fifty-year-old man. Matthew had traveled a good part of the trip with his legs crossed, and twice he'd barely made it to the side of the road to relieve himself without soiling his pants. With little to eat and drink, however, nature's callings turned less urgent. So far his captors had allowed him one hard-boiled egg, one *arepa*, a soft drink, and a few sips of water. He would have been hungry if he weren't so concerned about more immediate causes of death.

He wasn't gagged, and his feet weren't bound. He'd thought about yelling or kicking the sides of the truck to draw attention, especially during the early part of the journey while they were still in the city. But he'd read the U.S. State Department's travel advisories before leaving Nicaragua, and he'd followed the consular's official advice on how to behave when abducted in a foreign country. Kick and scream when in public, but once you're in the vehicle, quiet down and concentrate on surviving. You could end up beaten or drugged. Or worse.

Strange, but as yet he wasn't overly concerned for his own safety. He worried about Cathy and wondered how she'd handle this. Who would break the news to her? Would it come by telephone, or would someone visit the house? Thankfully, Nick lived close by. This was going to be tough on the whole family, but it was hard to feel too sorry for himself. Hours of darkness behind the blindfold had forever etched in his memory the horrifying image of his friends riddled with bullets, dead on the deck of the *Niña* as their blood ran together in a crimson pool. Hector and Liván, two good guys in the wrong place with the wrong gringo at the wrong time. That was the scariest part for Matthew. He knew nothing about his captors except for one telling piece of information: with impunity, they killed the innocent.

"Stop," said the guard. It was the first word of English that Matthew had heard since the abduction, but the commands quickly reverted to Spanish. "*Espera*." Wait.

Matthew was squinting. Even the twilight of early evening was more than his sensitive eyes could stand. The setting sun was a bright orange ball in a magenta sky that hovered above the jagged ridges of snowcapped mountains. There was a break in the clouds, and long golden rays streamed like lasers across the open valley. Suddenly the light was gone, and he was standing in the long shadow of two other guerrillas. The first thing that impressed him was their weapons. Both were heavily armed, one with an AK-47 and two bandoliers of ammunition crisscrossing his chest, the other with an Israeli-made Galil assault rifle and a pair of grenades hooked to his belt. The second thing to strike Matthew was the obvious youth in their faces. They were barely teenagers.

The stocky one motioned with his gun, directing

Matthew to a fallen log at the side of the road. *"El baño,"* he said.

Peeing in the weeds was just something Matthew was going to have to get used to.

Unescorted, he crossed the road and stopped at the log. The guerrillas were still watching as he unzipped, though he wasn't sure why, except to further humiliate him. Finally they turned away and shared a cigarette. They didn't seem overly concerned about his possible escape, probably because they were in the middle of nowhere. The dirt road they had traveled seemed to dissect an abandoned farm. Across the field, the dilapidated barn was barely standing. What was once a farmhouse had burned to its foundation so long ago that the remains were almost completely covered with weeds. Beyond were endless fields of some kind of crop. Sugarcane, was what it looked like. That gave Matthew a start. From his last trip to Colombia more than twenty years ago he remembered where most of the Colombian sugarcane was grown.

Good lord, they've dragged me as far as Cali. That gave him insight into the identity of his captors. The areas south of Cali were guerrilla strongholds of various Marxist groups.

He zipped his fly and glanced back at the guards. One was sitting in the truck with his hat over his eyes. The other was throwing stones at a fence post. Matthew took the moment of privacy to take stock of his possessions. Passport, gone. Wallet, gone. Ditto for his wristwatch. They'd left him with the clothes on his back and one essential that in these surroundings seemed like a luxury—his reading glasses. He didn't imagine he'd be doing much reading. These sons of bitches appeared to be the most desperate group of illiterates he'd ever encountered.

Again he glanced at the guards. Now they were both seated in the van, their backs to their prisoner. Matthew took a good look across the valley. The tall sugarcane wasn't that far away. In an all-out sprint he could reach it in sixty seconds, maybe less. It might take these stupid guards that long to notice he was gone. The downside, of course, was that he knew that these guys could shoot. Hector and Liván were the no-longer-living proof of that. One more look. The guy in the hat was sound asleep. The other was fiddling with the van's radio. This was an opportunity. It might be his *last* opportunity. His heart was pounding, as if waiting for the brain to send the message—*Run for it!*

Suddenly, out of the weeds, another guerrilla rose, then two more. They were standing between Matthew and the sugarcane, just ten yards away from him. They'd been hiding on their bellies, invisible in their camouflage fatigues. Had he run for it, he would have stepped right on them.

The one in the middle came forward. He seemed a good bit older than the others, maybe thirty. Matthew recognized the eyes from the shrimp boat. He was the leader, the one who'd sported the Australian-style hat. The one who had murdered Hector and Liván.

"You were thinking about it, weren't you?" he said in English.

"What?" said Matthew.

"You were going to run."

"No."

"You lie. I saw it in your eyes."

Matthew glanced back at the two guards in the truck. They were standing, watching and smiling. They'd set him up. The whole incident had been a test to see if he'd try to escape.

He stepped closer, then stopped, staring Matthew directly in the eye. "My name is Joaquín. You are a prisoner of war, and you are now my responsibility. You will never escape, so don't try."

"Whose war?"

"The people's."

"Who are you?"

"That is not your concern."

"What do you plan to do with me?"

"We intend to treat you as you deserve to be treated. If you are good, we are good to you. If you are bad, your family will be negotiating not for your release but for the return of your lifeless corpse for a proper burial. Do you understand me?"

Matthew was silent for fear of what he might say in anger. The audacity of this common criminal with a so-called cause was more than he could stand.

"Do you understand?" Joaquín said, more pointedly.

"I don't understand any of this. This is crazy. You and your whole idiotic group of teenage Rambos is crazy."

Joaquín glared. "Don Matthew, your attitude is not good. You have already cost me one good man. You are quickly proving to be more trouble than you are worth."

Matthew said nothing. Joaquín turned away, then said something in Spanish to the smaller guard that Matthew didn't quite hear.

"*Adelante*," said the little one. Another surprise: The voice was a girl's.

As commanded, he started walking back toward the truck, but she gave him a shove in the other direction, prodding him again with the AK-47. They walked through chest-high weeds until they came to a small clearing of softer grass with the cold black ashes of an extinguished campfire in the center. Two mules were tied to a tree, both bearing a mountain of gear and supplies. Beside them were two goats, a large black one and a smaller white one.

"Stop," she said in Spanish. "On your knees, eyes forward."

Slowly he knelt in the grass, his arms at his sides. He could sense she was standing behind him, but he didn't look. He felt vulnerable, defenseless, and now he regretted the insults he'd hurled at Joaquín. These losers had murdered his friends, but he'd have to hold his tongue. They'd kill him just as quickly, especially if he continued to antagonize their leader in front of his little band of juvenile delinquents. He braced himself for some kind of disciplinary action, possibly a beating.

He heard footsteps behind, heavy boots coming swiftly toward him. He didn't look back. He just gritted his teeth, expecting a swift kick to the kidneys. Joaquín suddenly whisked past him, then stopped, a long serrated knife in hand. He got down on one knee and began to sharpen it on a rock, the grinding noise piercing Matthew's ears. When he finished, he held the blade at eye level, the metal glistening in the setting sun.

Matthew could not tear his eyes away from the eight-inch blade.

Then, in one swift motion, Joaquín wheeled, reached behind him, and grabbed the smaller goat by the throat. He pinned the animal on its back, jabbed the knife in its underbelly, and slit upward, tearing the ribs from the sternum.

It screeched in utter agony, a sound unlike any Matthew had heard since his days in Vietnam. It convulsed and kicked, still alive, blood spewing onto the ground. Matthew could hear the last breaths sucking through the gaping wound, through the sliced lungs.

Joaquín rose, unmoved by the horrific sounds of pain. He simply watched and listened as the animal's screeches gradually weakened, its life-ending throes losing their kick. The agony lasted a solid minute, and then Joaquín seemed bored. He unholstered his pistol and shot the dying goat in the head.

Then he turned toward the prisoner.

My God, is this the way I'm going to die?

Matthew preferred to be shot making a run for it than to be mutilated by this butcher. His muscles tightened as Joaquín drew near. He was about to lash out, but he held back at the last instant, convincing himself in that tense moment that he was surely worth more alive than dead to Joaquín.

Joaquín wiped the bloody knife on Matthew's shirt, one flat side and then the other. "Don't ever run from me," he said in a low, threatening tone. "I promise, death will not come so quickly for you."

Matthew glared at him, wishing he could just deck this monster.

"Up," ordered Joaquín.

Matthew rose, saying nothing. So much for Joaquín's promise to treat him well. Matthew had the feeling it was only the first of many lies.

Joaquín said, "What you said before is true. This is crazy. We are all crazy." Then he turned to his guerrillas and shouted, "*¡Bienvenidos a Locombia!*"

They laughed. It was a wordplay on "Colombia" that Matthew had seen before in newspapers, with no exact translation. But he got the drift. *Welcome to Crazyland.*

At Joaquín's command, one guerrilla took Matthew by the left arm, the other by the right, as they led him to the pack mules.

8

I had a bizarre dream that night. My family owned a gold mine. We agreed to pay the kidnappers a king's ransom for my father's release. It was delivered in a dump truck, tons of glittering gold dust. The guerrillas came with shovels and wheelbarrow. When the last of the mountain had been hauled away, the rebels released their hostage. Out from the jungle walked an eighty-six-year-old man who was not my father. Frantic, I chased after the guerrillas and shouted at the top of my lungs that they'd made a terrible mistake. One of them finally stopped and turned, almost laughing as he answered in the exact voice of the Colombian police officer I'd spoken to on the phone last evening.

You are Señor Alvarez, no?

Some people find meaning in dreams. I usually dismissed the good ones as wishful thinking and the power of suggestion; the bad ones I chalked up to stress, anxiety, and the power of indigestion. This time I wasn't taking any chances. The next morning

I drove to the Miami field office for a personal visit with the FBI.

I arrived at half past nine, took the elevator to the second floor, and checked in with the receptionist who sat on the other side of the bulletproof glass. I told her my name and why I was there.

"You want Agent Nettles, our legal liaison for international kidnappings."

"I've seen him already. I'd like to see his supervisor, please."

"Do you have an appointment?"

"No. But it's no exaggeration to say that this is a matter of life and death. Please, I really need to see someone with authority."

She gave me a quick once-over, as if trying to determine whether I was a nutcase. "I'll see who's available," she said.

"Thank you."

I sat in the Naugahyde chair and waited. Rising from the table beside me was a three-foot-tall trophy from a regional softball league. On the wall were two plaques that bore the names of FBI agents who'd lost their lives in the line of duty. It was in chronological order. There seemed to be more in recent years, like everything else. More guns. More criminals. More dead FBI agents. More Americans kidnapped abroad.

Finally the door opened and the receptionist called for me. "Come with me, please."

She clipped a visitor's badge to my shirt, and I followed her down the brightly lit hall. We made several turns, then came to a larger room that was partitioned into smaller workstations by chest-high dividers. Dozens of agents and other personnel were busy in their pods, reviewing files, working at computer terminals, or talking on the telephone. Work here was done without the noise and confusion of police stations, where people always seemed to be shouting at each other or dodging some drunk who was about to vomit on their shoes. An FBI field office had an air of dignity, practically a church, compared to the zoo-in-blue downtown.

We stopped at a conference room. Three walls were windowless; the fourth was completely glass and faced the interior workstations. Inside were two agents who rose from the table to greet me. The older one was Agent Sam Huitt, a man about my dad's age. He had the same lines around his eyes as Dad did, too, not from years of squinting in the sun, I surmised, but from habitually narrowing his gaze with suspicion. The younger agent was Angela Pintero, a tall woman with olive skin and short brown hair styled into tight, efficient curls. We exchanged pleasantries and then took our seats, me across the table from the two of them.

"Are you Agent Nettles's supervisor?" I asked Huitt.

"Not directly, but I am a supervisory special agent. And I'm aware of the impasse between the bureau and the State Department."

"Good. Because I'm making it my business to break the impasse. Agent Nettles tried to help, but his hands were clearly tied. If you can't do better, I'd like to speak to your supervisor."

"I'm confident we can help."

"That's encouraging. Do you have anything specific in mind?"

"First, I propose to listen. You came to us. I presume you have some thoughts of your own as to how we can solve the problem."

Huitt sat back with hands clasped behind his head. Pintero was poised to take notes. They seemed to operate the way Duncan and I did, the senior guy running the show, the other playing backup.

"Here's the way I see it," I said. "The State Department insists that FBI negotiators can't be involved if they plan to assist the family in the payment of a ransom. After speaking with my father's business partner last night, my fear is that the kidnappers will demand a ransom that my family can't possibly pay. If that's the case, we might as well have the FBI negotiators on our side trying to get the kidnappers to release my father for no ransom. Let's just tell the State Department we'll play by their rules."

He smiled thinly, as if amused. "That's a little transparent, don't you think?"

"How so?"

"If I were the State Department, I would suspect that your overall plan is simply to get the FBI involved, get them entrenched in the case, and then ultimately ignore the no-concessions policy and pay a ransom."

The guy was onto me. "Do you have a better suggestion?"

"Yes. Take a step back and ask yourself why the FBI really declined the State Department's invitation to participate in this case."

I didn't like his tone. Things had suddenly moved

from a friendly discussion to a subtle confrontation, one I didn't fully understand. "You're going to have to help me out there, Mr. Huitt."

"Did you know that your father has been stopped and interrogated by U.S. customs nineteen times in the last five years?"

That one hit me like ice water. "No."

"Does it surprise you?"

"Not really. He probably fits an arbitrary profile the government has developed. As often as he travels alone between Miami and Central America, it honestly surprises me that he hasn't been stopped more often."

They just stared at me, silent accusers. Their gaze made me look away, through the conference room's glass wall. At one of the workstations outside the conference room, I noticed a bumper sticker tacked up on the bulletin board. It read, SO MANY COLOMBIANS, SO LITTLE TIME.

"Am I in the narcotics unit?" I asked.

"Yes. I'm a squad leader."

"My father's been kidnapped. Why am I talking to narcotics agents?"

"Because we're the ones you need to play ball with."

"What?"

"You give us something, we give you something. Quid pro quo."

"You'd better mean *squid* pro quo, because that's about all the Rey family can give you. My father's a fisherman."

"Fisherman, huh?"

"Yeah. Fisherman."

"Whatever you say. But if you stick to that story, we get nowhere in our efforts to resolve the so-called policy differences between the FBI and the State Department."

I leaned into the table and looked him in the eye. "Let me make sure I understand. You're telling me that this deadlock between the FBI and the State Department can be cleared up if . . . what?"

"If you cut the crap about your old man being a fisherman."

"But that's what he is."

"Humor us," said Huitt. "For argument's sake, let's say he's not."

I was getting angry. "Okay, let's play fantasy world. My dad's not a fisherman. Then what? You're saying that the FBI will help him get released from his kidnappers, but only if I give you information that will land him in jail the minute he returns to the United States? That's crazy."

"We're not after your old man. It's his business partner we want. The Nicaraguan, Guillermo Cruz."

"I barely even know Guillermo."

"That's our point," said the female agent, her only contribution.

I looked at her, then at Huitt. Both were deadpan. There was nothing I could say in Guillermo's defense. I'd met him only once in my life.

Huitt said, "Talk to your mother, see how much she knows. If you can come up with something compelling on Cruz, we're in business. We get the man we want. Your father gets an FBI negotiator working on his case. Your whole family can have immunity from prosecution."

"Prosecution for *what?*"

"Talk to your mother. And take my advice. Watch yourself around Guillermo Cruz."

They rose simultaneously, as if on cue. It struck me as pure intimidation, the strategic moment at which an experienced agent like Huitt liked to end meetings of this sort.

The younger agent opened the door to escort me back to the lobby. As she led me away from the table, I stopped for one last word with Huitt.

"Just out of curiosity," I said. "Of all those times my father was stopped by U.S. customs, how many times was he found to have broken the law?"

He said nothing.

"That's what I thought." I turned and headed out the door, the other agent at my side.

"Kid," said Huitt.

I was halfway down the hall with Agent Pintero. We stopped and looked back.

"It only takes once," he said flatly, then stepped back into the conference room.

I wondered if that was some kind of warning that he'd continue to dog my family until he got something on us. Or was he implying that he already had the goods?

I continued toward the lobby in silence, more confused than when I'd arrived.

9

"Notice of Death" were the three words that caught my attention. Alone at my desk, I read the caption on the pleading twice to make sense of it.

After the meeting with Agent Huitt, I'd driven straight down I-95 to my law firm. I quickly dismissed the idea of asking Duncan Fitz for advice on how to handle the government's accusations. My supervising partner would have been utterly unamused to hear that my father and his business partner were on the FBI's radar screen. Nevertheless, I rode up the elevator and went straight to my office, with no real purpose other than to be alone there. As my ex-fiancée had finally come to realize, my career was my cocoon. Bad news, a crisis of any sort—retreating to my cubbyhole and immersing myself in work could make just about anything seem to disappear. Countless times Jenna had begged me to crawl out of my cave and talk out a problem with her. Eventually I would emerge, usually with the proud announcement that I'd figured out everything by myself and that there was nothing left to talk about. It used to make her crazy.

And here I was again, going through my stack of mail, as if that would fix everything with the FBI. It wouldn't, of course, and what made the whole exercise even more absurd was that I didn't even need to be there. Duncan had arranged for another associate to review my mail while I was on personal leave for the week. Anything that was deemed bland enough to remain in my in-box until my return was about as compelling as reading the phone book, with the exception of the latest pleading filed by the plaintiff's counsel in the Med-Fam Pharmaceuticals case. A simple one-page "notice of death" advised the court of the sad turn of events.

Gilbert Jones was dead.

He had died of respiratory failure the morning after Duncan talked him into playing "Let's Make a Deal." We all knew he was going to die. No one expected it to happen this soon. He'd given up. Duncan had snatched away what little he had left to fight for in his life. Having met Gilbert, I felt bad enough. Dad's being kidnapped made me feel that much worse. Gilbert's death made me realize that everyone had a breaking point, maybe not the stomach to pull the trigger or jump off a bridge, but certainly the ability to act—or, more precisely, *not* act—on the realization that there was no escape and that pushing forward was utterly pointless. That Gilbert had reached his point of despair so soon after Duncan's ploy made me terribly depressed. The thought that Dad might someday follow had me downright distressed. Even the strong could snap at the hands of abusive kidnappers.

I pushed the mail aside. Being alone wasn't the answer. I needed to talk to someone.

I wasn't exactly sure why, but I found myself dialing Jenna's phone number. My mother had planted the seed in my head yesterday when she'd suggested that I tell her about the kidnapping. It had sounded like a bad idea then, and in some ways it didn't sound any better now. I was down in the dumps, however, and for some reason I wanted to hear her voice.

"Hello," she answered.

I almost hung up, but I knew that her cell phone had Caller ID. She'd think I was stalking her.

"Hi, it's me. Nick."

"I know. I recognized the number. How are you?"

"I have some bad news, I'm afraid."

"Your dad, I know. I'm sorry."

"You heard?"

"I saw Duncan Fitz at the courthouse yesterday. He told me."

Jenna was a trial lawyer at a small firm in Coral Gables. As she used to rub it in, lawyers at smaller firms actually had their own cases and got to see the inside of the courthouse, unlike the young paper pushers at law firms like Cool Cash.

"Well, I'm glad he mentioned it," I said. "I wanted you to know."

"I wasn't sure if I should call you or not. I wrote a little personal note to your mom. I know this might sound hollow, but if there's anything I can do, just call. I mean it. I feel terrible that this has happened."

"Thanks."

"You're welcome."

I paused, not sure where to take it from there. We'd been best friends and lovers for almost five years. How weird it was to think that if my father hadn't been kidnapped we might never have uttered another word to one another. My heart was pounding. I was nervous and confused. I felt guilty, too, thinking that in some way I'd used my father's crisis as an excuse to reconnect with Jenna, however briefly. Calling her had accomplished nothing. Or maybe it had proved too much. The mere sound of her voice had only confirmed that I wasn't over her.

"So, how are you doing?" I asked.

She said something beyond "Good," but it was garbled. The connection was breaking up.

"I'm sorry, what?" I said.

Her response was pure static. The connection was even worse.

"I think I'm losing you." As soon as I'd said it, the line went dead, and I realized the irony of my words. I placed the receiver in the cradle, sat back in my chair, and stared blankly off to the middle distance.

"I've definitely lost you," I said softly.

My cell phone rang. I snatched it from my pocket, thinking it was Jenna. It was my mother.

"Good news," she said.

"What?"

"I've been worried sick ever since Guillermo told us how those kidnappers think of your father as a gold mine. All I've been able to think is, What if we can't pay the ransom?"

"I know. We're all worried."

"Well, our worries are over."

"What do you mean?"

"If we have to, we can pay a gold mine and then some."

"How?"

"Your father once told me that if anything ever happened to him on one of his trips, I should check a special safe-deposit box he opened at Brickell Trust. The last couple of days I've been putting it off. I was afraid I would find a letter of good-bye or something on that order. This morning I finally went. You won't believe what was in there."

"Stop right there, Mom." On the heels of Agent Huitt's accusations, I was suddenly concerned that Mom and I might not be the only ones on this phone line.

"But this is really good news."

"We'll talk about it when I get home. I'll be right there." I hung up before she could say more.

I had no idea what she'd found, but I surely didn't want her blurting it out if there was any possibility that the FBI had tapped our lines and was eavesdropping. I returned the notice of Gilbert Jones's death to the top of my pile, then quickly headed out the door.

10

As a lawyer, I was embarrassed to admit it. But I couldn't lie to my own mother. I'd never heard of kidnap-and-ransom insurance for a fisherman.

That was exactly what Mom had found in the safe-deposit box: a K&R insurance policy issued to my father. I'd seen that type of coverage before, but only for the big multinational conglomerates. For companies with employees abroad, it certainly made sense to shift the risk of an abduction to an insurance company. The insurer was then on the hook for paying the ransom and, even more important, hiring a private security consultant to negotiate a safe release. When I thought about it, the concept made even more sense for a small business. A half-million-dollar ransom would do much more damage to Rey's Seafood Company than would a ten-million-dollar hit to a Fortune 500 company. Until now, however, I'd never realized how affordable it was even for the little guy.

I read the entire policy carefully, first page to last, while seated at the kitchen table with my mother looking over my shoulder. I was at once proud of my old man for thinking of it and excited as hell that he'd actually followed through and bought it. *Hot damn!* Dad was insured.

"This is good, right?" said Mom.

"It's fantastic."

"So I read it correctly? The insurance company pays the ransom?"

"Up to three million dollars."

Her eyes brightened, and she actually smiled. It was the most upbeat I'd seen her. "I wish your father had told me he had insurance. Why was he so secretive with the safe-deposit box?"

"It says right here in the policy that if the insured tells anyone that he has kidnap-and-ransom insurance, the policy is void. Apparently Dad took that pretty literally. He wouldn't even tell you."

"What happens now?"

"I'll call the insurance company and give them notice. If I read the policy right, they select the negotiator who will handle Dad's case."

"Is that better than using the FBI?"

I hesitated to tell her about the disastrous meeting with Agent Huitt. Her spirits were too high. "My guess is that these private consultants are former FBI hostage negotiators and the like. How can it get better than that? We'll have a skilled negotiator who doesn't have to work within the box created by bureaucrats and diplomats."

"If only I'd gone to the bank sooner. But when your father told me to check the safe-deposit box if anything ever happened to him, I thought he meant if he crashed in one of those little airplanes they fly into Puerto Cabezas or was lost at sea in a leaky old shrimp boat. I was so afraid to find something in the box that I wasn't ready to see, a last will and testament or—"

"I understand."

"Please be firm with this insurance company. You know how slow they can be."

I could hear the concern in her voice, her fear that she'd needlessly delayed things by not finding the policy sooner. "Mom, I don't care what it takes. Before the day's over, I'll speak to our negotiator. I promise."

As it turned out, keeping that promise proved almost too easy. Dad was insured with Quality Insurance Company, a Bermuda-based subsidiary of a worldwide underwriting group. More important, I quickly learned that Quality was a client of Coolidge, Harding and Cash. The connection wasn't surprising. While scores of companies offered kidnap-and-ransom insurance, the leaders in the industry—and the ones who had pioneered the concept—were the largest insurers in the world. Companies like that were the mainstay of the Cool Cash client roster.

The Miami office had never done work for Quality Insurance, but a woman in our New York office was their go-to lawyer in the United States. She was only too glad to help, which underscored the wisdom of my earlier decision to run a conflict check at my firm before placing a phone call to Quality. Having represented insurance companies myself, I'd anticipated needing to be aggressive, perhaps even a little nasty, to make the elephant jump. However, I recalled a fellow associate in our office who, on a purely personal matter, had written an ugly letter to an appliance discount store on Cool Cash letterhead. The scathing missive eventually landed on the desk of the partner in our Atlanta office who happened to represent that "sleazebag, bait-and-switch, two-bit operation." Two weeks later my friend was working in the county attorney's office. I learned from his mistake. Instead of being in the defensive posture of explaining to a New York partner why I was beating up on her client, I had the partner working for me from the get-go. She personally followed through to make sure the case was assigned immediately to a Miami consulting firm, and Duncan Fitz offered to sit through our first meeting in his office, just to make sure that Quality Insurance understood that this law firm had a keen interest in the case.

Thank God for small favors. Twice for big ones. This was huge.

"Alex Cabrera is here," Duncan's secretary announced over the intercom.

"Send him in," said Duncan.

Duncan and I rose as the door opened, both of us surprised to see that Alex was a her, not a him. I'd expected someone like Agent Nettles, but in walked a striking Latina woman with big brown eyes. She was dressed in a fitted gray business suit that was conservative only in color, as it did little to hide the fact that she took very good care of her body. I probably looked a split second longer than I should have. Any man would have done the same, and notwithstanding the one-two punch of Jenna and her dive-bombing seagull on the beach, I was, after all, still a man.

"Alexandra Cabrera," she said. "Call me Alex."

"My pleasure," I said, as we shook hands.

"I'm with Crowell Associates."

"A fine organization," said Duncan. "I've used your investigators for litigation support." He glanced at me and added, "They're one of the largest private investigative and security firms in the world."

"Actually, you're thinking of Kroll Associates. I said Crowell." She spelled it.

"Oh. Sorry."

"A lot of firms in this business have similar-sounding names. It gets confusing."

"So you're based here in Miami?" I asked.

"For the past two years. I spent seven years doing the same kind of work in Bogotá."

"Well, you come very highly recommended by our partner in New York. She says you're an expert on kidnapping and business extortion."

"Solving and preventing it," she said, "not committing it."

We shared a little smile over her joke, and then she turned serious. "I'm very sorry about your father. But you've come to the right place for help."

Duncan's secretary brought us fresh coffee. We took our seats, Duncan behind his desk, Alex and I in the wing chairs that faced him.

"Where do we begin?" I said.

"I want to hear your whole story, but I should tell you a little about myself, just so you know you're not wasting your breath. I was born in Bogotá. My mother was Colombian, and I'm told my father was from Italy. I won't burden you with the details of my childhood, but suffice it to say I grew up very fast. By the time I was a young teenager, I was already caught up in antigovernment activities. At age sixteen I joined Las Fuerzas Armadas Revolucionarias de Colombia. FARC for short."

"That might be the group that has my father."

"It's one of the largest and last remaining Marxist guerrilla armies on earth. More to the point, it's probably the biggest kidnapping enterprise that has ever existed. FARC and organizations like it account for over sixty percent of the kidnappings in Colombia."

"That's a lot of kidnappings."

"You have no idea. The more you analyze the numbers, the more ridiculous they seem. One out of every five kidnappings for ransom in the entire world happens in Colombia."

"How long were you with FARC?" I asked.

"Less than two years. Long enough to learn the kidnapping trade."

Duncan said, "I don't suppose you'd find many FBI stiffs with those kinds of credentials."

"You won't find any," said Alex. "I once thought of applying to the FBI, but with my past connection to FARC, I was told not to bother. It's their loss. My other life is exactly the reason I can help you in ways they can't."

"Don't be offended," I said. "But I have to be honest. I was expecting my negotiator to be a former law enforcement officer. Not a former member of FARC."

"First of all, I was sixteen years old when I left

FARC. Second, you won't find a former FBI agent or Scotland Yard negotiator with more experience in Colombia or a better success record than mine."

"Have you negotiated the release of an American before?" asked Duncan.

"Yes, and some Canadians as well. But if you're thinking it's any easier to negotiate for the release of a Colombian, you're wrong. Generally, these aren't politically motivated kidnappings. They're financially motivated. The nationality of the victim is relevant, if at all, only to the extent that it might affect the amount of ransom demanded."

"You certainly seem to know your stuff," I said.

"The most important thing is that you have confidence in your negotiator. Under your father's policy, the insurance company pays for a private consultant only if you use Crowell Associates. But if you don't like the specific consultant assigned to your case, you're not stuck. There are others in our organization to choose from. For example, we have a former CIA agent who's a crackerjack on Mexico. I'm sure he'd do a fine job in Colombia, much the way one of your bankruptcy lawyers would do just fine on a divorce case."

"I get your point," I said.

"You can also bypass private security altogether and rely on the FBI."

"That's not really an option. I'm at an impasse with them." I didn't elaborate in front of Duncan; the threat from the narcotics agents was best kept to myself.

"I'm sorry you had that experience," she said. "There are a lot of talented negotiators in the FBI who can be of tremendous help to families when the bureaucracy lets them do their job."

"It's pretty clear the bureaucracy's winning this battle."

"That's one of the benefits of private security. I'm totally responsive to you, and to you only. My approach is to tell you everything, each step of the way. I'll advise you of what to do, explain to you the significance of every little thing the kidnappers do, and offer my best guess as to what they might do in the future. Total honesty and openness is the best approach, as in any other relationship. And, believe me, this is a relationship."

"Not too long-term, I hope."

She didn't smile. "Didn't the FBI even tell you that much?"

"What?"

"The length of time it normally takes to bring a Colombian kidnapping case to closure."

"He wanted to wait and see who was involved before making any projections."

"That makes some sense. But you should be forewarned."

"Of what?" I asked.

"These guerrilla organizations don't exactly operate at breakneck speed."

"How long might it take? Weeks? Months?"

"I've had a few relatively quick resolutions. But for the most part we're definitely talking months."

"How many?"

"The average case, anywhere from six to twelve."

"A fucking year?" My astonishment was met with plaintive silence.

"I warned you, I don't sugarcoat."

"I prefer it that way. Excuse my profanity."

"No problem. You'll hear worse from me before this case is over. Assuming you want me on the case."

I shot a quick glance at Duncan. He seemed to be as impressed as I was. "Absolutely," I said.

"Great. Now, it's been very nice meeting you and Duncan, but I'd like to meet with you and the rest of your family as soon as possible."

"My sister's traveling, and we haven't been in touch with her yet. But I can drive you over to my mother's house right now."

"Let's go."

We rose to leave, but Duncan stole another minute of Alex's time. He needed surveillance work for one of his cases and wanted to know if Alex had any suggestions. *Right.* Ever since his divorce, Duncan seemed to draw personal validation from any attractive woman who would smile and talk to him, even if it was purely business from her standpoint.

I waited at the window and looked down thirty stories on the evening rush hour traffic. It was slowly snaking south on busy Brickell Avenue, an endless chain of fuzzy orange taillights at dusk. People were going home, the same old routine, not knowing how lucky they were to have their routines.

Could this possibly drag on for a year?

So much in a person's life could change in that much time. Look at me and Jenna, engaged one month, history the next. Could my father physically survive that long in some remote guerrilla camp? He'd survived Vietnam, albeit as a much younger man. What would the emotional scars be like, the effects of prolonged captivity? Not seeing him for that long was unfathomable.

Poor Mom, I thought, the reality sinking in. *Poor Dad.*

11

.

For only the second time in my life, I was taking a woman home to meet my mother and desperately wanted them to hit it off. Obviously the circumstances were very different, as were my motivations. Yet, I was strangely reminded of Jenna as Alex and I wove through traffic in my Jeep with the canvas top down. It was a rare comfortable evening in early autumn, without the persistent mugginess that usually lingered in South Florida until almost Halloween. Alex had removed her jacket and pulled her shoulder-length hair back to keep it from blowing in the breeze. Her profile was classic. Whether she was the more beautiful was hard to say, but, no slight to Jenna, she was definitely more intriguing.

"So, how'd you get caught up in FARC?"

We were stopped at a traffic light on Coral Way. Just ahead was the world's first Burger King restaurant. Decades later it was still there, but everything around it had changed as the new Miami took over the old Miami—"My-ama," my grandmother used to call it, an era as extinct now as the old notion of a "healthy" suntan. To my left was the original Latin American Cafeteria, where people waited in line outside for a chance to sit at the long, horseshoe-shaped counter and order everything from *medianoche* sandwiches to milkshakes made with exotic fruits like *mamey*. At the walk-up café across the street stood a group of Spanish-speaking men dressed in guayaberas, traditional Cuban shirts. Espresso served in little plastic cups inspired friendly arguments over *béisbol* and politicians who were too soft on Castro. Just ahead, the man in the intersection with the big straw hat was hawking bags of *limas* from the tree in his neighbor's backyard. It was the Miami I'd grown up with, the cultural mix I liked.

Alex said, "I wouldn't say I was caught up in FARC. I just joined."

"Why?"

"The usual burning philosophical issues that propel teenage girls to do anything."

"Meaning what?"

"My boyfriend was in it."

"I suppose we've all been there on some level. Except that the craziest thing I ever did was sign up for the glee club."

"Hmm. Not sure which of us was the bigger sucker."

"True. I got dumped about two weeks after I signed up. How about you?"

"That's about the size of it."

"Did he meet someone else?"

"No. He took a bullet in the head."

For a second I felt like I'd taken the bullet. "I'm sorry."

"Don't be. He was a drug-addicted worthless piece of trash who didn't think twice about kidnapping people like your father."

"Did he ever kill anyone?"

"Yes."

I hesitated, then asked, "Did you?"

"Why do you want to know?"

"Just thought it might come up with my mother. You know, the natural progression of things. 'Hello, how are you, ever been a revolutionary?'"

She smiled cryptically. "Would it make a difference to you if I had?"

I wasn't sure it would, but I was beginning to wish I hadn't asked. "I suppose not. Like you said in Duncan's office, that was your other life."

"Exactly."

The light turned green, and we were flowing with the traffic again. I waited for her to elaborate, but after several moments of silence it was clear that she wasn't about to. FARC was her other life. That was that. Maybe she had killed someone, maybe she hadn't.

Just don't piss her off, Nick.

"Tell me about your father," she said. "What's he like?"

"Just a regular guy." I reconsidered, then said, "Actually, he's pretty extraordinary. Dad never went to college. Went straight from high school to Vietnam in the early seventies, came home and fell in love with my mom. She was nineteen when she got pregnant. They married, and six months later it was the three of us."

"So you're a love child?"

"Yeah, but they didn't stay together for twenty-six years because of me. After all these years, after all they've been through, they really are still in love."

"Does your mom help in the business?"

"That's totally my dad's passion. He started it with one old lobster boat that on a good day broke down only once. Now his company has forty boats pulling twenty tons of lobster a week out of Nicaragua. It's a cutthroat business, but I daresay there's not a guy in it who doesn't trust my dad."

"Sounds like you think highly of him."

"I do."

"You two must be close."

That gave me pause. To hear me gush, it did sound as though we were close. I gave her the same kind of half-baked answer that she'd given me when I'd asked about her body count with FARC. "I'm sure we'd be closer if I'd gone into the fishing business with him."

We were a half block from my house when I noticed a van in the driveway, ACTION NEWS emblazoned on its side. The media had found us. I pulled up in the driveway beside it, jumped down from the Jeep, and confronted a couple of tech guys packing away their equipment. They were leaving, not coming.

"What are you doing here?"

"Our job," he said in a flat, sanctimonious tone.

"Did you interview my mother?"

"She was great. It's over."

Alex laid her hand on my shoulder, as if to calm me down. "It's okay," she said. "We'll deal with it."

I took it down a notch, but knowing how upset my mother had been lately, the thought of someone's sticking a microphone in her face really angered me. "Where's your reporter?"

"Gone. You're not the only news in this city. Just relax. No one was traumatized here."

Alex and I went inside. She waited behind in the living room as I continued to the kitchen. Mom was seated alone at the table, sipping a glass of orange juice. She was dressed nicely, with her makeup on, which I was glad to see. If she was going to be on television, it wouldn't have done her any good to have people saying that she looked as if she were falling apart. She smiled nervously as I entered, perhaps rethinking the things she'd told the reporter.

"I didn't know what to do," she said. "They just showed up at my door, no notice, and said they wanted a live interview for their six o'clock broadcast. I said no at first, but the reporter was very nice and convinced me that a little publicity might help your father's cause. I was going to call you, but she had to do it right then. I shouldn't have done it, I guess."

"It's okay. I'm sure you were fine."

"Can I say something?" Alex was standing in the doorway, not really eavesdropping. It would have been impossible for her not to overhear.

"Who are you?"

"Alex Cabrera. I'm with Crowell Associates."

"She's a private consultant," I added. "The insurance company pays for her."

"Mrs. Rey, dealing with media under these circumstances can't be pleasant for you, but don't second-guess yourself. Even the experts disagree on whether the families of kidnap victims should lie low or try to drum up publicity. Since cases of international kidnapping are often tinged with politics, some people think that publicity helps bring pressure on the politicians to resolve them quickly. Others think that if a case gets a lot of publicity, the kidnappers will infer that they've caught a really big fish, which inflates their demands."

"They already think they have a gold mine," said Mom.

"And nothing you said on the evening news is going to affect that view one way or the other. But from now on let's have an agreement, all right? No one talks to the media unless it's something we all agree on in advance."

"I only did the one interview."

"And that's probably enough for now. Once you get a ransom demand and we know for sure that FARC or whoever is behind the kidnapping, then we can develop a media strategy."

I offered Alex a chair, then pulled one up for myself at the kitchen table. "Shouldn't we also give some thought on how we might use the media? We haven't heard anything from the kidnappers yet. Maybe it's a way to get a message across."

"That's something to consider, but it takes planning. You have to ask yourself, what message do you want the kidnappers to hear? And how will it be interpreted by everyone else who hears it? The general public. The police. It's even possible that your father will hear you on Voice of America or RNC radio."

"I hadn't really thought of Dad hearing anything while in captivity."

"Some prisoners are more isolated than others, but I know that FARC does on occasion give radio privileges to some. So if we do decide to use the media—and I'm not saying we will—it might make sense to have more than one person in the family do interviews. The longer this drags on, it could be of psychological benefit for him to hear his wife's voice, then his son's voice, his daughter's voice, and so on."

"How do you know so much about these kidnappings?" Mom asked.

Alex looked at me, as if to say that the message would flow best from my lips.

"Remember that group Agent Nettles told us about, FARC? She used to be a member."

Mom blinked hard, as if my words weren't quite computing. After several moments of silence, she was slowly turning green.

"Are you okay, Mom?"

Her shoulders started to heave. "Excuse me," she said as she bolted from the table.

Alex gave me an awkward look. "Maybe I should leave."

A strange noise emerged from the bathroom at the end of the hall, like a goose honking. Mom sounded really sick.

"Wait here. Let me check on her."

The retching noise grew louder as I headed down the hall. The door was half open. I was almost afraid to look inside. After several moments of silence, I heard the toilet flush, then silence. Figuring the worst had passed, I tapped lightly on the door and entered.

Mom was kneeling on the floor, her arm resting on the rim of the bowl.

"I'm sorry, Mom. I should have warned you about Alex. I know you're under a lot of stress, and I—"

"It's not her. It's morning sickness."

"What?"

"It may be nighttime, but my stomach doesn't know it. All damn day long, I've got morning sickness. It was the same way with you and Lindsey."

"You're pregnant?"

"Yes. I'm pregnant."

"How?"

Her expression said, *How do you think?*

I checked my astonishment slightly, reminding myself that she'd become my mother just a year out of high school. "Does Dad know?"

"Yes. It wasn't planned, but he was actually excited. We both were. And now," she said, her voice shaking, "now, I might already be a widow and not even know it. This is such a disaster."

I sat on the floor beside her, my hand atop her stomach. "This is not a disaster. This is the most important reason in the world for Dad to reach inside himself and find the will to survive, no matter what happens. And it's the most incredible reason on earth for me to do everything I can to make sure he gets home."

Tears welled in her eyes. She reached out for me, our first hug ever on the bathroom floor. She wasn't just holding me; she was holding *on* to me. I'd never thought of my mother as weak. But if Alex was right—if this ordeal could last twelve months—I honestly wasn't sure how Mom would deal with it. Especially now.

"We'll be fine," I said as we rocked gently in each other's arms on the cold tile floor. "The whole new family is going to be just fine."

12

·

Matthew Rey lay sleeping beneath the make-shift remains of a shoddy old army tent. A cold rain dripped onto his foul-smelling bed, which was nothing more than a dirty blanket stretched atop a pile of corn husks. The canvas roof was so saturated from steady rainfall that it leaked even where there were no holes. It would have been im-possible for most people to sleep under these condi-tions. Matthew slept from exhaustion.

The first night he and his five armed escorts hiked for two hours. The valleys here were savanna, with a broad belt of trees about halfway up the mountain, then more savanna at the mountain crest. All of it was swampy, even the mountainside. Thick grass, clover, and mosses held rainfall like a sponge well into the higher elevations. Soggy ground made for tough go-ing in the moonlight, but the guerrillas seemed deter-mined to evacuate the grassy valley and reach the cover of tall trees before making camp. The next morning they'd risen at dawn and continued deeper into the forest, walking at a healthy clip beneath the canopy of bushy trees and twisted vines. The guerrillas didn't seem concerned that they were wearing boots and Matthew wasn't. The higher altitudes brought cooler temperatures, about a drop of three degrees centigrade for each five hundred meters. Matthew had no jacket and was still wearing the short-sleeved shirt in which he'd been captured.

As the sun descended toward the jagged mountaintops, the thinning air turned chilly, though not unbearable. Just before dusk they stopped to make camp, and Matthew was finally given a blanket. The guerrillas made a small fire and ate boiled goat, the one Joaquín had butchered in such cruel fashion. Matthew had only a tin of Vienna sausages and a hot cup of *sabayón*, a milky drink made from *aguardiente*, a local firewater that tasted like a bad imitation of French Pernod. They didn't tell him what it was until after he'd finished, and it was the first alcoholic beverage he'd had in almost fifteen years. It warmed him slightly, but in the fading afterglow of the sunset he had to focus hard on his surroundings to take his mind off his goose bumps. Their camp was near a field of onions intercropped with magnificent blackish-purple plants topped with bright scarlet flowers. In a country that boasts over a hundred and thirty thousand different plant classifications, Matthew couldn't even hazard a guess. *"Amapola,"* one of the guerrillas had told him. "Poppy," said another. The translation belied the beauty. It struck Matthew that few Americans had ever been this close to the raw materials for heroin.

No one had told him exactly where he was, of course. The endless peaks and valleys suggested western Colombia, the most mountainous part of the country. The five-thousand-mile Cordillera de los Andes runs the length of South America, then splits into three ranges in Colombia. Sandwiched between the peaks of Cordillera Occidental, Cordillera Central, and Cordillera Oriental are two great valleys, Valle del Cauca and Valle del Magdalena, whose two rivers run northward until they merge and flow into the Caribbean. Just the sight of moving water had Matthew thinking of possible escape routes, though escape seemed impossible this far from civilization. Last night at their campsite, Matthew looked up through the trees to the vast ocean of stars twinkling overhead. They were so brilliant and plentiful, he had to be hundreds of miles from any city lights. The world was so quiet at this altitude, and the weather changed so quickly. By the time he'd made up his tent and bedding, the stars were gone. Low-hanging clouds had turned the camp pitch-dark, and he slowly became more aware of sounds than sights. The river churned through the valley a thousand feet below, like static on the radio. The gurgling sounds just ten meters from his tent were from a stream of the sweetest, purest water he'd ever tasted. Ten meters in the opposite direction stood a patch of bamboo, the bathroom, from which a strange clicking noise emerged in the darkness. A bird, he assumed. Colombia was full of birds, more species in this one country than in all of North America and Europe combined. The lure had gotten many an unsuspecting bird-watcher kidnapped.

The last sound he'd heard before dozing off to sleep was the patter of raindrops on canvas. It continued until he woke at the crack of dawn the next morning.

"Up," said one of the guerrillas.

His eyes opened to instant disappointment. The shooting and kidnapping on the boat, the daylong ride in the back of a truck, and the hike through mountains had all seemed like a bad dream. The sight of a girl almost ten years younger than his daughter, armed with an M-1 .30-caliber carbine, only confirmed how real it was. She poked him with the barrel.

"*Por favor*," said Matthew, pushing the barrel aside. All the guerrillas had the dangerous habit of misusing weapons as pointers and prods.

For Matthew, breakfast was a cold, chewy roll. He ate alone beneath his dripping-wet military canvas. By the time he'd finished, the rain had stopped. The guerrillas started a fire with wood they'd kept dry beneath a canvas tarp that was far superior to the so-called tent they'd given to Matthew. Something was sizzling in a pan over the fire. It didn't smell very appetizing to Matthew, but he would have preferred it if only because it was hot. They gathered around the fire to eat as Matthew watched from several meters away. He noted that Joaquín, the leader, was not around. A minute later he was coming through the forest, instantly recognizable with his Australian-style hat.

"For you," he said as he handed Matthew a plastic sack.

Inside were a toothbrush, a tube of toothpaste, a roll of toilet paper, and a bar of soap. Matthew was torn as to whether he should say "*Gracias*" or "Don't do me any favors, you murdering pigs." Showing appreciation toward these thugs wasn't going to be easy, but they did hold his life in their hands. A rapport on some level was essential to his survival.

"All the comforts of home," he said. It was as close to "thank you" as he could muster.

"Later. Come with me now."

Joaquín and two other guerrillas led him back by the same route Joaquín had just taken. They walked for almost fifteen minutes along the edge of the poppy field, then another twenty minutes deep into the forest. Joaquín seemed to know where he was headed, even as the foliage grew thicker. Again the thought of escape crossed Matthew's mind, but it was quickly dismissed. Even if he could break away, he doubted that he could ever find his way out of this jungle.

Finally he heard voices ahead. In a minute they reached a clearing in the forest. A large cottage stood on stilts in the center. It was constructed of roughly hewn logs and a thatched roof. Several smaller huts were nearby, two with the doors open, three with the doors closed. It was a busy place, like a way station. Almost a hundred men and women in combat fatigues were standing around, sitting on rocks, walking from one place to another. A team of pack mules was hitched behind the cottage, munching hay. Goats picked at the garbage near the latrine.

Joaquín was smiling as he walked into camp with his catch. Matthew once again wanted to deck him, but he was even more incensed by the reaction of the other guerrillas. They whistled, some cheered. He felt like the prize fish on the dock.

"*El gringo*," said one of the guerrillas, smiling.

"*La mina*," said Joaquín. The name seemed to be sticking. Matthew was the gold mine.

Joaquín led them toward the cottage, slowly, so that he could soak up the praise. He especially enjoyed the adoring glances from guerrillas of the opposite sex. He even removed his hat once and took a bow. The girls—and they were just girls—giggled in response. Joaquín winked. He obviously fancied himself the ladies' man.

Matthew thought they were headed for the main cottage, but Joaquín led him past the entrance to a smaller hut behind it. Two armed guards were posted outside the door. One of them unlocked it. Joaquín pushed Matthew inside.

Inside it was dark. The floor was dirt, not even flat. The air was thick with a musty odor emitted from a thatched roof that was perpetually rain-soaked. A small rectangular opening in the door was the only source of daylight. Matthew peered through it and watched as Joaquín disappeared into the cottage. A noise from behind gave him a start. Rats, he feared, or worse.

"*Hola*," a man said.

Slowly, Matthew's eyes adjusted. The man was one of four seated on the floor, far in the corner. With all the shadows, Matthew hadn't noticed them upon entering.

"*Hola*," said Matthew.

"Are you the American?"

Just one word, and the man could tell. His friend Hector had been right: He was Juanito Carson. "Yes. Who are you?"

"An unlucky son of a bitch. Just like you."

The man rose and said, "Emilio Sánchez. From Bogotá."

Matthew shook his hand and introduced himself. "Who are these people?"

He took Matthew to the door. Together, they peered out. "See the insignia on the left sleeve?" he said, pointing toward the guard outside the door.

Matthew squinted to make out what appeared to be a dragon holding a sword of equal height. "Yes, I see it."

"That's FARC."

His heart sank. He'd heard of FARC, and what he'd heard wasn't good. "I didn't notice that insignia on the guerrillas who kidnapped me."

"That's because those guys aren't FARC."

"What are they?"

"Worse than FARC."

Matthew almost scoffed. "What could be worse?"

"You have to understand, kidnapping has become like an industry in this country, especially for groups like FARC. It's gotten to the point where they basically subcontract their work. They hire negotiators, intermediaries, people to house the kidnap victims, even people who pull off the abductions. All these extras might have nothing to do with FARC. They're just part of the industry."

"How do you know so much?"

"This is the second time I've been kidnapped in three years."

"Damn. That's awful."

"Tell me about it. But you learn. Some guards can be a good source of information if you talk to them the right way. That's how I got the goods on you. I know all about Joaquín, too."

"My kidnapper?"

"*Sí.* I saw him prancing around the cottage earlier this morning when I had my bathroom break. He was strutting like a big shot, so I asked the guards about him. They said he was bringing in an American."

"Who is he?"

"Who knows? Just some ex-guerrilla who's decided he can make good money selling kidnap victims to FARC."

"I'm being sold to FARC?"

"He's *trying* to sell you. The guards told me that he was asking for too much money. I guess he decided to come back with you live and in person, give it one more try. But if he doesn't strike a deal, you may be stuck with him."

Matthew looked around the hut. The other three men were silent, not part of the conversation in English. "Who brought you in? FARC?"

"No. The same group who got you."

"Joaquín?"

"Not him, personally. His group. The guard tells me he has about twenty followers. Not sure where they're from. Not even sure they're all Colombian. Part of his band brought you in. The others pulled a *retén* outside Cali three days ago."

"What's a *retén*?"

"Roadblock. They just throw some tires in the road, stop any cars that come along. They have a computer with Internet access right on site to run a background check on each person they nab. Anyone who looks like they have money goes in the back of their truck. The others lose their cars and walk home."

"How many did they take?"

"Six, including me."

"I only see four here."

"The women are in the other hut."

It sickened him that they'd take women, too. He thought of his wife or daughter at the mercy of teenage boys with automatic weapons.

Joaquín stepped out of the cottage. He didn't look happy as he walked toward the hut. Matthew and Emilio stepped back from the door. It opened, and the guard ordered everyone out. Matthew and the four others stepped into the daylight. The day was overcast, but Emilio and the others who'd been in the hut for hours still had trouble with their eyes. Joaquín walked to the other hut, the same drill. Out walked the women. One looked close to Cathy's age; the other, about the age of their daughter, Lindsey.

Joaquín and his two men herded the seven prisoners together. Four FARC guerrillas assisted. It seemed to be an unwritten rule that there were always at least as many guards as prisoners. Joaquín spoke to the group in Spanish.

"Welcome to the valley of smiles," he said.

The group was silent, unamused by his humor. He continued, "Some of you will remain here in the good hands of FARC. Some of you will leave here today. I have only one way to decide who stays and who goes."

He reached inside his knapsack and removed two billfolds. He opened one and held it up so all could see. It was a picture of a young boy. "Who is this?"

"My son," said Emilio.

"How old?"

"Six."

"Come forward."

Emilio stepped up, apart from the group. The younger woman started crying. "Please, please, señor. I have children, too."

Joaquín pulled another billfold from the pack and displayed it the same way, so that all could see. There were two children in this photograph, a boy and girl. "How old?" he asked.

"Rafael is two," she said, her voice cracking. "Alicia is four."

"Come here."

"Thank you, oh, thank you," she said.

With just a signal from Joaquín, the FARC guards herded the three remaining men and one woman back into the huts. They went quietly, though the expressions on their tired faces screamed with despair. The young mother was still crying and thanking Joaquín, even kissing his hand, as if he were the pope. She obviously thought they were going home.

Matthew could only assume that Joaquín had been unable to persuade FARC to pay the high price he wanted for the American. But that didn't explain why Emilio and the young mother had been segregated from the group along with him. Could this be some kind of humanitarian gesture? Maybe they somehow knew that his wife was pregnant, and they'd pulled out the mother, the father, and the father-to-be for special consideration.

"We have a long journey ahead of us," said Joaquín, still speaking in Spanish.

Then he looked at Matthew and spoke in English. "And these are the rules. Don Matthew, do not try to escape. If you try to escape and are captured, we kill the daddy. If you try to escape and succeed, we kill the mommy. And I assure you, it won't be quick and painless."

He patted the large knife attached to his belt, then reverted to Spanish. "Any questions?"

Emilio said nothing, having understood it all. The young woman looked confused, as she spoke only Spanish. Matthew was angry, but he felt foolish, too, for even having considered the possibility that this animal was capable of a humanitarian gesture.

"*Bueno*," said Joaquín. "*Vamos.*"

At gunpoint, the three prisoners marched past the FARC cottage, across the clearing, and back into the forest, back to the rebel campsite near the beautiful red fields of poppy.

13

My chance to confront Guillermo came and went.

Two days had passed since my meeting with Agent Huitt, and I'd spoken to my father's business partner on the telephone at least a half dozen times. He was still in Colombia, still the family's representative in dealing with the local police. Each time we spoke, I resolved to ask the questions that needed to be asked. Each time, I let it go. I needed more than vague innuendo from an FBI agent before questioning the integrity of a man who might be completely innocent. The last thing I needed was to alienate Guillermo and end up having to deal with the Colombian police on my own.

At least for now, I dealt with Guillermo as if the conversation with Agent Huitt had never taken place. Things were so normal that he was even delegating work to me in my father's absence. I spent the afternoon at the port checking on a shipment of scuba equipment to the lobster divers in Nicaragua.

I'd visited the port once before with my father,

when I was a teenager. I remembered it well, because it had shocked me. I'd expected to see the big white cruise ships docked like a string of pearls in the shadow of beautiful downtown Miami. This was an entirely different port, up the Miami River near the airport. Chain-link fences and barbed wire cordoned off ugly metal warehouses and mountains of metal container trucks stacked one on top of the other. The boats were rusty old freighters that looked barely capable of making it to the mouth of the river, let alone to the Panama Canal. Overall, it reminded me of the kind of place a serial killer might dump his bodies. In fact, I think one had a few years back.

This time I took my best friend with me. J.C. Paez was christened Juan Carlos by his Cuban parents, but his friends knew him only as J.C. We'd been friends since we were nine years old. In fact, it was J.C. who'd set me up with Jenna. It was a toss-up as to which of us had taken the breakup harder—a toss-up between me and J.C., not me and Jenna.

"I saw Jenna on Miami Beach the other night," he said.

I was trying to negotiate a parking space. I didn't say anything.

"She looked great," he continued.

I had to wonder, what was it that compelled friends to carry on about how incredible your ex was looking since the breakup? She wasn't Bigfoot; I didn't need every reported sighting. But now that he'd opened the door, I had to ask, "Was she with anyone?"

"You mean when she came in or when she left?"

"Don't mess with me. I know Jenna's not picking up guys at bars."

"She was with a girlfriend."

"Did you talk to her?"

"Yeah."

"Did she say anything about me?"

He smiled coyly. "Now why would you be interested in that?"

"Just forget it."

"Wait a sec, she did say something about you."

"What?"

"Something like, 'Wow, J.C., you do kiss much better than Nick.'"

I just rolled my eyes and applied the parking brake. He laughed as we got down from the Jeep. "You should call her sometime."

"Oh, right."

"Seriously. I think there's still something there."

As much as I would have liked to believe that, I didn't. J.C.'s parents had divorced when he was twelve, and some fifteen years later he was still clinging to the notion that someday his folks would remarry. That had a way of putting anything he said about Jenna in perspective.

"We'll see," I said, noncommittal.

We went around to the back of warehouse Number 3 to see a man named Paco. Shipments had a strange way of not making it onto the boat if you didn't see Paco—more precisely, if you and Ben Franklin didn't see Paco. He was busy, so we waited outside his office door. It was a beautiful sunny afternoon, bright blue skies. I wished I'd had my sunglasses.

"Hey, isn't that your Jeep?" asked J.C.

I looked over and saw a forklift pulling my Jeep

toward a huge freighter. I nearly knocked J.C. over, I flew past him so fast.

"What the hell are you guys doing?"

The forklift stopped. The driver shrugged and laughed. He said something in Spanish that I couldn't quite catch with all the engine noise. J.C. translated for me.

"He says you were blocking traffic. He was making room for the trucks to pass."

It was possible he was telling the truth, though it was also possible that if J.C. hadn't caught them, my beloved Jeep would have been a boat ride away from South American license plates. Four-wheel-drive vehicles were in hot demand down there—just ask any Miamian who *used to* own a Range Rover.

J.C. and I moved my Jeep to a safer place, a parking spot beside the warehouse that was inaccessible by forklift. As I killed the engine, I noticed the goofy expression on J.C.'s face.

"What?" I asked.

"I was just thinking, this is broad daylight. What must go on down here at one o'clock in the morning?"

"God only knows."

"Actually, I think God must look the other way."

"Yeah," I said. "God and my old man."

"Get out. Your dad's as straight as they come."

"You and I know that. But I have this feeling that everybody else lumps him together with every snake who's ever slithered down the Miami River."

"Why?"

"*Why?* It's like you just said, this is the day shift. Who do you think works here at night? Nuns?"

"You're making too much of that. So what if your dad spends a lot of time at the port. He travels back and forth from Nicaragua on fishing business. He has the bad luck of being kidnapped by Colombians. That doesn't mean . . ."

He stopped in midsentence, as if saying those things had made him see my point. "It's just a perception thing," he added.

The forklift drove by. The driver beeped his horn and waved. He was hauling a pallet of frozen grouper fingers. Or at least that's what the markings on the box said. Who knew what was really in there?

I looked at J.C. and asked, "What would you say if I told you that my old man had been shaken down by customs nineteen times in the past five years?"

He was trying hard not to look shocked. "Was he ever charged with anything?"

"Nope. Not a single time could anyone tag him with anything illegal."

"Then I'd say he's being harassed."

"Spoken like a true best friend," I said, though the accusatory look of Agent Huitt was still burning in my mind. "Of course, another man might say he's just lucky as hell he never got caught."

J.C. looked away, saying nothing. In silence, we walked back into the warehouse to see my father's friend Paco.

14

·

More than a week since Dad had disappeared, and still not a word from his kidnappers. Alex assured me that this was normal. The consul's office told me the same thing in my daily update from the State Department. Families always want the ordeal to end quickly, but the kidnappers move at their own pace. It's not that they're incapable of moving faster. They're simply in control, and they want you to know it.

On Monday morning I went to the office to see if Duncan would extend my personal leave for another week. He agreed, though we both knew the rules. At a large firm like Cool Cash, associates either billed twenty-two-hundred hours annually or took a pay cut. No slack for kids, kidney stones, or kidnappings.

Back in my office I logged on to my computer to enter my time for the week. Lawyers at Cool Cash recorded their time in six-minute intervals. Each billing day had entries for a twenty-four-hour day, as you never knew when you might be stuck in the

office till 3:00 A.M. cranking out a brief. I entered
zeroes across the board, ten slots per hour, two hundred and forty per day, twelve hundred for the week.
Staring at five days' worth of zeroes, I suddenly realized how incredibly long a day could be. It made
me think of Dad sitting in the jungles or mountains
somewhere in Colombia and counting each passing
minute, nothing to do but survive and wait for his
ordeal to end.

I checked my e-mails. Most were office memos,
easily deleted. I printed a half dozen updates from
the lawyers who were monitoring my caseload in
my absence. One that caught my eye was from an
address I didn't recognize. It had arrived just a half
hour earlier. I opened it, then froze.

"*I know where Matthew Rey is,*" it read.

I stared at the words. The sender's screen name
was an eight-digit number, not even a word. I scrolled
down to check the rest of the message.

"*If this interests you, please come see me.*" An address
followed, but no name and no telephone number.

At this stage of the game I had to take every lead
seriously. It was only instinct, and my thinking was
definitely colored by my meeting with Agent Huitt—
but I suspected that if this guy really knew where my
father was, he might also know things that were better not shared with the FBI, my negotiator Alex, or
even my friend J.C.

I wrote down the address. It wasn't too far. I could
be there in twenty minutes—alone, just me and my
family secrets.

As usual, a twenty-minute trip on the Palmetto
Expressway turned into forty. With no map, I tried

to find my way by using two handy mnemonic devices that helped drivers get around Miami-Dade County. The more well known one was STL: streets, terraces, and lanes ran east to west (think "St. Louis"). The one I seemed to remember better was courts, roads, avenues, and places. In Miami, as at Cool Cash, CRAP flowed north and south, top to bottom.

Unfortunately, someone had stolen most of the street signs in the neighborhood, and I finally realized I was in Hialeah, which had a different street-numbering system entirely. I stopped for directions at a gas station where a big Cuban flag was draped in the window. An old bumper sticker on the counter read, NO CASTRO, NO PROBLEMA. In Spanish, the attendant directed me to one of many rows of two-bedroom, sixties-vintage houses. Once upon a time Hialeah had been synonymous with pink flamingos gracing a manicured infield as powerful thoroughbreds raced around the famous old track. Many areas were beautiful to some, but I was in a declining neighborhood where the flamingos were plastic and front lawns were surrounded by chain link and barbed wire to keep away the car thieves.

I found the right house halfway down the street. An old Chevy was parked in the driveway. Beneath the carport was an aluminum fishing boat on a trailer with two flat tires. As with most of the surrounding homes, the windows and doors were covered with jail-like security bars. I had to wonder what this person could possibly know about my father's kidnapping. After my conversation with FBI Agent Huitt and his threats against my father's partner, Guillermo, I supposed it could have been just about anything.

I opened the gate, walked up the cracked sidewalk, and knocked on the front door. A man answered, dressed in sandals, shorts, and a Miami Dolphins T-shirt. It was only 11:00 A.M., but he had a healthy five o'clock shadow, the kind that was chic on a movie star but plain old scruffy on just about everyone else. A protective Doberman pinscher was standing behind him.

"I'm Nick Rey. You sent a message about my father?"

He smiled and unlocked the screen door. "*Sí. Come on in.*"

I glanced at the dog.

"Don't worry," he said. "She's friendlier than she looks." He led me down a dark hall to the kitchen. The window shades were pulled shut, and the only light in the house was from the lamp in the living room and the ceiling fixture in the kitchen. Incense burned in a small urn on the kitchen counter, filling the air with an almost sickeningly sweet odor.

"*¿Café?*" he offered.

"No, thanks."

He poured himself half a cup and filled the rest with milk. At his insistence I took the good chair, the one that didn't have duct tape covering splits and tears in the vinyl covering. He seated himself opposite me at the kitchen table, the dog at his feet.

"Who are you?" I asked.

He smiled and extended his arms like a preacher. "The answer to your prayers."

"I hate to be blunt, but you don't look like it."

"Looks don't matter. It's the message that's important. It was very powerful, no? '*I know where Matthew Rey is.*'"

"It brought me here."

"Exactly."

"So where is he?"

"In due time, we'll get there."

"Do you know my father?"

"No."

"Do you have some connection to the kidnappers?"

"In a manner of speaking."

At the risk of offending him, I had to speak my mind. "You have no idea where my father is, do you?"

"Not in the conventional sense. But I have access to a power that can lead us straight to your father."

"By power, do you mean a person?"

"No. Collective mind power."

I smelled a scam. "Are you supposed to be some kind of psychic?"

He leaned across the table and looked into my eyes. "Not the kind you're thinking of. Look around the room. There's no crystal ball, no dead chickens to dissect, no turban on my head. I don't work with tarot cards or birth dates. What I'm offering is a clean and legitimate opportunity to link your father telepathically to the most powerful minds in the world. I call it my deluxe power package."

"Does it come with a moon roof and CD player?"

"This is no joke. It's done by e-mail to a group of specialists selected by me. Each of my contacts around the globe is strategically located to enhance the flow of energy from one to the next. At a predesignated moment, each of them opens the e-mail and reads the exact same message: '*I know where Matthew Rey is.*' The timing is critical. It sparks their collective mind power. If it's done right—and this is where my expertise comes in—I guarantee that someone in that group will know where Matthew Rey is."

"Yeah, probably last seen with Elvis."

"Please, I understand your skepticism. But only after your father returns home safely will you realize that this was the best five thousand dollars you've ever spent."

I nearly laughed in his face. "Five thousand dollars? For what?"

"For my connections to the very best minds in their field. I have a woman who has helped law enforcement officers locate missing children all over the United States. There's a guy in the U.K. who gets patients through major surgery without anesthesia. An aboriginal tribe member in Australia can snap a butter knife in half using only her powers of concentration."

"I came here thinking you knew where my father was. You're lucky I don't snap *you* in half and kick your ass all the way to Colombia to go look for him."

"No need to kick me anywhere. The mind is all-powerful. I've been invoking the message for two days now. Don't be at all surprised if you experience a telepathic communication very soon."

I rose to leave. "You're a crackpot."

He glared, as if I'd just hurled the ultimate insult. "Your mother didn't think so."

"You've spoken to her?"

"Yes," he said smugly. "I saw her on the television news last week. She finally agreed to speak to me this morning. I just about had her sold on the deluxe power package, and then she backed off and said it was up to you."

"Well, the answer is no."

He sipped his coffee, unfazed. "For now, maybe. But a month from now, or two months from now, as this drags on with no end in sight, she'll turn to me. With or without your approval, she'll cough up the money. Probably more than once."

"You scum." I shot from my chair, ready to grab him by the shirt.

"Sergeant!" he shouted.

His dog leaped from the floor, up on its hind legs, and pinned me against the wall. It was growling in my face, mouth wide open, its long white canines an inch away from my carotid artery. One more command from its master, and I was a dead man.

"Release!" he shouted.

The dog retreated obediently to its master's side. "You've got thirty seconds to leave peacefully. After that, Sergeant drags you out by the throat."

"Where's your conscience, man? This family is suffering."

"I want my money."

"You talk as if we owed it to you."

"Wow. You must be psychic."

He was being coy, but he seemed to be saying exactly that. We *did* owe it to him.

"You've got ten seconds to be on the other side of that door," he said.

The dog growled. This was no time to pick a fight. I walked down the hall and let myself out. Halfway to my Jeep, I heard him say, "Hey."

I stopped and turned. He was standing inside the house behind the closed screen door.

"Tell your sister that Jaime Ochoa sends his regards."

He spoke as if the name should mean something to me. It didn't. "Sorry. I don't know where my sister is."

"I do," he said, his eyes narrowing into a piercing stare that chilled me.

I couldn't tell if he was bluffing, and he didn't give me a chance to ask. I stood there and watched, confused, as he closed the door and retreated into the house.

15

I called Alex for lunch. I figured it was time to level with my consultant.

We met at Scotty's Landing, a waterfront patio-style restaurant, where the specialties were grilled mahi-mahi sandwiches and bowls of delicious conch gumbo, served cold, like gazpacho. The place was essentially an open hut with a bar and a kitchen, flanked by a wood deck eating area with little round tables, plastic chairs, canvas umbrellas, fresh sea breezes, and nice views of the bay. It wasn't exactly in the heart of Coconut Grove, but to me the sign posted at the entrance captured the old Grove spirit. PLEASE WAIT HERE FOR NEXT AVAILABLE TABLE, it read, followed by separate, smaller signs in increasingly smaller print: IT DOESN'T SAY WAIT TO BE SEATED. SEAT YOURSELF. IF NOT UNDERSTOOD, START AGAIN.

We seated ourselves at the table nearest the water. Alex sat with her legs crossed, which I naturally noticed because the sundress and sandals she was wearing made her legs highly noticeable. It was actually the toe ring that had caught my attention, a little gold band around the middle toe, her longest. Feet like a ballerina, or so I recalled from the day Lindsey had come home from ballet crying because her teacher said it would be harder to stand on point if your first toe was your longest toe. She gave up dance and took up hell-raising.

"You like my toe ring?" she asked.

"What?"

"The ring," she said, wiggling her toe with the slender ankle flexed. "It seems to have caught your fancy."

"Yeah, I guess so."

She smiled. I looked away, embarrassed. We both knew I'd been staring.

The waiter brought us water and took our order. While waiting for our food, I told her all about Jaime Ochoa, which prompted the obvious question.

"Do you think he really knows where your sister is?"

"Probably in much the same way he knows that at age sixty-three Julia Roberts will give birth to triplets."

"You think he's ever met Lindsey?"

"My guess is that she probably stiffed him on payment for psychic readings somewhere along the line. When he saw Mom on television last week talking about the kidnapping, he decided to rip off the family as payback."

"Nice guy."

"I love my sister, but she has a habit of mixing it up with deadbeats, usually about as far away from home as she can get. She likes to think it's part of her adventuresome journalistic spirit, very Ernest Hemingway. One of her old J-school professors once told her that if you want to write a story about sewer rats, you don't interview swans. I wish he'd also pointed out that to write a story about suicide, you don't have to kill yourself."

"So, you think she met Jaime Ochoa doing research for a story?"

I looked away, then back. I wasn't a good liar, and there was no point pulling punches at this point. "That's what I'm hoping. But I'm starting to get a little worried."

"Where is she now?"

"Last time we talked, Nicaragua. Even though she and Dad are kind of on the outs, I always took some comfort in knowing that they were at least in the same country."

"How long's it been since you last heard from her?"

"A while. It's always a while. She calls when she's broke. But to be honest, it's a little different this time, now that Dad's missing."

"That's true. But I'd have to say that the odds are pretty low that both of them would be kidnapped at the same time in different countries."

"Unless the kidnappings are related."

She raised an eyebrow. "Let's not get ahead of ourselves."

I noted that she didn't totally dismiss the possibility.

The server brought our food and left. I popped

a french fry in my mouth, then said, "I've been thinking of going down there. I need to check on Dad's business anyway. Maybe I'd do a little checking on Lindsey, too."

"I recommend you at least wait until you hear from the kidnappers. Don't leave your mother here to deal with that herself."

I nodded, then glanced toward the bay, where a sunburned tourist was struggling furiously to tack his rented sailboat. "Maybe it would help to run a background check on Jaime Ochoa."

"Sure. I can do that."

"I'm sure he's just a crackpot."

"Then why did you go see him?"

I knew that the conversation would lead this way, but I also knew that it was high time I stopped keeping secrets from the person I was depending on most to bring my father home. "Does everything I tell you get back to the insurance company?"

"No. The insurance company pays your bill, as required by the policy. But my client is you, not the company. If you ask me to keep something in confidence, it remains in confidence."

That was the answer I'd wanted, but I still hesitated. Dad's problem with the FBI was not my favorite lunch topic. "I went to see him because I thought he might have something to do with some accusations I'd heard. About my dad."

"What, specifically?"

She listened without interruption as I told her about my meeting with Agent Huitt, the FBI's suspicions about my father's business. She seemed particularly interested in the bureau's apparent refusal to assist us in the kidnapping unless the Rey family cooperated in some as-yet-undefined investigation against Guillermo. When I'd finished, she said nothing. In fact, she looked a little miffed.

"Should I not have told you any of this?" I asked.

"You should have told me as soon as it happened."

"It's all such a crock. I didn't want you getting the wrong idea about my father."

My cell phone rang. I debated whether to answer till I'd cleared the air with Alex, but so long as Dad was missing, this was no time to be screening calls. It was my mother.

"A courier package just arrived from Colombia," she said, her voice racing. "I think it must be from the kidnappers."

I nearly fell off my chair. From the look on my face, Alex knew what it was. I waved her over so she could put her ear next to mine and listen in.

"Open it," I told my mother.

"I already did."

"Is there a ransom demand?"

"I can't read it. It's all in Spanish. There's a little note on the bottom that looks like your father's handwriting, but that's in Spanish, too. I just don't understand. Why would he write to his own family in a foreign language?"

She sounded so frazzled, I was about to suggest that she take it to one of our bilingual neighbors to translate. But this wasn't something to share with the neighborhood.

"Just hang in there a few more minutes. I'm with Alex right now. We're on our way."

"Should I call Agent Nettles at the FBI?"

I paused, and Alex seemed to sense the reason: I hadn't even talked to my mother about our problems with the FBI. "Let's not do anything till I get home and read it."

"Then hurry, please. It's killing me not knowing what it says."

"You and me both," I said.

16

W e reached my mother's house in ten minutes. She met us at the door.

"This way," said Mom as she led us to the kitchen. The letter was resting faceup on the table beside the opened courier package. I was glad Alex was with me. I probably could have translated it myself, but I suspected that a communication from a kidnapper would contain subtleties in word choice and phraseology that I would never be able to interpret. She seemed like the right person to discern the true meaning. I wondered if perhaps she'd even written a few letters like this before.

As Alex read the letter, I tried to read her face. "Is it FARC?" I asked.

"Could be."

"Oh, my God," said Mom.

"It's a little strange. Usually FARC comes right out and claims responsibility. They're not shy. This one reads like a FARC letter, but there's no explicit claim of responsibility by anyone."

"For heaven's sake, just read it to me," said Mom.

I looked over Alex's shoulder as she read aloud, translating. "'Dear Mrs. Rey—'"

"Read the bottom first," said Mom. "The part in Matthew's handwriting."

"It looks like they allowed him to write a short postscript," said Alex.

"Yes. Read it to me, please."

"'My dear family. I am well treated, so please don't worry. Cathy, I love you. Nick, give my love to Lindsey when you talk to her, and take good care of your mother and grandmother. Love, Matthew.'"

My mother was shaking. I hugged her as she sank into the chair across the table from Alex.

"That's it?" she said.

"It's a teaser," said Alex. "Kidnappers sometimes release bits and pieces like that to push the family's emotional buttons. Other times the family is kept totally in the dark. Either way, you're being jerked around."

"Why did he write in Spanish?"

"Because his kidnappers want to make sure they understand every word he writes. They're paranoid about something slipping by in what to them is a foreign language. Someone could be speaking in code to reveal their position. If it's in Spanish, they can control what's said."

"What does their letter say?" I asked.

Her eyes shifted back to the letter, and she read, "'Dear Mrs. Rey. We are your friends.'"

"Friends!" My mother nearly shrieked.

"That's a typical beginning," said Alex. She read quickly through a paragraph that set forth various

Marxist platitudes, guerrilla propaganda. The substance was in the last paragraph. "'We do not intend to harm your husband if our demands are met, but we regret that we cannot continue to communicate with you in Miami. All arrangements for the release must be made in Colombia, through you or your representative.'"

"They expect us to go to Colombia?" said Mom.

"That's not surprising," said Alex. "They want to play on their turf."

"Finish the letter," I said.

Her translation continued, "'At sunrise, twenty-two October, be in the park behind the church at the top of Monseratte.'"

"What's Monseratte?" I asked.

"One of the mountain peaks just east of Bogotá." She continued reading: "'Bring a two-meter-band radio. Instructions will follow. Do not involve the police or the army, or you will never hear from us again, and all chances for your husband's release will be lost.'"

"But . . ." Mom could barely speak. "But we've already involved the police."

"They know that."

"Then why did they threaten to kill Matthew if we called them?"

"They want you to stop talking to them. Mind you, they're not afraid of being caught. Even when the police are involved, maybe two percent of the kidnapping cases in Colombia are solved. What they're afraid of is that the police will try to dissuade you from paying a ransom. And their fears are justified. The police *will* do that."

"They must think like the State Department," I said.

"Everybody thinks that way, until their own son or daughter is kidnapped."

Mom asked, "Should we stop talking to the police?"

"Not necessarily," said Alex. "So long as you have a private negotiator who's putting money on the table, the kidnappers won't really care who you're talking to behind the scenes."

"Does that mean you'll be our family contact in Bogotá?"

"That's part of your insurance coverage."

"Will the police be with you?"

"No," said Alex. "Don't misunderstand me. When I said it's not necessary to stop talking to the police, I wasn't suggesting that we join ourselves at the hip with anyone in law enforcement, Colombian or American. Frankly, we don't need them if our intention is to pay a ransom. This is why your father bought insurance."

"So you're going alone?" said Mom.

"Shouldn't I be with you?" I asked before she could answer.

"No," said Mom, playing the same game.

Alex paused, clearly reluctant to weigh in on either side. "That's up to the family."

I said, "When you talk by radio to the kidnappers, they're bound to make threats or set deadlines. I don't want to have to rely solely on someone else's opinion as to whether they're for real or not. I want to hear with my own ears."

"But it could be dangerous," Mom said.

"I won't be going alone."

"That's exactly what your father said!" Her voice was sharp but quaking.

I looked away, saying nothing. Mom looked at Alex and asked, "Is this something we have to decide now?"

"No. Soon, though. We need to make plans."

"Tomorrow morning soon enough?"

"Sure," said Alex.

Mom looked me in the eye, then glanced out the window. I wasn't sure who she was talking to—me, Alex, or no one in particular. "I know my son," she said softly. "He's going to South America. I guess by morning we'll know if he's going with or without my blessing."

I watched from my chair as she rose and quietly left the room.

17

That night was more difficult than I'd expected. Seeing the letter with Dad's handwriting had been both a boost and a downer. The good news: He was alive and kidnapped. The bad news: He was alive and kidnapped.

Mom and I went to bed after the eleven o'clock news, but I lay awake in the darkness, listening to the palm trees rustling in the breeze outside my bedroom window. Those three royal palms had been two feet tall when Dad and I planted them, he with a shovel, I with my trusty plastic sandbox rake. Now the fronds were literally tapping on my second-story window. A quarter century, gone in a blink of the eye. Yet the last two weeks seemed like a lifetime. I tried not to be negative. Today's note from Dad had at least confirmed his survival of the shoot-out in Cartagena that had killed three of his crew. But I wondered how long ago he'd written those words, knowing that so many things could have happened since then, so many of them tragic.

Around 1:00 A.M. I heard a noise downstairs in

the kitchen. Mom and I were obviously on the same train of thought. I got out of bed, put on my robe, and walked downstairs. The kitchen light was on, but I didn't see Mom. I noticed a pad of paper on the table. I walked over and checked it out.

My dearest Matthew, it began. I didn't snoop, but the sheer length struck me. It went on for pages and pages, all written in Mom's longhand. Practically the entire notebook was already full.

"Don't read that."

I turned and saw my mother standing in the doorway. "I wasn't."

She took the notebook and held it to her bosom. "It's for your father. I'm writing down everything for him."

"You don't have to explain. It's a nice idea."

She sat at the table, apparently wanting to talk. I sat across from her.

"Your father was so excited about this baby. He wanted to be a part of the whole pregnancy, the birth. Fathers didn't do that so much when you and Lindsey were born. This was going to be a new experience for both of us."

I smiled sadly. One more thing the guerrillas had stolen from the Rey family. "I'm sure he'll be back in time to enjoy some of it."

"Next week is my first ultrasound. We'd planned on going together. Since he can't be there, I'm at least going to share it with him through my writing."

"It'll make good reading when he gets home."

"It's not for then. I'm going to send it to him."

"How do you intend to do that?"

"I called the Red Cross. They told me that under

the Geneva Protocol, all prisoners have the right to receive mail."

"Mom, Colombian guerrilla groups don't honor the Geneva Protocol."

She had a wan look in her eye. I'd seen it before in clients who suddenly had to face the difference between what the law prescribes and what the law can deliver. "Why not?"

"They just don't. There's no one to hold them accountable."

"I suppose I knew that," she said quietly. "Of course, that only confirms my suspicions about that little postscript on the kidnappers' letter."

"What do you mean?"

"If they won't let your father receive mail, I hardly think they would have let him write a letter to his family. I'm sure they wrote it."

"It was clearly Dad's handwriting."

"I don't mean so much the physical act of putting pen to paper. He may have written it, but they composed it."

"I disagree. Those were his own words. I'd bet my Jeep on it."

"How can you be so certain?"

"Because of the way he expressed himself toward me."

"But it was so short."

"It was long enough for me to know."

She gave me a curious look. "What are you trying to tell me, Nick?"

"Look at it this way. Let's say that a kidnapper is writing a letter that he hopes will pass for a letter written by a father to his son. If he's going to do it

right, the ghostwriter has to step into the shoes of
the father. For all the father knows, this letter could
possibly be the last words he ever conveys to his son.
As a ghostwriter, you'd probably throw in three
little words: 'I love you.' You'd do that because that
would be normal, right?"

Mom blinked. "Depends on what you mean by
normal."

"Exactly. Because normal in this house doesn't
mean a father telling his son 'I love you.' Normal is
what Dad wrote: 'Nick, give my love to Lindsey
when you see her, and take good care of your mother
and grandmother.'"

She looked at me with soulful eyes. That I'd committed his impersonal message to memory told her
that I'd given it much thought, that it had affected
me. "You know your father loves you."

"I suppose I do, yes. But it would be nice to hear it."

"That's a two-way street."

"You're right. We've never been great communi-
cators. That's what makes me sadder than anything.
In the last few days I've come to realize that in my
entire life I've never had an honest conversation
with my father."

"Your father doesn't lie to you."

"I don't mean honest in the George Washington
sense. I mean honest as in intimate. Two people bar-
ing their souls."

"Your father doesn't have many of those conversations with anyone."

I thought for a second. The kitchen was suddenly
so quiet I could hear the hum of the refrigerator. I
hadn't intended to raise the issue of the FBI tonight,

but this seemed like an opportunity. "Mom, how much do you know about the Nicaraguan end of the fishing business?"

"Some."

"How well do you know Guillermo?"

"Actually, I've met Guillermo only once. We hardly said two words to each other."

She said it with conviction, almost as if she didn't want to know Guillermo. Or maybe I was reading too much into it. "Do you trust him?"

"He's been your father's partner for over a decade. And I don't see anyone else volunteering to run to Colombia to deal with the local police on behalf of the family."

"No doubt he's been a help."

"Did something happen that makes you not want to trust him?"

I was thinking of Agent Huitt and his accusations, of course, but Mom seemed stressed enough without taking her down that path. "It's just that you don't know him, I don't know him. You get right down to it, we don't know Alex either. Someone from the family should be on the front line."

"You still want to go to Bogotá, don't you?"

"Yes."

She shook her head, almost groaning. "Why?"

"I just told you."

"I don't think you did." She seemed to sense there was something I hadn't told her.

"It's hard to explain," I said.

"Try."

"This kidnapping has made me stop and realize that something's missing between me and Dad, always has been missing. I have respect for him. He's courageous, strong, all that. Growing up, I'd always thought I wanted to be like him. Not necessarily a fisherman, but like him nonetheless. The last few nights I've stayed awake wondering if we really are at all alike, and it's occurred to me: I don't know him that well. And he doesn't know me either. Maybe that's why it's so important that I go on this trip. Find him. Maybe we can introduce ourselves."

From her pained expression it was clear that she still didn't want me to go. But she finally seemed to understand. "I don't know what I would do if I lost both of you. Please, be very careful."

I reached across the table and held her hand. "I will. I promise."

18

It was their third camp in seven days. Or maybe it was eight days. Matthew wasn't sure. The guerrillas had stolen his wristwatch, his only calendar.

At least a week had passed since they'd reached the mountains, almost two since the shoot-out in Cartagena. They'd traveled by foot and by mule, mostly climbing, but at times descending at angles as steep as forty degrees. More than once he was certain that they'd doubled back and covered the same ground. The exercise seemed designed to disorient the prisoners and discourage escape. Surely it had nothing to do with casting confusion to possible rescue teams. With guerrillas in control of almost half the country, a Rambo mission was out of the question. Even if these particular kidnappers weren't formally aligned with any Marxist group, the army would still have to beat back more organized leftist forces like FARC and the National Liberation Army, and then literally climb a mountain to free Matthew and the others. Fat chance.

The captives numbered six now, counting Matthew and the Colombian daddy and mommy that Joaquín had bargained away from FARC to help prevent his escape. Two nights ago Joaquín and his team had joined camp with another band of rebels who had three other prisoners in custody. Those guerrillas were apparently part of Joaquín's group, as they all obeyed his orders. Initially, Matthew hadn't known what to make of it. During a bathroom break it was again Emilio, the Colombian daddy, who'd explained.

"It's their division of labor," he said. "One team specializes in the abductions. The other focuses on housing and guarding the prisoners."

The three new prisoners, Matthew learned, weren't new at all. A Swede and a Canadian were in their second month of captivity, having been abducted together from a mining project near the Ecuadorian border. The Canadian was from Saskatchewan, a strapping, confident cowboy at heart who acted more like a Texan. The Swede was more reserved, more bitter about the whole experience. So far the only thing he'd told Matthew about himself was his name, Jan Lunden. The body language, however, seemed to place blame on the Canadian for the mess they'd gotten into.

The third new prisoner was another Colombian, a banker who'd simply driven down the wrong road on his way to work one day—sixteen months ago. Time in captivity had taken its toll on him. Pants that had once fit him now gathered around his waist. A thick beard covered his face, hiding the sunken cheeks. His skin was dry and flaky, the worry lines on his forehead seemingly carved in wax. His long hair was tangled in knots, and a strange shade of orange. Hair wasn't naturally that color on any human being. It had to have been malnutrition.

Most shocking of all, he was just thirty-eight years old.

His appearance had left Matthew speechless, which was just as well, since the prisoners were rarely allowed to speak to one another. That wasn't Joaquín's rule. The edict had come from Aída, a thirteen-year-old girl who seemed overeager to use her M-1 .30-caliber carbine. Aída was the low-level guerrilla designated to deliver meals to the prisoners, usually potatoes and a few beans. Routinely, she'd drop most of it on the ground while serving, feigning clumsiness. It was always intentional. She clearly relished her power over the captives, and she asserted it by spilling their small rations of food and giggling about it or by enforcing stupid rules, like no talking during meals. Matthew surmised that females, especially young girls, were low in the pecking order in Joaquín's group. Aída took it out on the prisoners, the only ones lower than she was.

For the third consecutive evening, the six ate in silence under Aída's watch. A total of six guards were on duty, but everyone except Aída was busy trying to see who, with a flick of the wrist, could stick a hunting knife into a tree stump from four meters away. One of their buddies was on the other side of the stump sleeping off a hangover. It was typical behavior from these fools. Knives, guns, and grenades were all sources of amusement, all handled like toys without regard for anyone's safety.

"¡*Idiotas!*" shouted Sleeping Beauty, adding a

stream of choice words. An errant throw had landed the knife in his lap. Luckily it was the blunt end and not the blade. The others laughed as he stormed off to the hut.

The hut was where the guerrillas slept, men and women together. It was possible that the guerrillas had built it themselves, but Matthew thought it more likely that it had been taken by force from mountain peasants. With mud walls and a crude thatched roof, it looked like something a primitive Indian tribe might have constructed ten thousand years ago. It didn't even have a chimney. A fire burned constantly to combat the cold mountain air, and smoke escaped through an open window. It reminded Matthew of the little shacks the Miskito Indians built along the Nicaraguan coast to smoke fish, only the Miskitos were smart enough not to smoke themselves.

The guards were still laughing, passing around a bottle. It was practically a nightly ritual, parties at sunset. A few swigs of rum, followed by *basuco*, a cheap and plentiful by-product of cocaine processing that would make them crazy out of their minds.

One of the male guerrillas caught Aída's eye from across the camp. She smiled in return, interested. She rose from the fallen log she'd been sitting on, losing the smile as she addressed her prisoners.

"Nobody goes anywhere," she said in Spanish. "And no talking." She turned and headed for the party, soon out of earshot.

"Can you fetch me a bourbon and Coke, honey?" said the Canadian. His name was Will.

Matthew looked up from his plate of cold beans.

Fortunately, Aída hadn't heard Will's crack, as she had absolutely no sense of humor.

The six were seated on the ground in a circle around a small pile of black, extinguished coals, the remnants of burned *chuzco* firewood. The campfire had burned out an hour before, not to be relit till the morning. Earlier, Matthew and Will had spent two hours gathering wood while three guerrillas almost forty years younger stood guard and watched. The prisoners carried back plenty, but every stick of it had gone to the guerrillas' fire in the smoky hut.

The prisoners ate in silence. The Colombian woman was shivering from the cold. Matthew, too, was feeling a chill. A cool breeze was blowing down from the surrounding peaks, and the inescapable dampness only made it seem colder. A huge mosquito landed on Matthew's forehead, and he squished it. The mosquitoes in the Andes were the biggest he'd ever seen, but they were slow-moving and didn't seem to bite. Too cold for them, too.

Twenty meters away, the guerrillas were getting louder and drunker. Two of them had a hand on Aída's ass, one on each side.

"Any bets on which one she blows tonight?" said Will.

No one answered.

"What's the matter with you people? You hard of hearing?"

"Quiet," said Jan, the Swede.

"Oh, so you *can* talk?"

"Quiet, you fool. Don't make trouble for us while the guerrillas are drinking."

"Aw, this is the biggest group of pussies I've ever

met in my whole life." He glanced at the Colombian woman, as if to confirm that she didn't understand his English slang. Then he looked at Matthew and said, "With the possible exception of the fisherman here."

"Nobody here's a pussy," said Matthew.

"That's not what you told me in the woods."

"I didn't tell you anything in the woods."

He smiled. "Got you there, didn't I, fisherman? Just a little joke. We're all going to go crazy if we don't have a few jokes."

Jan said, "Just shut up, will you please?"

The sudden crack of gunshot echoed in the valley. Another round followed, then two more. The guerrillas shouted, as if it were New Year's Eve. The drugs were kicking in. That was a sure bet when they started discharging their weapons like drunken cowboys.

"Crazy bastards," said Will. He was speaking loudly, not caring who heard him.

Jan glared. "I'm asking you nicely for the last time. Quiet, before you get us all in trouble."

"What are they going to do? Take away a couple of beans from our dinner plate?"

"They can do plenty." This time it was Emilio, the voice of experience—the one who'd been kidnapped before. "Trust me, so far we've been well treated. It can get much worse."

"Stop talking," said Jan. "All of you."

"Why should we?" said Will. "Because Aída the little bitch says so?"

"No," said Matthew. "Because she has a gun."

Across the camp, the two guerrillas who had laid

claim to Aída's ass were now arguing with each other, probably about whose turn it was tonight. These were the times that made Matthew most nervous, when teenage boys with raging hormones, automatic weapons, and *basuco* racing through their brains started arguing over a girl.

Will glanced at the Swede and muttered, "They're a bunch of punks. You gotta stand up to them."

Matthew intervened. "Easy, cowboy. Now's not the time to set them off."

"I guess I pegged you wrong, fisherman. Thought you had balls."

"I also have brains."

"Are you calling me stupid?"

"I'm not calling you anything."

"Because if you want to see stupid, don't look my way. At least I wasn't dumb enough to write a letter home just because Joaquín tells me to."

Matthew did a double take. Joaquín had pulled him into the hut to write the note, so he wasn't sure how Will knew. "There's nothing stupid about putting my family at ease."

"Fool. You're helping the guerrillas, not your wife. The only purpose of that letter was to prove that you're still alive, so the guerrillas can demand a big, fat ransom."

The Swede chimed in. "What were we supposed to do, refuse?"

"*Yes.* I did."

"They asked you to write a note to your wife, and you said no?"

"Damn right. My wife and I had an understanding before I came to this country. If some Commie-ass rebels kidnap me, don't pay the bastards a thing. No negotiation, no cooperation. Period."

Behind them there was a sudden stir in the bushes. Out walked Joaquín and two other armed guerrillas. They had been eavesdropping on the prisoners, as on that first day when Joaquín had hidden himself in the field to see if Matthew would try to escape.

He stopped at the edge of their circle, then spoke to the Canadian. "Commie-ass rebels, eh?"

Will said nothing.

"Get up," said Joaquín.

Will looked around for support, but the others avoided eye contact. There was nothing anyone could do. Slowly he rose.

"Your attitude needs improvement," said Joaquín.

"I'll work on it," said Will.

"I'll help you," Joaquín said through a thin, sardonic smile. At his command, two guards rounded up the prisoners at gunpoint and followed Joaquín across the camp. They stopped at the stump where the guerrillas had been playing stick-'em with the knife. The blade was still stuck in the bark. Joaquín yanked it out, then called the other guerrillas over from their party. Aída had the giggles, and two others were staggering. Each of them had a strained expression, as if struggling not to look too intoxicated in front of their leader. They gathered on one side of the stump, the prisoners on the other.

"Put your hand here," Joaquín told Will, pointing toward the stump.

Will didn't budge. Matthew wasn't sure if he was refusing to move or simply frozen with fear. It didn't matter. With a nod from Joaquín, two guerrillas grabbed Will, brought him forward, and placed his right hand on the stump, palm down.

"Don't do this," said Will, his voice shaking.

"Spread the fingers," said Joaquín.

"Please. I'm begging you."

"Spread them!" Joaquín shouted. "Or you lose all of them."

Will opened his hand, but not quickly enough. With a jerk, Joaquín forced the fingers as far apart as possible.

"This isn't necessary," said Will, his voice growing tighter. "I'll write that letter to my wife, if that's what you want."

"Of course you will," said Joaquín. "With your other hand."

Standing and watching, Matthew knew that one man couldn't stop this. Still, he couldn't stand silent. It was a long shot, but he could think of only one possible angle in a country where 95 percent of the population was raised Roman Catholic.

"God is watching!" he shouted in Spanish.

The drunks snickered, but Joaquín didn't. Just for an instant, Matthew saw a flicker of hesitation in Joaquín's eye. It seemed to be saying that he wasn't of the same ilk as the other guerrillas, that maybe he'd been raised with a conscience and had somewhere along the line taken a wrong turn. A very wrong turn.

Joaquín shouted back, "Shut up or you're next!"

He held the knife vertically, grabbing the handle like a ski pole and placing the tip between the prisoner's outstretched thumb and index finger. Slowly he raised it and brought it down carefully between the index and middle finger. Up again, then down between the middle and ring finger. Up and down once more between the ring and pinkie finger, and then he started all over again between the thumb and index finger, a little faster this time, counting as he moved from one to the next.

"*Uno, dos, tres, cuatro.*"

The guerrillas watched, riveted. Most of the prisoners looked past the spectacle. All was silent, save for the tapping. With each move the tip of the blade tapped against the stump, matching the rhythm of his count.

"*Uno, dos, tres, cuatro.*" Tap, tap, tap, tap.

Joaquín's face strained with concentration. His eyes grew wider. The pace quickened. The shiny blade moved from one position to the next faster and faster still. The tapping became like machine-gun fire, the counting like one long word. A wave of panic washed over Will's face as the guerrilla's motion built to what seemed like a frenzy—back and forth, thumb to pinkie, then back again. The knife was a blur, the tapping nonstop, the rhythm ever escalating.

Until finally a deafening shout pierced the silence.

Matthew looked away, then back. The Canadian was rigid, motionless. It wasn't Will who'd screamed. It was Joaquín. He let out a second one, even louder, as he thrust his unbloodied knife triumphantly into the air. It was a game for him, and he'd won. His steady hand and coordination had prevailed. The Canadian's fingers had been spared, untouched by metal.

Will was trembling. "*Gracias,*" was all he could say, thankful still to have all his digits.

"Now you try," said Joaquín.

Will looked around, not sure who Joaquín was talking to. "You mean me?"

"Yes. You." Joaquín handed over the knife. Two guerrillas aimed their assault rifles at Will's chest, just in case he had any ideas.

"What do you want me to do?"

"Exactly what I just did."

"I can't."

Joaquín removed a nine-millimeter pistol from his holster. "You will," he said flatly, aiming at Will's forehead.

Will swallowed hard and acquiesced. He spread his fingers once more atop the stump.

Matthew watched with his heart in his throat. Will grasped the knife firmly, though even from fifteen feet away Matthew could see it shaking in his hand. It seemed bigger, more unwieldy for Will.

He started where Joaquín had started, with the tip of the long blade between his thumb and index finger. He left it there for several long, silent moments, afraid to move.

Finally, Joaquín cocked his pistol. "Begin."

Will drew a deep breath, then slowly moved the blade from the first position to the second, then to the third, the fourth.

"*Rápido*," said Joaquín.

He picked up the pace. The tapping continued. A rhythm was building, though not as steady as Joaquín's. Will's eyes bulged, the intense concentration broken only by intermittent flashes of pain from the slightest of scratches. The first nick was to the ring finger, followed by several clean taps, then another glancing blow to a knuckle. Little white and crimson specks of flesh were starting to collect on the blade.

"Count it off!"

"One, two, three, four."

"¡Rápido!"

Will was too breathless to count. Joaquín pressed the barrel of his pistol to the prisoner's forehead. "¡Más rápido!"

Will turned it up a notch, his hand a blur, the tapping incessant, his breathing erratic, until he could maintain the pace no longer.

The tapping ended with a thud—then a bloodcurdling scream. It rolled across the mountain peaks, down into the valley, then returned in what seemed like three or four waves in a long, chilling echo. The knife was protruding from his hand, having made short work of the tender webbing between his thumb and index finger.

Joaquín grabbed the handle and held the blade in place, so that Will couldn't remove it from the wound without ripping the skin.

"Get it out!"

Joaquín held the blade firm. Then in one quick motion he jerked it down like a mini-guillotine, adding a little hop to bring down the full force of his body weight. The bone snapped with a loud pop. Another scream followed, this one even worse than the other.

The severed thumb rolled off the stump and landed at Joaquín's feet.

Even the guerrillas were stunned silent. Matthew started forward to help, but Aída trained her rifle on him, stopping him in his tracks.

"*Por favor.* He'll bleed to death!"

The stump was soaked in red. Will was holding his bloody hand between his legs. "You animal! You didn't have to do this to me!"

Joaquín gave a signal to Aída, who then allowed Matthew to pass. Another guerrilla tossed him an old gray scarf, which Matthew wrapped around Will's hand to stop the bleeding. The hand felt cold. His whole body was like ice, his face pale.

"He's going into shock!" said Matthew. "We need more blankets."

No one moved.

"If he dies, you get no ransom," said Matthew.

Joaquín seemed torn, as if giving the man a blanket might undermine the point he'd been trying to make in front of the prisoners. But Matthew could see in his face that his own point about the ransom was hitting home. Joaquín finally gave the order, and one of the guards disappeared into the hut for some blankets.

Will was shivering in Matthew's arms. "It's going to be all right," Matthew said quietly. "Just hang in there."

Joaquín took the knife and gave it one last flick. The tip stuck perfectly into the tree stump. Then he picked up the severed thumb and held it up for the other prisoners to see.

"No need for Don William to write a letter now," said Joaquín. "His wife gets this."

The prisoners stood silent. Finally the young

mother in the group began to weep. Joaquín started to walk away, then stopped and addressed the group in a flat, matter-of-fact tone.

"Soon I'll ask each of you to write another letter home. Not just to prove you're alive but, more important, to urge your families to pay your ransom. Write it. Write it with conviction." He turned away and headed for the smoky hut.

Matthew kept pressure on Will's bloody stump to control the bleeding. Part of him wanted to grab the knife and tell Joaquín that the Rey family would never pay either, but this man was evil, perhaps even psychopathic. There was no telling what he'd do to keep his prisoners in line, to squeeze a ransom out of their families.

Thank God I bought insurance, he thought as the Canadian groaned once more in pain, his body growing colder in Matthew's arms.

19

I wanted to see Grandma before going to Bogotá.
Maybe I was dreaming, but I was truly hopeful
that the kidnappers would let me speak to Dad on
the telephone once I got to Bogotá. I wanted to be
able to pass along at least one lucid thought from his
mother.

On the day before my scheduled departure, I woke
early and drove south to the Florida Keys, knowing
that Grandma was better early in the morning. The
Keys were better in the morning, too. Here, a ride
down U.S. 1 in a topless Jeep was the next best thing
to boating. A series of bridges connected one small
key to the next, with turquoise waters to the east and
west. Sunrise was like a starting pistol for fishermen,
though they moved out to sea at the pace of the tor-
toise, not the hare. The boats—some large, some
barely big enough for a man and his catch—dotted
the waters for miles. Another world. My normal A.M.
commute would have found me stuck in traffic on my
way downtown, car exhaust instead of fresh sea air.

As I approached the old Red Cross cement home

in which my father had been raised, I saw a young boy and his dad putting their boat into the water. It made me think back to my own childhood. My father and I had done that once. *Once.* One time in my whole life, my father had taken me fishing, just the two of us. We'd never fully recovered.

I was still hoping that someday we'd sort that out.

Grandma was around back on the patio, seated at a cast-aluminum table beneath a broad, shady umbrella. She invited me to join her for orange juice. That was a better start than last time, when she'd thrown me out of the house. Better, though not perfect. She still called me Matthew and obviously thought I was her son, but the nurse had a plan. She'd found an old photo album filled with pictures of Grandma and my father. My walking her through it might help clear her memory. I liked the idea. Grandma's mind was sharpest when trained on the distant past. For me, it was definitely an education. Some of the photos I'd never seen before.

"You were such a cutie," said Grandma, beaming. She was speaking of my father at a childhood birthday party.

"How old there?" I asked.

"Four. That was the year I gave you that fire truck. It didn't make it to your fifth."

So strange, I thought, this Alzheimer's disease. She could remember a gift given almost a half century ago, but she was too confused to realize that I was her grandson.

"Did I not take care of my things?"

"I wouldn't say that. You were just a boy. All boy."

"A regular troublemaker, huh?"

She looked at me with sad eyes, laid her hand on mine. "No, honey. You didn't have to make trouble. It found us."

I wanted to follow up, but I was beginning to feel guilty about pretending to be my father. Was I being deceitful? Or was it an act of kindness toward an old woman who for the first time in months was holding a conversation that she could enjoy, that she could at least think was normal?

"Who's that?" I asked as I pointed to another photo.

"Your sister, of course."

Sister? I didn't have an aunt. I'd always thought Dad was an only child. "Are you sure?"

"I know my own children," she said sharply.

I didn't point out the irony. At the same time I didn't dismiss her claim that this was her daughter. "Where is she now?"

Her eyes turned misty. Her hands began to shake. "Why do you do these things to me?" she said, her mouth tightening.

"Do what?"

She slammed the photo album shut. "Playing with me that way. Do you enjoy this? *'Where is she today?'*" she said, mocking my question. "What kind of nonsense is that? I have a good mind to crack you across the head. No, *both* sides of the head."

"I'm sorry, I—"

"Like hell, sorry. I don't give a damn if you're sorry."

The nurse appeared, having overheard the shouting. "Maybe we've had enough photographs for one morning."

"We've had enough *Matthew*, that's what we've

had enough of. Who invited you here anyway? Go away. Get out of my yard, out of my house, out of my sight!"

I couldn't move, neither my mouth nor my feet.

"Go!" she screamed.

The nurse took my elbow, and I rose from the chair. Grandma folded her arms angrily across her bosom and looked away. I didn't know what to say, so I didn't say anything.

My mind was awhirl as I walked alone to my Jeep. Her confusion had made it impossible to talk about the kidnapping, but strangely, the outburst had made me realize the true purpose of my visit. I hadn't come to tell Grandma about my father. I was hoping she might tell me something about him.

I drove away with the sinking sense that there was plenty to tell.

Friday at lunchtime was a standing date with my buddy J. C. for basketball, and I needed to blow off some steam.

We met at Jaycee Park in the Gables, an outdoor court that J. C. fancied his home turf, given the similar-sounding name. Not to brag, but I was bigger and quicker than J. C., and whenever my outside shot was on, he couldn't stop me with a bazooka. Today I was firing up air balls.

We finished around one o'clock. J. C. had to get back to the office. As it was, he was one of the few stockbrokers I knew who would duck out for basketball before the market closed, but such was the level of commitment from a guy who'd told his clients to buy Heinz simply because he liked ketchup.

He toweled off his sweaty head at courtside and packed up his athletic bag. "Not your day, huh?"

"Obviously not. The last time I lost three straight to you, I had a broken wrist from a skateboarding accident."

"Sour grapes," he said, then chugged his Gatorade.

Normally another witty comeback would have been in order, but my heart wasn't in it. I was thinking about my trip. "You mind checking in on my mother while I'm gone?"

"Sure. Be glad to."

"Thanks."

He glanced at his watch, and I knew he was already late. We'd played longer than usual today, a nice gesture on his part to try to lift me out of the dumps.

He laid a hand on my shoulder, looking at me with concern. "Have a safe trip. I mean that."

"I will."

He turned and headed for his car. I stayed behind and rested at the picnic table beneath a shady royal poinciana tree. For a moment I was actually at peace, watching a giggling four-year-old on the swing set nearby, her toes pointed and aiming for the sun. Every third or fourth pump she'd throw her head back until her long, curly hair almost touched the ground.

Halfway through my Gatorade, I heard a voice behind me. "Hello, Nick."

I turned, surprised to see FBI Agent Huitt. "What are you doing here?"

"It's a public park."

"You don't look dressed for the monkey bars. How did you know I was here?"

"It's Friday lunch, isn't it? Basketball's your routine. You know how easy it is to find people when they live their lives in routines. It's one of the things kidnappers look for when choosing their victims. I'm sure your consultant has explained all that to you."

I wasn't sure how he knew about Alex. I didn't answer. He seated himself across from me at the picnic table, meeting me at eye level.

"Consultants are full of all kinds of information and advice, aren't they?"

"I suppose."

His gaze tightened. "Have you given any thought to what you and I talked about?"

"There's nothing to think about. My dad's not a criminal."

"Maybe he is, maybe he isn't. What I'm telling you is, he got mixed up with the wrong people. I'm giving you a chance to unscramble the egg."

"Sorry. I just don't see it the way you do."

"Maybe it's because you won't open your eyes."

"I don't like the way you operate. My father's been kidnapped, and the FBI won't help unless I snoop around his business and try to find something to incriminate his partner. You haven't given me a shred of evidence to raise my suspicions about my dad, his partner, or anyone in any way connected to Rey's Seafood Company. Pardon the pun, but you're on a fishing expedition. And I'm not biting."

He drummed his fingers on the table and nodded, but not in agreement. "I know your consultant. Alex is good, as far as she goes. But she's steering you wrong here. I'm sure she's told you not to worry about the FBI. She's probably gone so far as to say you don't even need us." He leaned across the table, looked me straight in the eye. "Let me tell you something, Nick. You need us. More than you think. More than Alex knows. A lot more."

He rose and said, "We'll be in touch."

I watched as he cut across the park to his car. He walked in a perfectly straight line, eyes straight ahead. He didn't even notice the cute little girl on the swing, didn't return her wave as he passed her, probably didn't even hear her say hello to him. The hard-ass routine was evidently no act. Being a jerk came naturally.

I grabbed my bag from the picnic table and walked to my Jeep.

20

Mom and I had a quiet dinner at home. She didn't ask much about my visit with Grandma, and I didn't tell her about my meeting with Agent Huitt. The last thing I wanted to do was add to her worries the night before my flight to Bogotá.

We ate in the kitchen, a break with family tradition. When I was growing up, we always ate dinner in the dining room. That empty space at the head of the table—Dad's space—was something Mom didn't want to see. We sat on barstools at the granite counter, both of us picking at a tuna casserole one of her friends had brought over.

"You and Alex all ready to go?" she asked.

"We're ready."

"I figured as much. I'm sure she's done this many times."

"Too many."

Mom sipped her sparkling water. Her obstetrician had told her to cut out the caffeine, so San Pellegrino with lemon was now her drink of choice. "She doesn't think you'll be in the way, does she?"

"No."

"Are you sure?"

"Why would I be in the way?"

"You're another person she has to worry about."

"We've been over it a dozen times. Alex has told me what to wear, how to act, who to talk to, who *not* to talk to. She's handpicked our hotel, she's rented a car so we don't have to jump into taxis with strangers. Yesterday she sat down with me for an hour, going over what's safe and what's not safe. She even drew maps of the exact routes we'll travel. She used to live in Bogotá. As long as I'm with her and listen to what she says, I'll be fine."

Mom didn't answer. It was her last shot at keeping me home, a feeble one at that. I decided to change the subject.

"Did Dad have a sister?"

She looked up from her plate, a little taken aback by the question. "What?"

"This morning Grandma told me he had a sister."

"Your grandmother has Alzheimer's."

"I know. But she even showed me an old photograph of a girl about five or six."

"Did she look like his sister?"

"Not especially."

"Could have been anyone, then."

"So he didn't have a sister?"

"None that he's ever mentioned to me. None that anyone's ever mentioned, including your grandmother for the twenty-five years I knew her before she started slipping."

"Strange. She confuses me for Dad. Now she's created a missing daughter."

"She's probably thinking of your sister."

I thought for a second as I buttered a slice of bread. "When's the last time she saw Lindsey?"

"A long time, I suppose. But maybe your father planted some ideas in her head about Lindsey separating herself from the family."

"That's possible, I suppose."

"More than possible. For heaven's sake, your father has been missing for almost two weeks and we still haven't even talked to Lindsey. We don't even know where she is."

"That was the weirdest part with Grandma this morning. She totally blew a gasket when I asked her where this missing daughter was. She lashed out at me—at Dad, in her mind—for even asking the question."

Mom poured herself more water. "She's a very confused woman right now."

"Yeah," I said, almost speaking to myself. "I'm pretty confused, too."

The telephone rang. Mom and I exchanged glances, and then I rose to answer. It was Alex.

"What's up?" I said.

"Bad news, I'm afraid."

"Did something happen to my father?"

"No, not that. Not directly anyway."

Mom was ashen. She'd heard my question. I covered the mouthpiece and told her Dad was fine, then continued with Alex. "What is it, then?"

"I'm afraid I won't be going to Bogotá."

"Have you spoken to the kidnappers? Did they reschedule?"

"No. The meeting's still on, as scheduled."

"I don't understand. Are you saying you want me to go alone?"

"It's— The insurance company pulled me off the case."

"Why?"

"I can't get into that with you. I'm just calling to let you know I won't be accompanying you on your trip."

"So who's the replacement?"

She paused, seeming to struggle. "There is none."

"Excuse me?"

"I'm sorry, Nick. The insurance company is denying coverage on your claim."

I gripped the phone, not quite comprehending. "We have no negotiator?"

"No."

"And the ransom will be paid by . . . .?"

"By you. This is what I'm telling you. There is no coverage. No negotiator, no ransom. All of it— denied."

"How can this be?"

"I can't elaborate. I wasn't even supposed to call you. The insurance company is sending you official notice in accordance with the terms of the policy."

"Well, isn't that big of them? In less than forty-eight hours I'm supposed to talk to my father's kidnappers by shortwave radio from the top of some hill in Bogotá that I've never even heard of. Where the hell does this leave me?"

"I can't answer that."

"*Someone* needs to answer it. This has to be a mistake."

"It's not a mistake."

"Who can I talk to?"

"I would suggest the company's general counsel. The lawyers made the final call."

My heart sank. I was hoping that this was some kind of administrative screw-up. Not likely if the lawyers had already approved the decision.

"Come on, Alex. There has to be something we can do."

"Believe me, I've done everything in my power. I truly hope you have better luck than I did."

"So that's it? You're bowing out?"

"I'm sorry."

"What about my father?"

"Good-bye, Nick."

I couldn't even speak. The line clicked, and the dial tone hummed in my ear. Finally I turned at the sound of my mother's panicky voice.

"What just happened?"

I looked at her, stunned. "I wish I knew," was all I could say.

Part Two

21

I reached Miami International Airport at 6:00 A.M., two hours before my flight.

Even if I'd known how to contact the kidnappers, I wouldn't have dared to reschedule our first meeting. I'd done my homework, I was prepared psychologically, and logistically everything was set. With or without insurance, I was going to Bogotá. End of story.

I'd represented enough insurance companies to know that I wasn't about to resolve a coverage dispute overnight, so I didn't even try. I did call Duncan Fitz, however, and told him exactly what Alex had said. He seemed like the right person to get things moving in my absence. Since Quality Insurance was a major client of Cool Cash, he couldn't be adversarial and browbeat them into reversing their position. But Duncan felt confident that he could at least make an inquiry and elicit a more detailed explanation of their about-face. We agreed to powwow when I got back and figure out where I stood.

I checked in at the crowded international terminal,

then found a seat and killed some time reading a
Spanish-language magazine called *Semana*. One of
the things Alex had told me was to blend into the
Colombian culture while traveling. I left my *Sports
Illustrated* and John Grisham novels at home. Another piece of advice was never to let go of my travel
bag. I kept it right at my side. Interestingly, the bag-
gage tag was still on it from the last time I'd checked
it on a flight home from La Guardia to Miami International. "MIA" the airport abbreviation read, which
in this context struck me as ironic. I wondered if *I*
would end up MIA—missing in action.

The bag was filled with maps and travel books,
things I didn't dare pull out in public and effectively
announce to the world that I was a naive American
tourist traveling alone to Colombia. I'd already read
all of them several times anyway. The travel hype
made Bogotá sound vaguely like Miami, sophisticated in some segments, crude and violent in others.
It boasted futuristic architecture and old colonial
churches, world-class museums that showcased
everything from pre-Columbian to contemporary
art. It was a vibrant mix of all things Colombian—
culturally diverse, an intellectual center, its busy
streets a forum for the daily clash between rich and
poor, pack mules and Porsches. There was no short-
age of great restaurants either. It seemed like a city I
might have actually liked to visit under different circumstances, save for one glaring statistic: Every hour
someone got killed. Some deaths were accidents, but
as many as eight a day were homicides—more, if you
counted at least a portion of the twenty-five hundred
annual deaths from "unknown causes." The con-

firmed homicides alone added up to an annual murder rate higher than that in Miami, New York, Atlanta, and Los Angeles combined.

I turned my thoughts back to restaurants.

Forty minutes before the flight, the airline made the first boarding call. First class only. The entire waiting area started toward the gate. That was another tidbit Alex had shared.

"Don't expect South Americans to queue up like a bunch of Brits," she'd said. "Wherever you are—airport, movie theater, bus station—act like you're on the *Titanic* and they're loading the last lifeboat."

When in Rome, I figured. I joined the mob at least twenty minutes before my row would officially be called for boarding.

Through the crowd, an attractive Latina woman caught my eye. She was standing at the check-in counter, her travel bag draped over her shoulder. She wore a stylish, short-waisted leather jacket and jeans that fit extremely well. Her face was partially hidden beneath the broad rim of a felt hat, but what little I caught of her profile was promising. She finished with the airline attendant, then turned and shot me a discreet sideways glance. I definitely wasn't looking for it, but even my travel book had mentioned that there was more to Colombia's beauty than just countryside.

She started walking toward me, pushing through the semblance of a line, and then it registered. The long hair had been tucked up beneath the hat, and I hadn't recognized her.

"Alex?" I said.

"Surprise."

"What are you doing here?"

"I'm going with you."

Wow, I thought. *Duncan works fast.* "What happened?"

Clearly she didn't want to talk in the crowd. Neither did I. We gave up our places in line and moved to an open space near the finger-smudged window that looked out on our Boeing 767.

"Did the insurance company change its tune?" I asked.

"No. They're denying your claim. I had a long chat with their general counsel after you and I talked yesterday evening. My sense is that they're never going to change their minds."

"Then why are you here?"

"Because I think you're getting a raw deal."

"I'm glad someone sees it my way."

"It's hard for me, as a professional, to see it any other way. It's unethical what the insurance company did to you, pulling out just hours before your flight leaves for Colombia."

"How are you handling this with them?"

"I still need to think that through. I figured I'd get you through this first go-round with the kidnappers and then sort things out."

"I'd like to be able to pay your normal fee, but now that I'm without insurance, I'm worried about how I'm going to cover the ransom."

"For now let's just say this trip is a freebie. We'll figure out something. Maybe you can give me some free legal services someday."

"Thank you."

"No problem. All I ask is two things. One, from

this moment forward, you don't utter the word 'insurance.'"

"Done. What's the second thing?"

She smiled wryly. "Try not to embarrass me in my home country."

"How would I embarrass you?"

"You're a gringo. You'll find a way. Just remember the advice I gave you yesterday: *No se puede dar papaya*."

"I looked that up in my phrase dictionary, and it still doesn't make sense to me. It means, 'You can't give papaya.'"

She shook her head, still smiling. "It's an expression, genius. It means, 'Don't let your guard down, don't give anyone a chance to take advantage of you.'"

"Good advice."

"Come on. Let's get back in line."

We started back toward the mob. Even the pushing and shoving at the gate seemed to be less of a hassle with Alex on my team. My spirits were up, and with the challenges ahead, I sorely needed the boost.

I looked at her and said, "I'm glad you're back on the case."

"Well, you do need a negotiator."

"I know I do. And I'm glad it's you. I think my father would like you."

"I think I'd like him, too."

"Because of all those great things I told you about him?"

"No. Because the apple usually doesn't fall far from the tree. And I happen to think his son is a pretty great guy."

"Thank you."

"For a lawyer."

"Ouch."

"You're welcome."

She gave me a little wink, then nudged me forward. Together we pushed toward the gate. Just me, Alex, and two hundred Colombians.

22

Our car was a clunker. It wasn't even from a rental agency. One of Alex's friends loaned us a rusty Chevy Vega with eighty-nine thousand miles and worn-out shocks. It was part of her low-profile strategy. No fancy car, no wads of cash, no jewelry or wristwatch except my nineteen-dollar Swatch. And I could forget those nice restaurants I'd been reading about. At least we'd booked a reputable hotel.

"Hotel?" she said with a chuckle as we left the terminal. "I borrowed a flat from Pablo for a couple days."

Pablo was the guy who'd loaned us the car that was now limping down the highway. "What about my reservations at the Bogotá Royal?"

"You didn't really think we were staying *there*, did you?"

"Uh . . . yeah."

"Just a diversion. If someone comes looking for us, we won't be there."

I thought she was joking, but she wasn't smiling. "You're thinking someone would be following us?"

"They grabbed your father. Obviously someone thinks your family has money."

I suddenly felt vulnerable. I reached over and locked the passenger door.

She drove, and I rode in the glove compartment. That was what it seemed like, anyway. The passenger seat was stuck in the forwardmost position, so that my knees pressed up against the dash. The ride was bumpy, too many potholes for our little rust-bucket. We made decent time out of the Aeropuerto El Dorado, but traffic clogged as we headed east into the city. The drive from the airport was a foreigner's first taste of lawlessness in Bogotá. Horns blasting, red lights ignored, sudden maneuvers to avoid collisions—all performed to the endless symphony of vulgar gestures and the most violent insults ever hurled between motorists. Yesterday I'd been skeptical upon reading that each day three pedestrians were run over and killed by buses in Bogotá, to say nothing of the casualties caused by some nine hundred thousand private automobiles. Now that I'd arrived, I was beginning to think they'd understated the carnage.

Sometime after 2:00 P.M. we finally reached downtown. The cool, thin air surprised me. Bogotá was closer to the equator than Miami was, but the city was nestled high in a mountain basin against the jagged ranges of the Cordillera Oriental, about the same altitude as Aspen, Colorado. With over six million people, it was an aggressive metropolis. The mountains bordered the east, wealthy expansion had moved north, poorer housing and industry were to the south and west. The old city center was still vibrant, though some of the colonial buildings were in disrepair. At its best, the feeling was Madrid or New York, especially the old commercial center. There were impressive skyscrapers, wide boulevards, trendy shops, and well-dressed professionals walking with the ubiquitous cell phones. The air was thick with exhaust from plenty of clunkers and some nice cars, too, more than I'd expected. Of course there were beggars at the intersections. Sad, but street poverty was a fact of life in virtually every city in South America, not just Bogotá. The atmosphere didn't strike me as overwhelmingly friendly, but it wasn't especially scary either. Then we turned the corner and saw the rubble.

Beside a bank was a huge pile of loose bricks, broken concrete, twisted metal. Cleanup crews were shoveling shattered glass and burned-out furnishings into wheelbarrows and dump trucks. The skeletons of three scorched cars were still on the sidewalk, one of them upside down. The work area was secured with rope and barricades. A handful of uniformed officers stood guard, but the investigation appeared to be over. They were just sweeping up the mess.

"Last week's car bombing," said Alex.

"Terrorists?"

"*Claro.*"

"Who?"

"Who knows? It's at least the tenth one this year."

I wanted to be open-minded and say something like "*It could happen anywhere.*" But a bombing every month? This wasn't Madrid or New York. This was Bogotá, and once I'd seen the first sign of terrorism, I seemed to become more critical of everything else, or perhaps just more observant. A beggar approached our car at the next intersection. He was just a kid, his face and hands dirty, his clothes practically rags. This time I didn't just look past him. I looked right into his eyes, his face pressed against the passenger window. They were black, empty eyes. I noticed two other boys on the curb passing a big bottle of glue between them, sticking the nozzle up their nostrils. One looked right at me, but I honestly couldn't say that he saw me. He had that same vacant expression. Foreigners heard so much about Colombia and its drugs, but no one seemed to talk about the eight-year-old kids on the streets blowing their brains out with industrial-strength fumes.

The traffic light changed, and we were on our way.

Our meeting with the kidnappers wasn't until tomorrow evening. By arriving a full day early, we were sure not to miss it over a logistical problem like a flight delay or goats in the road. So far everything had gone without a hitch, which left us the rest of the day and a full day tomorrow with nothing to do. I thought I'd take the time to visit one of the organizations I'd been communicating with by Internet, Fundación País Libre, a private foundation whose main mission was to raise public awareness of Colombia's kidnapping epidemic and to push for reform. With their headquarters just blocks away, I felt rude not stopping by to thank them for the information they'd sent me.

"Skip it," said Alex.

"Why?"

"Because any time I'm in Colombia to negotiate with kidnappers, my basic rule is to trust no one."

"Not even the foundation?"

"No one."

"I don't have to tell them I came here to talk to the kidnappers."

"What are they going to think? Your father was kidnapped by guerrillas, so you decided this would be a dandy spot for a vacation?"

"No. They'll think I came all the way to Bogotá because my family is pursuing every possible angle to make sure my father is released as quickly as possible. How can that hurt?"

"Look, I'm not putting down the foundation. They do a lot of great things. But keep in mind that they helped push for the passage of Colombia's anti-kidnapping law in the early nineties. One of the things that law did was make it illegal for the families of kidnap victims to pay ransom."

"You mean if we pay a ransom, we're breaking the law?"

"Don't worry. That part of the law was declared unconstitutional by the Colombian Supreme Court. The government still opposes the payment of ransom, but I've done everything we need to do to make sure the authorities look the other way."

"What does that mean?"

"It means that you can't begin to understand the scope of the kidnapping and ransom problem in this country, and I don't want you making side trips to talk to people at the foundation or anywhere else. From now until the time we leave, I'd prefer that you stay within my line of sight."

"Come on, Alex. I appreciate all you're doing for me, and probably a little paranoia is understandable. But you're starting to sound worse than me."

She suddenly turned angry. "You want to see paranoid? I'll show you."

She steered down a side street and stepped on the gas. The tires squealed as the little car cornered up a winding road to the top of a steep hill. Minutes later we stopped at the side of the road, where the view of the valley was unobstructed for a good square mile. She stepped down from the car, and I followed her to the edge of the cliff. Below was a residential neighborhood, hundreds of middle- and upper-middle-class homes on the wealthy north side of Bogotá.

"Look," she said.

We had a bird's-eye view of the rooftops. The houses were nice, but they were little fortresses. Security walls surrounded each home, some topped with razor wire. Dobermans roamed many of the properties. Dozens had guards posted along the walls or at the doors, like sentries, armed with automatic rifles.

"When I was a little girl, this neighborhood was like the one you grew up in. Kids could ride their bicycles. Mothers could stroll with their babies. Hard to believe, isn't it?"

I nodded slowly, taking it in.

"That green house on the corner," she said, pointing. "FARC has their twenty-two-year-old son. The yellow house five doors down. They took a father of three. Shot him in the head six months later when he tried to escape, then came back and snatched his eight-year-old daughter while his widow was out making the funeral arrangements. That two-story house on the hill over there—"

"Okay, enough," I said. Reading the *País Libre* statistics was one thing. Seeing where the victims actually lived was quite another.

"These aren't drug dealers. They aren't even super-rich people. They're normal families who worked hard to have a decent home and a few nice things. Bankers, shop owners, lawyers like you. This is the way they have to live now."

I noticed her voice tightening. Obviously this wasn't easy for her to talk about.

"If you want to wander around Colombia against my advice, Nick, don't do it while you're my responsibility."

I looked at her, then back at the fortified homes. "I'm sorry," I said softly.

"Let's go."

We got back into the car, neither of us saying a word. What I'd seen had definitely made an impact. Certainly there was every reason to take precautions. As she'd said in the airport, "*No se puede dar papaya.*" But her refusal to stay at a hotel or drive a rental car seemed a bit overboard to me, not to mention her going so far as to make a phony hotel reservation purely as a diversion to would-be followers. And her fears of an organization like Fundación País Libre seemed almost irrational.

The ignition whined, then screeched, and finally the car started. As Alex struggled to find first gear, I was starting to wonder. Maybe she was being extra careful for my benefit. She feared for the safety of the gringo.

Then again, maybe it was Alex herself who was hiding from someone.

I glanced back once more toward the houses in the valley, then tucked my knees against the glove box as she drove us back into the city.

23

Two things struck me about television in Colombia. Well, one thing, really. I suppose I'd expected the daily toll of violence on the evening news—murders, kidnappings, muggings. You could get that in Miami. But the nudity was the real shocker, not in the programs but the commercials. To be sure, American TV had its share of scantily clad models selling beer, cars, cologne. But American ads were puritanical by Colombian standards. With the amount of flesh flashing here, who needed the Spice Channel?

Television was about all I saw during my first eight hours in Bogotá. Alex had me holed up in our flat all day. It wasn't a bad place actually. But by eight o'clock I was feeling claustrophobic.

"Want to get some dinner?" said Alex.

"You mean go out?"

"Yeah."

"Really?" I said, teasing. "I thought you'd have me disguise my voice and order pizza under an alias."

"Very funny."

I smiled, but in truth I needed to get out. Watching television in my distant-second language was tiresome, and I found myself slipping into nonproductive worries about my father. "Let's go," I said.

We drove north of downtown to a trendy area called Zona Rosa, a maze of music clubs, bars, restaurants, and cafés that seemed to compress into a small nucleus of vibrant Bogotá nightlife somewhere around Calle 84. We ducked into a tiny, relatively quiet bistro, where doting waiters wore traditional white shirts and black vests. Several teams of them hovered over a dozen small tables for two. A canopy of twinkling white lights hung in strands from the ceiling, reminding me of Christmas. Our table was in front by the window, with a view of the steady parade of cars outside. The rich were chauffeured in bulletproof Mercedes-Benzes and Renaults. Smartly dressed couples entered in the company of bodyguards. The women wore no jewelry, but once safely inside the restaurant, they opened their purses and applied their diamond earrings or emerald rings as a matter of course, the way American women might check their makeup. It was one of the safer areas, according to Alex, but people never let their guard down completely in Bogotá.

The restaurant specialized in food from Antioquia, one of Colombia's largest and richest departments, which included the city of Medellín. It was a region fond of parties and prayer, Alex told me, known for orchids, gold, coffee, and the distinctive architecture of rural towns that had stood for centuries. Most renowned of all were its native people, the *paisas*, famous for their hospitality and interesting customs. Alex ordered a glass of wine to start. I took only mineral water, as I was still having a little trouble with the trip from sea level in Miami to over eighty-six hundred feet in Bogotá, and alcohol wouldn't help the adjustment.

"Nice place," I said.

"After scaring you to death all day, I thought you should see another side of Bogotá. People haven't stopped living."

I tried a breadstick. "Do you think I was foolish to come here?"

"I understand why you did it."

"Do you think I made the right decision?"

"Can't really say. If the only thing to consider was the risk to you personally, that would be one thing. But every time you take a risk, you have to factor in the added anxiety it causes your mother and whoever else cares about you."

"It's really just my mother."

"What about your sister?"

"She still doesn't even know about Dad."

"Surely your girlfriend worries."

She tried to slip that in casually. Maybe I was flattering myself, but I sensed more than just passing curiosity on her part. "I'm unattached right now. I was engaged, but that ended a few weeks ago."

"I'm sorry."

"Wasn't meant to be, I guess."

"Yeah, right." She almost scoffed.

"You don't believe in fate?" I asked.

"Do you?"

"Sure. We all have our destiny."

"We make our own destiny."

"So you would deny me the comfort of thinking that Jenna's breaking up with me was all for the best?"

"It might be for the best, but it wasn't fate that got you there. When a relationship dies, it's usually because somebody finally came to their senses or somebody screwed up."

She had a way of cutting through the nonsense, which I rather liked. "You're right. I screwed up."

"What happened?"

"She told me it was because my job was too consuming. But that wasn't the real reason."

"What do you think it was?"

"She built up a lot of resentment over the years."

"Toward you?"

I nodded. "She never believed that I loved her enough."

A waiter came by and lit the candle on our table. Alex waited for him to leave, then asked, "*Did* you love her enough?"

"My, this is getting personal."

"I thought it was just getting interesting."

I took another sip of water and said, "Yes, I loved her very much. I just never . . ."

She waited for me to finish, then finished for me. "You never told her?"

"It took me a long time."

"How long?"

"Almost two years."

She made a face. "Why do guys do that?"

"I wasn't trying to be cruel. We met when I was on the rebound. I'd had two serious relationships in less than a year and was burned both times. I was starting to think 'love' was one of those words that got tossed around a lot without much behind it. So I decided the next time I told a woman that I loved her, it was going to be forever. I didn't realize it, but that little pact I'd made with myself had dug me into a hole. In my mind, telling Jenna I loved her would have been tantamount to asking her to marry me. So I couldn't say it until I was ready to pop the question. Does that make sense?"

She looked at me with utter disbelief, then finally let out a short burst of laughter. It was little more than a hiccup, completely involuntary, but I was crushed nonetheless. It was as if Jenna and her seagull had dumped all over my head again.

"What's so funny?"

She sipped her wine. "Don't tell me you actually believe what you just said."

"Yes. It's true."

"You may think it's true, but here's a news flash, my friend. You didn't love this Jenna."

"How can you say that?"

She was smiling with her eyes, but I could tell she wasn't completely kidding. "When it comes to matters of love, don't argue with the girl from Bogotá. She'll eat you alive."

The waiter brought menus, but Alex didn't need them. She ordered a traditional Antioquian dish for us to share, something that wasn't on the menu but that she and our overly attentive waiter concocted together. Finally he left us alone.

I was still mystified and a little miffed by her reaction to my Jenna story, but I decided to turn the tables rather than push it. "You still have family here in Bogotá?"

"I think so."

"You don't know?"

"My family's pretty screwed up."

"Isn't every family?"

She smiled weakly but didn't elaborate. "Come on," I said. "I just laid my heart on the line and got laughed at. You can open up a little."

She looked right at me, almost through me, as if deciding whether I was trustworthy. Then she just started talking, her dark eyes fixed on the candle's flickering yellow flame. "I never knew my father. He was an Italian businessman who traveled back and forth from Rome to Bogotá. My mother would see him one weekend a month till I was about ten. I always knew when he was coming, because I had to go stay with my aunt. For years my mother deluded herself into thinking he was going to marry her someday. Deep down she must have known he already had a wife back in Italy."

"So your mother raised you alone?"

"Yes, my older brother and me."

"You don't keep in touch with them?"

"No."

It was a flat "no," the kind that didn't invite inquiry. She sipped her wine and asked, "Don't you want to know why?"

"Only if you want to tell me."

"My brother is dead. He was killed."

"I'm sorry."

"My mother thinks it was my fault, so she doesn't speak to me."

I wasn't sure what to say. Almost reflexively, I asked, "Was it your fault?"

She looked away briefly. Then her eyes met mine and she answered in a soft, troubled voice. "I don't know. After all these years, I still don't know."

The waiter interrupted with the first plate. It smelled delicious, and he refused to leave until Alex had tasted it and told him how wonderful it was. Her somber mood was suddenly gone.

"Enjoy," she said. "With a meal this authentic, we must follow Antioquian custom."

"Which is what?"

"While we eat, we can speak of nothing but the food. It's an unbreakable rule."

I wasn't sure if that was truly an Antioquian custom, but one thing was plain: I wouldn't hear another word about her estranged mother and dead brother. At least not tonight.

"*Salud*," she said as she raised her wineglass, and I raised my glass of mineral water in return.

24

The NRA was laying down its weapons. Yankee fans were rooting for the Boston Red Sox. The French were eating English food and loving it.

Matthew was sure all those things were happening. His tent was leaking, he hadn't bathed in three weeks, his daily food ration had been cut to one plate of beans with rat droppings and a canned fish product that even he, a lifelong fisherman, couldn't identify. It had been three days since his clothes had been soaked in a rainstorm, and he could still wring moisture from them. The putrid overflow from the hole in the ground that was their bathroom had started oozing downhill toward Matthew's tent, but the guards only seemed amused by his complaints. Joaquín was still in charge, the Canadian was losing his fight with infection in his severed thumb, and the Swede was sniping at the other captives, certain that he was next in line for torture. Each night the young Colombian woman cried for hours in the darkness, praying to the Holy Infant and whispering the names of her children. No one held any realistic hope of a prompt release. All that, and temperatures were dropping by the hour. Late afternoon had brought their first hailstorm.

This was the proverbial cold day in hell, and Matthew was living it.

It had amazed everyone, Matthew included, the way the Canadian had maintained his backbone even after losing his thumb. The stub was still bleeding when Joaquín had returned with a pen and paper, insisting that he write a letter to his wife. Will told him it wouldn't do any good, that he and his wife had a firm pact: If he was kidnapped by rebels, never pay, no matter what. Only after Joaquín threatened to cut off his other thumb did Will finally acquiesce. With his left hand he wrote the exact words Joaquín dictated, an impassioned plea begging his family to break their no-ransom pact and cough up whatever money the kidnappers demanded. Joaquín had made a spectacle out of it. The entire letter was composed in front of the other prisoners, a form of intimidation, a demonstration of how even the most defiant prisoner eventually capitulated to the will of his captor. The Canadian dated it, signed it at the bottom, and handed it over to Joaquín. The boss man seemed pleased. Strangely, the Canadian had seemed even more smug as he returned to his seat around the fire with the other captives.

"I signed it 'Mickey Mouse,'" he whispered to the others.

They were all shocked—Matthew, Emilio the Colombian, Jan the Swede.

"They'll kill you," said Jan.

"These idiots won't even notice. I signed in real tiny letters. You need a magnifying glass to see it. But my wife will know right away it's not my real signature. When she looks closely and sees what I wrote, she'll know I was forced to write the letter and don't really want her to pay a ransom. Pretty smart, huh?"

"Joaquín has your passport," said Matthew. "He can check your real signature against the tiny scrawl you put on his letter. If he looks closely and sees Mickey Mouse . . ."

Will was suddenly ashen. Matthew wished he hadn't said anything.

Dark, ominous clouds moved in from the east. The jagged peaks in the distance disappeared behind thick, misty shades of black and gray, and night seemed to fall over their camp long before sunset. One of the guards brought them hot coffee. That was actually the one pleasure about captivity in the Colombian mountains. The coffee was the best Matthew had ever tasted. He sipped it slowly to prolong the enjoyment and warming effect. The chill was back just thirty seconds after the cup was empty. He had a wool blanket, but it wasn't big enough to cover his whole body. He had to alternate between warming his feet, then pulling it up to warm his torso. It wasn't raining, thankfully, but heavy clouds hung like a wet rag over their camp. This was going to be the coldest night yet, Matthew could tell. It was even too cold for the guards to drink their *aguardiente* outdoors. They were snug in their smoke-filled hut. Aída and another low-ranking rebel were ordered to sit outside and watch the prisoners alone. By nine o'clock they were all shivering. Matthew complained.

"We need a fire."

Aída walked over and said, "No."

"Why not?"

"No outdoor fires. *Chulos* are too close." She turned and walked away.

Matthew had no idea what she was talking about, having a vague recollection that "*chulo*" could mean either "pimp" or "buzzard." Emilio explained. "*Chulos* is what they call the Colombian army. Joaquín must have information that there's a military offensive going on against the guerrillas. He's afraid that a fire at night might give away our position."

"Then why do they have a fire in their hut?"

"Because they're the guards and we're the prisoners."

The Swede sat up, huddled beneath his blanket, his knees against his chin to stay warm. "This is absurd. There's no *chulos* out here in the middle of nowhere. They're punishing us because Will signed his name Mickey Mouse."

"Don't blame this on me," said Will.

"How else do you explain it? Coldest night yet, and they won't even let us have a fire. Way to go, Mickey."

"One more crack out of you and I'll cut off your Swedish meatballs."

Jan shot him a contemptuous glare but said nothing. The prisoners sat in tense silence for a moment, and then Emilio said, "We could huddle for warmth. We did that the last time I was kidnapped, and it worked."

"I'm up for it," said Matthew.

Jan glanced at the other Colombian, the thirty-eight-year-old with straggly orange hair who looked like an octogenarian. "Not him," Jan whispered. "He has fleas. I've seen them in his beard."

Matthew and Emilio looked at one another, as if thinking the same thought. It didn't seem fair for the five of them to huddle while a sixth slept alone and nearly froze to death. The man was the most antisocial in the group, having yet to utter more than one or two words to anyone, but he was still one of them.

"He can sleep on the end next to me," said Matthew.

Emilio quietly explained the plan in Spanish to the orange-bearded Colombian and the young mother from Bogotá. The six started to move closer together when Joaquín approached in the darkness. He had two other guerrillas with him.

"We're just trying to stay warm," said Matthew.

Joaquín didn't seem interested. He had fire in his eyes, but without the glazed and cloudy look that came from drink. This was raw anger. He glared at the Canadian and said, "You. Come with us."

"What now?"

Joaquín pointed his rifle. "Get up."

Will rose slowly. The others watched in silence as the two guerrillas grabbed him, one on each side, and pulled him toward Joaquín. It was eerily reminiscent of the day he'd lost his thumb.

The Colombian woman sat up in panic. "¿Qué hace?" she asked. What are you doing?

Joaquín answered her in Spanish. "The Canadian's

wife got his thumb by courier. She's agreed to pay the ransom." He shoved Will and said, "Move it."

Will started walking. The team of four walked quickly past the guerrillas' hut and continued toward the path that led into the jungle. Matthew and the others followed with their eyes until the group was out of sight in the darkness.

Matthew looked at Emilio and asked, "You think it's true? Could his wife have gotten the thumb already?"

"It's possible, I suppose. I just hope they didn't figure out that Mickey Mouse signature."

"They're following the same path they used to take me to the FARC camp," said Matthew. "Maybe they're going to try to sell him."

Jan said, "You heard Joaquín. His wife agreed to pay the ransom. The lucky son of a bitch is going home."

"This is bad." It was the old-looking Colombian, the one who never spoke. To the surprise of the others, he understood English. "Joaquín would never escort prisoners out of the jungle. He leaves that for his underlings."

"Then maybe he is going to sell him to FARC," said Jan.

"Too late for that. You have to understand, Joaquín is not in the business of housing prisoners. Whenever he makes an abduction, he takes the merchandise straight to FARC and sells it, if he can. He keeps a prisoner only when FARC offers him too little money. He wouldn't take the Canadian back to FARC a second time only to have FARC offer him less money than before. He'd sooner kill him."

"But then he gets nothing," said Jan.

"This time, yes, he gets nothing. But if he sells too cheap, he cuts his own throat in the long run. He has to keep the price up for his merchandise."

The Swede was getting edgy. For all his sniping at Will, he didn't like the way this conversation was headed. "They can't just kill him. That's ludicrous. There's too much of an investment."

"It's the way Joaquín does business. When someone doesn't look like they're going to pay off, he cuts his losses and gets rid of him."

"But what about you?" said Matthew. "You've been here sixteen months. If it's true he dumps the ones who won't pay, why are you still here?"

The deep-sunken eyes turned deadly serious. "My family has paid. Four times. I'm his annuity."

Matthew shuddered at the thought.

"I've seen this situation before," the man continued. "Joaquín isn't like FARC. His little group doesn't have enough supplies and guards to watch more than five or six prisoners, tops. If one of them isn't working out, he has to make room for a new one."

"You mean he lets one go?" Jan asked hopefully.

The man's voice dropped to little more than a raspy whisper. "I mean one way or another, he makes room."

A lone gunshot pierced the night like thunder. The Colombian woman shrieked. On impulse, Matthew's head snapped toward the dark path the guards had followed. The shot echoed in a long, almost continuous crackle that rolled across the mountaintops like an endless ocean swell. It was still rolling, faint but discernible, when Joaquín and his guerrillas emerged from the jungle.

It was just the three of them. Will was not among them.

The prisoners exchanged uneasy glances, saying not a word as Joaquín and his fellow executioners disappeared into their hut.

25

Nineteen hours in Colombia. I'd counted off every one of them, including the wee hours of a sleepless night.

Alex and I had returned from the restaurant before midnight. She went straight to bed. The couch was all mine. I nearly dozed off around 1:00 A.M., then shot bolt upright at the shrill noise of what at first sounded like a drunk screaming his lungs out on the balcony next door. Turned out it was actually a rooster crowing at the moon. Naturally this startled me, since it was hours before dawn and silly me had always thought it was the big orange ball on the horizon that got roosters to crowing. Once awake, I quickly put aside the whole question of this bird's lousy sense of timing and wondered, more to the point, what in the world a rooster was doing in an apartment building in downtown Bogotá in the first place. I had just about convinced myself that it was all a dream when, fifteen minutes later, the crazy bird crowed again, this time waking Alex. She came out to the kitchen for a drink of water and explained that roosters lose all sense of time when housed in a high-rise building. Her tone was so matter-of-fact, as if the whole world knew how screwed up an urban rooster could be. She went back to sleep without a problem. I, on the other hand, was awake for good, anticipating the cock's next untimely crow, checking the clock repeatedly, counting the hours and then the minutes to our deadline, even though the letter from the kidnappers had set a time for our meeting that wasn't determined by any clock or insomniac rooster: Sunday at sunrise.

At 4:00 A.M. I was dressed and ready to leave the apartment. Alex was in the shower. I waited in the living room, no television and no radio. Noise traveled freely in the old apartment, even through closed doors, and without moving from the couch I could still hear Alex humming what sounded like a bolero as streams of hot water pelted her firm body. The thought of her nakedness flashed in my mind, though I was far too stressed to be even remotely aroused. Last night's dinner and conversation still had me puzzled anyway. One moment it had felt like a first date, the next like a jailhouse interview with a convicted felon. The last thing it had resembled was a conversation with a trained negotiator the night before a first communication with kidnappers. Only now, as we were about to head out and accomplish the thing we had come here to do, did I finally see the wisdom in her curious method. We had prepared thoroughly back in Miami, and any last-minute discussion about the kidnapping would only have made me crazy with anticipation and worry. She'd taken my mind as far away from this morning's meeting as possible, teasing me with her past, even flirting a little with her eyes over a delicious Antioquian dinner. My friend J. C. would have said she was messing with my head. In reality she was just keeping my head screwed on before the most stressful event in my life. At least, that's what I assumed she was doing.

"You ready, Nick?" she asked as she emerged from her bedroom.

"I think so."

"You nervous?"

"I know so."

"I can go alone, if you want."

"Are you crazy? Let's do it."

It was almost two hours before sunrise when we left the apartment and drove east to Calle 20 in the historic Barrio la Candelaria, Bogotá's well-preserved city center. We parked near Quinta de Bolívar, an impressive colonial mansion that was once Bolívar's home, now a museum. More important, it marked the beginning of our climb to Monserrate, the lower of two impressive peaks that rise to the east of Bogotá.

Monserrate was a popular tourist destination. At over thirty-two hundred meters, the summit offered an inspiring view, though according to Alex the expensive French restaurant alone was worth the journey. It could be reached by a funicular railway and cable car, but not at five o'clock in the morning. At that time of day walking was the only option, and it took us about an hour and fifteen minutes with no rest stops. It turned cooler as we climbed, and in the early-morning dampness I was glad for a thick sweater and jacket. Alex and I took turns carrying the shortwave radio in the backpack. Fortunately, the path was comfortably graded, and dressed stone from bottom to top offered secure footing. To my surprise, we weren't the only climbers. The safety was marginal, but even bandits had to sleep, and Sunday at 5:00 A.M. was about the only time anyone in their right mind ascended Monserrate in the dark.

Four climbers in front of us headed straight for the observation deck near the old church. We walked in the same general direction, past the street vending stalls that were all closed, heading finally toward the picnic grounds behind the church. The kidnappers hadn't told us to ascend to the top of Monserrate to enjoy views of the city's tiled roofs and the plains that stretched beyond to the rim of the savanna. It was all about reception on our shortwave radio.

Alex set up the radio on a picnic table near the ridge. For miles below us stretched Bogotá and the suburbs it had swallowed to the north. The sun had not yet appeared, but its anticipatory glow was already brightening the horizon. It was that ambiguous hour between night and day. Block by block the shadows were disappearing. The city lights seemed fuzzy, still burning but fading fast, like persistent guests who'd overstayed their welcome. It would be daylight in a few minutes, and in a few hours the park would be crowded with visitors. For now, however, Alex and I were completely alone. She switched on the shortwave radio and set it to the frequency the kidnappers had specified in their letter. I heard nothing but static, but it wasn't quite sunrise. All we could do was wait.

"What if they don't call us?" I asked.

"They will."

She answered with such assurance that I didn't doubt her for a second.

The radio hissed in a low, empty tone that signified nothing. Alex listened, alert for any change in reception. For nearly twenty minutes we sat at that picnic table, the radio set to the same blank frequency. Through the trees I watched the top of the orange globe rise from behind the peaks to the east. With each passing minute it grew bigger, its arrival magnified by the low band of clouds that turned purple and pink, an endless ribbon stretching the length of the Andes. Slowly the ribbon burned away, and the sun was alone in the sky, too bright to look at directly. At that very moment the radio crackled. At first it was a subtle break in the hiss. Then we heard the voice in Spanish.

"Rey family. Are you there?"

Alex grabbed the microphone. "Yes. We're here. Go ahead, please."

"Good morning, my friend."

It sickened me to hear him call me "friend," but Alex just rolled with it. "Good morning. We've been expecting you."

" 'We?' " he said, his tone slightly suspicious. "Exactly who is there with you?"

"Don't worry, no police. Just me and a member of the family. That's it. I'm their representative. Call me Alex."

"All right. Call me Joaquín. I'm sure we will get along just fine. So long as the Rey family is prepared to pay us some money."

"We don't even have a demand yet."

"I thought we'd let you open."

"Excuse me?"

"You have a member of the family there, don't you?"

"Yes, but—"

"Who is it?"

"The son."

"That must be Nick."

It was strange to hear my name, but at least it confirmed that we were really dealing with the kidnappers.

"That's right," said Alex.

"Perfect. Ask him how much his father is worth to him."

"Knock off the games," she said harshly.

"It's not a game. I'm sitting here with his father. Tell Nick to make an offer. If it's enough, I'll let his father go free. If it's not enough, I'll kill him."

I looked at Alex, my heart pounding. "Could he be serious?" I asked softly.

She spoke into the microphone, "This isn't the way we do business. The family has come to deal in good faith. I was hoping you would do the same."

"Really? Well, how's this for good faith? I have a pistol to his father's head as we speak. Make an offer. Make it a good one."

"Stop this right now," said Alex.

"Are you offering nothing?"

I gave her a hard look, wanting to make sure she knew what she was doing.

She said, "We've come to listen to your demand. Not to make an offer."

"If the family was dealing in good faith, the son would know exactly how much to offer."

"What are you talking about?"

"He knows what his father is worth. I know what his father is worth. It's just a question of who is going to be the first to spit out the number."

"We're listening."

"No, *I'm* listening. I want to hear the son say it. If I don't hear the right number, the next sound you'll hear is the crack of my pistol."

"We don't play guessing games."

"You'll do what I tell you to do," he said sternly.

"Then tell us what you want."

There was silence on the line. My hands were shaking. Nearly ten seconds passed. I looked helplessly at Alex. I was sure the gun would go off.

"Three million dollars," he said.

Alex laughed. I snatched the microphone from her hand and covered it so the kidnappers couldn't hear. "Don't laugh at him! The crazy son of a bitch is going to shoot my father."

"I know what I'm doing," she said as she took it back from me.

The kidnapper said, "Do you think I'm joking?"

"*Claro*," said Alex. "Three million dollars? You might as well ask for three billion."

"That's our demand."

"Fine. Here's our demand. We need proof that Matthew Rey is alive."

"You get only what you pay for."

"No. Before we plunk down a cent, we need proof."

"What do you want?"

I knew what she was going to say. Alex and I had worked this out in Miami. "We want Matthew to answer a question. His son had a dog when he was a child. A golden retriever. What was his name?"

"Okay. We'll get that."

"You said Matthew was sitting there with you. Ask him now."

"Can't do that."

Alex covered the microphone and said, "I knew he was bluffing."

This time I wasn't so sure she *really* knew.

"Have the answer at our next talk," she told the kidnapper.

"Easy enough. Same time, same place. Four weeks from today."

I whispered, but it was still a shriek. "Four weeks!"

She gave me a little wave, as if to convey that the timetable was reasonable. "Four weeks it is."

"Of course, at that time I will expect you to have a commitment from the family to pay us three million dollars."

"We're not going to pay you three million dollars. The family doesn't have that kind of money."

"I know with certainty that they do. They'll pay it, or Matthew Rey is a dead man."

The radio hissed. We didn't hear another word.

"He's gone?" I asked.

"For now." Alex switched off the radio.

"What do you think?"

"First off, don't you ever snatch the microphone from my hand while I'm negotiating."

"Sorry. When you laughed at his demand, I thought for sure he was going to pull the trigger."

"The way I handled it is the way the game is played. I must have told you a dozen times that most kidnappers settle for ten to fifteen percent of the original demand."

"I know. This guy just didn't seem all that open to negotiation."

For a split second her tough exterior melted, and I saw a look of concern in her eyes. I asked, "What are you thinking?"

"I'm thinking that you may be right."

"What?"

"You heard how he was talking. The way he stressed that both you and he know your father is worth three million dollars."

"So you're saying what? He knows my father bought kidnap-and-ransom insurance?"

"I'm saying more than that. I'm afraid he might know the exact amount of coverage."

A chill ran right through me. "So my instinct is right? It's no coincidence that the policy was for three million dollars and he asked for the same amount?"

"It's possible it's a coincidence. Three million is a nice round figure, and kidnappers always demand millions for Americans, usually somewhere between one and five."

"But you don't think it's a coincidence."

"I'm reading between the lines, but I think he was telling us that much."

"My God. What could be worse than a kidnapper who knows we have a three-million-dollar policy and an insurance company that refuses to pay?"

She looked away. She clearly didn't have an answer for that one. And neither did I.

The morning sun was burning brightly now, but I still felt cold. We packed up the radio and started back down the mountain.

26

I returned to Miami with one priority: resolve the
insurance coverage issue.

The situation was touchy. My law firm represented
Quality Insurance, the Bermuda company that had
written my father's policy. I knew the realities of life
in a big firm. Not even the partners who liked me
would dare tell a paying client to do right by Nick Rey
or take their big book of business elsewhere. I was
Lawyer Number 1,826 in seniority at a firm so riddled
with turnover that nameplates were fastened to office
doors not with glue or nails but magnets, as if second-
year associates were as secure in their position as refrigerator art. My only hope was that just one lawyer
with clout would have the backbone to arrange a
meeting at which I could at least plead my case to the
right set of deaf ears. Duncan Fitz was my best shot.

Before my trip to Bogotá, Duncan had promised to
make some inquiries with Quality. I followed up first
thing Monday, my first day back to work since the
kidnapping. I felt guilty about resuming normal
activities with my father still in captivity, but my

mother encouraged it, and our financial situation required it, especially if we ended up without insurance to pay the ransom and Alex's expenses. Besides, I could think of no better way to get to the bottom of the insurance issue than to plant myself right in the hallowed halls of the law firm that represented the insurer.

The door to Duncan's office was open, so I poked my nose inside.

"Got a minute?" I asked.

He looked up from his computer screen and waved me in. "How'd the trip go?"

I closed the door and took a seat in the wing chair facing him. Perched on the corner of his desk, he seemed eager for an update. Over the next few minutes I recapped the details, with a nifty tap dance around any mention of Alex. Since the insurance company had officially pulled her off the case, she didn't want it known that she was helping me nevertheless.

"Wow," he said. "Three million dollars. That's a lot of money."

"I guess if you're a Colombian guerrilla, you think every American's a millionaire."

"I don't mean to insult, but I assume that if this insurance problem isn't worked out, your family doesn't have that kind of money."

"That's why I'm here," I said. "Did you find out anything?"

He rose and walked around to the credenza. "I like you, Nick. But this firm is even more tightly allied with Quality Insurance Company than you may realize."

"How do you mean?"

"We don't normally tell associates which partners serve as officers or directors of our clients, but in this case I'll make an exception. Maggie Johans is a vice president and general counsel for Quality Insurance Company. As a partner, I owe a duty of loyalty to every client, but you can see how the duty to Quality is, shall we say, heightened."

"I understand."

"That said, I'm not going to leave you twisting in the wind."

"Thank you."

He leaned forward, hands atop his desk, peering out over the top of his spectacles to look me right in the eye. "To be blunt, the partners in New York are calling for your head. Maggie is practically apoplectic. As a favor to me, she picked up the phone and lit a fire over there to get your father's case moving quickly. Imagine how she felt when her own investigators called to tell her that the Rey family was pressing a fraudulent claim."

"Fraud?" I said, nearly choking on the word. "Is that what they think?"

"They apparently uncovered evidence of collusion with the kidnappers."

"That can't be. What is it?"

"You know I can't tell you that. It's a matter of attorney-client privilege."

"This is ridiculous. Three of my dad's crew members were killed in the attack. Another one saw him pulled from Cartagena Bay by Marxist guerrillas. There's no collusion. He was kidnapped. He was lucky he wasn't killed."

"The insurance company isn't so sure it was luck." He lowered his eyes as he spoke, as if he were embarrassed to have said it.

"I can't believe I'm hearing this."

"I couldn't believe it either. But that's where we are. Your claim is being denied as fraudulent."

The silence between us was growing uncomfortable. The news was bad, but I didn't want to lose Duncan's support. I had to reel him back in somehow. "This may sound paranoid, but I suspect that the FBI might be behind this whole problem."

"How?"

"If I share this with you, can I have your word that it will be kept in strictest confidence?"

"Of course. I consider this whole conversation to be friend to friend."

"I had a meeting with a couple of hard-nosed FBI agents last week. They seem to think that my father's business partner in Nicaragua may be engaged in illegal activities. Essentially, they're blackmailing me. The FBI refused to help with my father's kidnapping case unless my whole family promised to cooperate in the Nicaragua investigation."

"What kind of illegal activity do they suspect?"

Already I was having serious second thoughts about going down this road. "They were narcotics agents."

He looked at me with disbelief, which slowly gave way to anger. "I almost wish you hadn't told me that."

"I'm sharing this with you because it's all a railroad. Everything was going smoothly with the insurance company until the FBI started flexing its muscles."

"You're not suggesting that the FBI is behind the insurance company's denial of your claim?"

"Think about it. No one in my family can be forced into playing informant for the FBI if we don't need their help negotiating with the kidnappers. What better way for the bureau to make sure we need them than to muck up our insurance coverage?"

"You were right," he said, scoffing. "That does sound paranoid."

"All I ask is that you check and see if anyone at Quality Insurance has talked to the FBI. Do me that one small favor."

"I'm not doing you any more favors!"

His forcefulness took me aback. I tried to respond in the most level tone I could muster. "I can't sort this out without your help."

"Then you shouldn't have deceived me."

"Deceived you? How?"

"The FBI is investigating your father's fishing company for running drugs, and you didn't even bother to tell me."

"It's my father's partner, not the business. And if Guillermo had anything to do with drugs, my father wouldn't have anything to do with him."

"We're talking about perceptions. I went out on a limb burning favors for you and your family, calling my partners and colleagues, using my contacts, all to get the FBI and State Department to make your father's kidnapping a priority. I put my own good name and the reputation of this law firm on the line. Now I'm told that I went to bat for someone suspected of drug smuggling."

"You're missing my point. The FBI is on a witch hunt. My father is the victim here."

"No, *I'm* the victim. You used me and this law firm with absolutely no regard for anyone but yourself."

"My father was kidnapped."

"That's a tragedy, but it's no excuse. You should never have put me in this position without telling me the whole story."

"I'm sorry you feel that way."

"'Sorry' doesn't cut it." His voice definitely had an edge to it.

"Look, I don't want this misunderstanding to come between us. Tell me what I can do."

"Leave," he said flatly. "The damage is done."

On past occasions I'd seen Duncan so angry he could scream. This time I sensed an anger of a different quality, not the kind that passed with a good venting but the kind on which grudges were built.

I rose and started for the door. He stopped me and said, "I wasn't kidding about New York."

"What about it?"

"They truly are looking to fire you."

I wasn't sure what to say, didn't know what he expected to hear.

"And you know something?" he said in a low, threatening tone. "The more I hear, the less inclined I am to stand in their way."

Our eyes locked. Then he opened the door and showed me the way out.

I went from the law firm to the doctor's office. My mother's ultrasound was scheduled for that morning, a routine procedure in the fourth month of pregnancy. Of course, Mom didn't believe anything was routine for a forty-five-year-old expectant mother. She didn't come right out and say it, but I knew she was worried and wanted me to go with her.

The technician did a good job of putting her at ease, so it wasn't necessary for me to hold her hand through the actual procedure. It would have been interesting to stay, I supposed, but there was something vaguely oedipal about seeing the inside of my own mother's uterus, even if it was just sound waves. I waited in the lobby, surrounded by some very uncomfortable women in various stages of pregnancy, most of them further along than Mom.

Mom's preoccupation with the ultrasound did have an upside. Last night when I'd returned, she didn't ask as many questions about Colombia and the kidnappers as she might have. Her mind was on her baby. I told her that the ransom demand was high and that we hoped to negotiate it down. She didn't ask how high. It was almost as if she didn't want to know how unobtainable it might be.

The door to the ultrasound lab opened, and the technician called to me. "You can come in now."

I put down my three-year-old copy of *Parenting* magazine and went inside. Mom was seated on the examination table.

"Well?" I said, a little too cheery.

She looked at me and clutched a tissue. Her eyes were red and puffy. I feared the worst—no fetal heartbeat. "Is everything okay?"

She nodded, then sniffled.

I went to her and held her hand. "Why were you crying?"

"It just makes me so damn sad that your father wasn't here to see this."

She laid her head against my arm. I held her for a minute, searching for the right thing to say. Before I could get it out, she handed me the picture the nurse had taken of the fetus. It was a ghostly white image against a solid black background, actual size, no bigger than a peanut.

"Holy cow, it's another Einstein. Look at the size of that brain."

"That's the placenta, wise guy."

I almost had her smiling. "Boy or girl?"

"I asked her not to tell me."

"Oh, come on. You're going to keep us in suspense?"

"I'm saving that. Your father and I will find out together once he's home."

Her eyes welled again. Just the mention of Dad in this setting seemed to choke her up.

"Please don't cry. You have a healthy baby. That's a lot to be thankful for."

"I'm just so sorry he missed this. I know he's sorry, too. We didn't get to do ultrasounds with you or Lindsey. He was so excited about seeing it."

"Dad really wanted this baby, huh?"

"As much as I did. Maybe more."

I paused, unsure whether to pursue my thought. But the morning talk with Duncan about the FBI had stirred up my curiosity, and I couldn't let it go. "If Dad knew you were pregnant, why would he take the risk of going to a place as dangerous as Colombia?"

"I can't answer that."

"You mean you don't know or you can't tell me?"

She looked at me funny. "I mean I don't know."

"Did he tell you why he was going there?"

"No. But that's just the way your father operates. It was dangerous to go to Nicaragua, too. But he didn't dwell on the risks, and he didn't give me all the scary details."

"Nicaragua's one thing. That's where the company is. I just don't understand what could have been so pressing about a trip to Colombia that he would take chances while you were pregnant."

"Your father has a different perception of risk than most people."

"But he still saw it as risky enough to buy kidnap-and-ransom insurance."

"That's true. Which leads me to believe that he must have had a very good reason for going there."

"I'm sure," I said, knowing that "good" didn't necessarily mean "legal."

Mom got up from the table, hit the eject button on the VCR, and grabbed the videotape that the technician had made of my future sibling. "Let's go home," she said.

"Sure. I'm right behind you."

27

On Tuesday night I met Alex for a drink.

It was business, of course, but she didn't want to meet in her office. She was on retainer with Quality Insurance Company, and so long as my family was in a coverage dispute, it was best for me not to visit her place of business or for her to be seen coming and going from my home. She suggested neutral territory, like a bar, trusting that I'd pick a place reasonably obscure. I told her I'd see her at Duffy's Tavern at eight.

Duffy's was on Red Road between historic Coral Way and what was once just plain old Eighth Street, now Calle Ocho, the main drag through Miami's Little Havana. The Duffy's side of Red Road was a commercial mixed bag, home to adult video stores, run-down repair shops, and a little Italian restaurant that served the best minestrone I'd ever tasted. The other side marked the boundary to Coral Gables, where expensive Old Spanish–style homes and manicured lots faced tree-lined streets with dreamy names like Valentia or Obispo. Of course, most of those picture-perfect side streets didn't feed into Red Road anymore. Many had been tastefully barricaded with recently erected metal gates, stone pillars, and thorny hedges. The idea was to eliminate quick escape routes for brazen thugs who followed wealthy women home from the grocery store and clubbed them over the head for an emerald ring or diamond tennis bracelet. As more residents became victims—some for the second, third, or even fourth time—more barricades went up, until it seemed that the ultimate goal was to turn the entire city of Coral Gables into one big gated community.

In a weird way it reminded me of Bogotá.

Duffy's was a curiously popular hangout that over the years had become something of a local institution. It was the kind of place my father's friends might have gone for a beer after a hot day of bone fishing, or where a group of University of Miami grad students might unwind over a pitcher of beer. Its brick facade and blackboard for daily specials were more suited to a South Boston tavern than the typical slick Miami sports bar. Inside, the floors were old wood planks that bore the stains of countless spilled drinks. Long shelves at near-ceiling height displayed a seemingly endless collection of empty beer cans, one after another, like an aluminum crown molding. Varnished-over baseball cards served as wallpaper. Pendants, posters, framed newspaper articles, and just about anything else that had ever commemorated a sporting event were mounted everywhere, including the ceiling. The U-shaped bar was crowded with beer-guzzling carnivores who enjoyed their weekly quota of protein and cholesterol in one meal-size patty with cheese while watching twelve television sets at once, each tuned to a different sports channel. A bumper sticker behind the bar proclaimed DUFFY'S—WHERE THE ELITE MEET TO EAT.

I took a table by the window and ordered a pitcher of beer and a basket of jalapeño poppers. The group next to me was counting aloud as one of their buddies pitched peanuts into the air and caught them in his mouth, never missing. It was part of the atmosphere, though I was beginning to wonder if it was Alex's style.

"Come here often?" said Alex as she slid into the chair across from me.

"Nice line," I said.

The college kid at the next table was choking, then finally coughed up a flying peanut that had gone down the wrong pipe.

"It's not a line," she said. "Do you *really* come here often?"

I poured her a beer into a frosty mug. "Don't be a snob."

"You're right. I guess this is one place I can relax and not worry about the CEO of Quality Insurance walking through the door and seeing us together."

"Actually, that's him right over there."

Across the room was a fat, drunk old man dressed in a tight T-shirt and spandex bicycling shorts that were at least two sizes too small. He was dancing a waltz by himself, eyes shut, his arms around his imaginary Ginger Rogers.

Alex snickered at the sight. Then she turned

serious, eager to hear the upshot of my meeting with Duncan Fitz. For the next several minutes she listened without a word. The last bit of news, I thought, was sure to elicit a telling reaction of some sort.

"The insurance company denied the claim as fraudulent."

"I know," she said without hesitation.

"You know?"

She nodded, as if no explanation were needed.

"Then why are you sticking with me?" I asked.

"Because you're cute."

I blinked twice and probably even blushed a little.

"That was a joke," she said.

"I know. But I'm still wondering why you haven't dumped this case."

"Because no one at Quality Insurance will tell me what the alleged fraud was. In my book a person is innocent till proven guilty."

"But you said it yourself in Bogotá. You thought the kidnappers not only knew my father had insurance, but they knew the exact coverage limit."

"That doesn't mean your father tipped them off and staged his own kidnapping. He could have been set up by someone else."

"Like who?"

"If I were you, I'd sit down and make a list of every person who could have known your father's travel plans and might have known that he had insurance."

"There's my mother, of course, but she's said all along that she didn't know anything about insurance."

"You honestly think she's a suspect?"

"No way. She's practically in mourning over this."

"Could be guilt."

"Yeah, theoretically. If you want to go down that road, the bad guy could be me, too, in theory. But it isn't."

I was thinking, and then a familiar voice snagged my attention. "Nick, hi."

I turned and saw Jenna, my ex-fiancée. She was wearing a softball uniform from a women's league, her cap on backward. It was normal attire at Duffy's.

I rose, unsure whether to shake her hand or give her a little kiss on the cheek. After a split second of awkward indecision, I did neither. "What a surprise to see you here," I said.

"My softball team comes here every other Tuesday after a game. Don't you remember?"

"Must have slipped my mind."

"Must have," said Alex, a tad sarcastic.

I took that as my cue to make the introductions. "Alex, this is Jenna, who I've told you about. Jenna, this is Alex."

"Very nice to meet you." They said the exact same thing at the same time in the same insincere tone. I wasn't sure why it mattered to her, but I could tell that Jenna suddenly wished she didn't look as if she'd just run off the baseball diamond.

"How do you know Nick?" asked Jenna.

"I'm not sure I do know him," said Alex.

I laughed too hard, then steered the conversation toward Jenna. "So how've you been?"

"Good. We won our first game tonight."

"Terrific."

"Not really. The other team didn't show up."

I glanced at the group of women in clean uniforms ordering drinks at the bar. "Well, any excuse to celebrate."

"Right." Her smile faded. "Is there any news on your dad?"

"We're making progress, I think. Long way to go, though."

She lowered her voice, as if to keep things just between me and her. "I wasn't just being polite when we talked on the phone. If there's anything I can do, please let me know."

I felt her touch my arm as she spoke, just the tips of two fingers resting an inch or so away from my pulse. It was hardly any contact at all, but it was the first physical connection since the breakup, and I could have kicked myself for allowing it to confuse the hell out of me.

"I'll definitely let you know. Thanks."

One of her teammates called from their table and raised a glass. Jenna looked at me and said, "Guess I better get back to the victory party."

"Sure. You go ahead."

She smiled weakly and was gone. I returned to my seat and took a long sip of beer, only to meet a cold stare from Alex.

"Are you playing games?" she asked.

"What do you mean?"

"You picked this joint because you knew she'd be here, didn't you?"

The accusation stunned me, but the strange

truth was, I'd been thinking about Jenna a lot since yesterday. The ultrasound had triggered memories of the good times between us—getting engaged, planning a wedding, dreams of our own future family. We'd even gone so far as to toss around possible names for children. We settled on none but were in complete agreement that there would never be a Moon Rey, Sting Rey, or X Rey.

"I swear, this was a total coincidence."

"I don't believe that for a minute."

"Why would I want to see Jenna?"

"You didn't. You wanted her to see you. With me."

"What purpose would that serve?"

"You tell me."

"You think I was trying to make her jealous or something?"

Alex didn't answer. She simply rose, dug in her purse, and threw a ten-dollar bill on the table to cover the tab. "I thought you could be more professional than this, Nick. I'm doing you a huge favor by staying on your father's case. Don't blow it by messing with my head."

"You have the wrong idea, totally."

She just glared, silent.

"Alex, please don't go away mad."

She left without another word, not so much as good-bye. I was about to follow when I sensed that someone was watching. I turned, expecting to see Jenna giving me a sideways glance from across the room. I saw only the back of her head. I scanned the entire bar. Not a single set of eyes was on me.

Yet the feeling of being watched was almost palpable.

It gave me a creepy sensation that I tried to shake off quickly. I finished my beer in one long swig and headed for the exit, resisting the urge to look back at Jenna—or whoever else it was who'd made me feel watched.

28

The Swede was beginning to freak. Matthew had been watching Jan closely the last few days, fearful that he might do something stupid. He'd been acting strange ever since the guerrillas took the Canadian into the jungle and shot him. One minute he was withdrawn, the next surly and angry. Perhaps it was his way of grieving. He and Will used to argue and hurl insults back and forth, and only after the execution did Matthew get the sense that the two men hadn't merely worked for the same mining company but had actually been close friends.

Just days after Will's death two new prisoners arrived, a young married couple from Japan. The woman spoke English and told Matthew what had happened. They were bird-watching along the Colombian border near Ecuador, one of the most beautiful hiking areas in the world. They'd felt safe because they were traveling with a guide who knew the area and, presumably, the dangers. Joaquín and four of his guerrillas surprised them near a mountain stream during their lunch break. The guide was Colombian and talked to Joaquín for nearly half an hour, at times a heated discussion. In the end the guide went free and the tourists were taken away at gunpoint. The woman had been angry at first, suspecting that the guide had pleaded for his own release and not theirs. Soon she realized that the more likely scenario was that she and her husband had been set up from the very beginning, led into Joaquín's lair by their own guide, who was probably haggling with Joaquín over his commission.

The arrival of new prisoners further unsettled a group that was already on edge from the execution. The threat of death had always been in the air, but the lone gunshot that had pierced the night and the empty space around the campfire the following morning had made it all too real. Each of them had submitted to captivity while clinging dearly to the notion that a prisoner was more valuable alive than dead. Surely Joaquín wouldn't discard his merchandise and deprive himself of a hefty ransom. Will's death and the wisdom of the old-looking Colombian with orange hair—"Flea Man," as Jan called him—had set them all straight.

"Sometimes it's just easier for a guy like Joaquín to negotiate with the family for the return of a dead body," said the Flea Man.

With tensions running high, Matthew was thankful for his new source of sanity: fishing. While Joaquín and his abduction team were out hunting for Japanese tourists, Matthew had convinced the remaining guards that he could fish trout from the stream. They were as tired of the bland diet as anyone, so they let him try. He fashioned a hook from a

small safety pin, and the line was a six-foot length of
thread he unraveled from the frayed hem of a canvas tarp. Worms and grubs were a plentiful source
of bait. In the company of two guerrillas, he fished
almost an entire afternoon and caught sixty-one
trout from a quiet eddy near a fallen log. They were
no bigger than his hand, but anything larger would
have snapped the line of thread and taken off with his
only hook. Last night Aída had grilled them over the
fire in the hut, and the guerrillas ate most of them.
She brought the five smallest ones to Matthew, his
reward for having caught them. The other prisoners
got the usual rice and beans. Matthew gave one fish
to each of them. Even with the heads on, they were
barely enough to add a little flavor to the rice.

Yesterday it had rained all day, so they didn't go
fishing. This afternoon, however, the sun was shining, and the guerrillas were hungry for more trout.
They'd found another safety pin, and Matthew rigged
up a second line with more canvas thread. He told
them he couldn't watch both lines at once without
risk of losing one of them, so they let him bring along
a fishing buddy. The prisoners drew straws to see who
could go. The Swede won.

They left camp after lunch and returned to the
same eddy, about a fifteen-minute walk. Four guards
went this time because of the extra prisoner. For
added security they chained the prisoners together
at their ankles. Aída and her boyfriend perched
themselves atop a rock in the sun. They were soon
groping each other. The two other guerrillas enter-
tained themselves with a Spanish-language travel
book that Joaquín had taken from the guide who'd

led the Japanese tourists into trouble. Every few minutes they hooted with laughter, pointing at yet another passage that read, "This area is safe for tourists." Travel books were like the kidnapper's guide to hunting and fishing.

In thirty minutes Matthew had caught eleven trout. The Swede hadn't caught any.

"Will you stop making me look bad?" said Jan.

"You're doing fine. Just be patient."

"Don't patronize me. These guerrillas are going to think I'm worthless."

Matthew smiled, thinking he was kidding. But Jan's expression was tense and deadly serious. "Lighten up, all right?"

"How do you expect me to lighten up? Can't you see I'm next on their list?"

"What list?"

Jan lowered his voice, as if to make double sure that the guards couldn't overhear. "Their list of expendables."

Matthew glanced toward Aída and her boyfriend. They'd moved from atop the rock to the bushes behind it. "You're giving these punks too much credit. They don't make lists."

"Go ahead, brush it off. You're now their fair-haired boy, Mr. Fisherman. But me, I'm just Will's friend. Will, the pain in the ass."

"They're not going to kill you just because of that."

"You heard what the Flea Man said. Joaquín's group has enough guards to handle five or six prisoners, tops. With this new Japanese couple, we have seven now."

"He also said Joaquín eliminates only the ones who look like they won't pay off. Will was stupid. He flaunted the fact that his family wouldn't pay."

"That wasn't just a pact he'd entered into with his wife. That's the philosophy of our whole company. Will and I got extra pay to come to Colombia, but we knew that if we were kidnapped, the company wouldn't pay."

"Joaquín doesn't have to know that."

"He'll know soon enough. I'm not married. I don't have a wife or family to come up with the money to get me out of here. Joaquín is sure to make a ransom demand on my company. And they won't pay."

Matthew lowered his eyes. A trout was skimming the surface, flirting with his hook. "You don't know that for sure."

"Management thinks exactly the way Will did. I'm telling you because I trust you. My only way out of here is on my own two feet."

"You mean an escape?" Matthew whispered.

Jan made a face, as if saying it would jinx things. "If I stay, I'm a dead man. And you're in the same boat."

"Why do you say that?"

"These little underlings might like you now that you're catching fish for them. But Joaquín, he's got a score to settle with you. That guerrilla who got killed in the shoot-out on your boat in Cartagena was one of his best men."

Matthew froze for an instant. He hadn't told anyone about Cartagena. "How did you know about that?"

"I keep my ears open. The guards talk plenty."

Matthew said nothing, thinking.

"So you with me or not, fisherman?"

Again Matthew lowered his eyes toward the fish. It was about to bite, then swam away from the hook. "I can't."

"Why not?"

"I have responsibilities here."

"What?"

"The two young Colombians. When Joaquín took us back from FARC, he said he'd kill Emilio if I tried to escape. He'll kill Rosa if I succeed."

"It's a bluff. He won't kill two prisoners with families willing to pay."

"I can't risk it."

"Don't be a fool. You need to look out for number one. You said your wife is pregnant, right? Your family needs you."

That was true, in part. The family needed him— the new family anyway, the baby who might never know his father. It would have been easy for Matthew to feel sorry for himself, but he felt even worse for the much younger parents who might never see *any* of their children grow. Matthew had been blessed with the chance to raise two children to adulthood. Sometimes he'd felt as though he'd screwed it up; often he wished he were closer to his children. But there was no denying he'd been given the chance. Whether he deserved a second one, he couldn't say.

"I just can't run out of here at someone else's expense."

"They'd do it to you, my friend. This is the law of the jungle. Survival of the fittest."

"I told you, I can't."

"All right. I'm on my own. But think about it, will you?"

"Sure," he said, but he knew that escape wasn't an option. It wasn't even necessary. Maybe Joaquín was angry about the shoot-out in Cartagena, but in the end a ransom payment would surely ease his grief and erase whatever anger he felt toward Matthew. Joaquín loved money, and Matthew's insurance company had plenty to give.

But why was it taking so long?

Just hope I picked a good company, he thought as he turned away from Jan and refocused on his fishing.

29

The week ended as it had begun, with me headed for a meeting with Duncan Fitz. This time it wasn't going to be the folksy chat in his office. I'd been summoned to the private conference room adjacent to the Miami managing partner's suite, and the bad vibes had already started in the lobby. The receptionist greeted me pleasantly, but the moment I'd passed, I got the strange sense that she'd picked up the phone to alert someone I was on my way. Secretaries seemed unusually busy typing or filing, no time to look up from their desks and say hello. A partner emerged from his office, saw me coming, and went right back inside. It seemed as though everyone had decided that my family had defrauded a client.

Seemed, I chided myself. *You're getting paranoid.*

I wasn't sure what Duncan had been thinking since the unpleasant ending to our meeting on Monday morning. My first clue came from his secretary in the form of a bare-bones E-mail telling me where to be and when to be there. Of course the meeting would deal with the insurance coverage issue, but beyond that I'd been told nothing. That was the norm at Cool Cash. As a rule, news from the management committee leaked first to certain secretaries, then to partners, next to the associates at large, and lastly to the poor slob most directly affected by the action.

I checked my watch: 10:00 A.M., right on time. I turned the final corner, started down the hall, and slammed right into Duncan Fitz's secretary, knocking her files to the floor.

"Gosh, I'm sorry," I said.

"It's okay, my fault."

Beverly was a sweet but plain-looking divorced woman in her late thirties who had given up her social life for the benefit of Duncan Fitz, which meant working till eight o'clock every night, a full day on Saturdays, and a fair number of Sundays. She was the most efficient and organized person I'd ever met. Every day she worked through a lunch that consisted of either an orange or a banana, one granola bar, and the latest live-forever vitamin cocktail that she'd ordered online from a health food Web site. She didn't have many friends at the firm or, for that matter, outside the firm. The only photographs at her workstation were of cats, especially a big white one with awesome green eyes. Maybe it was because I'd always made a point of asking how Puffy was doing, but for some reason she'd always liked me.

"I can't believe I did this," I said.

We were kneeling and facing each other, scooping up the scattered papers from the floor. In the midst of the cleanup she stopped so suddenly that I stopped, too. She looked me in the eye and whispered, "Be careful what you say in there. I've seen the memos."

She tucked the reassembled files under her arm, as if to end our conversation right there.

"Thank you," I said, rising.

With her eyes she seemed to say, "Good luck." Then she continued down the hall without another word.

I took a deep breath, knocked on the conference room door, and entered on command.

Dark suits were the order of the day. Seated at the conference table were three men dressed in various shades of navy blue, plus one woman wearing charcoal gray with burgundy accents. Duncan Fitz was at the far end, nearest the window. Sid Templeton, the managing partner of the Miami office, was at his side. The other two I didn't recognize.

"Martin Rush," said the man, "Chairman of the Ethics and Conflicts Committee." With the accent, he didn't have to tell me he was down from the New York office. He seemed tightly wound, a compulsive jogger, I imagined—wiry body, thin face, hair cropped a little too short, the red bow tie a bit too tight.

"Maggie Johans," said the other. I'd never seen her face before, but from the name alone I immediately recognized her as the lawyer Duncan had called in New York to help me—the partner who served as Quality's general counsel.

"Please, have a seat." She was evidently taking the lead, which didn't bode well.

"Thank you." I glanced at Duncan and Sid Templeton as I settled into my chair, trying to get a sense of any sign of support from the Miami contingent. Sid glanced out the window. Duncan lowered his eyes.

Maggie said, "This committee has been assembled to determine the proper response of our law firm to the dispute that has arisen between Quality Insurance Company and the Rey family. In making that determination, we wanted to afford you an opportunity to express your views."

"Are you sure you want to hear my views?"

"Why wouldn't we?" she asked.

"Because my family has been accused of fraud."

"That's true."

"My view is that the accusation is baseless. Quality Insurance Company has acted in bad faith, and I hope that somebody makes them pay for the added stress they've put on my mother and for every additional minute my father spends in captivity because of their refusal to pay the ransom."

She and the other New Yorker exchanged glances. Duncan shot me a look, as if warning me to tone it down a notch.

The skinny ethics chairman asked, "Is it your intention to sue a client of this law firm?"

I measured my response, mindful of Duncan's nonverbal admonition. "I hope it doesn't come to that."

Sid Templeton, the Miami managing partner, jumped in. "Before everybody gets their back up, can we simply talk a few things out?"

"Sure," I said.

"Whenever there's a disagreement, I find it helpful

to stand in the shoes of the other person. If you'll bear with me, Nick, you may gain some insights as to where the insurance company is coming from."

"I'm all for that."

Sid cleared his throat, then began, "Your father was a fisherman for almost thirty years, correct?"

"That's right."

"He never had kidnap-and-ransom insurance."

"No."

"Finally he buys a three-million-dollar policy and—bam!—not much later he's kidnapped. That's a red flag for an insurance company, wouldn't you agree?"

"I suppose it might be."

Sid shrugged, as if giving me an opportunity to explain away the suspicion. Before I could say a word, Maggie took over the line of questioning. "Why did your father purchase three million dollars' worth of coverage?"

"Maybe that was the most he could afford."

"Let me ask the more pertinent question. Why do you think the kidnappers demanded exactly three million dollars in ransom?"

"The dollar amount of the ransom is part of an ongoing confidential negotiation. Unless the insurer intends to pay it, I prefer not to share that information."

"You already told Duncan it was three million dollars."

I looked at Duncan with surprise. Obviously nothing we'd talked about on Monday had been kept confidential, or "friend to friend," as he had promised. "I don't know why the kidnappers demanded three million. You'll have to ask them."

"Or your father," she said.

"What are you implying?"

"It hardly seems coincidental that the ransom demand is in the exact amount of coverage."

"First of all, that doesn't mean my father defrauded anybody. Second, the insurance company didn't even know that the ransom demand matched the policy limit until *after* it denied the claim as fraudulent."

"Young man," said Mr. Ethics, "what prompted your father to purchase kidnap-and-ransom insurance after going without it for thirty years?"

"Circumstances change. Kidnapping for ransom is more prevalent these days. And I would imagine that my mother's pregnancy had something to do with it. He started to think like a future father again."

"So he jumped on his boat and headed for Colombia. That doesn't sound like the responsible future father."

"In hindsight, I'm sure he wishes he hadn't gone."

Maggie narrowed her eyes, leaning closer. "Of all the companies out there, what made him choose Quality Insurance Company?"

"I don't know."

"Was it your recommendation?"

"No," I said, surprised by the question.

"Did you tell your father that Quality might look more favorably on his claim, given your association with this law firm?"

"Absolutely not."

"Did you tell your father that you would use the

partners in this law firm to pressure the insurance company into paying the claim?"

"That's absurd."

"Then why did you ask Duncan Fitz to call me and use my influence with Quality?"

"Duncan offered to call you, I didn't ask. Tell her, Duncan."

He answered in a hollow voice, "As I recall, Nick, you came to me."

"Yes, and you offered to help."

Sid intervened. "It should be made clear that no one is suggesting that Duncan knowingly participated in any kind of scheme to defraud."

"There was no scheme by anyone," I said. "The only thing motivating me or Duncan was the fact that my father was kidnapped and needed help. Period."

No one seemed convinced, least of all the New Yorkers.

"Is that what this is about?" I said. "You think I told my father to buy a kidnap-and-ransom policy from Quality Insurance so that I could scam them?"

There was no answer, but I could see where this was headed—me and my father, co-conspirators. The warning from Duncan's secretary was ringing in my ear: *Be careful what you say in there. I've seen the memos.*

"This is a sham. You don't care what my views are. You've already made your decision."

Maggie said, "I assure you, we came here with an open mind. We had sincerely hoped to hear something from you that would allow a course of action other than the one we must now recommend to the management committee."

"Exactly what is your recommendation?"

"Suspension without pay until the dispute is resolved."

"Why?"

Mr. Ethics scoffed. "Your failure to see the reason only underscores the urgency of our recommendation."

"How do you expect me to get the help my father needs with no income?"

"It's my understanding that the FBI works for free," Maggie said dryly. "At least for families who aren't defrauding insurance companies."

I could have argued with her, but I saw no upside in explaining that the point of contention between my family and the FBI was not alleged insurance fraud but suspected drug smuggling out of Nicaragua.

I rose and looked each one of them in the eye, allowing my glare to linger a little longer on Duncan. "This is far from over," I said, shaking hands with no one as I left the room.

30

"**S**uspended." That was the word that stuck in my mind when I woke Saturday morning, once the initial anger had passed. I reminded myself that my ego was secondary, that the real fight was for my father. But it was hard not to take a betrayal like this personally, especially from Duncan Fitz, a guy who'd given me nothing but glowing reviews from the day I'd started working for him.

I wondered what the party line would be on my suspension. The firm couldn't announce that I'd been suspended for pressing a fraudulent claim on a kidnap-and-ransom policy. Quality prohibited anyone—including its own lawyers—from disclosing the existence of kidnap-and-ransom insurance. Of necessity, the explanation for my departure would be vague, which would only invite salacious speculation on Miami's legal grapevine. Soon the poor guy whose father had been kidnapped in Colombia would be known only as the idiot associate over at Cool Cash who'd been suspended for sleeping with the managing partner's sixteen-year-old daughter and kicking a blind cocker spaniel.

I could fight rumors, but on the more serious front, I wasn't sure who was the more formidable opponent, the Colombian guerrillas or Quality Insurance Company. Battling alone was foolhardy. I needed help.

Since Tuesday's uncomfortable encounter at Duffy's Tavern, I'd left Alex alone to cool off. On Saturday morning I phoned her at home to find out where she stood. I half expected her to hang up on me, but to my surprise she suggested we meet for lunch at the News Cafe on South Beach, near her apartment. I jumped at the invitation.

"See you there," I said, hanging up before she could reconsider.

I didn't get to Miami Beach often. It was only a few miles away, but traffic made the trip from Coral Gables only slightly less difficult than leaping across the Grand Canyon. Each time I went, however, I vowed to make a point of going more often. Beneath a perfect blue sky, with warm breezes blowing in from the ocean, South Beach was one of *the* reasons to live in South Florida.

The News Cafe was a popular sidewalk cafe on the corner of Ocean Boulevard and Seventh Street, if not the heart of South Beach, at least its left ventricle. Any outside table was prime entertainment, ideal for spotting a Brazilian supermodel, the dance troupe from the latest Latin MTV video, or morbid tourists headed for a macabre Kodak moment on the very steps where Gianni Versace had been gunned down. Street traffic was typically bumper to bumper, a slow parade of expensive convertibles, motorcycles, and rolling boom boxes that blasted out a variety of music, some that made you want to get up and move to the beat, some that made you want to get up and move to Iowa. Across the boulevard was a grassy park with palm trees and volleyball courts, and then there was the famous sandy beach beyond. Scantily clad skaters maneuvered around pedestrians with the skill of slalom skiers, weaving in and out, excusing the occasional brush of a sweaty body with a glib "Sorry, dude."

Alex showed up just seconds behind me, dressed in capri pants, a sleeveless blouse, and Chanel sunglasses. It was definitely the kind of look that would have turned my head if she'd been a stranger just passing by. We found a table in the shade of an umbrella, and the waiter brought us sparkling water with lemon. She seemed to be waiting for me to start the real conversation.

"I'm almost surprised you came," I said.

"Why?"

"Things have taken a turn for the worse at my law firm. I thought you'd be even more concerned than ever about someone from Quality Insurance seeing us together."

"Trust me. That doesn't matter anymore."

I sipped my bottled water, reluctant to ask the logical question. "Is that because you're done with me?"

"No. It's because Quality Insurance fired me."

"From my case, you mean?"

She removed her sunglasses to reveal the serious expression in her eyes. "They terminated my retainer agreement. They'll never send me another case."

I grimaced, knowing it was my fault. "I swear, I didn't tell anyone you were helping me."

"I told them myself."

"Why?"

"After you and I got together at Duffy's, they confronted me. Apparently someone saw us there together."

"That's so weird. As you were leaving, I sensed someone was watching us."

"Might have been someone from your law firm, but whoever it was has a pipeline to the general counsel for Quality Insurance."

"That's because the GC is also a partner in our New York office."

"Kind of incestuous, isn't it?"

"Tell me about it. So Maggie Johans called you?"

"Yeah. Wanted to know what the hell I was doing fraternizing with the enemy."

"What did you tell her?"

"That I didn't agree with the company's decision to deny coverage, and that I intended to continue helping you on my own terms."

"Damn, Alex. You should have said you were pumping me for information, setting me up for their benefit."

"Is that what you would have done?"

I thought for a second, then said, "No, but I still feel terrible. Quality Insurance has to be a huge source of business for you to lose."

"Don't worry about that."

"I do worry. If helping me is going to cost you an entire book of business, that's a debt I can't ever repay."

"I didn't come here to hand you a bill. If anything, I came because I felt like I was the one who owes you."

"Owes me what?"

She lowered her eyes and said, "An apology. For the way I acted at Duffy's the other night."

"You had a right to be mad."

"No. I should never have opened my mouth and accused you of playing games. Whatever is going on between you and your ex-fiancée is your business."

"There's nothing going on between me and Jenna."

"That's not the point. I was letting my personal feelings get in the way."

She caught me in mid-sip, and I nearly choked. "You mean for me?"

"No, I mean for Duffy's beer and popcorn. Yes, of course for you, dummy."

"When you say personal feelings, do you mean . . ."

"I'm not head over heels, okay? We've simply been spending a lot of time together lately, and—and would you please stop being so obtuse?"

"I just had no idea."

"I wasn't exactly trying to make it obvious, given our professional relationship."

"I'm sorry, I just didn't think that . . . you know, you and me."

"Now you're lying."

I wasn't accustomed to this kind of directness, but in a way it was refreshing. "Okay, so maybe I was sensing a little something. But there's nothing to apologize for."

"That's where you're wrong. Your father was kidnapped, and I offered to help. It's totally unprofessional for me to inject anything else into that equation."

"Maybe you should let me be the judge of that."

"No."

I waited for her to elaborate, but she didn't. "That's it?" I asked. "A simple no?"

"What more is there to say? You have my word that I won't send any more confusing signals."

I nodded, though the present signals were plenty confusing. "If that's the way you want it."

"I've thought about it all week. On principle, I refuse to back down and dump your case. I won't let any insurance company dictate my client list to me."

"I can respect that."

"Then I'm sure you'll understand that the only way I can be effective is if we agree to keep things strictly professional."

I was speechless. Here was an intelligent, beautiful woman confessing a vague but potentially romantic interest in me, and I'd been too wrapped up in my own world to recognize the signs. To be sure, a kidnapping could have made any man oblivious. My fear, however, was that the real hang-up was still Jenna.

"I can live with that," I said.

"Good."

"But if you're sticking with me on principle, you need to be aware that this is going to be a dogfight. From what the lawyers at my firm said yesterday, they might even accuse me of being a co-conspirator in the fraud."

"I'm not worried about that. I've checked you out."

"What does that mean?"

"Exactly what I said. You're not the type to scam an insurance company."

"I'm glad you think so. But the way the ransom demand matched the policy limit right down to the last dollar, I'd probably be suspicious of you if the tables were turned."

"Did you make that list I told you to make?"

"List?"

"Anyone who would have known your father's travel plans and who might have known he had insurance."

"I've mulled it over in my head, but I can't say I've physically made a list."

"Let me help you. Did your father pay for the policy out of his own pocket, or did he get it through his company?"

"I believe he bought it himself."

"The reason I ask is because insurance is the kind of thing he might have discussed with his partners. Oftentimes employees try to get their company to pay for it."

"You're suggesting that Guillermo might have set him up?"

"I'm saying that his partners might have known about the insurance. It's up to you to figure out if they set him up."

"I'll look into it," I said.

"I recommend it. Highly."

"Why?" I asked, half kidding. "Did you check out Guillermo, too?"

She smiled thinly, almost imperceptibly. Then she put on her sunglasses and turned her gaze toward the joggers across the street, as if she'd said enough.

I watched her, intrigued. One minute she was direct and assertive, bold enough to bare her feelings. The next she was a mysterious cipher pointing me toward Nicaragua. It was possible that she'd targeted Guillermo purely as a matter of deductive reasoning. I couldn't help but wonder, however, if something more was behind her suggestion—something that for some reason she wasn't telling me.

"I'll definitely check it out," I said, staring at her nebulous reflection in my tall, empty glass.

31

Monday morning was perfect for windsurfing. Sunny and eighty degrees, surf temperature almost as high, a steady breeze from the southeast. Not bad, considering that at least fifty million Americans to the north were already scuffle deep in fallen leaves and wiping frost off their pumpkins. I strapped the board atop the roll bars on my Jeep, drove to Biscayne Bay, and took off.

Key Biscayne is an island southeast of downtown Miami, and the relatively flat, shallow bay waters off the causeway that link it to the mainland are practically in the shadows of the office towers on Brickell Avenue. As I skimmed across the waves, chances were excellent that several of my colleagues at Cool Cash were peering out the window from thirty stories up, wishing they were that lucky guy windsurfing out on the bay. I could have waved. Or flipped them the bird. It seemed like a fitting way to begin my suspension.

As teenagers, J. C. and I had gone out on the bay every Saturday, a couple of thirteen-year-old studs in our own minds. Our not-so-secret desire was to meet that girl in the opening credits of *Miami Vice*, the one in the skimpy bikini whose board is knifing through the water at thirty miles an hour when she arches that incredible body, throws her head back, soaks her long blond hair in the bay, and keeps right on going. The bay was a great escape from school, the world, the hassles of being a teenager—and from my father. Finding my own passion on the water was a convenient way of telling him that the disastrous fishing trip we'd taken together was going to be our first and last. At age twelve I'd seen a side of him that I never wanted to see again. So I decided I'd never be alone with him again, at least not in a setting where he was not just my father but the captain of the ship. A drunken captain of the ship.

Seeing him that way had been bad enough. What he'd done that day changed us forever.

As I packed my equipment back onto my Jeep, I realized that the old wounds were very much a part of the pain and personal strife that had been brought on by the kidnapping.

"Lemonade, friend?"

I turned at the sound of the man's voice. It was Nate, a cheery old guy who in the past twenty years had peddled his frozen lemonade cart up and down the bicycle path enough times to circle the globe. Business today was so slow that he couldn't break a twenty, so I let him keep the change. That was only fair. He didn't recognize me, but J. C. and I probably owed him at least a hundred bucks for all the frozen lemonades he'd let us put on our tab.

I climbed into my Jeep and was about to start the engine when another voice startled me.

"Can we talk, Nick?"

He was right beside my Jeep, but with the sun shining directly in my eyes I wasn't a hundred percent sure on the ID. "Agent Nettles?" I said, squinting.

"In the flesh."

Nettles had been the initial FBI agent assigned to my father's case. I hadn't heard from him since the narcotics arm of the FBI had seemingly taken over. "What's there to talk about?"

"Your father's case, of course."

I released the parking brake, letting him know that I was leaving. "Look, you were much nicer than the drug agents who interrogated me, but I'm giving you the same answer I gave them. I think it's wrong for the FBI to tell me they won't help my father unless I play spy and help your narcotics agents pin some unspecified crime on his business partner."

"I agree with you."

That took me by surprise. "Then why did Agent Hard-Ass give me the 'come to Jesus' speech?"

"Not every cowboy who thinks he talks for the entire FBI actually talks for the entire FBI."

"Are you saying that the FBI is now willing to help, no conditions?"

"When your father comes home, you can bet that Agent Huitt will have a good long talk with him. But it's my job to get him home, regardless of whether you or anyone else in your family agrees to cooperate in any future investigation against anyone."

"Why the sudden reversal?"

"Let's just say there was an internal disagreement. We finally straightened it out."

"Or maybe it's just the old good-cop/bad-cop

strategy. I wouldn't bow to threats from Agent Huitt, so you politely insinuate yourself back into the kidnapping negotiations, work closely with our family, and snoop around while you're at it."

"That's not what this is about."

"Why should I believe you?"

"What choice do you have?"

We locked eyes for a moment, until the sun shining behind him finally forced me to look away. If I hadn't had Alex in my camp, I might have jumped at the offer. But I had to remember that this was the same guy who'd stonewalled me when the FBI had "declined" the State Department's invitation to work on my father's kidnapping.

"I'll think about it," I said, then started up my Jeep and drove away.

I spent the rest of the afternoon at my house in Coconut Grove, then headed over to my mother's for dinner. Since the kidnapping, I'd made a point of dropping by at least once a day to see her, and tonight she was in the mood to cook. Hearts of palm salad and grilled salmon with dill sauce beat the heck out of a cold bologna sandwich, so who was I to stop her?

I let myself in and found a note on the refrigerator saying that she was at the grocery store. Mom was a great cook but not a great planner. It seemed that no meal was complete without an emergency run to Gardner's Market for some missing ingredient. I helped myself to a soda, flopped on the couch with the newspaper, and turned straight to the "Americas" section of the *Miami Herald*. Before the kidnapping I used to skim right past it, but now I had a keen interest in the Colombian Army's latest clash with guerrillas or the most recent bombing by paramilitary forces.

I heard Mom's car pull up, the dull thud of a closing car door, the click of her heels coming up the sidewalk. It sounded as if she were running. The front door flew open. She burst inside and slammed it shut. I turned to see her with her back against the door, clutching her bag of groceries.

"Someone followed me home," she said in a nervous voice.

"What?"

She quickly headed for the kitchen. I followed. Her hands were shaking as she dropped the bag of groceries on the counter.

"A man in a blue car. I swear, he tailed me all the way from Gardner's."

"Did you recognize him?"

"No. Never saw him before."

I had a quick thought. "Could it have been Agent Nettles from the FBI?"

"No. This man was white."

Could have been Huitt, but in her state of near panic, now wasn't the time to tell her about the bullies in the FBI's narcotics squad. "Is he still out there?"

"I don't know. I ran inside."

"What kind of car was it?"

"I can't say. Maybe a Ford. Do you think it could be a messenger for the kidnappers?"

Before I could answer, there was a knock at the door.

"Don't answer it!" my mother said.

For thirty seconds we didn't move. Another knock

followed, harder this time. I looked at Mom and said, "Wait here."

"Nick, no."

I walked to the window and pulled the drapes away from the window frame only far enough to peer out. A blue Ford was parked across the street. Just the sight of it had my blood boiling—the nerve of this creep to follow my mother home. My dad had a Smith & Wesson revolver in the bedroom, but I had a sense that the ax handle he'd always kept hanging behind the refrigerator might set a more proper tone.

"Call the police," I said.

She picked up the phone. I grabbed the ax handle and started for the back door.

"Where are you going?"

"I can't just open the door and let him in. I'll walk around to the front and confront him."

"Please, wait for the police."

"How dangerous can he be? He rang the doorbell."

"So did the Boston Strangler."

"I'll be right back."

Over my mother's pleas I opened the door and stepped out, ax handle gripped firmly. I hurried across the back patio, turned at the corner of the house, headed up the side yard, and stopped at the front of the garage. From there I could see the Ford across the street. I could hear it, too. The motor was running. I took another step forward and looked across our front lawn. A short guy in a baseball cap was standing on our front porch. He was smaller than me, a good thing. I approached with as much bravado as I could muster and stopped at the base of the steps.

"What do you want?" I asked pointedly.

He nearly jumped. I'd caught him by surprise. "Are you Matthew Rey?"

"No. I'm his son. Who are you?"

He reached inside his shirt.

"Don't move!" I shouted.

In a flash he threw something that hit me in the chest. He leaped off the porch and sprinted across the lawn. I tried to catch him, but I'd gotten a slow start and this kid was lightning. In a matter of seconds he was inside his car. The motor was already running. He slammed it into gear and squealed away.

I tried to get the license plate number but missed it. I walked back to the front porch and found what he'd thrown at me. It was an envelope stuffed with papers. I opened it and immediately realized what had just happened. The guy was a process server. Someone must have told him that we'd try to avoid accepting service of court papers, so he'd planned a sneak attack.

My shock turned to anger as I saw the caption in black and white: *Quality Insurance Company v. Matthew Rey*, it read.

They were suing my father. Even more infuriating, two separate subpoenas commanded my father and me to appear in Miami-Dade circuit court at nine o'clock tomorrow morning for an emergency hearing. The gall. Dad was in a jungle held captive for ransom by Colombian guerrillas, and *they* had an emergency.

I flipped to the last page to see who the lawyer

was, though this kind of legal maneuvering left little doubt as to the perpetrator. Still, it nearly sent me spinning to see the name and address of my own law firm in the signature block and, above the signature line, the familiar scrawl of my supervising partner, Duncan Fitz.

"You son of a bitch," I said quietly. "I'll give you an emergency."

I folded up the papers and went back inside the house.

32

It was less than two hours till sunset, and they'd been marching since dawn. Joaquín and two others led the way through the jungle thicket with machetes, followed by three more guerrillas armed with AK-47s. The three Colombian prisoners were next, the young mother and father first, then the Flea Man. Close behind them were three more armed guards and the Japanese couple, the newest prisoners. Two more guerrillas followed with Matthew and the Swede. Four guerrillas brought up the rear, the best shooters in the bunch.

Their shooting skills were no secret. Yesterday afternoon they'd trotted out the prisoners to watch their target practice, not just to show off but to make their point. If any of them were thinking about an escape, they'd have to outrun a team of sharpshooters who could blow a Coke bottle off a stump at a distance of a hundred meters. The demonstration wasn't exactly a lift to anyone's spirits, but Matthew sensed that the Swede had been especially demoralized. Jan had been dispirited and crankier than ever since their talk at the river, when Matthew had made it clear that he wanted no part of an attempted escape. Of course Matthew had kept their discussion to himself, but strangely enough the guards seemed to have picked up on Jan's mood and were watching him more closely. Perhaps the guerrillas were experienced enough to sense when a prisoner was plotting an escape.

Or, Matthew feared, maybe they'd overheard him and Jan talking.

"Stop here," shouted Joaquín.

The human chain came to a halt. The guerrillas dropped their packs and began to make camp. It was a suitable place. Firm ground, not the swampy mosses they'd struggled through for the past hour. A thick canopy of trees overhead concealed them from sight. There were plenty of dead branches around for a fire, though it wasn't essential that they make one. It was noticeably less chilly here than at their other camp. All day long they'd climbed and descended along narrow mountain paths, but the net result was a slightly lower altitude. One of the guerrillas was in shirtsleeves, but that was a little crazy, a machismo thing.

The guards barked out orders in Spanish, and the prisoners were broken into three groups. Matthew and the Swede found a couple of large rocks to sit on beneath a tree.

Jan asked, "Interesting, the way they always keep you and me together."

"We're easier to guard this way."

"But look how they break up the lot of us."

"Seems logical. The Japanese couple is married,

the Spanish speakers are with the Spanish speakers, and you and I speak English."

"It has nothing to do with language, fisherman. Both the Colombian men speak English. You and I are the troublemakers. That's why we're together."

"Is that something you figured out by yourself?"

"Yes. And the sooner you figure it out, the better off you'll be."

Matthew sensed that Jan was going to raise the E word again—escape. "I told you, you're on your own."

"Yeah. That's what the Colombian said, too."

"You talked to Emilio?"

"Of course. Haven't you noticed the guards swarming all over me for the past three days? Emilio tipped them off."

"Emilio's no snitch."

"Like hell. Why do you think he got a new pair of boots for today's march? No one else got so much as a clean pair of socks."

"They gave him new boots because he needed them."

"I keep telling you, fisherman, it's every man for himself here. Can't you see that we have to do something?"

Matthew didn't answer. He glanced toward a group of guerrillas sharing a tin of sausages and some white beans. The prisoners hadn't eaten a thing since breakfast—half a cup of coffee and a handful of cold rice. Matthew had forgotten how it had felt *not* to be hungry.

"Open your eyes," Jan continued. "They've got too many prisoners. They can't even feed all of us, let alone guard us. Either we make a run for it, or it's like the Flea Man said: They'll whittle down the group one way or another. We'll both end up dead like Will."

"Nobody's going to end up like Will unless we do something stupid."

"You're wrong. In their eyes you and I are exactly like Will. If they can't make a quick buck off us, we're not worth the trouble. The docile ones like the Flea Man they'll keep forever. But guys like us, it's fish or cut bait. You can relate to that one, can't you, fisherman?"

"You're paranoid."

"It's the way these guerrillas think. They're bored, and we're their entertainment. They got rid of Will, and pretty soon they'll decide that somebody else is trouble and needs to go."

"So what are you saying? I'm next?"

"No. Clearly it's me. But once I'm gone, it's only a matter of time before they take care of you."

"They're not going to kill me and give up a ransom."

"Don't kid yourself. That Japanese couple is loaded, and the Japanese have a reputation for *always* paying. Joaquín doesn't need your ransom. One snag in the negotiations, he'll kill you for the fun of it."

Up ahead, the scouts emerged from the jungle and reported to Joaquín. Apparently they'd found what they were looking for. Two guards approached the Japanese couple. Joaquín and three others came for Matthew and Jan.

"What now?" said Jan.

"We're going for a walk," said Joaquín.

"Where?"

"You'll see."

They walked single file with the Japanese prisoners toward a densely forested part of the jungle. It was more overgrown and much darker than anything they'd covered all day. An animal growled from somewhere in the thicket, and the Japanese woman clung to her husband. He sniped at Joaquín in Japanese, and the tone if not the words conveyed his message. From behind, a guerrilla shoved him and brandished his weapon, threatening him into silence. The mysterious animal growled again. Hundreds of birds suddenly exploded from the tree branches high overhead. It was nearly deafening, the flutter of wings and all that screeching and cawing. They warned of danger. Unfazed, Joaquín and his two machete-wielding scouts led them deeper into the jungle, brushing back bamboo stalks and droopy green elephant ear plants. Five armed guerrillas followed closely behind the prisoners.

Matthew wasn't sure what was going on. It seemed odd that the three Colombian prisoners had been left behind.

"Stop," Joaquín said.

They'd reached a clearing at the edge of a cliff. A canyon stretched before them, a huge gorge with steep walls that descended at least seven hundred feet. A muddy river snaked tortuously below, its raging waters the only audible sound in the valley. With this view, Matthew gained a full appreciation of Colombia's nickname, "the Tibet of the Andes."

He focused on what at first glance looked like a huge bird swooping across the canyon, and then he realized it was a man—carrying a pig. A steel cable stretched from one side of the mountain to the other, which Matthew hadn't noticed right away, because it was covered in part by a low-hanging cloud. The man was seated in a rope sling, zipping across the canyon on a simple pulley-and-tackle system, easily topping thirty-five miles per hour. He was just fifty feet away from the cliff's edge and closing fast. The cable whined as he applied the brake, a crude wooden fork that the rider squeezed to create friction. The added weight of the pig had given him too much momentum, and he slammed into a wall of old tires that brought him to an abrupt stop. He picked himself up, and he and his pig scampered away without fuss. As if this were just an everyday trip from the market in a country with too few roads and bridges.

Matthew watched as one of the guerrillas strapped himself into the sling on a parallel cable that sloped in the opposite direction for return traffic. He pushed himself off the cliff, shouting like a bungee jumper as he sped away on the steel cable, hanging perilously above a river that churned two hundred meters below, and finally disappearing into the thick white cloud that filled the valley.

"What do you make of this?" Matthew whispered.

"I don't know," Jan said under his breath. "But I wouldn't count on it being good."

Matthew exchanged a wary glance with the Japanese prisoners, nervously waiting his turn.

33

Matthew could not believe his eyes.

After crossing the canyon, they'd walked for twenty minutes, mostly uphill along a narrow and at times overgrown jungle path. The last hundred-yard stretch had been downright frightening. The path was at its narrowest along the edge of a steep cliff. The rocks were slippery, the footing unsure. Any lapse in concentration could have meant a two-hundred-foot drop straight down into the ravine, instant death. But finally they'd reached their destination, a surprising reward.

"Will you look at that," said Matthew.

Before them was a large pond, a warm and wet hole in the jungle canopy where the sun streamed in. Clouds of steam wafted up from the calm, flat waters. Matthew could feel the heat in the soles of his shoes, and each step toward the water brought the audible crunch of ancient volcanic cinders beneath the overgrowth of fallen jungle foliage, grass, and mosses that had gathered over the centuries.

Joaquín had brought them to an extinct crater, a tiny geothermal paradise where nature warmed the waters to bath temperature. To a man who hadn't bathed in weeks, this was heaven on earth.

"You have ten minutes," said Joaquín. "Head above water at all times. If we lose sight of any one of you, we shoot everyone."

The guerrillas positioned themselves at evenly spaced intervals along the water's edge. The prisoners looked at each other with some humility. Without words, Matthew and Jan agreed not to lay eyes on the woman. Matthew removed his clothes eagerly and immersed himself up to his neck. On so many levels it was sensual overload, and for the first time in nearly a month he was actually smiling. The waters warmed him to his core, soothing the elbows, wrists, and other joints that ached from cold and wet mountain air. He would have loved to dunk his head under and swim to the bottom, but he didn't doubt for a minute that Joaquín would commence fire on him and the others the instant he disappeared from view. He swam the breaststroke, the first exercise he'd had since jumping off the boat in Cartagena—and the thought of Cartagena brought him back to reality. Here he was frolicking in the warm waters, almost grateful to Joaquín. Gratitude was the last thing he should have been feeling. He could never let himself forget that his Nicaraguan friends, Hector and his son Liván, were dead at the hands of this monster.

Floating on his back, Matthew glanced toward Joaquín on the shoreline. They didn't make eye contact. The guerrilla was fixated on the naked Japanese woman, having positioned himself perfectly for a peep show.

Ten minutes passed quickly. Joaquín called them back to shore. Matthew swam as close in as possible, then rose and ran to his clothes on the rocks. Jan was right behind him. The warm waters had turned his pasty pallor pink, and the air felt very cold. Ten meters to their left, the Japanese couple helped each other to shore. The woman covered herself quickly, still enduring the weight of Joaquín's stare.

"Leave the old clothes," shouted Joaquín.

They stopped dressing. One of the other guerrillas came forward and gave each of them clean trousers and a warm shirt. The Japanese bowed and thanked him profusely. Even Jan muttered a reluctant "*Gracias*." Matthew just took the clothes, in no mood to thank a murdering kidnapper for the necessities of life.

They dressed quickly, and Matthew was happy to leave his smelly garments behind. He hated to indulge himself in false hopes, but one thought consumed him: *Could this mean they're letting us go?*

Instantly, thoughts of Cathy flooded his mind. He wondered how his wife was handling the pregnancy, if she was showing yet, if she'd started decorating the baby's room. He wondered if she'd received any of the late-night messages he'd tried to convey through nothing more than mind power. He had no idea if telepathy worked, but it was all he had, and he concentrated very hard when he told her that he loved her every night. He thought of Nick and Lindsey, too, but that was risky. He'd made mistakes with his children, and the memories weren't always pleasant. A guerrilla camp in the mountains was no place for regrets, not for a man who knew that he might never even see his family again, let alone make things right.

Matthew was buttoning his new shirt, then froze. In all the excitement over new clothes, he hadn't noticed the dozen new guerrillas who'd descended upon them. Matthew didn't recognize any of them as being from Joaquín's group, though they were all just as young and dressed similarly in fatigues, bandannas, and a variety of hats. It was a goofy thought, but Matthew was suddenly reminded of the Friday's restaurant chain in the States, where all the waiters wore the same uniforms but showed their individuality through hat selection. These new guys could have been FARC, but the dragon insignia was conspicuously absent.

"I think they're ELN," said Jan.

Over dinner one night, Emilio had told Matthew about the National Liberation Army, or ELN, Colombia's other major Marxist guerrilla organization, second in strength to FARC and equally prolific at the kidnapping trade. Crossing the canyon by cable had evidently taken the prisoners into the ELN's territory.

"What do they want?" asked Matthew in a voice just loud enough for Jan to hear him.

"Us."

Matthew finished buttoning his shirt, watching the guerrillas closely. Joaquín was talking intensely with one of the ELN, a short guy with a thick black mustache. He and Joaquín were the only two guerrillas in the entire group who looked to be over the age of twenty. They spoke back and forth for several minutes, and then finally Joaquín brought him and two other ELN guerrillas down toward the prisoners.

The ELN guy strutted past Matthew, then Jan, then the Japanese. He stopped before each of them, glanced up and down, then moved to the next, as if he were General Patton inspecting his troops. When he'd finished, he and Joaquín walked to one side and continued their discussion.

"Joaquín's selling us," said Jan. "That's why he gave us all a bath and cleaned us up."

The thought of being spiffed up like a used car before trade-in infuriated Matthew. "He tried to sell me once before. To FARC."

"You better hope the ELN gives him his price. If he gets the idea that you're unsalable, that's not a good thing."

"I don't need that kind of trouble."

"We're already in trouble. I've said it all along: We're too many for Joaquín to handle. If ELN won't give him his price, he'll have to get rid of at least one of us."

"Maybe he'll turn one of the women loose."

"Dream on, fisherman. It's going to be either you or me. And he isn't going to sell us off too cheap, and he isn't turning anyone loose."

From a distance Matthew watched Joaquín more closely. The discussion with the ELN leader was well out of earshot, but they were standing in the open, and Joaquín was waving his arms with emotion. It was clear from the expression on his face that the negotiations weren't going his way.

Finally Joaquín shouted something in anger and stormed away.

"¡Vamos!" he told his men.

The guerrillas rounded up the prisoners. Without another word to the ELN, they headed back into the jungle, single file down the same path that had brought them there. No one talked, except Joaquín, who was cursing FARC and the ELN for their greediness. He was fuming, and as they continued down the overgrown path, it made everyone edgy, even the other guerrillas.

The path was becoming treacherous. The footing was unsure, and a misty rain made the rocks even more slippery than on the way up. The warm waters of the pond had actually made Matthew's legs rubbery, and after a full day of marching, fatigue was taking its toll. He forced himself to concentrate, especially on this narrow stretch of path along the cliff with the deep ravine below. For some reason going down was proving to be more difficult than climbing up. The grade seemed steeper on the descent, and if you focused on the river two hundred feet below, vertigo could easily overtake you. The group proceeded one at a time. Three guerrillas went first to show the prisoners the proper technique. They didn't walk straight down the path but took half steps sideways with their backs to the cliff and their chests toward the mountainside. Two hands were on the face of the mountain at all times.

Next it was Matthew's turn.

Despite the danger and his need to focus, he couldn't clear his mind of a terrible sinking sensation. He remembered what Emilio had told him after the FARC deal had fallen through. The worst place for a kidnap victim to be was with a rogue criminal like Joaquín. The survival rate was better with an established Marxist group that had the resources to hold prisoners for longer periods of time.

A scream pierced the jungle, the desperate cry of a dying man.

It was hard to tell where it had come from—Matthew could have sworn it was *below* him. Confused, he hurried ahead to the base of the narrow pass. He looked back and saw Jan, the Swede, and he was immediately concerned. The order of descent had been Matthew, the Japanese man, and *then* Jan.

Behind Jan was Nisho, the Japanese woman. She was hysterical. One of the guerrillas grabbed her and carried her down the rest of the way. Two other guerrillas were at the cliff's edge. Matthew hurried over and looked down into the ravine.

The Japanese man lay dead, facedown, his body smashed on the rocks near the river a hundred feet below. The wife was screaming inconsolably. Grief was what Matthew thought at first, but she was swinging wildly and cursing in Japanese, seemingly more angry than anguished. One guerrilla wasn't enough to control her. Two others finally came over to subdue her.

Joaquín was last on the scene, having doubled back from his lead position. "*¿Qué pasó?*" What happened?

Jan answered quickly, "*¡El americano le empujó!*"

Nisho was still screaming wildly, and Matthew wasn't sure if he'd heard Jan quite right. "I pushed him?" he said, incredulous.

Two guerrillas grabbed him. "No, no!" said Matthew.

"*Sí, sí,*" said Jan. "*¡Matthew le empujó!*"

Matthew locked eyes with the Swede. In a flash, that earlier nervous talk of Joaquín's having more prisoners than he could handle came back to Matthew, and he realized what Jan had done: Some prisoners needed to be eliminated, and Jan had made sure that he wouldn't be one of them.

The crying widow was fighting to break free of the guerrillas' grasp, trying to crawl on her hands and knees to the cliff's edge to see or perhaps join her fallen husband. The guerrillas restrained her to the point of exhaustion, but the wailing continued.

Joaquín had fire in his eyes as he walked up to Matthew and, without warning, delivered a monstrous sucker punch to the solar plexus. Matthew doubled over, sucking air, but the guerrillas held him up, forcing him to stand on his own two feet.

"He's lying," said Matthew, barely able to speak.

"*You're* lying," said Joaquín. He grabbed Matthew by the hair and yanked him straight up to the standing position. "And don't think you won't pay for this."

He unleashed another blow to the same spot. Matthew went down onto his knees, gasping for air. Another guerrilla kicked him from behind, an army boot directly into his left kidney, which sent him sprawling face first into the dirt.

Matthew coiled into the fetal position to fend off any further blows. He could hardly breathe, and the dizziness was making it almost impossible to see. Mustering all his remaining strength, he managed to turn his sights on the Swede, but his fellow captive just looked away. Jan had been saying it for days, though Matthew hadn't wanted to believe him. Now he knew it was true.

They were becoming their own Pitcairn Island. It was every man for himself.

34

The Miami-Dade County courthouse was practically ancient by Miami standards, an imposing stone tower and distinctive bump on the city's modern skyline. My first visit had been on a field trip in middle school, though it wasn't the massive fluted columns or tiered granite steps that had impressed me so much I'd decided to become a lawyer. It was the unbridled energy, the almost perpetual state of confusion.

On Tuesday morning it was abuzz with the usual chaos. From every direction swarms of people converged on the main entrance, squeezed through the metal detectors, and then raced across the lobby for a spot on a slow-moving elevator that would eventually land them before one of twenty-three judges on fifteen floors. It was a nonstop stream of lawyers and litigants, witnesses and jurors, court employees and members of the media. Thrown into the mix were the venerable retirees who had nothing better to do than pack a liverwurst sandwich into a paper sack and head over to Flagler Street to enjoy the real-life version of *The People's Court.* They were like unofficial court historians, capable of rattling off stories about the giants in Miami's trial bar the way baseball fans knew the legends of the sport. For them, trial was theater, at times the theater of the absurd, and the longest-running show around was right here in this old building. A few could even wax nostalgic about the old days when the courthouse also served as the stockade, well before my time. Criminal cases were no longer heard here. These days the docket was strictly civil.

"Civil." That wasn't exactly the word that came to mind as I braced for the sight of Duncan Fitz as opposing counsel.

The hearing was scheduled for 9:00 A.M. before Judge Korvan, roughly sixteen hours after I'd been served with the papers. I was well aware of the old adage that a lawyer who represents himself has a fool for a client, and I'd considered asking the judge to postpone the hearing. But searching for a lawyer and then bringing him up to speed on the facts would only have delayed matters. My father needed someone to get before a judge and plead the family's case as quickly as possible, and I knew the case better than anyone. At least for round one, I was on my own.

I was the last to arrive at Judge Korvan's chambers. Duncan Fitz and his New York partner, Maggie Johans, were seated on the battered plaid couch in the waiting room. They probably would have shaken my hand if I'd offered it, the hypocrites.

Maggie wasn't a trial lawyer, so I assumed she was here not in her capacity as Cool Cash partner but as an officer of Quality Insurance. She'd brought down a pair of sharp litigators from the New York office to assist Duncan, a man and a woman I'd never met. Unlike my peers in the Miami office, they'd have no personal reservations about filleting me like a flounder. No one had bothered with introductions, but I knew from their engraved leather trial bags that they were seasoned litigators. Trial bags were badges of honor at my firm, the more beat up and battle-scarred, the better. Litigators at Cool Cash took their image seriously. Unlike corporate lawyers, health-care lawyers, antitrust lawyers, and so on, lawyers who specialized in litigation were never called litigation lawyers. They were "litigators," a term that connoted more fighting than lawyering and that, quite appropriately, even sounded a little like "gladiator." When business dealings went sour, nobody ever threatened to call in the real estate department. If lawyers were sharks—a joke I heard far too often, being the son of a fisherman—then litigators were the great whites.

"The judge will see you now," announced her secretary.

The hearing would be held in chambers, rather than the main courtroom, which wasn't unusual when a judge intended to hear only argument from counsel with no live testimony from witnesses. There was no stone-faced bailiff, no high mahogany bench from which the judge presided. The intimacy of a proceeding in chambers, however, did not mean informality. The judge wore the same black robe and the lawyers were just as respectful as in open court. Her carved antique desk was at the far end of the chambers, positioned so that the judge's back was to the window. A table extended from the front of her desk to create a T-shaped seating arrangement. The lawyers sat on opposite sides of the table, the plaintiff to the judge's left, the defendant to the right. The court reporter was off to the side, near the floor-to-ceiling bookshelves.

"Good morning," Judge Korvan said in an amicable tone. She reminded me a little of my grandmother before the Alzheimer's, except that the smile seemed less genuine. Judge Theresa Korvan was a twenty-year veteran on the bench, who'd seen it all and had a reputation for smiling pleasantly no matter what she was doing, whether bidding you good morning or citing you for contempt.

The lawyers introduced themselves, four for Quality Insurance, two partners and two senior associates. And then me. Judge Korvan seemed amused by the lopsidedness.

"You must be quite a lawyer, young man."

Duncan said, "Excuse the crowd, Judge, but our client takes this case very seriously."

"So does mine," I said dryly.

Duncan met my stare, then looked away.

"Splendid," said the judge, still wearing her patented smile. "Now that we're all so serious, let's get started."

Duncan said, "This is basically an action by an insurance company to enforce the confidentiality provisions of a kidnap-and-ransom insurance policy. Matthew Rey is the insured, and his family claims he was kidnapped. Quality Insurance Company has denied coverage."

"I gathered that from your papers. Explain what you're asking the court to do."

"Essentially we're asking for a moratorium on any lawsuit that could have the effect of putting the kidnappers on notice that a dispute has arisen between Matthew Rey and his insurance company."

"Let me get this straight. You want to deny coverage, and you want me to enter an order that prevents Mr. Rey and his family from suing you?"

"Only until Mr. Rey is released from his kidnappers. In addition, we ask that the court seal the record in this proceeding, so that this action filed by Quality Insurance does not become public knowledge."

Judge Korvan made a face, confused. "Why is this such a big secret?"

"It's customary for a kidnap-and-ransom insurance policy to prohibit the insured from disclosing that he has insurance. The object is to keep the insured from becoming a target and to prevent kidnappers from making exorbitant ransom demands."

"I understand that. But once Quality Insurance has denied coverage, why should you care about secrecy?"

"In an ordinary fraud case we wouldn't. But this is no ordinary case."

"Enlighten me," she said.

"Me, too," I added.

"First of all, Quality Insurance company does not deny that Matthew Rey was kidnapped by rebels."

"A wise concession," I said, "given three dead bodies in Cartagena."

"Mr. Rey, please. You'll have your turn."

"Sorry, Your Honor."

Duncan continued, "If he had staged his own kidnapping, we could deny the claim and have nothing to worry about. But we believe that he is truly in the hands of some dangerous people. The basis for our denial of the claim is that the insured revealed to a third party that he had kidnap-and-ransom insurance. That alone voids the policy."

"You're not alleging fraud?"

"We believe there is fraud, but Quality Insurance doesn't have to prove that much to invalidate the policy. All we have to show is that he told someone he had insurance."

"So it's your contention that Mr. Rey told someone he had insurance, and then what?"

"Clearly the kidnappers are in cahoots with someone who knew that Mr. Rey was insured for a ransom payment up to three million dollars. That someone is getting a cut of the three million dollars. A referral fee, if you will."

"If the kidnappers already know about the insurance, then why do you need secrecy?"

"At this point it's not the existence of the insurance policy that needs to be kept secret. It's the denial of the claim. If the kidnappers find out that Quality Insurance Company is refusing to pay, Mr. Rey will be in serious danger."

"Then pay the claim," I said.

"Mr. Rey, enough," said the judge.

"I'm sorry, Judge. But it's impossible for me to sit quietly and listen to Mr. Fitz suggest that it's in my father's best interest for the court to enter an order that prohibits him from suing the insurance company that denied his claim."

"You'll have your turn," she said sharply.

I backed off. Duncan continued, his tone indignant. "Quality Insurance Company has no obligation to pay this claim. That doesn't mean we want to see Mr. Rey's father murdered when the kidnappers find out that the insurance company is refusing to pay."

"I see," she said, as if finally catching on. "If a jury were ever to decide that your denial of the claim was wrongful, the last thing you want is his death hanging over your corporate head."

"It wouldn't be on our head, Your Honor. We had a meeting with Nick Rey in our office last week, and he made certain comments that led us to believe he was foolish enough to jeopardize his father's safety by filing a lawsuit that would make our dispute public. If the court allows him to do that, it's on his head. And with all due respect, Your Honor, it's on yours as well."

I glared but held my tongue. Duncan had managed to push the judge into my corner, so I didn't have to speak.

"I don't really care whom you wish to blame, Mr. Fitz. I still don't see how your proposed moratorium works. You want me to prohibit Matthew Rey from suing until after his release from the kidnappers, correct?"

"Yes. Then, once he's released, he can sue to his heart's content, and a jury can decide whether the insurance company's denial of coverage was justified."

"Here's the problem: How would the family ever pay the ransom to gain his release?"

"We can't," I said.

"They can," said Duncan.

One of the associates from New York handed him a file. Duncan said, "I didn't want to have to raise this issue in the context of this hearing, but the truth is, we've been in contact with the FBI."

It was as if he'd punched me in the chest. Finally I was gaining some insight as to why the FBI had been breathing down my neck.

Duncan continued, "We have in our possession a detailed analysis—or perhaps 'unwinding' is a better term—of bank accounts that the FBI has traced back to Rey's Seafood, Inc., a Nicaragua-based fishing company. Collectively, the cash on hand is close to ten million dollars."

My jaw nearly dropped. The judge looked suspiciously at me, but she said nothing.

Duncan said, "Matthew Rey is a substantial shareholder of the company. I can list any number of banks that would loan three million dollars to anyone who can pledge cash assets of ten million as security."

"Nicaraguan fishing company, huh?" she said, smirking at me. "What do you say to *that*, Counselor?"

"All I can say is that I've never seen this FBI financial investigation or analysis that Mr. Fitz is waving before the court."

"It's for real," said Duncan. "I have here an authenticating affidavit from a supervisory special agent in the narcotics unit of the FBI's Miami field office. His name is Sam Huitt."

Agent Huitt, of course. I was wishing now that I hadn't been so quick to rebuff Agent Nettles's offer of the FBI olive branch.

"Thank you, Mr. Fitz. I believe I understand your position." She turned and faced me. "Mr. Rey, what's your response?"

I was almost reluctant to say anything, for fear of what other missiles might come flying out of the trial bags of my opposing counsel. "Your Honor, what I would like most is the time to prepare an intelligent response. By offering this FBI affidavit, Mr. Fitz has turned his request for a moratorium into an evidentiary hearing. I've had no chance to call witnesses on my own behalf and no opportunity to cross-examine any adverse witness."

"How much time do you want?"

I thought quickly. My next communication with the kidnappers was less than three weeks away. I needed to have the insurance issue sorted out before then. "I'd like fifteen days."

"I'll give you ten."

"Your Honor, my father is kidnapped. I have other time commitments."

"All right, fifteen. But there will be no extensions. If you can't get it done yourself, find a good co-counsel."

Duncan said, "If I may make a suggestion. Rather than co-counsel, it would probably be advisable for Mr. Rey to retain substitute counsel, since it is very likely that he will himself be a witness at the up-coming evidentiary hearing."

"That's ridiculous, Judge. There is no legitimate need for Mr. Fitz to call me as a witness. These are simply more bully tactics. Last week the law firm suspended me without pay, and now they want me to pay for a lawyer."

"I have two responses to that," said Duncan. "One, it's true that Mr. Rey was suspended, and in the interest of fair disclosure I should note for the record that the decision has already been made to terminate his employment."

"Very classy way to tell me."

He ignored me. "Second, there very definitely is a good-faith basis to call him as a witness. I assume that Your Honor will require us to make some showing at the hearing that the decision of Quality Insurance Company to deny the coverage was justified."

"That's correct."

"Quality has two theories in that regard. The first is as I described earlier: Matthew Rey told the wrong person that he had insurance, which the court may or may not decide was sufficient grounds for Quality to deny coverage. Our fallback theory is that denial of coverage was justified on grounds of fraud, and Nick Rey is a material witness in that regard."

"I'm unclear. Is it your position that Matthew Rey defrauded you or that he simply has a big mouth?"

"In a way, both. He told someone he had insurance. That person then arranged for his kidnapping in an effort to defraud Quality Insurance Company out of a three-million-dollar ransom payment."

"How is it that you intend to link Matthew Rey to a fraud committed by someone else?"

"The person who committed the fraud is some- one very close to him."

"How close?"

I was fighting to stay quiet, but I couldn't. "Your Honor, I can see where this is headed, and I have to object to Mr. Fitz's continued efforts to prejudice this court against my father by making further base- less accusations against his business partner in Nica- ragua. Springing that surprise financial affidavit was despicable enough."

"I wasn't talking about any business partners," Duncan said smugly.

My heart skipped a beat. The judge asked, "Then just who is the unnamed mastermind behind this scheme?"

"It's a member of the Rey family."

I nearly leaped from my chair. "Now you've done it, you—"

"Mr. Rey, please!"

"I'm sorry. But this is just a continuation of the charade that started last week when they sus- pended me. Mr. Fitz and his committee of hench- men cooked up this ludicrous theory that I steered my father toward Quality Insurance Company. Now they have the audacity to suggest to this court that I actually arranged for my own father's kid- napping."

"No one is accusing Nick Rey of anything," said Duncan.

My mouth opened, but no words flowed. Duncan looked at me coolly and said, "The person who set up this kidnapping is his sister, Lindsey. Matthew Rey's own daughter."

I was utterly unable to speak, outraged that Duncan would make such a wild charge.

The judge broke the silence. "I've heard enough accusations for one day. We'll convene in fifteen days for an evidentiary hearing. Until then I will temporarily grant the request of Quality Insurance Company for a moratorium, as Mr. Fitz calls it. Neither party will make any court filings or public disclosures that might lead the kidnappers to believe that a dispute has arisen between the parties over the payment of the ransom."

"What about Mr. Rey's status as counsel?" asked Duncan.

"I can't tell in a vacuum whether he will or won't be called as a witness. Since it's a possibility, Mr. Rey, you had better have capable co-counsel who can step in and take your place in the event that you are called to the stand. Anything else?"

No one said a word.

"We're adjourned," she said.

The Cool Cash team left quickly, which was Duncan's style. After any hearing that had gone his way, he always made a run for the door before the judge could change her mind.

I gathered up my briefcase slowly, almost shell-shocked. So much had landed on me, way more than I'd expected. Bank accounts with ten million dollars in cash. Cool Cash working arm-in-arm with the FBI's narcotics division. The thought of being a witness at the upcoming hearing. All of those things were daunting enough, but they were nothing compared to the simple hurt and embarrassment of having a clever lawyer—my former supervisor—accuse my own family of fraud. In the heat of the moment I could easily have leaped across the table and grabbed him by the throat. Once he'd left, however, my anger dissolved into something much more disturbing. Deep down I was incapable of rejecting out of hand the possibility of Lindsey's involvement in our father's kidnapping.

Slowly I grabbed my briefcase and walked out of Judge Korvan's chambers, alone completely.

35

With so many problems, I wasn't sure which to tackle first. I sat down and made a list. Several lists, actually. I ranked them in order of importance, then chronologically, then from easiest to hardest to solve, from most amazing to least amazing. It was getting me nowhere. In a snap judgment I made it a top priority to fire myself and find a new lawyer. One who didn't make lists.

But first I needed to have an honest talk with my mother.

I entered the house through the back door and found her seated at the kitchen table. I checked my ominous expression at the door for fear that she'd think something horrible had happened to her husband. But I didn't hold back on the truth. We were in a legal battle with a nasty insurance company that was represented by one of the most powerful law firms on the planet. This was no time for any surprises from my own family. I told her everything. The meetings I'd had with the FBI narcotics agents. Dad's share of a fishing company with ten million dollars in hidden assets. And finally the suspicions about Lindsey.

Mom didn't answer for a time that seemed like forever. At last she said, "Your father doesn't have a dishonest bone in his body."

"What about Guillermo?"

"I only met him once. That brunch with your father in Palm Beach. Honestly, I don't really know Guillermo."

"I'm beginning to wonder how well Dad really knew him."

"Your father never even hinted that the company had that kind of cash on hand."

"It's possible he didn't know. The FBI's financial analysis is a pretty sophisticated unraveling of a rather elaborate corporate structure. None of the bank accounts were held directly in the name of Rey's Seafood Company. It was all a matter of tracing the accounts of wholly and partially owned subsidiaries back to the parent corporation. Rey's Seafood was the ultimate parent. Or so they claim."

"I can assure you, your father never saw a dime of that money."

"How can you be sure?"

I saw anger in her eyes. Without a word, she got up and left the room. Two minutes later she was back at the kitchen table with a file folder.

"This is how I'm sure," she said, sorting through the papers for me. "This is a second mortgage on our house that your father took out two years ago to pay off a shrimp boat that capsized in a storm off San Juan del Sur. No insurance. Unfortunately for us, he personally guaranteed the loan from the bank to pay for the boat. Two hundred and fifty thousand dollars." She moved to the next file. "Here's an unsecured line of credit that we've maxed out at ninety thousand dollars. Here's the cash advances we've taken on Visa, MasterCard, Discover—anyone who'd give us unsecured credit."

"I had no idea things were so tight for you."

"Your father's company hasn't turned a profit in eighteen months. At least, none that he's seen. Now, does that look like the financial portfolio of a man who holds the keys to secret bank accounts with millions of dollars?"

"No, but . . ."

"But what?"

"I'm trying to think like Duncan Fitz."

"And you're thinking what?"

"This does sound like a man who might defraud an insurance company."

"Your dad didn't defraud anyone." She rubbed her eyes, as if a headache were coming on. She got up and went to the sink for a glass of water. From the side, the pregnancy was definitely starting to show.

"I guess the baby on the way only added to the financial stress."

"What are you suggesting? You think your father bought a kidnap-and-ransom policy so that we could build a life for our new baby on the proceeds of insurance fraud?"

"Not at all. It's just that these credit cards are like a black hole. I wish he'd come to me. I could have helped out."

She looked at me as if I were crazy. "Do you think

in a million years that your father would come to his own son asking for money?"

"I suppose not."

"You *suppose*. Nick, he used to agonize for two days before getting up the nerve to call you on the phone and invite you over for dinner."

"That's not my fault."

"And that's the whole problem between you and your dad. Neither one of you is ever at fault."

"You know the truth, Mom. You know how he used to be."

"That's in the past. You have to forgive him for that."

"I have."

"But have you ever told him that?" Her tone made it sound more like an accusation than a question.

"I think so."

"Yes, and I'll tell you why you think so. Because you've had the conversation in your mind so many times that it feels real to you. But it never happened. You have to make it happen."

"I will. Or I'd like to anyway. But what do you expect me to do about it now?"

"Stop blaming your father for the way he used to drink, the way he used to be. A fifty-one-year-old man shouldn't be made to feel like he has to start a whole new family to find a child who loves him."

"What?" I said, incredulous.

She brought a hand to her mouth, as if wishing she hadn't said that.

"This is crazy," I said. "You know I love Dad. He knows it."

"I'm sorry. I didn't mean to say that."

"But you meant it."

Her eyes clouded as she laid a hand on her pregnant belly. "It's not that your father has given up on his children. He just wanted another chance."

"I'll give him as many chances as he needs."

"Maybe you will. And when he finally comes home, maybe you can look him in the eye and tell him so."

Her take on me and Dad was so simplistic, I knew she didn't understand. The issue wasn't whether I could forgive him for his drinking. I could have certainly done that. The man hadn't touched alcohol in fifteen years. That's why she had forgiven him. For her, Dad's drinking had been a chronic weakness, a dark chapter in their lives that they'd put behind them. For me, it all boiled down to a single moment on a single day—the one and only day he'd ever taken me lobster diving with him. The hurt that had lasted all these years stemmed not from his alcoholism but from the words that seemed to flow instinctively from his mouth in a moment of crisis on the boat that day, something no twelve-year-old boy should ever hear from his father.

I didn't even try to sort that out with my mother. But there was one thing we'd left unresolved.

"Mom, we haven't talked about Lindsey."

"Yes, I think we have." She gave me a long look, as if to say that everything that had gone wrong between my father and me applied double to his daughter.

"It's a very serious accusation they've thrown at her. But so far it's just an accusation."

"I haven't spoken to your sister since her birthday."

"Has Dad?"

"Yes."

"When was the last time?"

"I don't know. But I think they've actually even seen each other a few times down in Nicaragua."

"Was it an ugly thing, or were they on good terms?"

"Let me put it this way. Your father and Lindsey have never been that close. But they were never, *never* that far apart."

"Thanks, Mom. That's a help."

She nodded as if to say "You're welcome," then quietly left the room.

36

She didn't immediately say no. That I took as a real positive, since it was the biggest favor I'd asked of Jenna in the five years I'd known her, and the asking had come two months after our busted engagement.

Admittedly her name hadn't been at the top of my list, but Judge Korvan had ordered me to find co-counsel, and I was having trouble finding someone. The lawyers I knew best either worked for Cool Cash or were Cool Cash alums who earned a good chunk of their annual income on referrals from their old firm. No one was willing to cut off that gravy train just to take my case. I couldn't blame them, especially since I couldn't pay them. With no job, I had no income. If my father had a Nicaraguan company with millions of dollars in hidden assets, as the FBI suspected, his loved ones had seen no evidence of it. As it was, Mom and I would have to borrow money to pay the ransom. I needed an attorney who would take the case on a handshake and a promise to be paid somewhere down the line. And it had to be someone I could trust with a potentially dark family secret.

After eleven strikeouts and considerable agonizing, I put my ego aside and finally called Jenna. I'd talked to her twice since the kidnapping. Both times she'd told me to call if there was anything she could do to help. Both times I'd been unable to conceive of any possible circumstances under which she might actually lend a hand. Slowly, however, as one lawyer after another concocted an excuse, I talked myself into asking her to work by my side, not really sure what to expect. Certainly I hadn't banked on the good twenty seconds of silence that preceded her reply.

A good sign, I told myself, waiting. *An immediate answer would never be yes.*

Finally she spoke. "We should talk about this."

I nearly dropped the phone. "Sure. Whenever you like."

"I can meet you tonight for dinner."

With that, I actually did drop the phone but quickly got myself together. She selected the restaurant, one that the two of us had never been to together. A wise choice. No ghosts.

"Meet you there at seven," she said.

"Terrific."

She was about to hang up, but I caught her just before she did. "Jenna?"

"Yes?"

"Thank you."

"I haven't said yes yet."

"But you had every right to give me a flat-out no."

I imagined she was flashing the faint smile that I knew so well. "Maybe so," she said.

"I just want you to know that I'm grateful you'd even consider doing this for me."

She paused, then said, "Don't take this the wrong way, all right? But if I decide to do this, it will be for your dad."

I detected no animosity in her tone. Still, I wasn't sure how to take it. "That's as it should be," I said.

"Right. As it should be. I'll see you tonight, then?"

"Sure." I said good-bye and hung up the phone.

I'd always thought of Jenna as wiser than me. We'd met at the University of Florida when she was a third-year law student and I was still an undergraduate headed for law school in the fall. After six months of dating, we moved in together. She took a job as a prosecutor in Gainesville, bought a house not too far from the law school campus, and for the next three years served as my best friend and live-in tutor for contracts, torts, civil procedure, and, of course, the real-life version of domestic relations. I aced all but the last of those subjects, though she didn't present the failing grade until after we'd moved to Miami.

We didn't agree on everything, but that had kept things interesting, and only once had it made me nervous. I didn't realize it at the time, but it was the prelude to our breakup. We were bicycling through Coconut Grove and stopped at the water's edge in Kennedy Park. It was a sunny and warm Saturday in February, the kind of day that made you realize why you lived in South Florida. Picnic blankets dotted the green landscape, parents were out playing with their children all over the park, a clown was entertaining a flock of children at a birthday celebration. I couldn't help noticing that most of the moms and dads in that particular group looked even younger than I was. Just the thought of making a lifelong commitment so early in life had me both in awe of them and scared for them.

"What makes them so sure?" I asked, almost to myself.

The question had come out of the blue. Jenna and I had been sitting on the grass in silence, but she knew exactly what was going through my mind. She always did.

"It's a process," she said. "It doesn't start with kids, or even the thought of kids."

"Where does it start?"

"Physical attraction."

"What?"

"Every successful romantic relationship is built on physical attraction."

I gave her a strange look, but she was serious. "That's ridiculous. You think the most important thing is looks?"

"Physical attraction encompasses a lot more than looks."

"Like what?"

"Millions of things. You might think I'm smart. On one level that might make you want to be in my study group. On another it might make you want to romp naked with me in a big bowl of Jell-O. Physical attraction can flow from anything about me that makes you want to touch me."

"And that's the basis of every successful romantic relationship?"

"Yes."

"I don't buy it."

"Then you should move in with your sister and adopt children."

"Come on. You're saying that what makes all these people want to get married and take their kids to the park on the weekend is physical attraction?"

"No. I'm saying that it's what makes them want to rip each other's clothes off and jump in the sack. And if we don't want to do that, there aren't any kids to take to the park on weekends."

I wasn't sure I agreed, but I nodded and smiled. Back then it didn't take much for Jenna in spandex to make me nod and smile. "So are you physically attracted to me?" I asked.

"Are you asking if I want to get married and have your kids?"

"No," I said, smiling wider and shaking my head. "No-no-no-no-no-no."

She rose quickly from the grass and walked toward her bicycle. My stupid grin quickly faded, and I hurried after her.

"Jenna?"

She continued down the bike path, no answer.

"Jenna, wait."

She strapped on her helmet and got on her bicycle. I grabbed the handlebars to keep her from taking off. She looked me in the eye and said sharply, "A single no would have sufficed, jerk."

Our eyes locked for a moment longer, as if she were waiting for me to say something to redeem myself. Before I could speak, she broke free, leaned into the pedals, and took off.

"Damn it," I said beneath my breath. I was angry at myself for having played this game, for having said no so emphatically just to preserve the big surprise. Her thirtieth birthday was a week away. I'd planned to pop the question then. After this blowup, I didn't think she'd ever believe that I'd bought the ring two months earlier.

I watched in silence as she sped down the bike path, keeping her in my sights until she was almost too small to see.

Not once did she look back.

37

Late Wednesday afternoon a package arrived. It was about the size of a box of checkbooks and wrapped in brown shipping paper. Torn at every corner, it was held together by multiple straps of clear plastic tape picturing a colorful parrot atop a blue box that read *"Corréos de Colombia."* The metered postage was stamped ADPOSTAL SANTA FÉ DE BOGOTÁ D. C.

I assumed it was from the kidnappers.

Interestingly, it was sent to my house in Coconut Grove, not to my mother in Coral Gables. That made some sense. Alex had told them I was with her during the radio communication in Bogotá. Perhaps they'd decided to communicate with me directly, and my father could have given them my address. The thought of his telling them anything lifted my spirits. It meant he was still alive.

I was eager to open the package, but I proceeded with caution. I shook it lightly. Something moved inside. My mood suddenly shifted from curious to macabre. The warnings of Duncan Fitz at yesterday's court hearing came flooding back to me, the gloomy picture of what dangers my father might face if ever the kidnappers learned that the insurance company had denied coverage and refused to pay. Could someone have tipped them off to the dispute? I suddenly feared that the box might contain some gruesome warning from the kidnappers, something that my father would have given up only after a struggle, something so shocking that he would have begged them to send the package to his son and not his wife.

My hand began to shake. I'd heard of kidnappers sending ears or fingers to the family in the mail, and this box was the perfect size. I closed my eyes and forced myself to bring it to my nose and sniff for strange odors.

I detected nothing, but the contents could have been sealed in plastic. From the kitchen I phoned Alex and told her my concerns.

"Open it," she said.

"But what if it's—"

"I think I know what it is. Open it."

I put the phone down and switched Alex to the speaker. Slowly I peeled away the already torn paper. The box inside was sealed with more tape. I slit it with a kitchen knife, drew a deep breath, and flipped open the box.

"It's an international pager," I said.

"I knew it. Those bastards."

"What? This has to be a good sign. They wouldn't send me a pager unless they wanted to be able to contact me on a moment's notice. They must be getting ready to turn Dad loose."

"That's what they'd like you to think."

I was only half listening. "There's a note here," I said, already translating in my mind. "They want me to wear the pager at all times. It says they'll be in touch."

"It doesn't say when, does it?"

"No."

"Of course not."

"I would assume they'll call when they're ready to make the exchange."

"Stop it, Nick. You're doing exactly what they want you to do."

"How do you know?"

"Because I've seen it a dozen times. It's a psychological ploy. They give the family a beeper, and the reaction is always the same: Resolution is near. But the beeper never sounds. You'll wear it every day, check it every ten minutes, wonder if it's broken, take it to a repair shop, drive yourself crazy. Finally you'll get a message, but the number you're supposed to call will have a few digits missing, which is intentional on their part. You'll think your father is going to die because the stupid pager didn't work. It's all a game for them. It's how they wear you out, make you pay the big bucks."

I held the pager in the palm of my hand. I wanted to cling to the idea that my father might soon be released, but the dose of reality from Alex had turned most of my hope to anger. "What should I do with it?"

"Keep it, of course. Just don't drive yourself crazy with it."

I wanted to throw it against the wall but calmed myself and took a seat on the barstool at the kitchen counter. "I'm tired of the games on all fronts. The kidnappers, the lawyers, the FBI. It's wearing me out."

"I know. You could use a little help. By the way, how's your search for co-counsel coming?"

Alex and I had talked about the court hearing last night. She knew that the judge had ordered me to find another lawyer. "Fine, I think."

"I have the name of a pretty good plaintiff's lawyer for you. Lots of experience suing insurance companies, if you're still looking."

"Actually, I may have found someone."

"Who?"

"I'm thinking about Jenna."

Silence. I moved closer to the speakerphone. "Hello?"

"Yes, I heard you. Do you think that's really such a good idea?"

"I don't have many choices. Yes, she's my ex-fiancée, but Jenna is still someone I can trust. She's an excellent lawyer. She had tons of trial experience as a prosecutor, and she's done strictly civil litigation ever since she moved to Miami."

"I'm sure she's competent. I was talking more about your personal history. It can get very complicated, working with someone you used to be in love with."

"Then I suppose I have nothing to worry about. You said it yourself at that restaurant in Bogotá: I was never in love with her."

"That was before I saw the way you looked at her at Duffy's."

I chuckled nervously. "I don't know what you mean."

"Yes, you do."

She had a way of stepping on my tail, no wiggling away. "Alex, I'm just trying to do the right thing here."

"I think you're testing my theory."

"That is so not true."

"Then, if you think Jenna's the answer, by all means, go with her."

"I'm hoping to make a decision tonight."

"The sooner the better. Just remember one thing, will you?"

"What?"

"Do what's best for your father."

Her delivery was mellifluous, but it still felt as if I'd been hit between the eyes. "Of course," I said. "That's all this has ever been about."

"Let me know what you decide."

"I will," I said, but there was a click on the line before my response was out. She'd hung up without saying good-bye.

I met Jenna for dinner in Coral Gables at seven o'clock, as planned. She'd chosen an unpretentious Vietnamese restaurant near her office, called Miss Saigon Bistro. It was the kind of place where Mom cooked her own recipes while her grown kids waited tables, dressed in traditional Vietnamese silk wraps. The tasty smells of beef with lemongrass and steamed soybeans greeted us at the door, as did a singing waiter named Richard, who told us that it would be about an hour before he could seat us.

We ordered a couple of Bahamian beers and waited outside. Jenna had walked straight from her office on Alhambra Circle and was still wearing her lawyer uniform. I was sporting what might have been called the casual-chic, I'm-out-of-work-but-my-kidnapped-father-has-ten-million-bucks-stashed-somewhere-in-Nicaragua look. We made small talk for a few minutes, but Jenna seemed to sense that I was eager for her answer.

"I've decided to do it."

"Do you mean it?"

"I wouldn't kid about something like this."

"That's fantastic," I said, raising my beer in a toast. "Have you cleared it with your firm?"

"To a point."

"What does that mean?"

"We have a small office. It's just eight of us. If I spend a substantial amount of time on your case, they naturally would like to know if there's any hope of getting paid."

"There's no hope for a big hit, if that's what they're wondering. The policy limit is three million. Most plaintiff's attorneys would want a cut of the cash recovery, but in this case the entire amount has to go to the payment of the ransom. That's the main problem I had in talking to other lawyers."

"You talked to other lawyers?"

My foot was squarely in my mouth. "Yes. But only because I didn't think you'd say yes."

"That's okay. I didn't think I'd say yes either."

We exchanged a little smile, and then she turned serious. "My partners will be happy with whatever fee the court awards over and above the damages recovered. That's if we win, of course. They're more concerned about what happens if we lose."

"I'll pay your hourly rate, but you'll have to give me terms. Say, six months to pay it off?"

"Nick, I'm not going to charge you."

"That's crazy."

"That's my decision."

"I can't let you do that."

"It's not your decision. Like I said on the phone, I'm doing this for your dad. I owe him that much."

"You owe him?"

She lowered her eyes, the way she always did when touched by emotion. "When my father died last year, I was devastated."

"I remember."

"It was the worst thing I'd ever gone through. There were days when I wondered if I was ever going to be myself again. Now, of course, I realize I was just fortunate to have been that close to him."

"That's true."

"But I was also lucky to have someone like your father to talk to."

"My dad?"

"He was wonderful. That was such a dark time, and he filled a void for me. Just to have someone to turn to for fatherly advice was important to me. That's something I'm truly indebted to him for."

"I never knew that."

"That's the kind of person your father is. He works quietly."

I smiled wanly. "Thank you for telling me. I feel better."

"About what?"

"Honestly, it hurt me at first, the way you stressed that you weren't doing this for me but only for my dad. Now that you've explained, it's nice to hear that someone loves him."

"Everyone loves your dad."

"That's what I always thought. But there have been some strange goings-on since the kidnapping. Even his own mother has been saying horrible things about him."

"Doesn't she have Alzheimer's?"

"Yeah. But it still bothers me, the way she treats me. She thinks I'm my father. The last two times I visited her, she threw me out of the house. Screamed at me, called me a lousy son. She even made stuff up about a sister that my father never even had, as if to suggest that my dad had somehow mistreated her."

"I don't know about the mistreating part. But your father did have a sister."

I did a double take. "He did?"

"Yeah. He mentioned her in a conversation we had right before my father's funeral. My mother wanted an open casket, and I didn't want to see him that way. Your dad said he felt the same way when his sister died. Didn't want to see her dead. Of course, he was only six or something like that at the time."

"How did she die?"

"He didn't say. He didn't really want to talk about it, and I suppose I was too wrapped up in my own grief to probe."

"Why didn't you ever tell me this?"

"I guess I figured you knew."

"I *didn't* know," I said, with too much edge.

"I'm sorry. But that isn't my fault."

I took a step back, mindful that I'd been coming on too strong. "You're right. It's not your fault."

"Forget it. I know you're under a lot of pressure."

"Pressure isn't the half of it. It seems like I learn something new about my dad every day."

"You need to stay focused. Is any of it really all that important?"

I glanced toward the bar across the street, the lights playing tricks with swirls of cigar and cigarette smoke inside. "Honestly, I don't know what's important anymore."

"What does that mean?"

I looked her in the eye and said, "Do you think you could hold down the legal fort a few days if I went away?"

"Sure. What do you have in mind?"

"If we're going to bring my father home, the first thing I'd better do is maybe find out who he is."

"Where do you plan to do that?"

She seemed amused, but I was completely serious. "I'll start in Nicaragua."

Part Three

38

It looked dead. Perfectly still, milky green, no sign of life, Lake Managua stretched for miles below me. As the commercial jet turned to make its final descent, I noticed a lone fishing boat below, no lines cast. I doubted that anything edible could be pulled from these waters.

I'd done a little homework for my trip, enough to know that Nicaragua was the largest country in Central America and one of the poorest. Tourism was virtually nonexistent, though extreme hikers liked to explore its extensive rain forests in the north-central mountains and along the eastern coast. Ninety percent of the population lived in the Pacific lowlands to the west, mainly in the capital city of Managua, tens of thousands surviving in open-air, tin-roofed shacks like the ones around Sandino International Airport. The lake was the repository of all things to be expected from a city with too many people and too little infrastructure.

My flight was an hour late. We taxied down the runway, past the old machine-gun stands that had defended the airport during the bloody Contra-Sandinista war of another decade. Nicaragua was at peace now, but with my father kidnapped by so-called revolutionaries in Colombia, I had to wonder what those former Contras were doing these days with all the leftover guns and ammunition that my own country had so freely provided.

"*Bienvenido,*" said the customs agent. "Welcome." I passed without a search. No one seemed to care what I was bringing into the country. It was what people took out that raised eyebrows.

"Señor Rey?"

I turned to see a young man holding a cardboard sign with my name on it. "I'm your driver," he said in English.

My first instinct was to thank him and hand him my bag, but I remembered Alex's words of caution in Colombia. I couldn't take anything for granted. "Who sent you?"

"Señor Guillermo Cruz."

"What's your name?"

"Ignacio."

That was the name Guillermo had given to me in the previous night's telephone conversation. Satisfied, I followed Ignacio outside and loaded my bags into the new Mitsubishi Montero waiting at the curb. Ignacio drove us to downtown Managua.

Last night I'd told Guillermo very little about the purpose of my visit. I'd simply said that some business and personal matters needed to be hashed out. He graciously invited me to stay as long as I wanted.

"Hold on!" said Ignacio as he slammed the brakes.

A herd of goats crossed the busy street in front of us. A group of boys was playing baseball in the wide median, and the goats had been eating the grass in left field before being shooed away.

Ignacio put the SUV in gear, then stopped short again. This time it was an old guy riding some three-wheeled contraption. A huge basket in front held two squealing hogs—big ones, larger than my old golden retriever. They were throttling each other in a futile effort to break free, their twisted legs protruding through the basket's wire mesh. One was upside down, on its head. The shrill screeches made me want to jump out and slap the owner. Animal cruelty was something that really bothered me, but this wasn't Coral Gables.

"Dinner," said Ignacio.

This was my introduction to the nation's capital and its bustling city center, to the extent it had one. The real heart of Managua had been leveled by a 1972 earthquake that had left six thousand dead, and the temporary shelters that had sprung up were still here. Shacks along the road sold everything from used tires to mattresses. Newer stores abutted vacant lots, crumbling old buildings, and other signs of a thirty-year-old disaster that had yet to be cleaned up. Shoeless kids with dirty faces and tattered clothes were at every intersection, hawking radios, cashews, cigarettes, steering wheels, live parrots in home-made cages, and anything else they could get their hands on. Skinny horses pulled rickety wooden carts laden with vegetables. The taxis were mostly dilapidated old Russian cars, probably from Cuba. If Times

Square had its neon signs, Managua had its floppy, hand-painted banners, one after another stretched across the busy streets advertising events and products. Up ahead was the Palace of Justice, its walls bearing the work of Nicaragua's extremely busy graffiti artists. The most popular image was that of Augusto Sandino, the assassinated revolutionary hero who, from beneath his broad-brimmed sombrero, seemed to survey the country from every available wall and lamppost. A few blocks past the palace, overlooking an urban field of rocks, weeds, and cardboard homes, was the famous black, three-story statue of the *campesino* with a machine gun over his shoulder.

"Have you met Señor Cruz before?" asked Ignacio.

"Only on the telephone. I honestly don't know much about him, other than that he's my father's partner."

"I see."

"Is he a good man?"

"You mean Señor Cruz?"

"Yes."

He steered through the intersection, smiling at my question. "He's my boss," he said simply. I waited for more, but he left it at that.

We reached headquarters around three o'clock.

Just the word "headquarters" had me thinking that I was headed for an office building. Rey's Seafood Company, however, was based in an old ranch-style house that had been converted to commercial use. Security bars covered the windows. Big red flowers brightened the tiny front lawn. Inside, I was greeted by a team of extremely friendly people, none of whom seemed to have any qualms about working a full day on a Saturday as a matter of course.

"So *you're* the son of Señor Rey," I heard about a dozen times. Invariably some expression of concern for my father followed.

"We have been praying to the Blessed Virgin every day," said the receptionist. She was young and quite pretty. All the women here were young and pretty. I wondered if my father was in charge of hiring. For Mom's sake, I assumed it was Guillermo.

"Is Guillermo here?" I asked.

"In back," said Ignacio. "I'll take you."

We walked through another part of the old house that appeared to have been a garage at one time. A stack of cans filled with marine paint lined the hallway. The branded hide of a brown-and-white cow was draped on the other. We continued through one added-on room after another, somewhere well beyond the footprint of the original house. These were purely administrative offices, not the processing plant. The lab was in one room, where they tested small samples of products that were ready for export. Freezers were in the next room, chain-locked, of course, to keep the frozen shrimp from walking out the door. In the back was the employee kitchen, which smelled of beans and seafood. Finally we reached the end of the hallway. A crucifix was on the door.

"Señor Cruz is in the chapel."

"The chapel?"

"Of course," Ignacio said, as if every office had

one. "He prays every day. The last few days, twice a day."

"For my dad?"

"He wants it to stop raining on our shrimp farms near Honduras." He seemed to catch himself, then added, "I'm sure he prays for your father, too."

We were talking loud enough to be heard in the next room, and sure enough the door opened. Out walked Guillermo.

"Nick, good to see you."

He gave me a hug, which seemed a bit too affectionate coming from a man I'd never met in person. He must have sensed my stiffness.

"I feel like I know you, I've heard so much about you from your old man."

"A few good things, I hope."

"Only good things. He's very proud of you."

"That's nice to hear."

"Come back to my office, where we can talk."

Ignacio left us, and I followed Guillermo down yet another hallway. He was making small talk about Nicaragua, all the things I needed to see while I was here. The volcanoes, the big cathedral in Granada.

Guillermo was younger than I'd expected, or at least younger-looking. He was almost as tall as I was, a good six feet, which definitely wasn't the norm among Nicaraguan men. His smile was as smooth as his walk, and those big, dark eyes would have served him well if he were a Latin singer of love songs. Now that we'd met, I was certain that he, and not my father, had hired all the pretty young girls out front.

"Good flight over?" he said as we entered his office.

"Fine." I took the chair facing his desk. He went around to the other side. I opened my carry-on bag and dumped the box of pastries on his desk. "Here's the goodies you asked for."

"Ah, thank you so much. You know, it's not that you can't find guava and cream cheese in Managua. But you just can't beat the Cuban bakeries in Miami." He unwrapped one and gulped it down. "So how can I help you?" he said with a mouthful of goo.

I paused, not sure where to begin. It didn't seem wise to jump into the FBI allegations about my father's business partner less than five minutes after meeting him. "My mother and I are getting concerned about Lindsey."

"In what way?"

"Granted, it's not unusual for us to hear nothing from her for weeks, sometimes months. That's the way she's decided to live her life. But with Dad kidnapped, we're starting to worry."

"When did you last hear from her?"

"About two weeks before the kidnapping."

He nodded, then reached for another pastry. "Not sure I can help you there."

For the first time since the introductory hug, he'd finally stopped smiling. I said, "Last time she called, she was somewhere in Nicaragua. So I was thinking maybe . . ."

"That I was hiding something?"

"I didn't say that."

"You didn't have to."

He seemed too defensive. "Don't get me wrong. I'm not here to accuse anyone of anything, least of all you."

"I'm glad you feel that way. But why don't we just clear the air right away? It's over between me and Lindsey."

The words hit me like ice water. "What do you mean, 'over'?"

"Done. Finished. I know your father didn't approve. Your mother probably didn't even know."

"Are you saying that you and Lindsey . . ."

He arched an eyebrow. "You mean you didn't know either?"

"I didn't know anything."

"I thought you came here to talk about Lindsey."

"I did, but— What were you doing going out with my sister?"

He leaned back in his chair, seeming to look past me as he spoke. "It started a few months ago, maybe longer. We saw each other once every couple of weeks, then once a week. Pretty soon she was dropping by here pretty regularly, and people started to talk."

"What did my father say?"

"In a nutshell: Keep your hands off my daughter. He had a million reasons. I'm too old for her, it's bad for the business, he doesn't want his daughter hanging around the office . . ."

"You're married," I said, using my Earth-to-Guillermo tone of voice.

"Well, that, too."

"So you broke it off?"

"Not exactly. She did. She said your father wouldn't allow it."

"Not to deflate your ego, Romeo, but if my father wouldn't allow it, that would be all the more reason for Lindsey to keep right on seeing you."

His wounded expression slowly gave way to a wry smile. "I know that. Hey, maybe I *was* too old for her."

"Or too married."

"Jeez, you're really fixated on that."

"Must be a faulty synapse or something. Marriage. Fidelity. Not sure why those concepts are linked in my brain."

"Okay, I get your point. You're the big brother, and I understand how this is touchy for you. But the bottom line is, I haven't seen your sister in at least a month."

His phone rang. He excused himself, picked it up, and grunted a few clipped "Uh-huh"s to whoever was on the other end of the line. He hung up and said, "Sorry to break this off, Nick, but I have to meet a customer. How about dinner tonight?"

"Sure."

He walked me to the door. "I'm sorry about this Lindsey situation. Didn't mean to drop a bomb on you."

"Hey, Lindsey's always been a box of surprises."

"Surprises aren't good. I always say it's best to get things out in the open. So tonight I'll treat you to some Flor de Caña, best rum in Central America. I'll tell you whatever you want to know."

"Deal."

"Call me around seven," he said, then closed the office door.

My smile faded as I headed down the hall, past the chapel, wondering if there was enough rum in all of Nicaragua to get Guillermo talking about the ten million dollars the FBI seemed to think he was worth.

39

M atthew had expected some form of punishment. But not this.

After the death of Nisho's husband, it had been straight to solitary confinement for Matthew. Not in a thatched hut or wooden shack, like the one in the FARC camp where he'd met Emilio. This was five days in a hole in the ground. It was deep enough for him to sit upright but not stand. He could lie on his side in the fetal position, but there was no room to stretch out to his full length. The roof overhead was at ground level, made of chopped branches, wide jungle leaves, and thick mosses. It kept out the daylight but not the steady mountain rainfall. In a matter of hours the sides and bottom of his pit were nothing but slimy mud. Last night it had rained hard, and today the chilly water was up to his ankles, as the ground was too saturated for it to drain away.

Matthew still couldn't erase the sight of that man sprawled on the rocks beside the river. Joaquín had left him there, of course, no proper burial. All the way back from the tragic sight, Matthew had protested his innocence. Nisho, the new widow, hadn't seen anything, so she couldn't say whether Matthew or Jan was lying. Joaquín didn't have time to sort out the truth. Immediately upon their return to camp, Joaquín ordered his men to start digging. Matthew was thrown in one hole, and Jan went in another one twenty yards away. Better to punish the innocent than to risk letting a guilty man go free. Justice according to Joaquín.

Matthew tried to think of Cathy, his family—anything to take his mind away from this place. He recounted fishing trips he'd taken, bonefish in the Bahamas, peacock bass in Venezuela. That only brought to mind the ancient fisherman's motto—"Allah does not subtract from the allotted time of man the hours spent fishing." He wondered about the hours spent kidnapped, knee-deep in mud in a dark hole in the earth.

He suddenly cringed. There it was again, that sharp pain in his belly. It had first come upon him two days ago after lunch, a violent episode. Ironically, he'd thought the guards had acted out of kindness in allowing him to eat in daylight with the roof pulled back. Turned out they merely wanted to watch the show. Within ten minutes of finishing his cornmeal, he was doubled over in pain. The vomiting and diarrhea were utterly uncontrollable. He couldn't even climb out of his hole, and the guards wouldn't lift him out. They only laughed, and he knew that they'd slipped him something to make him so sick.

It was back again, the same stabbing sensation in his lower abdomen.

"Son of a bitch!" he shouted as the pain ripped through his body. He fell on his side in the darkness, mired in filthy water. His body twisted and erupted in the same violent motions, but after two days of this, there was nothing left to expel. His stomach had kept nothing down for at least thirty-six hours. The guards refused to give him more than a few sips of water, insisting that it would only make the diarrhea worse. That wasn't additional punishment. These morons just couldn't comprehend the concept of dehydration.

His body shivered. The water in the bottom of the hole was very cold, but he was too sick to sit up. A thought crossed his mind, a sure way out. If he could just force himself to roll over, he'd be facedown in the thick mud. The water was more than deep enough to drown in. The question was, Could he hold himself down? The survival instinct was strong, but perhaps his body was too weak for his mind to engage it.

With both fists clenched, he pounded the mud in anger. He was furious with the guards, naturally, and with himself for even having considered the coward's way out. Mostly he was angry in ways that even he didn't fully understand. The nausea, the weakness, the darkness in the hole—it was all ganging up on him, pushing him to the brink of hallucination.

His shivering stopped. The pain remained in his belly, but it was on some other level, a more conscious level, a level at which he was no longer operating. In the darkness he could suddenly see himself as a boy in the Florida Keys, back in the old Red Cross house in which he'd grown up . . .

"Leave her alone!"

He was five years old and shouting at his father. His terrified sister was standing right behind him, two years older than Matthew but dressed in a diaper. She'd wet the bed the night before, and their father's solution was to send her off to the school bus dressed in nothing but a diaper, so that all the other kids could see what a baby she was. That would break the habit.

"Stay out of this, boy!" His father was drunk, as usual. Six o'clock in the morning, and he'd been out all night.

"Run, Stacy!"

His father pulled off his belt, slapped the leather strap on the couch. "Don't move, you little bastards!"

Matthew charged straight at him, a fifty-pound bull of a boy plowing into a two-hundred-pound drunk. He knocked his old man flat, shattering a lamp in the tumble.

"Run!" shouted Matthew.

His father was cursing and swinging wildly, trying to get off his back.

"Run, Stacy! Run!" Matthew turned to escape, but just as he did, a huge hand grasped his ankle. "Let me go! Let me go!"

"¡Silencio!"

Matthew was suddenly shaken from his memories. The voice in Spanish had come from somewhere above his dark, covered hole, a place beyond the misery of his childhood. He'd been unaware of his own shouting, though it had obviously been loud enough for the guards to hear.

The leaves rattled overhead. Someone was opening the roof. Matthew prepared himself for the sudden burst of light, but even on a cloudy day the brightness was too much for eyes that lived in darkness. He couldn't look up.

"Lunch," the man said.

The familiar voice surprised him. It wasn't a guard, he knew, since none but Joaquín spoke English. Slowly he looked up toward the hole in the roof, and his eyes began to focus. "Emilio?" he said.

"Yeah," he said, then made a face. "Man, it stinks in here."

Matthew was still woozy. "What—what are you doing here?"

"Bringing you lunch."

"Are you crazy? They'll shoot you."

"No. I'm a trusty now."

"Huh?"

He handed down a tin plate with two cold sausages. Just the sight of processed meat had Matthew on the verge of relapse.

"Joaquín trusts me now, so he gives me little tasks."

His head was pounding, his belly racked with cramps. It was all so confusing. "Why?"

"He just does."

Matthew slowly rose to his knees, looked Emilio in the eye as best he could from his hole. His thoughts were jumbled from fever, but he struggled to string the truth together. "You ratted on Jan, didn't you?"

"What?"

"Jan and I talked, just before Nisho's husband was killed. He accused you of telling Joaquín that he was planning an escape. I told him he was crazy. But it wasn't paranoia, was it? You told."

Emilio checked over his shoulder, as if to see whether any of the guards were close enough to overhear. "Of course I told," he said softly.

"I can't believe you did that."

"I had to. That Swede is trouble. That first day we left the FARC camp, Joaquín warned us what would happen if you tried to escape. If you failed, Joaquín would kill me, the daddy. If you succeeded, he'd kill Rosa, the mommy."

"He made those rules to keep *me* from escaping."

"Not just you. He had the same rules for Jan. And then the idiot came to me, asking me to escape with him. He expected me to leave Rosa behind for Joaquín to execute. Wouldn't you have snitched?"

Matthew tried to focus, but in his weakened, sick condition, things were starting to spin. Murders, false accusers, snitches. This *was* Pitcairn Island.

"If Joaquín trusts you," said Matthew, "then get me out of here. You know I didn't kill Nisho's husband."

"Just because Joaquín lets me bring you lunch doesn't mean I can sit down and negotiate with him."

"Try," he said, his voice breaking. "Somebody has to get me out of this hole. I'm going crazy in here."

"Hang in there, okay? I don't think you'll be in much longer. He let Jan out yesterday."

"Him?" Matthew said, nearly losing it. "Why *him*? Why am I getting the worse punishment?"

"Maybe Joaquín thinks your spirit is stronger. He wants to break it."

A wave of nausea hit him, chipping away at his will to endure. "If he's going to kill me, tell him to just do it. Please, I don't want to go through this hell and end up dead anyway."

"You can't give up, Matthew. I don't think he'll kill you, even if he thinks you killed Nisho's husband."

"How do you know?"

"The guards tell me that the Japanese guy wasn't such a big loss, at least from Joaquín's point of view. He thinks Nisho's family will pay as much for her release as they would have paid for both of them. It's not like buying two cars with a price tag for each of them. These kidnappers just come up with a big number that they think the family can pay. Joaquín's not going to lower his price just because it's only Nisho's life on the line and not Nisho and her husband."

"So I guess he's glad her husband is gone."

"I wouldn't say 'glad.'"

"I would. Have you seen the way he looks at Nisho? He's more than happy to have her husband out of the way."

"I haven't really noticed."

"Then take notice. I don't care if you are a trusty, Emilio. I know you're a decent man. If somebody doesn't stand up to these guards, they're going to have their way with Nisho, then Rosa, then Nisho again, and again, and again. I can't do anything from in here, so it's up to you. Don't let it happen, you hear me?"

Their eyes locked. Matthew was stone-faced, unflinching.

"I'll see what I can do."

Emilio pulled away. Matthew just watched as the leaves and fronds returned to their place on the roof overhead, and his hole returned to darkness.

40

Guillermo canceled on me. I didn't get a specific reason, just a message at my hotel that he couldn't take me out for the Flor de Caña rum and additional rounds of truth-telling that he'd promised. Somehow I wasn't surprised.

I ate dinner in my room, alone, then called my mother to let her know that I hadn't been eaten by cannibals, thrown into a raging volcano as a human sacrifice, or otherwise victimized in any of the horrible ways that she'd imagined were commonplace in Central America.

I didn't tell her about Guillermo and Lindsey.

By nine o'clock I was bored out of my mind. I went to the balcony and checked out the street life three stories below. Pretty dead, except for the usual sights. Teams of kids in the intersection were still selling junk and begging for *córdobas*. I was pretty sure they were the same kids I'd seen almost eight hours ago. The boy with one leg I definitely remembered. Ditto for the girl with the baby face who already had two babies of her own, one in each arm.

Farther up the street the strip club with the big red lips painted on the door seemed to be hopping. Groups of men would walk in drunk, get all steamed up, and then come out, one at a time, to cut a ten-dollar deal with one or more of the thirteen-year-old girls who walked the street in their fishnet stockings and five-inch heels.

What in the hell were my father and sister doing here?

I went back inside. I was feeling lonely, a little depressed, and definitely confused. I picked up the telephone and started to dial Alex's number. I hung up on impulse and called Jenna instead.

"Hey, it's Nick. You got a minute?"

"Um—okay."

I suddenly realized it was Saturday night, almost 11:00 P.M. in Miami, and that she might be with someone. "I can call back."

"No, it's okay. It's my fault for answering. Now you know I'm one of those lonely girls who sit at home Saturday nights watching reruns on Lifetime."

Shame on me, but that made me feel good.

I talked a little about the legal case against the insurance company, but only as a pretext for having called her. She steered the conversation toward what she'd done all day, I brought it back to the amazing things I'd seen since landing in Managua, and the rest just flowed. It was easy, reminiscent of countless nights after midnight that we'd gone back to her place with a pint of ice cream and just talked, not really noticing how the time was passing until one of us would look at the clock and say, "My God, it's four A.M."

"You think you'll find Lindsey?" she asked.

It was a hard question to answer without giving her the background. I hadn't told my mother, but another perspective would have been helpful. Jenna's point of view was one I'd always respected, so I told her.

"Wow," she said. "Didn't expect that out of your little sister."

"Tell me about it. We didn't expect Duncan Fitz to accuse her of masterminding my father's kidnapping either."

"I don't want to give Duncan's theory too much credence. But still, have you given any thought as to which way the affair with Guillermo cuts?"

"How do you mean?" I asked.

"Let me step into Duncan Fitz's shoes for a second," she said. "You start with the idea that your father wasn't very happy about his twenty-four-year-old daughter having an affair with a married man twice her age. He forbids her to see Guillermo. It's at least plausible that Lindsey arranged her father's kidnapping as retaliation for his trying to control her life."

"Pretty diabolical, don't you think?"

"Or it could be collusion," said Jenna. "Lindsey and Guillermo may have teamed up and gotten rid of your father because he disapproved of their winter-spring romance."

"Now you're thinking more like Duncan Fitz than Duncan Fitz does."

"Are you saying that you're not even considering those possibilities?"

"Are you saying I should?"

She didn't answer. I tried to read her silence, but my thoughts were interrupted by a knock on the door. I checked the clock. After midnight. Even without two spoons and a pint of Oreos 'n' Cream, we'd lost track of time.

"Someone's at the door. I better go."

"Ditto. It's two o'clock here."

I hesitated, afraid to push the personal issues too far. "Jenna?" I said, as if testing the waters.

"Yeah?"

"All this Lindsey stuff aside, it was good talking to you. I mean, really talking. I miss that."

I sensed a smile on the other end of the line. "Anytime."

I smiled to myself.

"But, Nick?"

I winced. I hated those "But, Nick"s. "What?"

"Don't ignore what I said about Lindsey. And be very careful down there."

Her voice had a tone that I knew well. She really meant it.

"I will," I said. "Good night."

Her "good night" was followed almost immediately by another knock on my hotel door. I hung up the phone and walked to the peephole. The light in the hallway was burned out, however, and I saw only a silhouette in the darkness.

"Who is it?"

"María."

"María who?"

"Portilla. From Rey's Seafood. We met this afternoon, remember?"

I looked again through the peephole, and now the shape was familiar. It was the pretty young receptionist who'd said she'd been praying to the Blessed Virgin for my father. "Just a second."

I was wearing only jogging shorts, since my "air-conditioned" room came with a noisy old window unit that was, frankly, more full of hot air than Guillermo was. I pulled on a T-shirt, then unchained the lock and opened the door. María stepped in without waiting for an invitation. She seemed a little nervous as I closed the door.

"I'm sorry to come by this late."

From the expression on her face, I could tell this was important. "That's okay. I was awake anyway."

"I just came from dinner with some of the girls from the office. I didn't know, but one of them said that she thought you were here looking for your sister."

"I didn't really want to announce that. But, yes, that's one of the reasons I came here."

She seated herself on the edge of the bed. I pulled up the desk chair and straddled it, my arms atop the backrest.

"I might be able to help you," she said.

"How?"

"I was one of the few friends Lindsey made here. I was the only one she told about her and Guillermo."

"So it's true they were lovers?"

She made a face. I wasn't sure if she was struggling for the right words in English or just struggling with the brutal truth. "Guillermo was in love. Lindsey was—I think the term is, 'using him.'"

"Using him for what?"

"Information."

"About what?"

She started to answer, then stopped. "I care very much about Lindsey. But my job is very important to me, to my whole family."

"I can understand that. I'm not going to repeat anything, if that's your concern."

"The best thing is for me to show you. That way, if anyone ever asks who told you, you don't have to say it was me."

I assumed that by "anyone" she meant Guillermo. "Okay, show me."

She rose and said, "In the morning. Pack your bags tonight. I'll pick you up at six in front of the hotel."

I stood silent, which she seemed to take as acceptance. She walked to the door and opened it herself.

"Where are we going?" I asked.

She hesitated, as if debating whether she should even tell me that much. "Puerto Cabezas" was all she said.

The door closed, and she was gone.

41

We reached the airport at sunrise. María had picked me up right at 6:00 A.M. I'd thought we were going to drive, but she laughed.

"Did you really think there are decent roads to Puerto Cabezas?"

The choice was between two local airlines, but it really boiled down to one. I made it a policy never to travel on any airline that limited its passengers to only one carry-on iguana.

It was just the two of us and a pilot in an old and noisy single-engine Cessna. We flew slightly north and then east, directly into the rising sun. For ninety minutes an endless green forest unfolded below us, rugged in places, rolling elsewhere. Low-hanging clouds curled around the mountains, misty wisps of white that created the illusion of snow-filled valleys. Blue lakes and crystal rivers glistened with the first streaks of daylight.

And then I saw the ocean. Old, almost primitive-looking fishing boats bobbed peacefully on undulating seas of midnight blue. A narrow ribbon of sand stretched for miles to the north and south, not a soul in sight, not a footprint anywhere. It was practically virgin beach, the famous Mosquito Coast—*La Mosquitia*.

"Our country is very beautiful, no?" María shouted over the whining engine.

I nodded and smiled to myself, realizing finally why my father had come.

Ten minutes later we landed. After the picturesque views from above, it was like falling out of bed in the middle of a tropical dream. María had neglected to mention the lack of a runway. Heavy rains had washed out the major part of the airstrip. I didn't ask how that made landing in a field any safer. Once on the ground, María and I hopped a ride in the back of a banana truck, bounced our way down a muddy trail, and jumped off at the edge of town.

Puerto Cabezas was the largest city on Nicaragua's eastern shore, the largest for hundreds of miles along the entire Mosquito Coast. Buildings were old, some made of blocks and some of wood, nearly all in need of paint and basic repairs. Some of the roads were cobblestone, as in Managua, but we'd found a rutted street that was under heavy construction. Within minutes I was exhausted, the mud pulling at my boots like quicksand. Puddles were like land mines, in the sense that it was impossible to tell which one might actually be a flooded storm sewer with no grate. One careless step and I could have disappeared from the face of the earth, no one to rescue me. It was a sleepy place, especially on a Sunday morning, which added to the very palpable sense of isolation. The city was geographically remote, bordered on the east by the Atlantic Ocean and separated from the rest of the country by mountains, coastal plains, and the largest remaining rain forest in Central America. Culturally it was distinct, no shadows of Sandino and Che Guevara, so omnipresent in the west. This area was home to some seventy thousand Miskitos, the largest remaining group of *indígenas*, a proud and somewhat autonomous people.

"Where are we going?" I asked.

"We need a boat."

Ankle-deep in mud, I thought she was exaggerating only slightly. As we continued down the hill and toward the dock, however, I realized that what she meant was a boat to take us offshore.

The dirt road to the ocean was lined with shacks and grounded fishing boats that had been washed ashore some years earlier by Hurricane Mitch. The boats looked abandoned, but the laundry line and the naked little kids playing out back made me realize that they'd been converted into homes. The path grew narrower as we neared the water, and finally we broke through the thicket onto the beach.

The sounds impressed me most. The gentle waves lapped the shore in a rhythmic, soothing whisper. Seagulls cawed overhead. The warm breeze was barely strong enough to have kept a sail from luffing, yet I could see it moving across the water, little ripples on the surface. My father had taught me how to do that, to see the wind when others couldn't.

"He wants three bucks."

María's voice snapped my daydream. "What?"

"He'll take us where we want to go for three bucks."

A shirtless old man was standing beside his little wooden boat, ready to go. I dug the bills out of my money belt and gave them to María. Wherever we were going, a few bucks seemed reasonable.

On the thirteenth pull the small outboard started. We headed straight east for about ten minutes, then veered north toward an eighty-foot fishing boat. From a hundred yards away I could see the rows of extra scuba tanks on deck. I'd never seen them in action, but nearly all my life I'd heard my father's stories about the famous Miskito divers. For thousands of years sea turtles had been their favorite target. A lone diver would swim alongside the turtle, rope it, and then hold on for a rapid descent to the deep, risking digits as he clamped the turtle's mouth shut with his bare hand and forced it to surface. If the diver could hold on long enough, an entire Indian village had food for a week. Sea turtles were a protected species nowadays, but the fishing companies had tapped in to those same skills for the harvest of lobsters.

The old man killed his little engine, and my ears stopped humming. The waves were bigger this far out, and the small boat rocked a good bit now that we were adrift.

"Is that a Rey's Seafood boat?" I asked.

"No. But it's just like the ones we use."

I saw only a few people on deck. "Divers are all down, I guess?"

"Yeah. This is where the money is. Probably about twenty-five of them scooping up lobster."

"They don't use any traps at all?"

"Some. But mostly it's just send the divers down

and stuff lobsters in a bag. They are all over the place out here."

"Must be quite a haul."

"Sure it is. These divers are Miskitos. They're experts. Each one will bring up about forty-five pounds of whole lobster a day."

I watched the waves, not sure what the point of this journey was. "So is this what you brought me to see?"

Her eyes were fixed on the dinghy a hundred yards away. A diver suddenly broke the surface and clung to the side. She handed me a pair of binoculars and said, "*That* is what I brought you to see."

I trained the binoculars on the diver. He looked exhausted, half drowned, his skin turning a strange shade of blue as he coughed up seawater. A frantic crewman finally dragged him into the dinghy.

"Looks like he ran out of air."

"Of course he did. They don't use gauges."

I did a double take. "That's crazy. How long do they stay down?"

"They come up and down as they think they need it. Some are better than others at figuring out how long is too long."

"With no gauges? They could drown, get the bends."

"Some of them do."

Her voice had an ominous tone. I lowered the binoculars, looked her in the eye. "So this is what Lindsey saw?"

"Plenty of people have seen it. Lindsey was going to write a story about it."

"How did she find out about it?"

"Señor Cruz. I told you, she was using him."

"Isn't that a kick in the teeth? Some young American girl sweet-talks him into exposing the Achilles' heel of the industry, then dumps him and runs off to her typewriter for her first coup ever as a wannabe journalist."

"That's Lindsey."

"He couldn't have been too happy about that."

"A lot of people weren't happy."

"My father included, I imagine. Which probably made the story all the more attractive to her."

I looked again toward that diver lying in the boat, still coughing and trying to recover. Something wasn't adding up. My father, the man I knew, was the last guy on earth who'd exploit these Indians.

"Did my father know about this?"

"You probably should talk to Lindsey about that."

"That's the whole point. I don't know where she is."

"I told you, people don't want this story told. She's in hiding."

"How do you know?"

"Because I helped her find a place to hide."

"You know where Lindsey is?"

She nodded.

"Can you tell me how to find her?"

"No."

"Why not?"

"Because you were barely able to handle the streets of Puerto Cabezas. You'd hardly manage your way through the rain forest."

My eyes followed hers, till they came to rest on

the thickest part of the jungle north of the city. "My sister is in *there*?"

"Not far. But too far for you to find her."

"Why don't you try me?"

"Why don't I take you?" she replied.

I smiled wryly and said, "Why didn't I think of that?"

In Spanish I told the old guy to take us back to shore. He shook his head firmly and said, "*Veinte*." Three bucks to take us out here, twenty to bring us back. I'd seen this one coming.

It was just a little thing, but as I handed him a twenty-dollar bill, I realized how easy it was to get yourself into trouble out here. The boat turned and pointed toward the rain forest.

I couldn't help but wonder, How deep was the mess that Lindsey had gotten herself into?

42

Matthew was no longer alone in his hole.

The rain had stopped, and the standing water had finally drained away. Out of sheer exhaustion he'd finally lain flat on his back, knees bent. For perhaps as long as an hour he'd been staring at the dark thatched roof overhead. His eyes had definitely played tricks in the darkness, but the tiny sliver of light at the far corner seemed real. Without a doubt, an almost imperceptible crack of moonlight or sunlight—he didn't know which—had broken through the thick covering. It was just bright enough to reveal a set of red, beady eyes at the other end of the hole.

It seemed to be staring at him, whatever it was. He listened for its breathing but heard nothing. The eyes were fixed, motionless. They were surely inside the head of some creature, but it was too dark to see any part of the body. If the frozen eyes were any indication, however, the entire creature was locked in some unshakable pose. Stiffened with fright, maybe. Or poised for an attack. A primitive thought crossed his mind, as if he were suddenly inside the small brain of his visitor.

Is that thing over there edible?

The piercing eyes glowed brighter, and finally they blinked. A chill raced through Matthew; fear gripped his heart.

Do anacondas have eyelids?

He suddenly heard breathing—his own. He didn't dare speak aloud, but silently he was talking himself out of his worst nightmare, assuring himself that it couldn't be an anaconda, that it was too cold up here in the mountains.

Unless Joaquín brought it here.

It would be the ultimate execution, a wrestling match with a hungry eighteen-foot snake. Ten horrific minutes of rolling in a hole as this monster coiled around his body and squeezed the life out of him, its massive jaws locked on to his head in a desperate effort to swallow him whole.

Matthew was shaking, and the creature seemed to sense his fright. Slowly, not more than a centimeter at a time, the eyes were creeping closer.

It was decision time. If he burst out of the hole, he could well be shot by the guards. If he stayed put, God only knew what was in store for him.

Carefully he sat up, drew his knees in toward his body, and planted his feet on the ground. On the mental count of three he summoned all his strength and shot straight up from the hole. His hands broke through the branches first, sending the makeshift roof splintering in all directions. A screeching noise followed him out of the hole, which only propelled him faster. He was clawing at stalks of bamboo, giant leaves, anything to get a grip and pull him-self out.

"Don't shoot!" he shouted, fearing it would look like an escape. He rolled to the ground outside his hole, tangled in the wet remnants of the thatched roof. He was swinging wildly in self-defense, not sure where those red eyes had gone. Something was at his ankle, then at his leg, and climbing up his belly. He rolled frantically and shouted, "Don't shoot!"

A gun went off, and a hot, red explosion covered his torso.

"*¡No se mueve!*" the guard shouted.

Matthew froze, obeying the command to stop, though his chest heaved in panicky breaths. Slowly his eyes adjusted to the daylight, and the glob of flesh beside him eventually came into focus.

It was the biggest dead rat he'd ever seen.

Joaquín and another guerrilla stood over him, laughing. Behind them were five others nearly fall-ing over in hysterics.

Matthew was fuming. "Is this your idea of a joke? Turn a rat loose in my hole?"

Joaquín's laughter faded. His eyes turned cold, colder than the rat's. "*Your* hole?" he said, glaring.

The others fell silent. Matthew stared back, but he couldn't match the black intensity in Joaquín's eyes. He suspected drugs.

"It's not your hole," said Joaquín. "You have noth-ing here. Not even this hole. Do you understand?"

Matthew was silent.

"I asked you a question."

He still refused to answer. Joaquín raised his rifle

and took aim at Matthew's chest. "Answer me," he said harshly. "Or you *will* own this hole. Forever."

Matthew stared down the long steel barrel. Finally he said, "I understand."

Joaquín jerked the rifle and fired off two quick rounds that splattered the rat beyond recognition, most of the mess landing on Matthew. Joaquín and his cronies laughed in chorus.

"You smell better now," he said.

Matthew didn't doubt it. After all that time in the hole, he felt like a human pest strip.

Joaquín shouted to his men in Spanish. Matthew didn't catch it all, but it had something to do with the river. And he thought he heard the name Nisho, the young Japanese widow. With the guerrillas' reaction, he knew that he'd heard correctly. Two of them howled and started racing back to camp.

"Nisho!" they shouted, sounding more stoned than ever. "Nishooooooo!"

They reached the river in two groups. Three armed guerrillas led Matthew to the bank. Ten meters behind were Joaquín, another guerrilla, and Nisho.

The makeup of the group gave Matthew concern. Joaquín, he'd decided, was just a sick sadist. Two of the guerrillas were bona fide sharpshooters, just itching for the chance to pop someone's skull. Two others were confirmed hell-raisers who passed the boredom at camp with drugs and silly target-practice. They'd get crazy out of their minds and shoot mice with AK-47s, ant mounds with .45-caliber Lugers. Today they seemed more wired on *basuco* than Matthew had ever seen them. All the way to the river they'd been loud and pushing each other. It was a dangerous combination: drugs, fully loaded automatic weapons, and a bunch of dead-end teenagers with zero respect for life.

"Stop," Joaquín said in Spanish.

They'd reached a calm eddy in the river behind a huge fallen tree and a boulder as big as a house. The guerrillas positioned themselves along the bank, two on the log, two others atop the boulder.

"You can bathe here," said Joaquín.

Matthew was more than ready. He started to remove his clothes, then went to the river's edge and tested the water. The cold was just about unbearable, so he retained a layer of clothing for warmth. He waded knee-deep into the eddy, hand-washing himself without full immersion, thankful to clean off the thick layer of filth that had crusted his clothes and body.

"You, too," said Joaquín. He was speaking to Nisho, who had not yet moved. With some reluctance she stepped toward the river and dipped her toe in.

"Clothes off," said Joaquín.

The guerrillas were watching and grinning, almost giddy with anticipation. Matthew could see the fear in Nisho's eyes, and the direction this seemed to be taking had him worried.

"It's too cold," she said.

"Leave your clothes," Joaquín said sternly. "Now!"

Slowly she removed her jacket and sweater, and then her boots. She was down to a blouse and pants.

"The rest," he said.

"She'll freeze!" shouted Matthew.

One of the sharpshooters fired a warning shot. It splashed in the water just inches from Matthew's knee. He backed off.

Nisho looked nearly paralyzed with fright. Her eyes darted from one gawking guerrilla to the next as her trembling hand unbuttoned her blouse. The catcalls started. The show was in full swing.

Matthew turned his gaze toward the guerrillas. They were a repugnant group, themselves in need of bathing. The fat guy was especially disgusting, a hideous tattoo covering the entire left side of his face. The word *"cerdo"* came to mind—"pig."

"The pants," said Joaquín.

Matthew heard the zipper, then the hoots. The guerrillas atop the boulder were sharing a bottle of something. The fat one with the tattoo stood up and started dancing, which quickly degenerated into a vulgar pelvic thrust. The others applauded, egging him on. He jumped down from the boulder and went toward Nisho.

She was wearing only underpants, her arms covering her breasts. *Cerdo* grabbed her clothes, then wadded them into a ball and pitched them to Joaquín. He held the bundle in open hands, as if offering Nisho her clothes. She came toward him, pleading as she reached for the bundle. He laughed in her face and quickly pitched it back to the fat guy. He made the same phony offer, and again Nisho fell for it. He tossed her clothes back to another guerrilla. She was soon running back and forth, still trying to cover herself, tears streaming down her face.

"Stop it!" shouted Matthew.

The sharpshooter responded with another warning, this one even closer. Matthew stopped in his tracks, still knee-deep in the eddy.

"Nisho! Nishooooooo!" Joaquín shouted.

She was bouncing back and forth, one guerrilla to the next, as they played keep-away with her clothes. As she raced by Joaquín, he reached out and grabbed her by the panties, ripping them off. She screamed and fell. The guerrillas shouted with excitement as Joaquín waved the panties over his head. The guerrillas formed a circle around her, tossing her clothes from one to the next, over Nisho's head, behind her back, howling each time she reached up and exposed her nakedness. Joaquín put his gun aside and grabbed her from behind, taking a breast in each hand. She kicked and swung wildly as he lifted her from the ground, then bit his arm.

He cried out and slapped her across the head.

Matthew seized the moment and dived for Joaquín's gun. He got a hand on it, but only for a split second. *Cerdo* rapped him across the head with the butt of his rifle. Matthew fell to the ground hard, bleeding from the head.

Her screaming grew more shrill and desperate. The guerrillas were shouting, no longer laughing. It was more like a barbaric chant.

Matthew sensed that someone was standing over him, but his head was throbbing, his vision blurring. Gradually the noises faded. He raised his head one last time, just high enough to see three men drag a screaming Nisho off behind the rocks, and then his world turned black.

43

María and I had traveled by boat up the coast from Puerto Cabezas, then hiked another half hour into the thick of the rain forest. The Mosquito Coast was living up to its name. I was covered with insect repellent, but nothing short of dousing myself in gasoline and setting myself on fire could have deterred these monsters. I was sure they'd drawn at least a pint of my blood by the time we reached the first clearing. We stopped for water from our canteens atop a barren, muddy hill. Hundreds of short sticks were protruding up from the ground.

"What's with all the sticks?" I asked.

"Mudslide. The last hurricane. Used to be a village here. The sticks are where we found the bodies."

I took a wider look and saw even more sticks. Hundreds more in every direction, up one slope and down another. It was the jungle version of Arlington National Cemetery, except that everybody here, children included, had been washed away at the same horrific moment in the same giant river of mud.

María fell silent, eyes closed, as if in prayer. I bowed my head and said a little one of my own.

That was our last real break of the afternoon. We walked nonstop for two more hours, sharing water along the way, until we finally reached an old Miskito Indian settlement at dusk. It was little more than a small clearing in the trees. There were no real roads, only footpaths that led from the hub to the forest in all directions, like the spokes of a wheel. In the center of the clearing was an old wooden building that appeared to be a combination church and schoolhouse. About a dozen tumbledown shacks surrounded it. A group of Indian children came out to greet us as we entered their village. I was suddenly surrounded by outstretched hands, some of them tugging at my backpack. They knew María by name, which lessened my anxiety.

"I used to teach here," she said over the incessant chatter of the children.

"Teach what?"

"Bible school."

I suddenly understood what had drawn her to Lindsey, a lost soul if ever there was one.

María said something in the native Miskito language, and the smiling children backed away, allowing us to pass. I followed her around to the back of the church, where she stopped at the door to a small cottage. She knocked twice, and the door opened. A woman with short blond hair was standing in the doorway, the first Caucasian I'd seen since leaving Managua. The short hair threw me. In the waning daylight I almost didn't recognize my own sister.

"Nick?" she said.

"I came to see if you want to change your long-distance carrier."

She smiled, appreciating the humor, then came out and gave me a rather unexpected hug. "I can't believe you're here."

"I can't believe *you're* here," I said.

We didn't tell María that we wanted to talk alone, but on her own initiative she headed off to chat with her former pupils. Lindsey led me inside, closed the door, and lit the oil lamp on the table. It was a one-room shack, and the lamp was the only source of light. The bed was a woven hammock. A pitcher and washbasin were resting on the nightstand beside it. The floor was a collection of straw mats on dirt. We sat at opposite sides of the table on the only two chairs in the room. She offered me a tin cup of water.

"You've had your shots, right?"

"I got them before I went to Colombia."

"You went to Colombia?"

The way she'd asked, it was clear that she didn't know about Dad. She seemed genuinely shocked as I told her all about the kidnapping. It took several minutes. I finished with the part that I assumed would be of greatest interest to her.

"The insurance company thinks you're behind Dad's kidnapping."

"That's preposterous."

"That's what I thought. For starters, how would you even know he had kidnap-and-ransom insurance?"

She paused, then said, "Actually, I think I did know that."

"What do you mean?"

"Dad never came right out and told me he had it. But he wanted to buy a policy for me, and I guess I sort of assumed he had it for himself."

"Now I'm really confused. The last time you and I had a phone conversation, you said that you hadn't spoken to Mom or Dad since Christmas."

"The last time you and I talked was almost three months ago."

"Are you saying things have changed between you and Dad?"

"Honestly, we were becoming . . . close."

I put down my tin cup, leaned into the table, and looked her in the eye. "Lindsey, knock off the games. María told me about you and Guillermo. I know all about the story you were writing on the plight of these divers."

"Did she also tell you that Dad was my source?"

"She said it was Guillermo. An unwitting Guillermo at that."

"Anybody who asked, I told them it was Guillermo. This is a dangerous story. Dad was really sticking his neck out by feeding me information."

"So you decided to put Guillermo's neck on the chopping block?"

"He deserved it. The creep never told me he had a wife in Florida."

"You didn't know he was married?"

"How would I? She's never here. I guess she prefers Palm Beach to Managua."

"Go figure."

"Anyway, after Dad dressed me down for dating his partner, we started meeting for coffee twice a week, that sort of thing. It didn't take long for him to realize that my journalism career was going no-where. That's when he asked me to write this story."

"You expect me to believe that he asked you to expose the abuses of his own company?"

"It's not about his company. Rey's Seafood trains its divers and uses the right equipment. Its divers get paid very well, too. That's why Dad's practically going out of business. He can't compete with some of these other companies that send untrained divers down all day long with no gauges."

"So it's your job to write the story that will blow the competition out of the water. Literally."

"Exactly. And they're not too happy with me right now. Which is why I'm hiding out in this shack."

"Why didn't you just come home?"

"Because the story isn't finished yet," she said without a moment's hesitation.

That was the most grown-up statement I'd ever heard my sister utter. I smiled with my eyes and said, "I'm proud of you."

"So was Dad."

"I'll bet he was. But what about Guillermo?"

"Honestly, he thinks Rey's Seafood should shut up and do business the way some of his competi-tors do."

"Did he tell you that?"

"Sure. Training and equipment cost money. I wasn't exaggerating when I said it was practically put-ting the company out of business. That's why Dad went to Colombia."

"I don't understand."

"Last time Dad and I talked, he said there were some good boats for cheap in Cartagena. Every extra boat they add to their fleet increases cash flow by about fifty grand a month. So Guillermo gave him two choices. Cut the diving costs or go get the boats."

"Guillermo sent Dad to Colombia? He never told me that."

"Take it from me and his wife. He's not the most honest person I've ever met."

"So I'm learning," I said, staring blankly at the flickering flame in the lamp.

"What are you thinking?"

After a moment or two I looked back at my sister and said, "I think it's time I had a serious talk with Guillermo."

I woke to the sound of screaming monkeys. At least I thought it was monkeys.

Lindsey and I had stayed awake late, just talking. I'm not sure what time we'd finally gone to bed, if you could call straw-covered earth a bed. I woke several times during the night with a horrendous backache. It made me think of my father, sleeping on the cold ground in some mountain jungle night after night.

A beam of sunlight was streaming in through a hole in the east wall. I rolled over to keep it from hitting me in the eyes, but sleep was out of the question anyway. I thought the screaming monkeys were at it again, and then I realized that all along it had been the unfamiliar ring of the satellite phone I'd rented for this trip. If I'd been insistent on going to Nicaragua, Alex had been equally insistent that I be reachable anywhere at any time, just in case of an emergency.

I answered with trepidation, fearful of what an "emergency" might mean in my family these days.

"Nick, I'm so glad I got you." It was Jenna. She was one of three people who had the satellite number, along with Mom and Alex.

"Is everything okay?"

"Don't worry. It's only some legal maneuvering. I just got out of a hearing."

It seemed early for court, but then I realized that she was two time zones ahead of me. "What happened?"

"I've been trying to keep the pressure on the insurance company while you're away. I got in front of the judge this morning and forced them to produce a company rep who will tell us exactly why your father's coverage was denied."

"That's great."

"The bad news is that Quality Insurance is a Bermuda-based company. Duncan Fitz convinced the judge that we have to go there if we want to take the deposition."

"When is it?"

"That's why I'm calling. It's tomorrow."

"Yikes."

"It's the old adage: Be careful what you wish for. I told the judge we wanted to move as quickly as possible for your father's sake."

"You did exactly the right thing. Unfortunately, I'm literally in the middle of nowhere right now."

"You want me to try to postpone it?"

"No. I'll do what I have to do to get home tonight."

"Anything I can do here to help?"

"Buy me a pair of knee socks and Bermuda shorts?"

"With those knees? Forget it."

I laughed, then said, "You're coming to Bermuda with me, right?"

"Do you want me to?"

"Well, I'm up against my old firm. It's such short notice. We'll practically have to prepare on the plane as it is. I mean—"

"Nick, I just asked a question: Do you want me to go?"

She wasn't being testy. She was just bringing me back to the only thing that mattered. "Yes. I want you to go."

"Then I'll go."

I smiled. "I'll call you tonight, okay?"

"Sure. Have a safe flight."

As I switched off the phone, I felt upbeat that the deposition was set and that Jenna was coming with me. But the part we'd left unspoken was more than a little awkward, even ironic.

Bermuda was the place we'd planned to go for our honeymoon.

44

·

At 11:00 A.M. Jenna and I were seated side by side in the St. George's office of Cool Cash. Frankly, I'd been unaware that the firm even had a Bermuda office. Nice place to hold firm retreats for partners, I presumed. The office had just one resident barrister, who was currently seated at the end of the table reading the *Wall Street Journal.* The real warriors were seated across the table, Duncan from Miami and Maggie Johans from New York. As general counsel, Maggie was evidently staying right on top of every phase of the case.

It had taken some doing for me to get out of Nicaragua in time for the deposition, and I never did get to talk with Guillermo. That would have to wait.

"Swear the witness, please," I told the stenographer.

Jason Lee was a vice president of Quality Insurance Company based in St. George's. He was a large man, husky but not fat, with salt-and-pepper hair that was thinning on top. His attire was the Bermuda businessman's uniform, khaki shorts and knee socks, oxford-cloth shirt and blue blazer.

I covered the requisite preliminaries, and just as soon as I started asking questions of substance, Duncan jumped on me with objections. It was getting annoying, and I prepared for the worst as I moved to the heart of the matter.

"Mr. Lee, why did Quality Insurance deny coverage?"

He sipped his water. "Legal reasons."

"Not to be flip, but the whole point here is to determine whether the reasons were legal. So let me try again: Why did Quality Insurance Company deny coverage?"

"We denied coverage on the advice of our legal counsel."

Duncan grumbled and said, "At this point I wish to caution the witness not to divulge any communications with the company's legal counsel. Those are protected by the attorney-client privilege."

It was the kind of speaking objection that was designed to coach the witness, and I wasn't going to let Duncan get away with it. "I'm not asking the witness to tell me what his lawyer's advice was. I simply want to know the factual basis for the company's decision to deny coverage."

Lee answered, "I'm afraid I can't possibly tell you the factual basis without revealing the nature of the legal advice."

"Just tell me the facts that you presented to your lawyer."

"It's all intertwined. It's protected by the attorney-client privilege."

"This is the most ridiculous interpretation of the attorney-client privilege I've ever heard."

"Then take it up with the judge," said Duncan.

"The court has already ordered your client to tell us why it denied coverage. Either Mr. Lee is going to answer my questions or I'll file a motion for sanctions."

Duncan raised his hands, mocking me. "Oh, gee. In that case, we give up. I'll have a cashier's check in the full amount of the three-million-dollar policy in your hands before the close of business today."

Maggie chuckled and said, "Or perhaps your family and its so-called Nicaraguan fishing company would be more comfortable dealing with a suitcaseful of cash."

They shared a good laugh, and then Duncan glanced at the stenographer and said, "Those last remarks are off the record."

"No way," I said. "I want it all on the transcript."

The Bermuda barrister at the end of the table looked up from his *Wall Street Journal*, made eye contact with the stenographer, and simply cleared his throat. It was clear that the remarks would be off the record.

Maggie smirked, pleased with the teamwork.

"Tell you what," I said. "Let's call Judge Korvan in Miami right now. See what she has to say about your objections."

The barrister jumped in again, sounding very British. "Actually, the proper procedure in these particular circumstances is to petition a judge who has jurisdiction in Bermuda. I'll ring Uncle Henry straightaway, get a direct answer for you chaps."

"Excellent idea," said Maggie.

"Thanks, but no thanks," I said flatly. "We'll call Judge Korvan, who's nobody's uncle."

"How long is this going to take?" asked Lee. "I have a two o'clock tee time at Mid Ocean."

"You'll make your tee time," said Duncan.

"Don't be so sure," I said.

"Oh, I'm quite sure," said Duncan. His tone was beyond confident, as if somehow he knew it was an absolute certainty.

I could feel my anger rising, but Jenna reeled me in with a gentle tug on the elbow.

Duncan said, "Go ahead, hotshot. Make your phone call."

We exchanged a cold glare, then I picked up the phone and dialed Judge Korvan's chambers.

All eyes were on the speakerphone in the center of the conference table. We were waiting to hear the voice of the Honorable Judge Peñas.

My telephone call to Judge Korvan had been re-routed. For reasons unexplained, Judge Korvan had just today recused herself from the case. Her replacement was Humberto Peñas, a puppet who owed his seat on the Miami-Dade County bench to none other than Duncan Fitz.

Finally his secretary announced his arrival, and we heard the judge's voice over the box. "Good afternoon to all of you."

Duncan seized the lead and introduced everyone. When the judge asked Duncan about his kids—identifying them by name, grade in school, and favorite sport—I knew I was in trouble.

"So what seems to be the trouble in Bermuda?" the judge asked.

I said, "Your Honor, there's a dispute over discovery—"

"Let me stop you right there, Mr. Rey. Why is there any discovery going on in this case?"

"Because the insurance company has denied coverage, and we need to prove they were wrong."

"I spoke to Judge Korvan about this case, and I have to tell you, I think she totally missed the boat. I don't see why Mr. Fitz's client should be subjected to intrusive discovery into its business decisions at this stage of the game."

"It's hardly intrusive, Your Honor. My father's been kidnapped, and they won't provide coverage."

"I understand that. But your insurance policy is a reimbursement policy. It reimburses you for any ransom payment that you make. You don't have a claim until you make a ransom payment and have an out-of-pocket loss."

"That's technically correct. But if the insurance company hadn't denied coverage, I could have used the policy as security to borrow the ransom money. No bank is going to issue a line of credit against an insurance policy that is allegedly tainted with fraud."

"That's very speculative, Mr. Rey."

"The insurance company is also supposed to pay for my negotiator. They aren't doing that."

Duncan said, "That's a disingenuous argument he's making, Judge. We happen to know for a fact that the negotiator we originally assigned to this case is still working with Mr. Rey under some kind of agreement they've worked out."

"Is that true, Mr. Rey?"

"Her decision to stay on is certainly no doing of Quality Insurance Company's."

"I asked you a simple question: Is she still helping you?"

"Yes, and I still have to pay her."

"How much have you paid her so far?"

"Nothing yet."

"Has she billed you?"

"Technically, no. She said we'd work that out later. I fully intend to pay her something."

Duncan was smiling. Maggie poked him in the ribs, urging him on. "Judge, this wasn't the point of the telephone call, but I think we've gotten to the nub here. My client's only purpose in bringing this matter before Judge Korvan was to enforce the confidentiality provisions in the policy. With all due respect to Judge Korvan, you seem to have a better handle on things than she did. The resolution of Mr. Rey's claims is for another day."

"But—"

"I think I've got it," said the judge. "I'll fax you an order before five o'clock. Good day."

The judge disconnected. Maggie hung up from our end, then looked at me and said, "That went rather well, don't you think?"

"Go to hell, all of you." I glanced at the stenographer and said, "You can put that on the record."

45

It was a Dark 'n' Stormy night.

Two or three Dark 'n' Stormies, actually. That was the signature cocktail of Bermuda. Two parts ginger beer, one part dark rum. It fit the bill, as Jenna and I were in need of something pretty potent back at the bar in our hotel.

The faxed order from Judge Peñas put a stay on all discovery, which meant that the entire case was at a halt. No depositions were to go forward—not of Jason Lee or anyone else. The evidentiary hearing was canceled, with no date rescheduled. It was as if Duncan Fitz himself had written the order.

Deep down I suspected that he had.

"Any thoughts on what we do now?" asked Jenna.

"I guess we file an appeal to try to get the case back on track. But that could take months, which doesn't do my dad any good."

Jenna stirred her drink, mixing the dark rum on top into the fizzing—stormy—ginger beer. "Last week I couldn't understand why Duncan wasn't scheduling any discovery or doing any of the things a lawyer would normally do with an evidentiary hearing less than three weeks away. I wonder if he knew back then that the hearing was going to be canceled."

"Of course he knew. Granted, cases get reassigned all the time even without any string-pulling, but it can't be an accident that this one landed in front of Peñas. Duncan couldn't have handpicked a more favorable judge."

"Why is he being such a bastard?"

"Because he truly believes that my family defrauded him and his client. Duncan pushes hard in any case, but he'll push to the limit if he thinks he's been screwed."

"Then why not just let his client say it under oath?"

"Maybe he has the same questions about Guillermo that I have. He doesn't want his client to go on record saying that Lindsey's the bad guy till they've sorted it all out."

"I feel so awful for your father."

I signaled the bartender for two more Dark 'n' Stormies. I hadn't eaten all day and already had a decent buzz. I knew better than to drink and drive, of course, but that didn't seem to keep me from blundering my way down certain metaphorical roads.

"Did you feel funny about coming to Bermuda with me?"

Jenna seemed to stiffen at the sudden turn in conversation. "What do you mean?"

"You know what I mean."

"The fact that we were going to have our honeymoon here?"

"Well, *yeah*."

"Not really."

I raised an eyebrow.

"Well, maybe a little." She cracked a smile and said, "Okay, a lot."

"Why did you come?"

"Gee, with questions like these, I may need Duncan Fitz to defend me." She was trying to make light of it, but the way she was playing with her hair, I knew she was uncomfortable.

The bartender set up our drinks. I finished the old one and started on the new. "When you first agreed to help me with the case, you said you were doing it for my dad, not for me."

"That was probably harsh. I'm sorry."

"You don't have to apologize. I'm bringing it up only because it's an important piece in a big puzzle that's come together for me since the kidnapping. After all the disappointment that you and I went through, you still love my dad. My mom, after the drinking and everything else they went through, is still totally in love with him. Yesterday I saw Lindsey, and even she seems to have made a connection. It was last night, while I was trying to fall asleep on the floor in Lindsey's hut, when it hit me. Nobody seems to have any issues with my dad. Except me."

"You've always said that, and to this day I don't understand what you mean. What issues?"

I paused, thinking how best to put it. "Did you ever know you loved someone and know that they loved you, too? And then this one thing happens. It might be a stupid thing. But for some reason, you won't allow yourself to look past it. Forever and ever it's stuck there, right between you."

"I don't know. Maybe."

"The crazy thing is, you know it doesn't belong there, keeping you apart. Yet for some reason neither one of you steps up and clears it away. It just festers. And before you know it, that stupid little thing actually defines your relationship. It might even destroy it."

She blinked hard, as if my words were hitting too close to home. It was unintentional, but I knew where I'd led her: to that day in the park when I'd been such an idiot and told her no, no, no, I wouldn't marry her, my well-intended but misguided way of keeping it a surprise that I'd already bought a ring to give her on her birthday.

"I can see where something like that could happen," she said, staring into her drink.

Part of me wanted to seize the opportunity and make this conversation about us. But it promised to be an awfully long plane ride home if I took that leap and fell flat on my face now. I chickened out.

"Anyway, that's kind of what happened between me and my dad."

"I'm sorry. What was the little thing?"

"What little thing?"

"The one that became such a big thing between you and your father?"

"Just something he did to me when I was twelve."

"You want to talk about it?"

"It's really not worth it."

She seemed reluctant to pry. "You two do seem to have a strange relationship," she said vaguely.

"You noticed, huh?"

"A week ago you said you didn't even know that your dad had a sister."

"No one ever told me."

She sipped her drink and said, "She died very young. Drowned. Seven years old."

"My dad told you all that?"

"We had just that one short conversation at my father's funeral, the one I told you about. He only mentioned that he'd lost a sister. The rest I learned on my own."

"When?"

"After I talked with you last week, my curiosity sort of ran away with me. I did a computer search on obituaries for anyone named Rey from the Florida Keys. Had to go back quite a ways, but I found it. Her name was Stacy."

"How did she drown?"

"A boating accident was all it said. I made a copy, if you want it."

"Sure, thanks. I'd like to see it."

I selected a couple of cashews from the bowl of mixed nuts on the bar, then shook my head. "This is exactly the sort of thing I don't understand about my father. Why wouldn't he tell me he had a sister who drowned?"

"Maybe it goes back to that thing you were talking about. When you were twelve."

"What could that possibly have to do with his sister's drowning?"

"Hard for me to say, without your telling me what it was. And I'm not suggesting there's a direct link. More likely it just turned out to be one of those pivotal moments in your relationship when your father decided that you didn't care. So he never got around to telling you about the sister he'd lost. He probably didn't tell you a lot of things. It wasn't worth it anymore."

I could have told her that she had it backward, that what had happened when I was twelve wasn't something *I* had done. It was something *he* had done to me. But I said nothing, knowing yet again that she wasn't really talking about me and my father.

She was talking about us.

"Another round?" asked the bartender.

Jenna and I exchanged a quick glance. She looked sad, and I would have liked nothing more than to fix things. But she hadn't believed me then, and I didn't see why she'd believe me now. She probably never would believe that I truly had bought the ring before that blunder in the park, that I hadn't just panicked and asked her to marry me to keep her from running away.

"No, thanks," I told the bartender. "I think we've had enough for one night."

46

Jenna and I caught the morning flight to Miami. She was going to cab it home, but I talked her into letting me give her a lift. Driving out of the airport, I plugged my cell phone into the cigarette lighter and phoned my mother to let her know I was back. She was frantic.

"I've been trying to reach you. Why didn't you answer your phone?"

"Battery ran out. I'm sorry."

"We got a package this morning."

"From . . . them?"

"It's a videotape of your father."

"Have you watched it yet?"

"Yes."

I was almost afraid to ask. "Is he alive?"

"Yes," she said, straining. "Oh, Nick, he looks so awful."

I steered toward the exit for Coral Gables. "I'll be there in fifteen minutes. Call Alex."

"I did. She's on her way here."

"Great. You did exactly the right thing."

She fell silent, as if collecting her composure. "It barely even looks like him," she said in a weak, shaky voice. "I almost didn't recognize him."

"I know it has to be a shock, but believe me, this is such good news. He's alive. We know he's okay."

I was trying hard to lift her spirits, but she didn't respond. I was about to say more, then stopped. At that moment words couldn't possibly have helped. I knew that the best thing was to let her have her cry. I steered with one hand and held the phone to my ear with the other, racked by the sounds of my mother's painful sobs.

It was probably my longest drive home ever, but Mom had regained her composure by the time Jenna and I arrived. She and Alex were in the family room in front of the television.

I was about to make introductions, but the women were ahead of me. "I'm Alex," she said as she and Jenna shook hands. "We met once before at Duffy's."

"I remember. I'm helping Nick with his lawsuit against the insurance company. We had to go to Bermuda."

"Bermuda, eh? Tough assignment."

"Actually, it was all work, no play. You know how that is."

"Sure."

I sensed a little tension, and it was only sidetracking us. "Let's watch the videotape."

"Good idea," said Mom. She popped it into the VCR. The women took a seat on the couch. I pulled up a bar stool from the counter.

The screen was blue. Mom had the remote in

hand, ready to start. "The whole thing is less than thirty seconds. There is audio, but they don't let your father say much. Most of the talking is from the kidnappers."

I nodded, signaling that I was ready. Mom hit the "Play" button. The blue screen went snowy, and then the image appeared. Even my mother's sobbing on the telephone hadn't prepared me for what I saw.

"My God," I said, completely involuntarily.

They'd videotaped him indoors, from the waist up. His face was thin, and his skin so lacked color that for a moment I thought the adjustments on the television set were off. Dad never had been able to grow a beard, so his unshaved growth looked especially shabby. His hair was dirty and uncombed. He showed little expression, neither a smile nor a frown. He was looking directly into the camera, then lowered his eyes and read from a prepared script.

"This message is to my family," he began.

I stepped down from my bar stool and walked to the set, drawn by his voice, as if compelled to be closer to my father's image.

"I am being treated well. I will be safe as long as you obey all instructions."

He laid the script aside and picked up a copy of *El Tiempo*, a widely distributed Bogotá daily newspaper. The camera zoomed in on the headline and the date.

"Three days old," I said. "That's pretty good."

The camera zoomed out, again showing my father.

"It's interesting he's wearing only a T-shirt," said Mom. "I guess they're keeping him someplace warm."

"They do that to confuse you," said Alex. "I'm sure they're in the mountains."

Back on-screen, my father put down the newspaper, then seemed to turn to someone off camera, as if looking for instruction.

"Freeze the frame," I said.

Mom hit the pause button. I walked right up to the screen and checked the side of his head. The rest of the video had shown him straight-on only, but these last few frames had caught his profile.

"It looks like somebody did a pretty lousy job of stitching up a good three-inch gash on the side of his head."

Alex came forward to have a look. "I'm afraid you're right."

My mother let out a combined groan and whimper. It was time to move on. "Hit the play button, Mom."

My father's image was on-screen for only a few seconds longer. Then it went black.

"What's going on?" I said.

Mom said, "This is the part where the kidnapper talks in Spanish."

Alex took a notepad from her purse, ready to translate. I leaned closer to listen, as if that would help my mediocre Spanish.

It was a man's voice, the same one Alex and I had heard over the shortwave radio in Bogotá. I'd had no trouble understanding him then, but here he was speaking too fast for me to pick up every word. Mom and Jenna looked even more clueless. Alex was scribbling feverishly on her notepad.

In twenty seconds he was finished. Mom switched off the tape. I was perplexed, not sure if I'd heard the last few words correctly. I asked Alex, "Did I hear him right?"

"Let me start at the beginning. He says that the radio contact scheduled for Sunday the nineteenth of November is canceled."

"What?" I hadn't caught that part.

She shushed me, then continued. "'Mr. Rey has proved to be a difficult prisoner,'" she read. "'We will tolerate no more delays. We will contact you by radio in our usual place on Sunday, the twelfth of November, at sunrise. The safety of the prisoner can be guaranteed no longer if you do not pay two hundred fifty thousand dollars at this time.'"

"Two-fifty! That's what I thought he said. They've come off their own demand."

"Why would they do that?" asked Jenna.

"It's like Alex told me from the beginning. Most kidnappers end up settling for about ten to fifteen percent of the initial demand. Dad's a pain in the neck," I said, smiling. "They must want to cut through all the back-and-forth negotiation and get rid of him. God, I love him!"

"It's not what you think," said Alex.

I stopped cold. From the expression on her face, I knew that it wasn't time to celebrate. "What do you mean?"

"The word for ransom in Spanish is '*rescate*.' That's not the word he used."

"He said two hundred fifty thousand. Even I understood that."

"They want two-fifty to keep your father alive. He didn't say they'd give him back. It's not a ransom. It's what they call a safety guarantee."

My mother looked ill. "What the hell kind of sickos are these people? Whoever heard of such a thing as a safety payment?"

"I've seen it before," said Alex. "Especially when a prisoner violates a rule or gets in some kind of trouble. From the looks of that gash on the side of Matthew's head, he's probably been more trouble than his kidnappers bargained for."

"This is absurd," I said. "They expect us to hand over a quarter million dollars for nothing?"

"It's not for nothing," said Alex. "They'll kill him if you don't."

My mother looked at me, her face etched in fear. "What do we do?"

The room was spinning, I was so upset. I went to the window and looked out at the yard. "What choice do we have?" I said quietly.

47

Sunday came too soon. Even with my father's life hanging in the balance, pulling together a quarter million dollars had proven more difficult than expected.

My parents had poured their life savings into the seafood company, and with my suspicion of Guillermo still running high, he was the last person I wanted to be beholden to for money. I considered trying to borrow against the insurance policy, but Quality's allegations of fraud made that worthless as collateral. I ended up taking a second mortgage on my house in the Grove. J. C. gave me ten thousand of his own money—a true lifelong pal—and Jenna loaned me another thirty. Cash advances from credit cards filled in another nineteen. Financially speaking, I was about as liquid as dried cement.

And we were still fifty thousand dollars short.

Physically getting all that cash out of the country was a logistical and legal problem in itself. The money was wired to a Colombian bank, which by law could give us only pesos. Alex had "sources" in Bogotá who could change the pesos back into dollars. I didn't ask how it would work. I wasn't sure I wanted to know.

"Was it this cold the last time?" I asked.

It was almost 5:00 A.M. Alex and I were huddled at the same picnic table that we'd used for the last shortwave communication with the kidnappers, behind the old church atop Monserrate. It was damp but not raining, though the fog was so thick I couldn't even see the city lights of Bogotá nearly six hundred meters below us.

"It was even colder. You just don't remember."

She was probably right. Who could blame me for having blocked that experience out of my mind?

I paced for nearly twenty minutes. Last time we'd spotted a half dozen sightseers at this same hour. This morning offered no views, however, and the hikers had stayed home. The observation deck near the old church was empty, itself nearly invisible in the fog. Even the moon and stars found the blanket of fog impenetrable. Flashlights were our only source of light.

The shortwave radio rested on the picnic table, emitting only static and garbled noises. Alex listened for any signs of reception. Finally a hint of dawn filtered through the clouds, just enough to make the floating mist glisten. The faint light of morning gave the fog an eerie density, slowly changing the mountaintop from a black, claustrophobic place to a swirling, mystical setting within the clouds.

It was sunrise, and as if on cue, the radio crackled.

The familiar voice was back, the man who called himself "Joaquín."

"Good morning, Rey family," he said in Spanish. "Are you there, Alex?"

She grabbed the microphone. "We're here. Go ahead."

"You received my tape, no?"

"Yes. Very nice work. I think there's a future in music videos for you."

"What?"

"Nothing. I have the son here with me. His Spanish is good, but he wants to be sure he doesn't miss anything. So if you want your money, we're going to do this in English this time."

"Very well," he said, switching to English. "But I hope you are as cooperative as I am. Do you have the money?"

"It's in the city."

"Don't give me that," he said harshly. "The videotape was very clear. It must be paid today."

"You didn't expect us to bring it all the way here, did you?"

"I warned you, no more delays."

"Don't sweat it. You can have it today. A hundred thousand dollars."

"A hundred? I said two-fifty!"

My heart was in my throat. I knew we were going to have to do a little horse trading when I'd come up fifty thousand dollars short on his original demand, but the simple fact was, we weren't talking about horses.

"This is not a wealthy family," said Alex. "We have

a hundred thousand dollars, and we had to scrape to get it. Come on, Joaquín. You're a smart guy. You know as well as I do that nobody pays two-fifty for a mere guarantee of safety."

He didn't answer right away. Alex and I exchanged anxious glances, and I wondered if her counteroffer of a hundred grand was pushing too hard, with double that in our war chest. The silence was insufferable; at this juncture even the slightest pause made my stomach flop. Finally the radio crackled with a response.

"Go to Hotel Los Andes on Carrera Seis. One block over from Plaza de Bolívar."

I could breathe again. Alex gave me a thumbs-up, then spoke into the microphone. "That's in La Candelaria, no? Lots of inexpensive hotels in that area."

"Correct. This one is small and has no private baths. There's a shared bath in back, right next to the rear entrance to the restaurant. At three o'clock take the money into the men's room. Enter the third stall and check behind the toilet. You'll find a note that tells you what to do. Is that clear?"

"Yes, clear."

"That's all for now, then."

"Hold on," said Alex. "We need something in return."

"You're getting plenty. The prisoner's safety is guaranteed."

"We need a date. When will he be released?"

"He's not being released for anywhere near a hundred thousand dollars."

"*Claro.* But let's call that the first half."

He laughed. "Alex, *mi amiga.* You're dreaming."

"I told you before, we aren't going to pay three million."

"You'll pay," he said, losing his chuckle. "Unless the widow prefers to have her husband's heart hand-delivered in a plastic bag."

"Don't threaten us."

"Then don't con me," he said angrily. "I'm letting you off cheap here, but the ransom is firm. We know he has insurance. It's three million dollars, not a penny less."

A sick feeling washed over me. We'd suspected that they knew, but this was the first time he'd come right out and said it.

"It's not as clear-cut as you think," said Alex.

"It is for me. The final exchange will be very soon. The details will be in the note you pick up this afternoon. That's all I have to say."

"Wait, one more thing. We need proof that he's alive."

"We just sent you a video."

"We want proof he's alive *today*."

"*No es posible.* The prisoner is not here with me."

"Put the proof in the note that you leave in the bathroom."

"What proof?"

"We want a proof-of-life question answered."

He groaned, then said, "All right, what is it?"

"Just one second." She looked at me and asked, "You know any secrets about your dad?"

"Like what?"

"It has to be a question that Joaquín can pass along to your father. Something that only your father would know."

"What's his favorite color?"

"Nothing subjective," she said. "Make it a verifiable fact."

"How about the question we used the last time? The name of the golden retriever I had when I was a kid."

"I need a new one. They could have asked him that two weeks ago and killed him yesterday."

"What's his wedding anniversary?"

"No good. If their plan was to kill him and pretend he was still alive, they surely would have gotten every birthday and anniversary out of him before pulling the trigger."

Put on the spot, I couldn't think of anything. I sensed urgency from Alex. Finally it hit me, the drowning that Jenna had told me about.

"How old was his sister when she drowned?"

"Perfect," said Alex.

Immediately I wanted to retract it, but Alex was already passing it along to Joaquín. He wrapped things up with a simple *"Adios, amigos."*

Alex switched off the radio, took one look at my expression, and asked, "What's wrong?"

"That question I asked you to pass along to Joaquín. It's not a good one."

"Nonsense. It was exactly the kind of thing Joaquín wouldn't be able to find out unless your father was alive to tell him."

"The problem is, Dad never told *me* about his sister."

"You mean you don't know the answer to your own question?" she snapped.

"I know the answer. But it's something that my

father never shared with me. It's obviously a subject that he has difficulty talking about, maybe even something he just didn't want me to know. The last thing I wanted to do was ask a proof-of-life question that upsets him."

She stowed the radio in her backpack, threw it over her shoulder. "Don't take this the wrong way, but your dad has more things to worry about than whether his son knows or doesn't know his personal demons. Three million more things, to be exact."

I couldn't argue.

She turned and started down the stone trail. I followed, the two of us descending deeper into the fog.

48

Matthew's head was still smarting. The blow he'd taken from the rifle butt during the attack at the river had rendered him unconscious for nearly a full day. The three-inch gash had been crudely stitched by Aída, a thirteen-year-old girl of a guerrilla who claimed to know how to sew. She knew nothing about the need for sterilized needles, however, and trying to get the wound properly cleaned and bandaged was about as likely as room service. All day long Matthew would search himself for a few square centimeters of clothing that weren't covered in grime, and then he'd dab the pus away. It galled him to think that after all he'd been through he could seriously end up dying from infection.

"*El vaso, por favor,*" he said to a passing guard. One of these lowlifes had stolen his only possession, a cracked rice bowl that he'd been using to collect clean rainwater, both for drinking and for washing his head wound.

The guard just kept walking, not his concern.

Matthew could easily have exploded, but he forced himself to remember that he was better off this week than last. He was out of his hole in the ground, though still held separately from the other prisoners. He spent his days beneath a stretch of canvas behind the guerrillas' smoky hut, while the others were housed on the other side of the slope in army tents that had come with the last mule train of supplies. He'd seen Nisho once, but only from a distance. He'd passed the entire group on his way to a bathroom break. Jan, Emilio, the old-looking Colombian, and Rosa were seated around a small fire, eating. Nisho was off to the side by herself, curled into a ball beneath a blanket.

It was hard for him to say how long it had been since the rape. The weather was in such a cold, drizzly pattern that one day was utterly indistinguishable from the next. He wished for a pen and paper just to mark the passage of time. The guards who brought him food or took him to the latrine would generally tell him nothing. He would ask how long he'd been in captivity, what day it was, how many days till Christmas. Their response was always along the lines of *"¿Qué te importa?"*

What does it matter to you?

It had gotten to the point where he just didn't talk to the guerrillas and they didn't talk to him. Except for this morning. A few hours after dawn Aída had brought him breakfast, the usual slop. Silence was the normal routine, but this time she'd placed the tin at his feet and, out of the blue, asked the strangest question.

"How old was your sister when she drowned?"

It had so completely thrown him that, instinctively, he almost asked her to repeat it. But he was certain he'd heard her correctly. "Who wants to know?"

"Your son. Now answer the question."

"Seven," he replied.

Without another word, she turned and left.

Elation had been his immediate reaction. The videotape had been a good sign of progress, but this question from Nick was the first real confirmation that his family was in contact with his kidnappers. All along, his biggest fear had been that his wife and children wouldn't know whether he was dead or alive, and that not knowing would make their lives an even worse hell than his.

As the morning passed, the elation gave way to more complicated emotions. His sister's drowning had always been a very private matter, one he'd never even mentioned to his son. It disturbed him to know that Nick was aware of it, and he worried what, exactly, Nick had been told about the whole horrible incident. His mother had her version. The coroner had another. For Matthew the worst version of all was his own. Because it was the truth, and he'd seen it with the eyes of a five-year-old boy.

It was raining again. Heavy drops pattered loudly atop his canvas tarp. The pattering was softer in the background, a soothing sound of a light shower on the jungle canopy. He stared off to the middle distance, letting his mind escape this place. Part of him resisted, but he needed to go back to that rainy morning in the Florida Keys almost fifty years ago . . .

"Run, Stacy, run!"

Matthew was struggling to get free, his drunken old man sprawled on the floor and pulling at his ankle. Out of the corner of his eye he saw his mother rising from behind the couch, her nose bloodied. She lunged forward and kicked his father in the groin.

He yelped, but it had worked. Matthew was suddenly free. His mother wrestled his old man down the way he'd seen her do it so many times before. She held him in a contorted hammerlock with his left arm behind his back. His right arm she pulled straight down, between his legs, and out the back side like an inverted tail. Anytime he squirmed, she tugged, and he felt it right where it hurt most.

"Go, kids!" she shouted.

Matthew froze. His mother was a small woman, and he knew she couldn't hold a man as big and drunk as his father for long.

"Mom, no!"

"I said, go!" she shouted.

"I'll kill you!" his father growled. "I'll kill every one of you bastards!"

"Take your sister and go!" his mother shouted.

"But, Mom!"

She locked eyes with her son, her face straining with intensity. "Listen to me, Matthew. Go right now! Go far away!"

He didn't want to leave her, but he never disobeyed her. He grabbed his sister by the arm, and together they ran out the door. They raced down the stairs, across the lawn, and into the street. They were sprinting at full speed in the rain, Matthew leading his sister by the hand. Stacy was still wearing nothing but the diaper her father had forced on her as punishment.

"Where are we going?" she shouted, her voice shaking as they ran.

"Away!" he shouted. "Mom said to go far away!"

They were huffing and nearly out of breath as they turned down the wet, sandy road that led to the shore. Stacy was about to collapse as they reached the water.

"Help me," said Matthew. He was pushing the little fishing boat into the water.

"What are you doing?"

"We have to go far away. Mom said far away!"

His feet sputtered in the sand. He pushed with all his strength, and finally the boat slid back into the water. The rain was falling harder.

"Get in!"

Stacy jumped into the seat up front. Matthew was in back, tugging at the starting cord on the little outboard motor.

"Do you know what you're doing?"

"Mom showed me." One more tug and the engine started. He turned the throttle and the little boat roared away from shore.

"Matthew, slow down!"

"We have to go far away! Mom said so!"

The engine whined, the stern went down, and the bow rose as the boat headed straight into the gulf. The waves were beginning to crash. The rain and salty sea-splash pelted their faces.

"Slow down!" she shouted.

Matthew couldn't hear her. The wind was blowing harder, the engine straining just inches from his little ears. All he could hear was his mother's order. *Go away! Go far away!*

A loud crack rocked the boat, and the sudden jolt sent him tumbling forward over the seats. Stacy screamed as she sailed over the bow and into the sea. The boat continued on its own till Matthew got his bearings and killed the motor. He was alone in the boat.

"Stacy!" he cried.

He tried to stand, but a large wave knocked him over. He grabbed the engine and scalded his hand, but it kept him from being tossed overboard. He glanced back and saw the buoy bouncing in the waves, and he realized that the boat had hit it at full speed.

"Stacy!"

The storm was intensifying. The waves were now whitecaps, splashing into the boat. The sky had gone from gray to black. Sheets of rain were practically coming sideways, propelled by a chilly north wind. He stood at the back of the boat, his eyes searching frantically for any sign of his sister on the choppy surface.

"Stacy, where are you!"

He waited anxiously for her to shout back. He heard nothing, saw only wind, waves, and rain, rain. More rain. Nothing but rain . . .

Matthew stared blankly into the jungle, numbed by his memories, chilled by the endless cold mountain rain. His face was soaked, partly from the leaky tarp, but mostly from the tears that thoughts of his painful past had unleashed.

Stacy's death had haunted him all his life. It had been an unspoken tension between him and his mother. Outwardly, she had always blamed her abusive husband. But another side had emerged with her Alzheimer's, her senseless but painful accusations that Matthew had killed his sister. He knew that it was the disease doing the talking, that she didn't really mean it. Still, one tragedy seemed to pile atop another in his life, all stemming from Stacy's drowning. It was his deep sense of guilt that had driven him to drink as a younger man, and it was the drinking that had led to the blowup with his own twelve-year-old son some fifteen years ago. One stupid fishing trip, way too much alcohol, and their relationship was changed forever.

He and Nick. Another tragedy at sea.

The wound on his head was throbbing again. He removed his soggy boot and rinsed the pus away with rainwater, wondering what his son would think of him now.

49

W e reached the Hotel Los Andes at ten minutes before three. No need to ask where the shared bathrooms were. I just followed my nose, literally.

The hotel was in the colonial barrio of La Candelaria, the oldest part of downtown Bogotá. The heart of the area was Plaza de Bolívar, the original town center. Though the square itself was surrounded mostly by government buildings and modern architecture, the neighborhood to the east retained many old houses from the Spanish era. Some were restored and brightly painted, others dilapidated and on the verge of falling down. Scores had been converted into budget hotels that were popular with foreign travelers. Hotel Los Andes was on the lowest end of the spectrum. It hadn't seen a coat of paint in decades, and chunks of stucco had fallen from the walls. The roof was sagging, and those windows that weren't boarded up were covered with rusty iron security bars. A handwritten sign on the door offered rooms for the Colombian equivalent of about three

American dollars a night. I didn't need to go inside to tell that it would have been a rip-off at any price.

We followed a narrow side street to the hotel's rear entrance. I carried the cash in a nylon backpack. Alex was at my side, armed with a concealed SIG-Sauer P 228. Muggings happened every day in this area, but Alex assured me that anyone who made a play for my backpack was in for a nine-millimeter surprise between the eyes.

"You nervous?" she asked.

"Should I be?"

"Just remember what I told you. There's nothing you can do here today that is going to get your father released. This is all about showing the kidnappers that we can follow instructions. No heroics. Just go inside, get the note, and do exactly what it tells you to do."

We stopped at the bathroom entrance. Behind us was the restaurant. Clanging kitchen noises filtered through the torn window screens. A sleeping drunk was on the doorstep, snoring. Sewage ran in a little stream from the bathroom to piles of garbage stacked high behind the restaurant. On a warm afternoon like this one, the mixture emitted a sweet, nauseating odor.

"If I don't come out in five minutes, come in and get me."

"I was going to give you two," she said.

"Thanks for the vote of confidence."

I clutched the sack of money and entered the men's room. As the door slapped shut behind me, the immediate assault on my senses nearly knocked me off my feet. The place smelled like an open sewer. Along one wall was a trough urinal. It was clogged with paper and the scummy yellow-brown runoff from toilets that had overflowed. The wet floor had the same disgusting brown tint of watery feces. The lone sink was cracked and rust-stained. The wall above it showed the painted outline of a mirror that had evidently been stolen. In the back were showers for hotel guests. To my shock, two were actually occupied.

I walked cautiously toward five dirty white stalls. The first one was empty. Behind the closed door of the second I could hear a man struggling, presumably with his bowels. I stopped at the open door to stall number three, the one Joaquín had designated for the drop-off. It had an old-fashioned toilet with a pull chain overhead. There was no toilet seat. The rim was splattered and filthy. Flies buzzed over the unflushed waste that had collected in the bowl.

One thought consumed me. *What in the hell am I doing here?* It made me realize, however, that I couldn't possibly imagine the conditions under which my father had been living. In accordance with the kidnappers' instructions, I closed the door and checked behind the tank.

There I found the envelope. I tore it open immediately. It was written in Spanish, but fortunately I could read my second language better than I could speak it.

"Stacy was seven years old when she drowned," it read.

I read that first proof-of-life sentence twice, almost in disbelief. This was for real, I realized. My father was alive. I continued to the next paragraph: "Slide the money under the divider to the stall on your left. Say nothing. Information about the release of Matthew Rey will arrive in ninety seconds. If you leave your stall before then, or if anyone follows the money, you will receive no further information."

To my left was stall number two, the same stall from which I'd heard noises on my way in. With a discreet glance I noticed a pair of feet beneath the divider. The groaner was here to take my money.

My mind raced with thoughts of who this person might be. Alex had told me that kidnappers used "mules" for transactions like these, neighborhood kids who would deliver drugs, pick up ransom money, or do just about anything else for a few pesos. They were extremely reliable. If they screwed up or tried to run off with the loot, their entire family would be slaughtered.

I held my backpack close to my chest, unable to move. I wanted to hop right over the flimsy partition that separated us and ask this stranger where my father was. But it would have been pointless. As Alex had said, the guy was surely a know-nothing mule.

I took a deep breath, leaned over, and slid the backpack underneath to the other stall. The stranger picked it up.

Instantly a wave of conflicting emotions ran through me, from hope that the money would keep my father alive to hatred of these bastards for all the grief they had caused. Somewhere in the mix was the visceral sensation that I'd just been robbed. Even though Alex had talked him down to a hundred thousand dollars, more than half of my entire net worth had just passed to a total stranger beneath the graffiti-covered walls of a bathroom stall.

Alone in the stench, I checked my watch and counted off the seconds until the promised arrival of further information. I heard the stranger's footsteps as he left, then the slamming of the bathroom door. Ninety seconds passed, and I heard nothing. I waited another fifteen and was beginning to feel scammed. I ran out of the stall and checked the one next to me. There was no sign of the stranger or of any forthcoming information. I raced outside and found Alex.

"Did you see him walk out?"

"Who?"

"The guy with my money."

"No one came out."

"I heard a door slam. There must be another door!"

"Nick, don't try to follow!"

"In ninety seconds we were supposed to receive information about the final exchange. There's no one here!"

I ran straight to the back. Sure enough, beyond the showers was another exit door. I opened it and froze, struck first by the noise and activity, struck second by the irony. I'd assumed that my money would be laundered. I'd had no idea that the Hotel Los Andes shared bathrooms with a busy Laundromat.

A minute later Alex was standing right behind me. "Just let him go."

"How perfect," I said cynically. "People come and go all day long with bundles in their arms. How would anyone know which one was walking out with my money in his basket?"

"I'm sure it's just a mule. There's no point in tailing him. In fact, if he delivers the money and says we tried to follow, that's bad news for your father. We might never do the real exchange."

"Joaquín promised that the note would have information about my dad's release. The note said to wait ninety seconds and it would be here. Those sons of bitches gave us nothing."

"I believe this is what you're looking for," she said, holding a yellow sheet of paper. "It was taped to the back of the door."

I couldn't believe I'd missed it. I grabbed it and started reading, but I wanted to know the bottom line faster than I could translate. "How much time did they give us to raise the money?"

She averted her eyes, a clear signal that the news was bad.

"A month?" I asked hopefully.

"A week," she replied.

"That's impossible. Short of walking into the corporate headquarters of Quality Insurance Company with a gun, I can't resolve a claim dispute and have three million dollars in a week."

"All the kidnappers know is that you have a policy worth three million dollars."

"Then we have to tell them that the insurance company has denied our coverage."

"They'll think we're stonewalling. Or, worse, they'll decide that your father isn't worth keeping alive."

"So what should we do?"

"Next Sunday they expect us to be atop Monser-rate for the next radio transmission. Maybe I should go alone and tell them you're working out a few details. Something minor but believable, so they don't get concerned. It might buy a little extra time."

"How long do you think you can string it out?"

"I wish I knew."

I sensed that she didn't like her answer any more than I did, but no one had a crystal ball. "God help us," was all I could say.

50

I n a city of eight million people, I felt completely alone.

It was well after midnight, and Alex had retired to the master bedroom more than an hour before. A cozy bed awaited me in the guest room. Though our return flight to Miami was just hours away, I couldn't possibly sleep. I sat in the living room at the open window, looking out onto a relatively quiet street below. A faint nightlight from the kitchen left me in dim solitude. Headlamps from the occasional passing car sent shadows dancing across the living room wall behind me. One by one the lights blinked off in the apartment buildings across the street. The minutes passed slowly, yet each time I checked my watch I got the same sinking feeling that time was running out.

I wondered how many others in Colombia were at that very moment living the same nightmare.

Sudden shouting from across the street jarred me. A man and woman in a second-floor apartment were arguing over something. On a balmy night with windows open, sound traveled freely. After several heated minutes, it ended with the loud slamming of a door. I watched from my window as the man angrily left the building, his footsteps clicking on the old cobblestones below.

"You still up?" asked Alex.

I turned to see her standing in the hallway. "I think the whole neighborhood is awake now."

She smiled a little, then crossed the room and sat in the white wicker armchair beside me, facing the window. She didn't wear pajamas. She was dressed in her preferred sleeping clothes, running shorts and a rather skimpy athletic top that was little more than a sports bra.

"Are you going to stay up all night?" she asked.

"Probably. I'm worried about this deadline. I almost wish you hadn't pushed Joaquín for a release date. Don't you think it would have been smarter to leave it vague till we had some hope of scraping the ransom money together?"

"I felt like I needed to push him today. We can't always appear to be stalling. If we do, that's dangerous for your dad."

I looked out the window into the night, neither agreeing nor disagreeing.

"Have you considered borrowing the money from Guillermo?" she asked.

"Are you serious?"

"I just wondered if you'd considered it, that's all."

"I don't see how I can. After today it's more clear than ever that someone told the kidnappers about Dad's insurance. If I had to guess who the rat was right now, I'd guess Guillermo."

"Then you should definitely ask him to front the ransom money. Play on his sense of guilt."

"I'm not following you."

"If Guillermo is behind this scheme, I firmly believe that he went into it thinking that the insurance company would simply cough up the money. Guillermo would take his cut, the kidnappers would get theirs, and your dad would come home safe and sound. It probably never occurred to him that the insurer would refuse to pay and that your father might be harmed."

"Then why wouldn't he just call the whole thing off and tell the kidnappers to let my father go?"

"Because he didn't team up with Moe, Larry, and Curly. I can tell from talking to this Joaquín that he's for real. One of his men even got killed pulling off the abduction in Cartagena. I hate to say it, but if somebody doesn't pay him . . . well, let's just say it wouldn't be good for your dad."

I appreciated her discretion, but I knew what she was saying. "So let's say I tell Guillermo that there's no insurance money and that Joaquín's going to kill my father. What really makes you think he'd suddenly develop a conscience and pay the ransom himself?"

"I don't know. Some people call it instinct. Others call it the hostage negotiator's time-honored WAG method."

"What's the WAG method?"

"Wild-Ass Guess."

Even as stressed as I was, I had to crack a little smile. "Got to respect your honesty, lady."

She returned the smile, though hers was even

weaker than mine. She seemed to sense that I didn't really want to talk about it anymore.

We sat in the dim glow of the city lights, saying nothing. Her feet were up on a coffee table, long bare legs bent at the knee. She'd probably considered her sleepwear more comfortable than sexy, but from my perspective it appeared to be both. Not that I intended to do anything about it.

Suddenly the street filled with the sound of an acoustic guitar. Alex rose and walked to the window. I joined her.

"He's back," I said. "It's that same guy who was arguing with his girlfriend."

He was sitting on the curb outside the woman's apartment, strumming his guitar beneath a streetlamp.

"He's serenading her," said Alex. "Men still do that here. I think that's so romantic."

Together we listened as he wailed about his broken *corazón* and *la mujer* with the dark brown eyes who was the lost love of his life. It was unusual by American standards, but when *la mujer* actually came to the window to listen, I found myself pulling for him.

"He plays a very good guitar," I said.

The beat picked up. He made a skillful transition from the sappy love song to a more vibrant Spanish guitar that reminded me of the Gipsy Kings, though the sound was less full with a one-man show. Still, he was giving it his all.

Alex started to move her hips to the music, then took my hand. "Here. I'll teach you to dance Colombian style."

"I really don't feel like dancing."

"No better reason *to* dance."

I thought for a moment. "Good point."

She pressed the palm of her right hand against the palm of my left. She took my other hand and placed it on her hip. I could feel the warmth of her skin and the rhythm of her movement. Instantly I was more connected to the music.

"Do you feel that?" she asked.

"How do you do that without even moving your feet?"

"Listen for the counterrhythm."

"What's a counterrhythm?"

She smirked. "You'd be pathetic if you weren't so cute. Follow my lead."

The guitar was booming in my head, I was trying so hard to concentrate. She moved one way, I moved opposite.

"Sorry."

"That's okay," she said.

We tried again, and this time I was with her. She counted the steps for me aloud, then pushed my hand more firmly into her hip, as if to help me feel the motion.

"You got it," she said, smiling.

We moved back and forth, side to side, hips moving, face-to-face. I crushed her foot once, but she just smiled and kept counting. After a full minute of no squished toes, her counting stopped.

"Look at you, you're dancing!"

"I think I do have it," I said.

Our guitar-playing friend was singing again, his voice stronger. The pace quickened, but I kept right up with it. Alex moved closer, shrinking the space between our bodies.

"You're pretty good for a gringo."

"Why do you say 'for a gringo'?"

"Because a Colombian man would never let me lead."

"I think you'd lead if you were dancing with Fred Astaire."

"Fred who?"

"He's a famous—"

She pinched my ribs, smiling. "I know who he is. *No se puede dar papaya*," she added, her favorite expression.

"Don't be so naive," I said, translating.

"That's right," she said softly. "I might just walk all over you."

The music stopped, but we didn't pull apart. We remained in our dance pose, her right hand in my left. Slowly her left hand slid from my hip toward my back, then up gently toward my shoulder blades. Instinctively I did the same to her, my fingers traveling from the gentle curve of her hip to the small of her back. Our bodies drew closer, so close that the space between us was almost gone. I tingled with the imagined feeling of her breasts pressed against me. Her breath caressed my neck as she looked up at me, *la mujer* with the dark brown eyes.

She moved her hand across my back, caressing me. Almost involuntarily I duplicated the light swirling motion across the warm, bare skin of her back. It was firm and very smooth, until the tips of my fingers found a slight ridge in the skin, then another ridge below it. Faded scars that I hadn't noticed before.

Now that my touch had discovered them, I could actually see them as I looked past her shoulder at the reflection of her back in the window behind her.

She stiffened in my arms, seeming to have sensed my discovery. "Do they frighten you?"

"What?" I said, playing dumb.

"You found my scars, no?"

"They're nothing, really."

"You're lying."

I counted five of them, each an inch long and about a quarter inch wide. They appeared to be the remnants of old wounds that had never been treated properly. "It looks like . . . you were stabbed."

"That's because I was."

She pulled away and stepped back, as if suddenly self-conscious.

"I'm sorry. I didn't mean to upset you."

"It's all right. It was a very long time ago. I was a sixteen-year-old girl."

"What happened?"

"I tried to quit FARC."

"They stab you for that?"

"It's a lifelong commitment. They don't like quitters."

I tried not to look stunned. "Isn't it dangerous for you to come back to Colombia?"

"For Sonia Bernal, yes, it would be very dangerous. If she were alive. But she was stabbed five times in the back and left for dead in a gutter at the side of the road outside Cali almost fifteen years ago."

"Sonia was your real name?"

"That was my FARC name. And to answer your question, none of that seems real to me anymore."

"I'm beginning to know how you feel."

She came toward me and patted me gently on the cheek, sort of symbolically slapping me out of my daze. "Don't worry. It only makes me tougher inside. More determined to get your father back. Good night, Nick."

I watched as she turned and headed back to her bedroom alone. I tried not to stare, but I was strangely fixated on the scars on her back.

It was wild to think of her as having been one of *them.*

For some reason I thought back to that first day we'd spent together in Bogotá, when she'd snapped at me for trying to inject even the slightest diversion into her scheduled itinerary. To prove her point, she'd angrily driven me up to the top of the hill to see the once-pleasant neighborhoods of northern Bogotá that crime had transformed into little fortresses. I'd wondered back then if her concern went beyond *my* safety. Even now I didn't know what to think, though one thing I was sure of.

I'd never known a woman like Alex.

51

Customs at Miami International Airport was a breeze. At least it was for Alex. She sailed through without a bag search. Apparently an unmarried white male in his late twenties who'd made two very short trips between Miami and Colombia in the last month set off all kinds of bells and whistles. My bags they wanted to see.

I told Alex to go on without me.

"You sure?"

"Yeah. We'll talk later."

She was gone just a second before the customs agents exposed to the world my dependency on American-made toilet paper. I stuffed my personal items back in the bag, closed it up, and was ready to move on.

"Would you mind coming with us, please?" asked the agent.

I took a half step back, surprised. The elderly couple behind me took about five steps back, as if to announce that they weren't traveling with me.

"What's this about?"

"We'd like to ask you some questions. Could you please step out of the line?"

At this point my lawyerly instincts were kicking in, but I didn't want to make a scene. "Sure," I said. I grabbed my bag and followed the agent through an exit designated for airport employees and law enforcement. The agent used his electronic passkey to get us through another set of secured doors. On the other side was FBI Agent Huitt.

"Long time no see, Nick," he said.

His sidekick was with him, the young female agent who rarely said anything but looked as if she could break me in two if she'd wanted to.

"Am I being detained?" I asked, knowing the legal significance of the word.

"Not at all," said Huitt. "Just want to ask you some questions. You're free to go if you don't want to talk."

"Then it was nice talking to you," I said. "See ya."

As I turned, he said, "Where'd you get the two hundred and four thousand dollars?"

I stopped, but I didn't answer. Two-oh-four was the exact amount we'd wire-transferred, even though we'd ended up paying only a hundred.

He said, "Your Miami bank filled out a suspicious-transaction report. You must have acted nervous when you went in to wire the money, Nick."

"It's my money. If I want to wire it to Bogotá and walk out of the bank with a suitcase full of cash, that's my business."

"Sure, so long as it really is your money. For your sake, I hope it didn't come from your father's partner."

The remark had me thinking of Alex's advice to borrow the full ransom from Guillermo. "It didn't come from him."

"I promised to get you and your entire family full immunity if you'd help me expose Guillermo Cruz for what he is. No way in hell the U.S. Attorney's going to go for that deal if you start spreading around dirty money."

"I pulled together every penny of that money with help from no one but my closest friends. I mortgaged my house, I—"

"Yeah, yeah. Spare me the sob story."

"Then spare me the grief. We don't need your immunity."

"Let me give you a little advice. You keep crawling around with snakes, you're going to get bitten. It happened to your old man, it can happen to you."

"What do you know about my father?"

He stepped closer and spoke in a low, threatening tone. "I know that kidnappings like this one are rarely a case of an innocent person being in the wrong place at the wrong time. I know that your father went down to Colombia with five Nicaraguans to buy three shrimp boats that I suspect haven't been used for shrimping in a very long time. I know all about the people he bought the boats from, and I know how vindictive they can be when someone double-crosses them in their particularly unseemly line of commerce. What do *you* know about your father, Nick?"

His words hung in the air, more an accusation than a question. I looked at him coldly and said, "Enough to know that you're totally full of shit."

I picked up my bag and walked out the door.

* * *

From the airport I drove straight downtown to the Miami-Dade County Courthouse. Though I'd refused to let him see it, Huitt had gotten to me. He made me realize that no matter how badly I needed the ransom, Guillermo really wasn't an option. I had to do everything possible to get the money out of Quality Insurance Company.

I reached the courthouse just a few minutes before the lunch hour, and I planted myself at the top of the tiered granite steps at the south entrance to the building. In the shadows of massive stone columns, I waited. Though she clearly hadn't remembered me, I'd second-chaired a weeklong trial in front of Judge Korvan about eight months earlier, which meant that I did little more than carry the trial bags back and forth from the courthouse to the offices of Cool Cash. If nothing else, the experience had taught me that Judge Korvan was a creature of habit when it came to the lunch hour. I knew she'd be passing by any minute on her way to the Boston Sub Shop.

"Judge Korvan," I called out.

She kept walking, donning her huge dark sunglasses. I followed her down the first tier of steps, calling her name once more. She slowed her pace but didn't stop.

"I'm Nick Rey," I said, walking alongside her.

"I know who you are."

We passed the hot dog cart on the street, then continued to the crosswalk. For an older woman, she walked at quite a clip.

"I have to talk to you, Judge."

"Is this what I think it's about?"

"My father's case against Quality Insurance."

"Then stop right there. You have a new judge."

"Are you aware that the case has been put on hold?"

"I have nothing to say about that."

The light changed, and we continued across busy Flagler Street.

"Do you think that's a fair result?"

"I've recused myself. It doesn't matter what I think."

"It matters to me."

"It's completely inappropriate for you to confront me this way."

"You're right, but I'm running out of options."

"Maybe I should report you to the Florida Bar, and we can see what they think."

"Maybe I should invite you to my father's funeral so that it's clear I don't care what they think."

She stopped cold on the sidewalk. "Did something happen?"

"It's about to. I have a week to raise three million dollars or they're going to kill him."

From the look on her face I could see that I'd pegged her correctly. She had a well-known reputation for fairness, and I'd sensed that she was a woman of compassion.

"I wish I could help you, but I can't."

"Why did you remove yourself from the case?"

"I can't tell you that."

"Judge, a man's life is at stake here."

Cars were passing in the street, a steady flow of pedestrians racing by us on the sidewalk. She seemed edgy. "This discussion should not be taking place."

"I know what the rules of ethics say."

"I'm not talking about the rules of ethics," she said in a hushed but urgent voice. "I'm telling you this for your own good and mine. This conversation should *not* be taking place."

Her tone chilled me. I thought I knew what she was telling me, but I wasn't sure. "Are you saying that you stepped down because—"

"Every judge has skeletons in her closet. They found mine."

I stood mute. She clearly had more of a conscience than I'd thought, and the shocking candor was perhaps her way of apologizing for having bailed out of my father's case.

She touched my hand and said, "Watch yourself, young man. Quality Insurance Company does not intend to lose this case."

With that she left me. She was well out of earshot by the time I uttered my reply.

"Neither do I," I said beneath my breath. I cut across Flagler Street to my Jeep.

52

Matthew got a new pair of boots. "Replacement" boots was a more apt description. They were better than the old ones, but definitely not new. He recognized them as the Swede's.

"What happened to Jan?" he asked the guerrilla. It was the fat guy with the tattoo on his face, *Cerdo*. "He's gone."

"Home?"

He smirked, then said with a chuckle, "Yeah, home. Now, let's go."

"Where to?"

"You'll see."

Matthew rose slowly. He didn't like the vibes, but he tried to be rational. They wouldn't have brought him a better pair of boots just to take him out and shoot him.

"Bring everything with you."

"Everything?"

"Are you deaf? Yes, everything."

Matthew pulled on the boots and buttoned his coat. It was a cold morning, so he was already wearing every stitch of clothing he owned. Two shirts, a pair of pants, a wool sweater, and a knit cap that one of the guerrillas had pitched aside because it was too full of holes. He also had two pairs of socks, one for his feet and one that served as mittens on really cold nights.

He looked around his sleep area beneath the canvas tarp, making a mental inventory of "everything." Beyond the clothes on his back, there wasn't much. He unfastened the tarp from the trees and shook out the water. He rolled his blanket inside and strapped the bundle to his back. He felt like a Great Depression–era hobo about to hop a train.

"Got it all?" asked the guerrilla.

"That's everything."

"Make sure. We're not coming back."

"What a pity," said Matthew.

Matthew's spot was down the hill from the guerrillas' main hut. He followed *Cerdo* up the path, then stopped short, startled by what sounded like machine-gun fire in the distance. It was faint, but he recognized the sounds from his tour in Vietnam.

"What's the shooting?"

"*Chulos*," he replied. That was the guerrillas' word for the Colombian army.

Was the army moving in for a rescue?

That had been Matthew's first thought, but his hope faded quickly. Rescue didn't seem possible. This place was too remote. It had to be just another skirmish in the decades-old war between the army and the leftist guerrillas. Or the guerrillas and the right-wing paramilitaries. Or the guerrillas and some group of Ecuadorian or Peruvian bandits. Or a turf

war between FARC and the ELN. Or right-wing
extremists dragging unarmed *campesinos* into the
street and murdering them in front of their families
just because they were *suspected* of being sympathetic to the guerrillas.

Out here, there were just so many ways to get
killed in the crossfire.

They reached the hut at the top of the hill. Matthew followed the guerrilla to the front, then stopped
short at the sight.

The camp had been completely transformed.
Joaquín and his men were standing to one side, guns
in hand and their packs strapped to their backs.
Several dozen other guerrillas—men and women
whom Matthew didn't recognize—had taken posi-
tions around the hut, including a long trench that
they'd dug and fortified with fallen trees. Near the
hut, guerrillas were rolling black ink onto their
weapons and striping their faces with black grease-
paint. Someone was anticipating some night fighting. From the dragon insignia on the fatigues,
Matthew recognized them as FARC.

"Sit here," said *Cerdo*.

Matthew quickly searched for the driest patch of
earth and seated himself in front of the hut, to the
right of the door.

"Matthew," someone whispered.

He peered around the corner of the hut and spotted Emilio, the Colombian prisoner, seated along
the side of the hut just a few feet away.

"What's going on?" asked Matthew.

"Army's getting close. FARC's gearing up for a
battle."

"I thought Joaquín wasn't part of FARC."

"He's not. They're kicking him out of their territory. FARC commanders put up with him so long as he was selling his kidnap victims to them. But he's been asking for too much money lately."

"Where are the other captives?"

"FARC took them."

"What?"

"I think it's like back rent. Joaquín's been a squatter on their turf, so they just took four of his prisoners. They let him keep two."

"Why us?"

"Just a guess on my part. Joaquín thinks I'm the least trouble. And you're worth the most money."

It sickened Matthew to think that things were so bad with Joaquín he almost wished he'd been sold to FARC.

"Up," said the guerrilla. It was a girl this time. *Cerdo* was gone. At gunpoint she marched Matthew and Emilio across the busy camp toward Joaquín and the rest of his band. Joaquín was in a serious-looking conversation with one of the FARC commanders. They were checking a map, apparently deciding on the best way out.

Matthew glanced back toward the hut. From about thirty meters away he caught sight of Nisho and the Colombian woman seated on the ground near the campfire. On the other side of the fire, closer to Matthew, *Cerdo* was talking with two FARC guerrillas. He was laughing and pointing back toward the women. Finally, he got down on his knees, hands together in the praying position, whining and begging in Spanish, *"Please, stop, you're hurting me!"*

The men all laughed, but *Cerdo* laughed hardest, and Matthew realized what was happening. He was recounting their rape of Nisho, as if telling the FARC boys what they had to look forward to.

Joaquín called his men together. He had his map, and he apparently had FARC's blessing on his way out. Turning over Nisho and the Colombian woman had guaranteed his right of passage.

"*Vamos*," said Joaquín. *Cerdo* came running along, his belly bouncing.

Matthew glanced back one last time at their camp, toward the two women prisoners. He thought of his own wife and daughter and felt an almost uncontrollable urge to grab a gun and do the right thing. But between Joaquín's group of bandits and the FARC guerrillas, he would have been killed before firing a single shot.

"*¡Te amo, Nishooooooo!*" shouted *Cerdo*. A chorus of laughter followed from Joaquín and the others who'd been at the river that day.

Filled with anger, Matthew forced himself to put one foot in front of the other as they marched down the side of the mountain. He didn't know where they were going, and it no longer mattered. At that moment he vowed that wherever they ended up, he'd seize the first opportunity. He'd kill Joaquín first, *Cerdo* second.

Whoever else he could take with him would just be gravy.

53

I'd wanted to sleep on things, but that night was fitful. I needed three million dollars. Time was short and options were limited. I could go the legal route and be stonewalled by the insurance company. Or I could ply quick and dirty money from Guillermo and worry about the consequences later. Problem was, Guillermo, too, had stonewalled me on my visit to Nicaragua.

By morning I'd settled on a new angle.

I knew from my visit to Nicaragua that Guillermo's wife spent six months a year in Palm Beach. According to Lindsey, that was the reason she hadn't known Guillermo was married. I wasn't sure I completely believed her on that, but he certainly could have led her to believe that he wasn't *happily* married. The important thing was that with just an introductory phone call from me that morning, Vivién Cruz had agreed to a noon meeting at the historic Breakers Hotel in Palm Beach.

"Mrs. Cruz?" I said, approaching her at poolside. She was reclining in a chaise longue, wearing a

bright yellow bathing suit that set off her dark suntan. The suit was cut high at the hips, giving her
shapely legs the illusion of even greater length. She
sat up and removed her designer sunglasses, revealing a face much younger than I'd expected. There
were a few telltale lines at the eyes, but it was still
clear that Guillermo had not married his high-school
sweetheart.

"My, don't you look like your father," she said,
smiling. "You must be Nick."

We shook hands, and she settled back into her
chaise. I sat in the deck chair facing her, the hotel in
the background. The Breakers was a beautiful old
hotel that evoked the grandeur and style of the Italian Renaissance, its impressive towers, ornamental
stonework, and iron balconies inspired by the Villa
Medici in Rome. The manicured croquet grounds
were adjacent to the pool, and the ocean was just a
short walk east, beyond the seawall. Aside from the
usual old money, it catered to a wealthy international
clientele—Arabs, Germans, and, evidently, pretty
wives of rich Nicaraguans.

"Something to drink?" she asked.

"No, I'm fine."

"I'd say you're extremely fine, but you still must
be thirsty." She signaled to the waitress, who headed
off to the bar for two of whatever Vivién had been
drinking.

The "extremely fine" remark seemed calculated
to rattle me, but I let it go. "I visited your husband
in Managua a couple of weeks ago."

"Oh, how's he doing?"

"You haven't talked to him in two weeks?"

She drew a deep breath, thinking. "Let me see . . . no. We've played message tag, but I don't think we've actually caught each other." She sipped the last of her drink. "Has he helped with your father?"

"At first he was a big help, especially on site in Cartagena right after the kidnapping. Less so as of late."

"I would have expected Guillermo to be right in the hunt."

"Honestly, I haven't asked him to do much."

"Don't be shy. I'm sure he'd be happy to do whatever you asked."

"I'm a little nervous about asking."

"Why?"

I paused, measuring my words. "I've had some discussions with the FBI. Seems the bureau doesn't have a very high opinion of your husband."

"No kidding."

The flip response took me by surprise. "Would you like to hear what they told me?"

"Why not? I suspect that's the reason you're here."

"They think he's sitting on a fortune in illegal money. From the looks of where you hang around on a typical weekday afternoon, I'm almost inclined to believe them."

"Don't be fooled. Guillermo's a cheapskate. I don't even have a membership here."

"Then how do you get in?"

She glanced at the muscular young lifeguard posted at the entrance to the pool area, then looked back at me. "Let's just say I give a great . . . back rub."

"That's probably more information than I needed."

She smiled, as if enjoying the shock value. "I'm not bragging. Just being honest."

"Being totally honest, what if I were to tell you that the FBI thinks your husband is hiding drug money to the tune of about ten million dollars?"

She laughed, as if it were ridiculous. "He's been dodging those accusations for years."

"I'm hoping they're just accusations."

"Guillermo came into a lot of land after the revolution. He also found himself in a nasty divorce with his first wife. Every time he sells a piece of real estate, she's supposed to get half. It's a game they play. He makes a sale, he won't give her the money, she calls her lawyer. Then the race is on. He starts moving the money around from company to company, from bank to bank, trying to hide it like . . . well, like a drug dealer. It usually ends with her going to the DEA or FBI, threatening him with trumped-up drug charges that never pan out."

The waitress brought our drinks. Gin and tonic with lemon. I sipped mine lightly, since it was a bit too early in the day for me.

"I'm surprised my dad would let him move that kind of money through the fishing company."

"Between you and me, he does it without your dad even knowing it. The plain fact is, your father is a minority shareholder. Guillermo can do whatever he wants."

"Just so long as whatever he wants doesn't include drug dealing."

"No way. He would never."

"But he would try to cheat his ex-wife out of the money she's legally entitled to."

"The woman's a bitch."

"She's also the mother of his eight-year-old son and six-year-old daughter, right?"

"What's your point?"

"I'm simply trying to get a feel for what he would or wouldn't do for money."

"Specifically, what?"

The question stuck in my throat, but at this stage of the game I couldn't be subtle. "Did you know that it was Guillermo who sent my father to Colombia?"

"No. But I don't see how that matters."

"This wasn't a random crime. The kidnappers knew that my father had kidnap-and-ransom insurance, and we think he was targeted for that reason."

"Are you asking me if my husband set up your father?"

"I'd love you to convince me that he didn't."

She took another one of those deep breaths that seemed to help her think. "Seems to me that the issue isn't whether Guillermo sent your father to Colombia. The key question is: Who knew that your father had insurance?"

"Are you saying that Guillermo didn't know?"

Her expression turned serious. "I'm telling you that he *did* know."

"How can you be sure?"

"I was sitting at the same table the day they discussed it."

"Where?

"Right here in Palm Beach. Back in August we met here for a Sunday brunch. Your poor mother had the worst morning sickness I've ever seen. On her third sprint to the bathroom I guessed she was pregnant. Your dad confirmed it but swore us to secrecy, since they hadn't even told you or Lindsey yet. Anyway, that's when Guillermo suggested he should look into kidnap-and-ransom insurance. A bit of friendly advice. A good thing for a new family man to have."

"You mean he bought insurance on Guillermo's recommendation?"

"Actually, your father said he already had it."

I did a double take. Technically, my father's telling anyone was enough to void the policy, but as a practical matter it seemed reasonable for Dad to have shared that information with his own partner. "Did he mention the amount of coverage?"

"A lot. Like three million."

I looked toward the pool, sorting things out in my own mind. "This doesn't exactly lower my suspicions about your husband."

"Did you expect me to lie for him, stand by my man?"

"Maybe."

"I'm through coming to his defense. I know he was sleeping with your sister."

My eyes shifted toward the lifeguard she'd pointed out earlier, the one who got the great "back rubs."

She said, "He's a symptom of my marital problems, not the cause. I was faithful to Guillermo."

I sensed genuine anger in her tone. I hadn't planned to be so blunt, but I saw an opportunity. "Do you think Guillermo set up my father?"

"We all have our theories about what happened."

"What's yours?"

"A married, fifty-year-old Casanova's obsession

with his business partner's twenty-something-year-old daughter. Two people were standing in the way of their getting together. Guillermo sends me to Palm Beach and sends your father to Colombia. So long as the shops are open on Worth Avenue, he knows I won't be headed back to Nicaragua anytime soon. Getting rid of your father was a little more complicated."

"I've talked to Lindsey. I think you're reading way too much into her and Guillermo."

"Are you sure?" she said, challenging me.

I looked her in the eye but didn't answer. She smiled thinly, seemingly satisfied that she'd made her point.

"Neither of us can be sure of anything, can we, Nick? We weren't there."

I was staring blankly, not really watching as she applied more suntan lotion to her thighs. "I suppose not," I replied.

She capped the tube of lotion and said, "Anything else I can help you with, honey?"

"Not unless you have three million dollars you can loan me."

She leaned back and closed her eyes to the burning sun. "You're so funny."

"Yeah," I said with a sardonic smile. "I kill myself."

54

"You and Alex shared the same apartment?" asked Jenna.

We were having dinner together, our first opportunity to regroup since my return from Colombia. Over a glass of red wine and an appetizer of steamed mussels, I'd told her all about the trip, and she'd asked intelligent questions. This last one had seemed to leap from her lips, as if she'd finally figured out the sleeping arrangements.

"It's a big place, owned by one of her friends," I said. "Alex had one room, I had another."

"You don't have to explain."

"I feel like I do. You asked."

"I'm sorry, I shouldn't have. I'm your co-counsel, not your . . . whatever."

The waitress brought us more baguettes, then smiled and said something in French as she left. Le Bouchon in Coconut Grove was one of my favorite bistros. It was a cozy place with wooden tables and chairs, Tour de France posters on the walls, and tasty French food at prices that even a guy who was hard up for three million dollars could afford.

"Does she ever ask about me?" asked Jenna.

"Who, Alex?"

"Yes. She must think it's strange, your ex-fiancée helping you."

"Mmm. She's never really said anything."

Jenna smiled knowingly. "You're such a bad liar."

I smiled back. "Okay, it might have come up."

"What's her take on it?"

I sipped my wine, tore off a piece of bread, brushed the crumbs away. Basically I was stalling, wondering how she'd feel if I were to tell her that Alex's first take on Jenna and me was that I'd never really loved her.

"She definitely had the wrong idea about us at first," I said vaguely, knowing how completely wrong Alex had been. "But she has a much better understanding now."

"What does that mean?"

"She thinks it takes a pretty special person to step up and help me the way you have. And so do I."

Our eyes locked for a moment, then a moment longer. It had been months since I'd looked so deeply inside her. It could have been awkward, but it wasn't.

The waitress politely interrupted and took our plates. Jenna looked away, and by the time the waitress had left, so had the moment.

"Tell me about Guillermo's wife," she said.

"Uh, sure," I said, stumbling as I shifted gears. Once I'd refocused, it took only a few minutes to fill her in.

When I'd finished, she asked, "Are you going to go after him?"

"How do you mean?"

"You were suspicious of Guillermo before you met his wife. The only missing piece in the puzzle was whether Guillermo knew for a fact that your father had kidnap-and-ransom insurance when he sent him on that trip to Colombia. Now you know."

"It still bothers me that in court the insurance company pointed the finger at Lindsey, not Guillermo."

"Maybe they suspect a lovers' pact. Daddy didn't approve of the May-December romance, so they got rid of Daddy. While they were at it, they split a three-million-dollar insurance policy with the thugs they hired to kidnap him."

"There's no way Lindsey did that."

She took a little more wine, then said, "If you're sure of that, then maybe you'll like my new idea."

"What is it?"

"First you have to tell me that you're sure about Lindsey. Because if we go this route and it turns out your sister isn't squeaky clean, you could end up sending her to jail for a very long time."

"I'm as sure as I can be. And I hate to say it, but if I'm wrong, I guess Lindsay deserves what she gets."

She leaned into the table, seemingly excited about her pitch. "Tell the government to forget about the immunity that Agent Huitt has been offering you in exchange for incriminating information on Guillermo. Tell them you want reward money."

"What kind of reward?"

"I did some research while you were in Colombia. The Diplomatic Security Service oversees a reward program for informants who come forward with information against international terrorists. Kidnappers are considered terrorists. If Guillermo set up your father, he's a coconspirator, a terrorist in his own right."

"Sounds interesting in theory. But we're pretty pressed for time."

"They might bite fast. The FBI sure seems eager to nail him on something. Terrorism is a lot juicier than just another drug-smuggling case."

"Except that our pitch still has holes in it."

"Such as?"

"Start at the top," I said. "As far as we can prove, the only talk Guillermo and my father ever had about kidnap-and-ransom insurance was at the brunch where Guillermo's wife figured out that my mother was pregnant. That was back in August."

"So?"

"These policies are country-specific. The trip to Colombia wasn't even on the map back then."

"The original policy didn't cover Colombia?"

"Heck no. You don't buy coverage for Colombia unless you know for certain that you're going there. It jerks the price way up."

"Then how did your dad get coverage for Colombia?"

"That came later. The insurance company issued a Colombia rider before the trip."

"Couldn't Guillermo have been in on that?"

"We can't prove that he was. The policy was issued to my dad, not the company. The only thing we can prove is that two people knew about the extension of coverage to Colombia—my dad and the insurance company."

My words hung in the air. We looked at each other, Jenna seeming to read my mind.

"Maybe that's enough," she said.

"Does it make sense?"

"Think it through. Why would an insurance company tip off rebels to kidnap one of its own policyholders?"

"It wouldn't. But a renegade employee might."

She smiled, the proverbial light seeming to go on. "That would certainly give Quality Insurance Company something to hide. Which would explain their scorched-earth litigation tactics."

I felt the excitement between us, but it was checked by the daunting reality that we both fully appreciated as lawyers.

"The question is, how do we prove it?"

55

I called Duncan Fitz in the morning, repeatedly. Each time his secretary insisted that he was "unavailable."

I knew that Beverly was simply running interference. She had a reputation for being difficult, but this was the same considerate woman who'd literally run me down in the halls of Cool Cash to warn me that she'd "seen the memos" and that I'd better be careful in my ill-fated meeting with Duncan and the henchmen from New York.

"I don't want to get you in trouble," I said finally. "But if Duncan won't take my phone calls, then let's assume that I don't want to speak to him either. Hypothetically speaking, is there any place I shouldn't go today, just to make sure we don't run into each other by accident?"

She paused. I crossed my fingers and hoped that God would reward me for those late work nights with Beverly when I'd smiled and listened politely as she droned on about all nine lives of all seven cats with whom she shared her one-bedroom apartment.

"Well, hypothetically," she said.

"Yes?" I encouraged.

"I suppose you shouldn't go anywhere near the inner loop of the People Mover before his three o'clock hearing in federal court. If you were to bump into him on the tram, you'd be trapped and couldn't get away. Wouldn't that be awful?"

"Horrible. Thanks for the warning."

"You bet," she said, then hung up.

From two o'clock on, I perched myself on the elevated platform at the Brickell Station. With the water table so close to the surface, the city of Miami has no subway, just rubber-tired trams that run on cement tracks elevated anywhere from two to ten stories above the city. I stood to one side of the platform, behind the elevators, watching the trains leave every few minutes. Finally I spotted Duncan climbing the escalator, toting his own briefcase for a change. The tram had stopped momentarily for loading and unloading, both sets of doors open. He entered at the set farthest away from me. I waited until the chime sounded, then hurried out from behind my hiding spot and jumped aboard. The final chime sounded, the doors closed, and the tram left the station. Duncan and I were alone in front.

"Hello," I said.

He seemed surprised but handled it with his usual aplomb. "Mr. Rey, how are you?"

After working side by side for over a year, we were now on a last-name basis. "I spoke to Judge Korvan yesterday. She tells me that she was blackmailed off the case."

"That's absurd."

"It's true. She said it herself."

"I'm not in the business of blackmail."

"I'm sure you're not. But your client would do it behind your back. Quality Insurance Company has something to hide."

"Your family defrauded my client. End of story."

"No, that's *their* story. Ask your client how they got the case taken away from Judge Korvan and re-assigned to a judge who sits in your hip pocket. The answer isn't dumb luck."

"Cases get reassigned every day."

"Not the way this one was."

"Look, I've been doing this law thing a little longer than you, junior. Don't tell me how to represent my client."

"Duncan, I wouldn't have this conversation if I didn't know you to have a conscience. All I'm asking is that you do the right thing and ask your client the hard questions. It's no less than you would have expected from me as your protégé."

He stared out the window of the moving tram, silent. For an instant I thought I was getting through to him, but slowly his disposition changed.

"You're the one who should be asking himself the hard questions. I've heard plenty from the FBI. Now, stop following me around on trains. Or I'll tell Agent Huitt to add stalking to your list of indictable crimes."

His mind had been poisoned, clearly. It would have been futile to argue my innocence, but I was too angry not to say what I really thought of him.

"Gilbert Jones killed himself, you know that?"

"Who?"

"The overweight cop, the last case we worked on together. After you made him gamble away his settlement money playing 'Let's Make a Deal,' he couldn't look at his children. He went home that night and turned off his oxygen."

"How do you know that?"

"I guess you either know these things or you don't. Like the first hearing you ever sent me to, when I refused to go into court and argue that one of your other insurance companies didn't have to pay fifty bucks a week for 'respiratory therapy' because it technically wasn't 'physical therapy.' Would that have been a victory in your book, keeping a twelve-year-old kid with cystic fibrosis from loosening the phlegm in her lungs so she could breathe?"

"You're making this personal. And you're going to regret it."

"It already is personal. And my only regret is that it took my father's kidnapping to open my eyes."

The chime sounded and the tram doors opened. Even though we were five stops away from the courthouse, Duncan started for the platform. On his way out he glared at me and said, "This was low. Even for you."

He stepped off, the doors closed, and the tram pulled away from the station.

It had actually felt good to air my true feelings, not just about the kidnapping but about the kind of lawyer Duncan had tried to mold me into. But watching him through the window as he hurried down the steps to street level, my heart sank with the fear that another precious door had just closed on my father. For good.

56

·

$\mathbf{M}$atthew had no idea where he was. Without the benefit of pack mules they'd marched deep into the valley. At the first sighting of a real road, the prisoners were blindfolded, first Emilio and then Matthew.

They walked about another hundred meters, the barrel of the rifle poking him in the back, urging him forward. They stopped on command. He heard a car door open, and he was shoved into the back of a van. He heard Emilio bang his head and curse, which strangely comforted Matthew. At least he knew he wasn't going alone. The door slammed, the engine started. The van pulled away, a very bumpy ride at first, then a little smoother. It felt like the same road that they'd taken from Cartagena when this whole nightmare had started, but with the blindfold he had no way of knowing.

"Emilio?" he whispered.

"*¡Silencio!*" said the driver.

He recognized the voice as Joaquín's. Matthew retreated into darkness, strangely deprived of more than just his sight by the thick blindfold. Bouncing in the rear of the van had put his entire equilibrium off.

He lay on his side on the metal floor, the tires of the van whining just below his ear. Seated in front were at least two guerrillas. Matthew sensed the presence of others, but he'd heard only two voices. The driver was definitely Joaquín, and he was pretty sure the other guy was *Cerdo*. He was complaining that his new street clothes were too tight, but Matthew's mind had already raced beyond the petty gripes. If they were wearing new clothes, they were leaving their guerrilla fatigues behind. Matthew knew what that meant.

They were headed for the city.

He tried not to start the emotional roller coaster, but his spirits soared anyway. A trip to the city could certainly be a sign that his release was in the works. The blackness behind the blindfold was suddenly a happy place. He saw Cathy's smiling face, his hand on her pregnant belly. He saw Thanksgiving dinner in Coral Gables with Nick and Lindsey at the table. He saw hot showers and razor blades and juicy sirloin steaks.

He didn't care if silence was the rule. He needed to ask a question.

"*¿Adónde vamos?*" Where are we going?

"*¡Silencio!*" shouted Joaquín.

It was risky to act up, but Matthew was tired of the abuse, tired of knowing nothing. "*¿Adónde vamos?*" he asked once more.

The other guy, *Cerdo*, said something that made

Joaquín laugh. Matthew didn't understand what he'd said.

"*¿Dónde?*" he said.

Neither one answered. Joaquín was still chuckling softly to himself. Finally Matthew heard a whisper from Emilio in English.

"He says we're headed for the hostage hotel."

Matthew retreated into dark silence. Somehow it hadn't struck him as all that funny.

57

Dinner was at Mom's house. I worried about her a lot lately, and tonight's dinner only heightened my concerns. Since the kidnapping we'd made it a practice to eat only in the kitchen, never in the dining room where she and Dad had normally shared dinner. Tonight, however, without explanation, she methodically set three places at the dining table. One for her. One for me. And one for Dad.

I sat across the table from Mom eating my beef Stroganoff in silence, trapped by fear. It might have helped to talk things out, but I didn't want to risk showing Mom how worried I was. Alex and I were supposed to deliver the ransom in a matter of days, and I still had no idea where the money would come from.

"Dinner was delicious," I said as I planted a kiss on her forehead.

"My obstetrician says I'm not gaining enough weight. I make the most fattening food in my cookbook, and I'm still the skinniest pregnant woman in his office."

"That's because you've hardly touched your food. Please, try to eat something."

Her eyes drifted toward the living room in an empty gaze.

I took my plate to the kitchen, then came back to the table and reached for the clean plate at Dad's chair.

"No," she said sharply. "That stays until your father walks through that door."

I backed off. Whatever helped her to get from one day to the next was healthy in the big picture, I supposed.

"Have you talked to Grandma this week?" I asked.

"I saw her on Monday. She's slipping more and more each day. I doubt she'll know her son when he returns."

"I know about that," I said, thinking of the way she'd booted me out twice. "It's good that you visit her. Maybe it will keep some spark alive somewhere inside her."

"I hate the way she talks about your father. He was such a good son to her, and she somehow has it in her head that he's good for nothing."

"Alzheimer's can make people say horrible things. Things they don't mean."

"I know. I went through a little bit of the same thing with your father when he used to drink. Every now and then I used to wonder if the disease was making him say things he didn't mean. Or if it was unleashing his true feelings. Is that silly?"

"Totally," I said as I squeezed her hand in mine.

"I shouldn't even be thinking of that. Every day

since your father has been gone, I've tried to remember the good times. But tragedy has a way of bringing back the bad times as well. Is it that way for you, too?"

I could see the pain in her eyes. I moved closer, held her in my arms. "Try to think of what's good," I said, hoping that she wouldn't notice the way I hadn't really answered her question.

I felt like a hypocrite. There I was, telling Mom to think only good thoughts, when for fifteen years I hadn't been able to purge my own heart.

Ironically, the physical separation caused by the kidnapping had made me realize how stupid I'd been to let things fester all these years. The emotional gap between my father and me wasn't exactly oceans wide, but it was definitely born of the sea. Dad had always taught me to respect the ocean, but he'd pushed me to conquer all fears of it as well. Perhaps it was somehow connected to the loss of his sister in that boating accident, which I'd known nothing about until Jenna had told me just a couple of weeks before. Whatever the root, it had always seemed somewhat irrational to me. When he drank, it could get downright ugly.

Alone in the family room, I felt my mind drifting, but I didn't want to go there. I had to follow my own advice and think only of the good times.

I grabbed the remote control and started to channel-surf, lying on the couch. A hundred stations of nothing to watch, as usual. I switched off the set, and my gaze drifted toward my father's big saltwater aquarium across the room. The angelfish were fighting as always, chasing each other around the submerged plastic shipwreck at the bottom. As a child I used to imagine myself diving around that wreck and pulling up treasure. I could see myself in mask and fins knifing through the depths, the world's greatest diver who didn't even use tanks. A diver was what I'd wanted to be—before my worst day ever with my father, our last on the water together. I was twelve years old. Dad and I had joined a group of other fathers and sons on a boating trip to Biscayne Bay, skindiving for lobsters. I tried never to think of that day, and I didn't want to think about it now. But I was getting lost in that aquarium, lost in my past . . .

Gulf stream waters felt warm all around me, caressing my skin, making me almost giddy. Though completely submerged, I could glance up and see the sun. So clear was the water that intermittent clouds were actually casting shadows across the bottom of the bay. I was skin diving at a depth of fifteen feet with a mask and snorkel, no scuba tanks, poking around some rocks.

Other boys around me were gathering lobsters into sacks. We'd come upon a huge colony. The floor was moving with crustaceans. I saw a big one scamper over a grassy hump, then behind some rocks. I swam right to the hole and reached inside.

Suddenly an eel lunged from a crevice. I immediately pulled back, but its powerful jaws locked on to my forearm. I struggled to get away, but the rear half of the eel was coiled around a large rock. My diving gloves extended up to my elbow, so the bite didn't break the skin. But the eel was too strong, and I couldn't shake free. I needed to surface for air, but it was holding me under. In my panic I was taking in water, a little at first, then huge mouthfuls.

My father swam over to help. He poked at the eel with a stick, but it only tightened its grip on my glove. My father grabbed a rock and hit it. Its tail uncoiled from the rock that had anchored it, but the snakelike head was still staring me in the face, locked to my arm. It was at least three feet long—monstrous to me. Dad grabbed the eel and me, pulling us up. We broke the surface, and I gasped for air. I wasn't even sure what was happening. My arm felt numb, but the eel was still with me. Dad pushed us to the dive platform at the stern, then climbed up and pushed us into the boat.

I was screaming, more shocked than in pain. The eel was flopping on the deck, refusing to let go. My father was screaming, too—at me.

"I told you never to poke your hands in those rocks. Use a stick!"

"Get it off me!"

"If I hadn't been there to pull you up, you could have drowned!"

"I'm sorry!"

I just wanted this awful thing off me. Even as a boy, I knew that an eel would never let go. The only way to get free was to cut off its head.

"Cut it off!" I cried.

"You do it!"

Dad handed me the knife. But I was too afraid, too shaken.

"Do it, Nick!"

"I can't, I can't!"

He grimaced and grabbed the knife, shouting, "Damn it, Nick! For one lousy day in your life, can't you just *act* like your father's son!"

He lopped off the head. The long body fell limp to the deck.

I rolled away sobbing, more stunned by my father's words than by the bite of the eel. I was lying on the deck, holding my arm, my lips quivering. I'd have a bad bruise, for sure, but the diving glove had protected my skin.

I looked up and saw immediate contrition in my father's eyes. He knelt beside me and took me in his arms. Tears were streaming down his face. "God, I'm so sorry, Nicky!"

I could smell the liquor on him. I didn't know which to believe, the outburst against me or the tearful apology. But it was too late for forgiveness anyway. I looked up and saw the stunned faces aboard the boat that had anchored beside us.

I'd been utterly emasculated in front of my five closest friends and their very sober fathers . . .

The chiming clock on the wall roused me from my memories. It was 9:00 P.M., and time was marching toward a deadline we might not be able to meet. But mercifully, time also had a way of healing. I had long ago gotten over the embarrassment of that diving trip, and Dad had won his battle with alcoholism. What had yet to be laid to rest, however, was the underlying fear that Mom had verbalized earlier tonight—that his drinking had perhaps unleashed his true, inner feelings. In all honesty, I didn't always act like my father's son. But I was still his son, always would be.

I vowed that when he came home—just as soon as he walked through the front door and sat down for dinner at the place Mom had set for him—I'd say those exact words to him.

Finally we'd be past it.

"Nick!" my mother called.

I shot bolt upright. It was almost eleven, and I'd dozed off on the couch.

"Come here!"

The urgency in her voice propelled me down the hall. I found her in the living room holding an envelope.

"I just took out the garbage and saw this tucked under your wiper blade."

It was a plain white envelope, no addressee, no return address, no markings of an international courier service. It was unlike any of the past deliveries from the kidnappers.

I opened it. Inside was a single sheet of paper.

"What is it?" asked Mom.

I read it, but the point didn't register. "Just a guy's name and address. Jaime Ochoa."

"Sounds Hispanic. You think he works for the kidnappers?"

I started to answer, then stopped. The name was suddenly familiar to me. I checked the back side. "Oh, my God."

"What?"

"I don't think Mr. Ochoa works for the kidnappers. Check this out."

She read aloud. " 'Nick. Ask why he got fired.

A friend.'" She looked up at me and asked, "Who's 'a friend'?"

It was just a guess, but the only person who came to mind was Duncan's secretary. I smiled thinly and said, "Thank you, Beverly."

Part Four

58

I was in Hialeah before the morning rush hour. I hadn't bothered with a phone call before starting out on the road. From what I remembered of my last meeting with Jaime Ochoa, hitting him cold was the way to go.

The note was cryptic, but it was just enough to set my thoughts in motion. Jaime was the so-called psychic who'd sent me the e-mail a little more than a week after my father's kidnapping, claiming to know his whereabouts. I'd thought it was a total scam. With this latest note, however, I had a compelling sense that Jaime really did know something and that his knowledge was linked to the vague question of "why he got fired."

I knocked twice before he came to the door dressed in shorts and a T-shirt, no shoes.

"Hey, Mr. Nick, I knew you'd be back."

A predictable greeting from a guy who'd claimed to "know" everything. "I wanted to follow up on some things. Got a few minutes?"

"Sure." He opened the door and led me back to

the kitchen. I entered carefully, checking for that Doberman pinscher that had pinned me against the wall last time. I heard barking outside, looked out the window, and was relieved to see Sergeant chained to the doghouse.

Jaime went to the espresso machine on the Formica counter and measured out a scoop of ground Pilón. "Have you reconsidered my power package?"

"Let's not waste time with that psychic stuff again, all right?"

"I do know all."

"But not because you're psychic." I was pushing it, but I had to pretend to know more than I did. "It's from your other job, isn't it? The one you were fired from."

He placed his espresso cup beneath the drip and said, "Jaime Ochoa has never been fired from any job."

"I'm not talking about just any job," I said, still fishing.

"I know exactly what you're talking about. Jaime Ochoa never worked for Quality Insurance Company."

My heart raced. He was in denial, but at least he'd confirmed my suspicions that we were talking about Quality Insurance. "That's not what I hear," I said, bluffing.

"Then you heard wrong. Jaime Delpina was fired from Quality Insurance. Not Jaime Ochoa."

"Who's Jaime Delpina?"

The little espresso cup was full. He downed it in one swallow, then said, "Yours truly."

"You changed your name?"

"They made me change it."

"The company?"

"*Claro.*"

"Why would you let them do that?"

"Because they gave Jaime Delpina a choice. Go to jail or disappear."

"I'm pretty sure I know the reason, but you tell me. Why did they want you to disappear?"

He smiled thinly. "Sorry, my friend. For the rest of the story I must tap into my inner clairvoyance."

"Huh?"

"That's all you get for free, Jack," he said flatly.

"You expect me to pay *you* money?"

"Absolutely."

"That's extortion."

"It's just business."

"Not when the business is kidnapping. Maybe I'll call the state attorney and see what she thinks it is."

"You'd be a fool to do that."

"Watch me." I started for the door.

"Hold it."

I stopped.

He said, "Let's be reasonable about this. The policy limit is three million dollars. You'll probably deliver the ransom by pack mule through two or three intermediaries. Do you honestly think the kidnappers will even notice that you slipped a little something to me?"

"You've seen the policy, haven't you? That's how you know it's three million."

"I told you, I know all."

"And you're going to tell all, too."

"Surely, for fifty thousand dollars, cash."

"I don't have to pay you fifty cents. I'll subpoena you."

"And I'll forget everything I know."

With that, something snapped inside me. I was tired of being extorted by kidnappers and scumbags like Jaime. I started toward him and said, "Maybe I'll just beat it out of you."

"Bad move," he said as he grabbed a big kitchen knife from the counter.

I stopped cold, then took a step back. "Take it easy, pal. I wasn't serious."

"You looked serious."

"There's no need for a knife."

"I don't see any other way to keep you from walking out that door."

"Just let me pass, all right?"

"Can't let you go to no state attorney. I changed my name to stay out of prison."

"No one's talking about prison."

"I seen what they did to my brother in his cell. Guys like us don't do well in prison. Somebody's boy."

"You don't have to explain. Just put the knife down."

He was grimacing, almost whining, slowly unraveling before my eyes. "Damn you. Why did you have to go and threaten me like that?"

"Let's forget it, okay?"

"A little money. That's all I wanted. Just a small percentage, and you turn around and threaten to put me in jail."

"Just put the knife down. I won't say anything to anyone."

He laughed mirthlessly. "You expect me to believe that?"

"I promise."

" '*Promise,*'" he said in a sissy voice, mocking me.

Slowly all traces of sarcasm drained from his expression. In his rage-filled eyes I could see that he felt abused, perhaps more by his former employer than by me. At that moment, however, I was the only target in front of him. In a weird way, he must have seen himself as the victim.

"Please, Jaime. Don't do something stupid."

"You're the stupid one."

He charged across the kitchen and came at me, leading with the knife. I dodged out of the way. He fell but sprang right back. I had my hands in front of my body defensively. A perverse smile came across his lips as he began to toy with me. We moved strategically in a circle, like two boxers looking for an opening. He kept lunging at me and pulling back, taunting.

Blood oozed from a cut over his right eye. He'd apparently injured himself in the initial fall. He wiped it away, then suddenly seemed to realize that the blood was his own.

"You son of a bitch!" he shouted as he lunged toward me, swinging wildly.

The knife cut through my shirtsleeve, and I felt the sharp metal against my skin. It was just a glancing blow, but it sparked my survival instincts. Somehow I found the strength and quickness to grab his arm. Locked together in a struggle for the knife, we whirled across the kitchen and slammed against the sink. I hammered his wrist against the basin, hard.

Once, then again. The third time I heard bones pop. He cried out in pain as the knife fell to the floor. He gouged my eye with one hand, but his injured limb was hanging limply. Still pinned against the sink, I grabbed the good arm and twisted it behind his back in a half nelson, then wheeled him around and shoved the broken hand down the opening to the garbage disposal.

He screamed as his knuckles met the sharp, still blades. I shoved even harder, jamming his hand deeper into the disposal. Finally he was in up to his elbow. His arm was stuck and he couldn't pull it out, not even after I let go. I kept his other arm locked behind his back as I reached for the switch.

"I'll turn it on!"

"No, not my hand!"

"Then talk!"

"Let me go, I'm begging you, man. I'm your friend."

The word "friend" made me think of the note. Maybe it hadn't come from Beverly. "Are you saying you're *a* friend?"

"I'm your only friend, man."

I wasn't sure what he was saying, but I wasn't backing down. The cut on my arm was throbbing and bleeding. He'd sliced it deeper than I'd thought. "Tell me what you know, or I swear I'll grind your fingers to the nub."

He grimaced, shaking his head defiantly. "No, no, man! Not for free!"

"Don't make me do this."

"Please!"

"You got till the count of three. One. Two—"

"Okay, okay," he said, his whole body shaking. "I'll tell you anything you want to know."

I took my hand off the switch and prepared to listen.

59

·

I had everything, but in effect I had nothing. That was the legal conclusion Jenna and I reached in her office that afternoon.

Jenna was seated behind her desk. I was in the silk wing chair facing her. She'd listened to my detailed recount of Jaime's confession without much apparent amazement, as his story jibed with our own theory: It was an inside job.

"We have the same problem we've always had," I said. "How do we prove it?"

"You think Jaime's long gone?"

"Absolutely. He was happy to sell me information on the sly, but he wasn't about to walk into a court-room and testify against Quality Insurance Company under any circumstances. He's terrified of them."

"The way they strong-armed Judge Korvan into recusing herself from our case, I guess he has good reason to be afraid."

"Even if I could somehow corral him, could you imagine the cross-examination?"

Jenna was right with me, breaking into role. "Mr. Ochoa, exactly how close did your hand come to being ground into a Quarter Pounder before you spit out the lies that Mr. Rey wanted to hear?"

Her saying it made me wince. "I wouldn't have actually done it, you know."

"Done what?"

"Flipped the switch."

"I wouldn't have blamed you. The creep handed your father over to kidnappers."

I stared out the window, thinking. Jenna said, "Have you thought about making good on your threat to Jaime? Why not go to the state attorney?"

"I need three million dollars by Sunday. Can you think of anything that would make a company circle the wagons and pay me nothing faster than the threat of a criminal investigation?"

"I suppose you're right."

I rose and started pacing across the Oriental rug. "There has to be something we can do."

"I don't know what, short of finding another witness."

I stopped. A wry smile came upon me as I looked at her and said, "Now *that* is a great idea."

60

Matthew smelled rum. He was in the slow, disorienting transition between dreams and the dark reality of life behind a blindfold, and he thought surely that his mind was playing tricks as he woke. His last cocktail had been more than fifteen years ago, but he could have sworn that a strong Cuba Libre was right beneath his nose.

He raised his head from the floor and sniffed the air. Giving up the sauce hadn't robbed him of his memory. The place definitely smelled of rum and Coke.

A screech pierced his darkness, the shrill sound of a chair sliding away from the table on a hard tile floor. He heard footsteps, and it finally registered that he was no longer in the van. He had no memory of being moved into a building, and he couldn't possibly have *slept* through that. The throbbing pain behind his eyes made him guess drugs.

As the footsteps drew closer, he instinctively raised his hands for protection. Chains rattled. The slack quickly disappeared, and metal handcuffs pinched his wrists. His wrists were cuffed in front of his body, rather than the more restrictive behind-the-back method. But the range of motion was still only about a foot.

"*Buenos días*." The slurred Spanish had sounded like bad Castilian, *Buenoth, díath*. The voice was definitely *Cerdo*'s, but the inescapable breath was Bacardi's. As hot as this room was, Matthew surmised that the sweat oozing from his captor was about eighty proof.

Matthew answered in Spanish. "Man, how much have you had to drink?"

"Enough to make me wish you were Nisho."

Just the smell of this pig had him pitying poor Nisho. *You're gonna wish you'd never laid a hand on her.*

"Where are we?"

"Can't tell you."

"How long was I asleep?"

"A while."

"How long do I have to wear this blindfold?"

"As long as I say."

As stupid as he was, *Cerdo* could handle questions with the skill of a politician. "Just take it off, would you? I already know what you look like."

"True," he said. *Cerdo*'s thick fingers fiddled with the knot behind Matthew's head. The blindfold fell from his face.

His eyelids fluttered in the sudden burst of light. The room was dimly lit, but the adjustment from total darkness came slowly. It seemed to take forever for him to focus, and even then he had to alternate eyes, closing one and then the other to alleviate the discomfort.

Images slowly began to materialize. He was on the floor, chained to the frame of a metal bed with a lumpy mattress and no linens. The small room had no other furniture and no window. The walls were filthy, paint peeling away, graffiti everywhere. He could only guess at the original color of the floors, they were so dirty. The only source of light was a low-wattage bulb hanging by a wire from the ceiling. The door was open, and in the hallway outside were a chair and a small table, *Cerdo*'s guard post.

His eyes turned back to his captor, settling on the hideous paisley-pattern tattoo that covered the left side of his face. This close, Matthew got a full appreciation of the tattoo's purpose. It did a fair job of hiding a ghastly scar that started at the corner of *Cerdo*'s mouth, curled back across the cheek, and then up over the ear. It looked as though, years ago, someone had tried to remove the skin from his skull with dull scissors.

"What are you looking at?"

Matthew rubbed his eyes. "Nothing. Takes a little getting used to the light, that's all."

"I could put the blindfold back on you."

"No, that's all right." He tried to hand it up, but with the chains he could only reach so far.

"Keep it," said *Cerdo*. "You may want it."

"For what?"

"When families don't pay, Joaquín always shoots his prisoners in the face. Seven, eight times. He never returns a handsome corpse."

Matthew had hoped that release was near, but now he feared a snag.

Cerdo shaped his hand into a pistol, aiming at

Matthew's nose. He made a clicking noise, as if to pull the trigger, then tossed the blindfold in the prisoner's lap. "Believe me, those last ten seconds, you'll beg for one of these."

Matthew was more sickened than afraid—to think that good lives had ended at the hands of this worthless thug.

Cerdo snatched back his gift and stuffed the rag in his pocket. "What the hell was I thinking? Joaquín doesn't allow blindfolds."

He laughed at his own joke as he crossed the room, then hit the light switch and closed the door on his way out.

Matthew sank low to the floor in total darkness. It was no better or worse than being blindfolded. The whole exchange had gained him nothing, save the unwelcome insight into how he might die.

61

It was almost 10:00 P.M., and Jenna was still at my place. We'd filed an action in federal court that afternoon. An emergency hearing was set for two o'clock tomorrow afternoon, and we'd been preparing all day, even working through dinner. It was a long shot, but it was clearly my last chance.

"Ouch," I said.

She was changing the bandage on my arm. Luckily I hadn't needed stitches, but the knife wound was pretty ugly. And sensitive.

"Double ouch," I said as she dabbed it with alcohol.

"Men are such wimps."

"Give me a break, I was stabbed."

"You were scratched. I've done more damage to myself with an eyelash curler." She reapplied the butterfly bandages. "There. All set."

I checked it out. "Nice work. Do you do back rubs?"

"I think you know everything I do and don't do."

It was one of those half-serious, half-flirtatious

remarks in her Kathleen Turner voice that I hadn't heard in a long time. It left me speechless.

"Sorry," she said. "I think that crossed the line."

"It's okay. I'm not really sure where the line is anymore." I sipped my beer. "You mind if I ask a personal question?"

"Depends on what it is."

I took another drink, a longer one this time. "Have you dated anyone—you know, since we broke up?"

She smiled coyly, as if she'd been expecting that question for some time. "Actually, no."

"Me neither."

She gave me a serious look. "I didn't see much point in getting to know anyone new here. I'm moving to Tampa."

"You're what?"

"I listed my town house a few weeks ago. As soon as it sells, I'll be moving back."

"Wow. That's . . . amazing."

"It's where I grew up. It still feels a little like home to me there."

"Sure."

"I talked to my partners. They're all for opening a Tampa office."

"Sounds like you have it all figured out."

"It just seemed like the right thing to do. At the time."

"Does it still seem like the right thing to do?"

She dropped her egg roll. Jenna was a natural with chopsticks, so my pointed question had made her nervous, clearly. "I don't know."

I wasn't sure where to go from there, but she didn't

seem comfortable with the direction so far. "So how much are you asking for the town house?"

"Why? You want to buy it?"

"No, but I don't want to see you get hurt in a fire sale. It's a really nice place."

"How much do you think I should ask for?"

"Just don't grab the first offer. It might mean having to stay here a little longer, but I'd hold out for maybe . . . six million."

"You," she said, smiling. She uncrossed her legs, rose from the floor and started clearing away the empty Chinese food cartons. I grabbed the empty bottles and followed her into the kitchen. The conversation seemed unfinished, but I sensed that she had enough on her mind already.

"Are you feeling any better about tomorrow's hearing?" I asked, shifting gears.

"Honestly? No. We're going to be bounced out of court so fast it's not funny."

"Just trust me, all right?"

The phone rang, which made me flinch. Lately every time it rang a part of me expected the worst. I placed the empty bottles in the recycling bin and grabbed the phone on the third ring.

"Hello?"

"Duncan Fitz here."

He said it as if he were the president of the United States. "Nick Rey over here," I replied with equal self-importance.

"What's this crap you served on my client this afternoon?"

"It's called a complaint and an emergency motion

to prevent Quality Insurance Company from intimidating witnesses."

"That's preposterous. My client has done nothing improper."

"Then you have nothing to worry about."

"Look, you can't just bounce around from state court to federal court."

"I didn't file in state court. You did. And that was nothing more than an action to enforce the confidentiality provisions of the agreement. That's over."

"We'll still oppose this."

"I'd expect no less from you. But once a federal judge hears our newly discovered evidence, we'll have a whole new ball game."

"What evidence?" he said, scoffing.

"You'll hear it all at tomorrow's hearing."

"Are you planning to call witnesses?"

"Just one."

"Who?"

"Me."

He laughed, then it faded. "You're not serious?"

"Here's your chance to tear me to shreds."

He paused, then said smugly, "I'll look forward to it. Forget what I said about opposing the hearing. This is going to be fun."

The line clicked, and he was gone.

"That's what you think," I said as I hung up the phone.

62

J enna and I reached the big center courtroom a few minutes before the scheduled two o'clock hearing. We were in the oldest section of the federal courthouse, which was also the most beautiful, done in the Mediterranean style with colorful frescoes on the arched walls and ceilings. The center courtroom had the largest area for public seating, big enough to accommodate events like the investiture of new judges or the trial of a Panamanian dictator. It was an impressive place, even for the most jaded of lawyers. Yet as I sat waiting at counsel's table with Jenna at my side, the cavernous surroundings made me feel even smaller in relation to Quality Insurance Company.

"You still worried?" I whispered.

"I told you from the beginning, you can't just take the stand and repeat everything Jaime Ochoa said to you. It's all hearsay. It won't come into evidence."

"Maybe Judge Weinstein will cut us some slack."

"Maybe she'll spit in my eye."

We heard a knock, and a side door opened.

"All rise!"

Jenna and I were immediately on our feet. Standing at the other table, farthest from the empty jury box, was Duncan Fitz. Beside him was the one lawyer at Cool Cash who seemed to hate me more than my old boss did—Maggie Johans.

The judge settled into her leather chair as the clerk called the case and announced, "The Honorable Judge Sylvia Weinstein presiding."

"Good afternoon," the judge said. "Please be seated."

She spoke without looking up from the open file before her, making eye contact with no one. I might have felt a little better had she glanced my way and conveyed just a hint of sincerity in her greeting, but it wasn't her style to buddy up to lawyers in any fashion. Judge Weinstein had a reputation for being a scholarly thinker and a sharp-tongued talker. I supposed that was a step up from state court, where we'd had to settle for spineless and corrupt.

Finally she peered out over the top of the gold-framed reading glasses that had slipped down to the tip of her nose.

"I've read the motion that is the subject of today's hearing," she said. "Witness intimidation is a serious charge. Frankly, there's virtually nothing in the filed papers to support it. I scheduled this emergency hearing only because of the immediate danger faced by Mr. Rey's father. While the court is sympathetic to his plight, the plaintiff had better have some evidence."

"We do," I said.

"Then call your witness."

Jenna rose slowly, as if she were headed for the gallows. She clearly didn't believe in the plan, and now that we were actually in the courtroom, neither did I. I realized that desperation had blinded me and that Jenna was right. No way could she put me on the witness stand and fight off Duncan's objections.

I stopped her with a gentle touch, then looked at the judge and said, "The plaintiff calls Maggie Johans."

"What?" said Duncan, rising.

Jenna shot me an equally surprised look.

Duncan said, "I spoke with Mr. Rey last night, and he told me that the only witness he and his girlfriend planned to call at this so-called hearing was himself."

"First of all, Ms. Davies is my co-counsel, and I would appreciate it if Mr. Fitz would show her the respect of not referring to her as my girlfriend."

"That was rather tacky," said the judge.

"I apologize, Your Honor."

"More important," I said, "had Mr. Fitz told me that Ms. Johans was planning to fly down from New York to be in the courtroom today, I would have told him differently."

The judge shrugged, nonchalant. "That's the way it goes, Mr. Fitz. I've seen lawyers pluck witnesses out of the balcony. It's the risk you run if you show up in the courthouse. I'm afraid we may have to put *your* girlfriend on the stand."

"But this is not an ordinary witness. Ms. Johans is a lawyer, and—"

Maggie tugged his sleeve, interrupting.

"Excuse me, Your Honor." Duncan stooped over to take her comment. Maggie cupped a hand to her mouth to prevent the judge from hearing, but she whispered loudly enough for me to overhear. I presumed it was intentional.

"How many jury trials has this kid had?"

I didn't hear Duncan's answer, but I did see the smile on Maggie's face.

He straightened up and said, "In the interest of bringing this hearing to a rapid conclusion, Ms. Johans will take the stand."

Maggie rose, stepped around the table, and shot one quick glance at me as she passed. It wasn't overdone, just a subtle signal that I couldn't get a thing out of her with a blowtorch.

"Swear the witness," the judge said.

Maggie raised her hand and recited the oath, placing particular emphasis on the words "the whole truth, and nothing but the truth." She'd said it with such genuine conviction. Liars always did.

I exchanged one last glance with Jenna. She whispered, "What are you going to do now?"

"Plan B."

"Which is?"

"It'll come to me."

The judge said, "Mr. Rey, please proceed."

I stepped toward the witness, stopping ten feet away from her icy stare. She stated her name, and I asked, "What position do you hold with Quality Insurance Company?"

"I'm general counsel."

"So you're an officer of the company?"

"Correct."

"And you're also a partner with the law firm of Cool Cash. I mean Coolidge, Harding and Cash, which serves as outside counsel to Quality Insurance Company."

"That's correct."

That was about as far as my prepared questions would take me. At that point there was nothing to do but go for the throat. "Have you ever heard the name Jaime Delpina?"

"Objection." Just the mention of the man's name had pushed Duncan's button.

The judge said, "Give the young man a chance, Mr. Fitz. Overruled."

"Yes," Maggie answered tentatively.

"He was an employee of Quality Insurance, correct?"

She glanced at Duncan, then answered, "That's correct."

"He was one of the people who processed my father's application for kidnap-and-ransom insurance, correct?"

"One of several, yes."

"How many of those several employees have had their employment terminated?" I said with just a touch of sarcasm.

"To my knowledge, only Mr. Delpina."

Duncan rose, "I don't see how any of this is relevant."

"You will," I said. "How many applications for kidnap-and-ransom insurance did Mr. Delpina process this year?"

"I don't know."

"More than fifty?"

"I don't have any idea."

"Come now," said the judge. "You must have some idea how many of these policies are written. Quality Insurance isn't exactly Lloyds of London."

"Fewer than fifty," she said.

"In fact, the exact number is thirty-one, isn't it?" Showing a command of the facts was a good way to control a witness—I'd learned that from Duncan.

She shifted uneasily and said, "That sounds right."

Duncan was again on his feet. "Your Honor, the witness shouldn't be forced to guess."

"Fair enough," said the judge. "Don't guess, Ms. Johans. But remember that you're under oath, and *I'm* the one who evaluates credibility here."

Maggie looked at the judge, then at me. "The answer is thirty-one."

"Isn't it also true that one of Mr. Delpina's policies resulted in a kidnapping for which the company denied coverage?"

"That's why we're here. That one isolated policy is your father's, which was denied on grounds of fraud."

"Am I also correct that Mr. Delpina's remaining policies have been sold to secondary insurers on the reinsurance market?" I had to hold my breath on this one. It was what Jaime had told me, but I wasn't sure what Maggie would say.

"That's true, but that's not uncommon."

"Just so we all understand, selling the policy to a secondary insurer shifts the risk of loss to the new insurer, correct?"

"Yes."

"So if those other policyholders are kidnapped,

the ransom won't be paid by Quality Insurance Company, will it?"

"That's the whole point of reinsurance."

"Let me put it another way. *When* those other policyholders are kidnapped, the ransoms won't be paid by your company."

"Objection."

"There's no jury here," said the judge. "Let's see how the witness handles the question."

"I'm not sure I understand it."

"I think you do. You know it's only a matter of time before others are kidnapped, just like my father."

"I have no such knowledge."

"I renew my objection," said Duncan. "These questions are simply wild accusations. There's no evidentiary foundation whatsoever."

"Mr. Rey, I'm trying to give you your day in court, but the man has a point. Why don't you move on to more solid ground?"

"Surely. Ms. Johans, is it fair to say that Quality Insurance treats information about kidnap-and-ransom insurance as highly confidential?"

"Absolutely."

"That's because a policyholder might become a kidnapping target if it were known that he had kidnap-and-ransom insurance, correct?"

"I don't believe that would ever happen. But that's the theoretical fear."

"So the company takes certain internal precautions to maintain a level of secrecy. For example, policies are coded so that names are not readily accessible."

"That's right."

"The policies themselves are kept in a locked vault."

"Yes."

"A limited number of employees are given access to the codes and policies."

"True."

"Jaime Delpina had access to the names, codes, and complete terms of all thirty-one policies we just mentioned, didn't he?"

She paused, again looking at Duncan. He started to rise, but the judge nipped the spurious objection in the bud. "Sorry," the judge said. "I didn't hear the witness's answer."

"Mr. Delpina had access," said Maggie.

"Do you know where Mr. Delpina is these days?"

"I have no idea."

"He no longer works for Quality, does he?"

"No."

"You terminated his employment."

"Yes. I believe it was an issue of habitual tardiness."

I couldn't stop myself from smirking. "Before he was dismissed for 'tardiness,' he found the time to process thirty-one kidnap-and-ransom policies."

"That was my testimony, yes."

"The dollar amount of coverage for ransom under your policies is typically in the millions, isn't it?"

"We don't write it for less than a million. On average, it's two to five."

"Theoretically, if all thirty-one policyholders were kidnapped, the company could be out as much as a hundred and fifty million dollars in ransom payments alone?"

"That would never happen."

"At least another ten million for investigator expenses."

"Like I said, that would never happen."

"You're right. I suppose it was more the bad publicity that worried you."

"Excuse me?"

"It wouldn't be good for business if word got out that one of your employees was selling the names of policyholders to would-be kidnappers."

"Objection."

"Overruled."

"But, Judge," said Duncan, groaning.

"The witness shall answer."

"No, it wouldn't be good for business. But that's not what happened here."

"Jaime Delpina was selling that information."

"Not true."

"That's why he was terminated."

"No. Tardiness."

"That's why you made him disappear."

"Objection!"

"Sustained."

"You denied my father's claim to hide your *own* fraud."

"Objection!"

"Mr. Rey, please."

"You knew that my father was just the beginning. You sold Jaime's other policies to get off the hook for thirty more disasters."

"Objection."

"Sustained!"

The judge banged the gavel, but I pushed on, louder. "You cheated my father, you defrauded other insurers, you allowed thirty people to wander the globe without bothering to tell them that their names have been sold to dangerous criminals. You covered up the whole thing to minimize your exposure and prevent a publicity nightmare that would have cost you millions!"

"Objection, objection! No foundation, no facts in evidence."

"That's enough!" the judge shouted. "Mr. Rey, I'm going to jump down there and tackle you if you take one step further without establishing some evidentiary basis for these questions."

I paused to collect myself. A tense silence filled the courtroom. "Your Honor, I'd like to give Mr. Fitz the opportunity to withdraw his objection."

"What?" he said, incredulous.

"If he doesn't, I'll be happy to call another witness who can lay the foundation for this entire line of questioning." I looked straight at my old boss and said, "I know where Jaime Delpina lives. Or should I say Jaime Ochoa."

He went white. Without words, Maggie seemed to be screaming for help from the witness stand. The name "Ochoa" was my trump card, my way of letting them know that I knew all about Mr. Delpina's newly assumed identity. I'd clearly played it right.

"Judge, I'd like a brief recess to confer with my client."

"She's in the middle of her testimony," the judge replied.

If I was going to get my money *today*, I had to let Duncan talk to Maggie. "I'll dismiss the witness, if I can have the right to recall her."

"Fine. We'll take five minutes," the judge said with a loud bang of the gavel.

The lawyers rose on command, and Judge Weinstein exited to her chambers.

Maggie stepped down and went straight to Duncan, seemingly ready to burst. Together they raced down the aisle to the rear exit. The big wooden doors slammed as they made their way out to the courtyard.

I nearly collapsed in the chair next to Jenna, my heart pounding.

"That was amazing," she said.

"You're not kidding."

"And you didn't even need any help from your girlfriend."

I did a double take, then realized that she was playing on Duncan's little jab at the beginning. "Oh, right."

The doors in the back of the courtroom creaked open. "Nick," Duncan shouted, his voice booming through the courtroom. "We need you."

Jenna and I hurried up the aisle, out the door. Maggie was pacing nervously in the courtyard, smoking a cigarette. She walked up to me and said, "I know you're bluffing."

"Do you?"

"You know there's no way Mr. Ochoa is going to walk into this courtroom."

"The question is, do *you* know that?"

Her eyes narrowed. She looked ready to hit me.

Duncan touched her shoulder, forcing her to step back.

"Let's keep our heads about this," he said. "I suggest that we all go back to the office and see if we can't work something out."

"No," I said.

Jenna gasped. Now I thought *she* was going to hit me.

"No?" said Duncan.

"I'm not going anywhere. If you want to settle, it's right here, right now. No more delays. No more stonewalling. Three million dollars, and not a penny less. Period."

Maggie's face reddened. The hatred for me was obvious, not for what I was doing now but for what I'd discovered—about her.

"All right," said Maggie, her eyes narrowing. "You can have three million. But that buys your silence. We sign a strict confidentiality agreement that prohibits you from breathing a word about this to the press, to the police, to anyone."

"No way on earth."

"No confidentiality, no money."

Part of me said take the money and ignore the agreement. But that would have made me no better than her. "I'm not signing any agreement. Three million dollars is what it takes to keep me from calling Jaime Ochoa to the witness stand right now and from calling every news station in Miami to come down here and listen to him."

She stared me down coldly, but I didn't flinch. "One point five million. No agreement of confidentiality. Take it, you cocky son of a bitch, before I change my mind." She stepped closer and said, "I swear, even if Jaime Ochoa does walk into that courtroom, we'll appeal. It'll be years before you get dime one to buy back your father."

It pained me to compromise, but at bottom I was bluffing about Ochoa's willingness to testify. And if I were to drag him here, his recollection of the garbage disposal surely wouldn't include the part where he pulled the knife. With a Sunday deadline, I didn't see a choice.

I looked her straight in the eye and said, "Deal."

She looked stunned, as if the last thing she'd expected was for me to leave money on the table today so that justice could be done later. But for no amount of cash could this company buy my eternal silence.

"Let's tell the judge," said Duncan. He pulled Maggie away. Side by side, they returned to the courtroom. Jenna and I followed. The bailiff went for the judge. In less than a minute she was back on the bench, all parties standing before her.

Duncan said, "Your honor, the parties have reached a settlement."

"Is that true, Mr. Rey?"

I had a moment's hesitation, imagining the look on Alex's face when I told her that we were short by a million and a half dollars. But I had to take what I could get. "Yes, Your Honor."

"Glad to hear it. File a notice of dismissal once you've finalized matters." She rose, then looked at me and said, "Good luck to your father. I mean that."

"We'll need it," I said quietly.

She banged her gavel and stepped down.

For a moment I couldn't move, paralyzed by my own mixed emotions. I was relieved finally to have *something* with which to bargain for my father's freedom. But I was so angry that I'd had to fight so hard to get less than everything from the very bastards who'd gotten him kidnapped.

Jenna touched my hand, as if sensing my ambivalence. "Come on, Nick."

I followed her back to our table to collect our briefcases. I felt as though I were moving in slow motion. Finally Duncan crossed to our side of the courtroom and handed me a yellow sheet of legal paper that he'd folded into thirds.

"Here's a list of information we'll need from you to wire the funds," he said.

"I'm pretty familiar with what's necessary."

He pressed the paper into my hand. "In this case there are some special instructions."

I looked at him, puzzled. Without another word he turned and started down the center aisle with his client.

I had a sick feeling that he was up to his tricks. I quickly unfolded the note, dreading what I might read. Immediately I saw that it had nothing to do with wiring instructions. But it wasn't even close to what I'd feared.

It was a quote attributed to the centuries-old teachings of the Talmud. It read, "The duty of ransoming captives supersedes charity to the poor."

I faced the rear of the courtroom and caught sight of Duncan just as he was heading out the door. He glanced my way, pausing a moment till his eyes met mine. No words were exchanged. He simply gave a quick nod, then continued out behind his client.

"What was that all about?" asked Jenna.

"What?"

"That little thing between you and Duncan."

I tucked the note in my pocket. "I'm not sure."

I picked up my briefcase and started out, wondering if the note was simply Duncan's way of wishing me and my father well, no hard feelings.

Or was he trying to tell me that *he* was "A Friend"?

63

I drove straight from the courthouse to the FBI field office. All along I'd felt that if I had a friend at the FBI, it was Agent Nettles, the first agent who'd visited my mother after the kidnapping. Maybe I was kidding myself, maybe I just wanted to prove to the FBI that my family wasn't at all the way Agent Huitt had painted us. Whatever it was, I called Nettles on his cell phone to give him an inkling of my discovery.

Less than a minute after my arrival, Nettles and I were in the office of Raul Carreras, the assistant special agent in charge, the second-highest-ranking agent in the office. I had the distinct feeling that my case had been assigned a new level of priority. They listened, took notes, sipped coffee from big blue mugs emblazoned with the FBI shield. When I'd finished, the men exchanged glances.

Agent Carreras looked at me and said, "Explain to me again how Mr. Ochoa came to tell you all this."

It made me nervous, that being the first question.

"Like I said, I threatened to go to the state attorney. He pulled a knife. There was a skirmish and . . . well, I sort of forced it out of him."

"I don't understand. What do you mean 'forced'?"

"In the fight he broke his wrist."

"And then what? You threatened to break his other one if he didn't talk?"

"No. The wrist got caught up in the garbage disposal."

Carreras leaned back, stroking his mustache. "I'm having trouble visualizing. How does that happen?"

"I sort of forced it in."

"Did you turn it on?" he asked, grimacing.

I felt as if I were shrinking before their eyes. This was the cross-examination I'd feared, the reason I couldn't possibly have called Ochoa as a witness in my hearing. "I only threatened to turn it on."

Once again they exchanged glances. "I see," said Nettles.

Carreras leaned forward, elbows atop his desk. "Let me get this straight. Your evidence so far comes from a fired employee who promised to say bad things about his former employer if you would pay him fifty thousand dollars, and who ultimately ended up spilling his guts after you threatened to make his left hand suitable for Hamburger Helper."

"I'm not proud of the way this came to light. But it's not a case of a disgruntled former employee making up horrible stories about the company that fired him."

Nettles put his notepad aside and said, "We'll check it out."

"You *have* to check it out. There could be thirty other policyholders at risk if you don't."

"I said we would. We will."

"I'm not hearing much conviction in your voice."

"My apologies."

I came to the edge of my seat, moved by anger. "The FBI needs to understand, I took a million and a half dollars less in settlement money from these bastards so that I'd be free to talk to you. They were willing to pay me three million dollars to keep my mouth shut. Doesn't that tell you something? Every minute you delay gives them another minute to pressure Ochoa into shutting *his* mouth forever. You need to talk to him, you need to get the names of those other policyholders, and you need to warn them."

Carreras rose and extended his hand. "Thanks very much for the information. We'll take it from here."

We shook hands. "I'd like to know what happens. Will you keep me posted?"

"As best we can."

Nettles led me out of the office, down the hall, to the lobby. The elevator doors opened. He thanked me once more as I stepped inside. I stopped the doors from closing and said, "Please, you need to follow through on this."

"Like we said, we'll take it from here."

"You know, I wasn't kidding about what I said in there. It cost me a million and a half dollars to come here and talk to you. I wish I could say it felt worth it."

He said nothing as I allowed the elevator doors to close between us.

Mom had Jenna and me over for dinner. We ate outside at the round, glass-topped patio table by the pool. It had been intended as a celebration dinner of sorts, but no one was fooled into thinking it was time to celebrate yet. I wasn't sure what the FBI was up to, but I would have liked more assurances on the follow-through, just for the sake of the other policyholders who were potentially at risk.

We did have our money. The funds had been wired directly to the same Bogotá account we'd used for the last trip. Alex and I would withdraw the cash when we got there, and she'd again work her black market contacts to convert pesos to dollars. Funny, only a month ago the mere mention of a currency black market would have made me suspicious, but I now realized that it was just a fact of life in Colombia, and not just for the kidnapping trade. Thank goodness I had Alex, who was savvy enough to watch out for counterfeiters.

By eight o'clock Mom was finished with dinner and fed up with mosquitoes. She went inside. Jenna and I lit up a citronella candle and watched the moon rise.

"Thought any more about Duncan?" she asked.

"Only constantly."

"Still think he's 'A Friend'?"

"It's hard to imagine any lawyer doing that. Ethically you can't betray your own client, no matter how despicable they might be."

"A lawyer doesn't have to help a client commit murder. If those kidnappers kill your father, the blood is on the hands of the insurance company, if you ask me. Maybe Duncan sees it the same way."

"Maybe."

She sipped her chardonnay. "You think one and a half million will get your dad home?"

"Alex is pretty nervous."

"I didn't ask what Alex thought. What do you think?"

"If Alex is nervous, I'm nervous."

The sliding glass door opened behind us. I turned and saw Mom coming toward us, her head down.

"What's wrong?" I asked with concern.

She stopped at the edge of the swimming pool, then looked at me and said, "Guillermo said no."

"What?"

"I called him to ask if he could loan us the other half of the ransom demand." She was staring past me, a vague expression in her eyes. "Said he just can't do it."

Without another word, she retreated into the house.

Jenna said, "I'm sorry, Nick."

"I expected that. Guillermo's own wife told me he was a cheapskate."

"What are you going to do now?"

"The only thing we can do. We're going to get my father home for a million and a half."

She refilled her wineglass, no response.

I looked away, shaking my head. "This makes me sick."

"What?"

"Here I am, worrying that I settled too cheap.

Somewhere across town, I bet Maggie and Duncan are out celebrating this very minute. Another success story. Damage under control."

"So you don't think Duncan had his epiphany in the end?"

"That note he slipped me could have come from the heart or it could have been pure showmanship. You just never know with Duncan."

"If you're having doubts, you should follow your gut instinct."

"My gut tells me that someone needs to be punished for this."

"That's up to the FBI now."

"I just didn't get the feeling that they're going to run with it."

"Then before you go to Bogotá, call the state attorney."

"The problem is, the more agencies I get involved, the more likely it is to get in the news."

"Quality Insurance deserves all the bad publicity it gets."

"Of course I'd love to see the media rip these people to shreds—Ochoa and Maggie and whoever else had a hand in it. But it's not as simple as just calling a reporter. I'm seriously worried how my dad's kidnappers might react if they hear all about the unraveling of this scandal on CNN. Maybe these same thugs thought they were going to have two, three, five more victims sent their way. They won't be inclined to cut my father's ransom in half if they think he's the end of the gravy train."

"I'm not saying you should alert the media. Just go to the state attorney, ask her to please keep her investigation confidential until your father is released."

"Have you ever heard of that working?"

"I see your point."

"So what should I do?"

"Jaime Ochoa handled thirty policies besides your dad's. I'm not saying that thirty other people are going to end up kidnapped, or ten more, or one more. But do you want to leave that to chance?"

I looked at the moon and sighed. "I guess there's no reason to give the FBI an exclusive on this. I'll call the state attorney in the morning."

She reached across the table and took my hand. "That's the right decision."

I squeezed her hand and said, "It feels right."

"You should go with it, then. You should always go with what feels right."

Our eyes met, and I wasn't sure if she was trying to convey a double meaning, but her words, her touch, had definitely sparked me. For the first time since our breakup, something finally felt right to me. "Jenna, before I go to Bogotá again, there's something I've been wanting to say."

"What?"

She didn't pull her hand away, which warmed me inside. "You remember that day we went cycling in Kennedy Park, and you got mad about the way I reacted to the idea of us getting married?"

"Let's not go back there, please."

"I only wish you would believe that I'd already bought the ring. I didn't propose marriage just to keep you from leaving me."

"I know that."

"You know?"

"I don't *know*, but I believe you. The thing is, Nick, that wasn't our whole problem. It really came down to what each of us was willing to do to make this relationship work. I completely changed the direction of my own career to move to Miami with you. As soon as we got here, you basically gave me up for yours."

"That's the old Nick. Or more like the temporarily insane Nick. I wasn't that way in law school. We were great back then. Remember?"

"Yes, I do. That's why I came to Miami with you."

"I just got caught up in the whole Cool Cash mystique. For a while."

"And now the kidnapping has you feeling otherwise."

"It's not just that. It's the egos, the twisted values, the Gilbert Joneses of the world and 'Let's Make a Deal.'"

"Who?"

"All I'm trying to say is kidnapping or not, I was finally coming to my senses. The last thing on earth I wanted to be was the next Duncan Fitz."

"I wish I'd heard you say that six months ago."

"Better late than never, right?"

She smiled weakly, saying nothing. I wondered if her silence was a sign of a rekindling inside, or if she was simply too kind to tell me "Too little, too late."

The swimming pool glistened in the moonlight. Shadows of a flickering candle flame danced slowly against her hair. At that peaceful moment I did know one thing. I would happily sit there by the pool and hold her hand just as long as she'd allow it.

64

Around nine I dropped Jenna off and went home to get ready for my trip. Alex and I had a noon flight that would get us into Bogotá in plenty of time before our third Sunday-morning ascent of Monserrate. I hadn't looked forward to any of the radio contacts with the kidnappers, but this one had me especially apprehensive.

I packed my bag in ten minutes, then sifted through the mail to make sure I hadn't missed anything important. Next I scrolled through a flood of e-mail messages between Mom and a network of family friends that stretched across the country. The e-mail that caught my eye, however, wasn't one of hers. It was from someone who used an eight-digit number as a screen name, which gave me pause. The last time I'd opened an e-mail like this one, it had turned out to be from Jaime Ochoa.

I clicked the mouse, and the message popped onto the screen.

"I know where Matthew Rey is," it read.

I stared at the words. It was the same e-mail message that Jaime had sent to me at my office right after the kidnapping. This time he'd added a teaser. *"Come see me, and I will show you."*

I printed the message and checked the time of delivery: 5:12 P.M. Just a couple of hours after the court hearing. My gut wrenched, wishing only that it had come two hours *before* it. I'd been so afraid to subpoena Jaime as a witness for the hearing that I'd decided to play the bluff. I'd been certain he would have come down with a convenient case of amnesia or, worse, told the judge that I'd shoved his hand into the disposal not in self-defense but simply to coerce a false confession. Things had gone badly between us at yesterday's encounter, but perhaps things had just gotten out of hand. Perhaps I'd misread him.

Perhaps he was "A Friend."

I got up quickly and grabbed the keys to my Jeep. I had to pay Jaime one last visit.

It took me twenty minutes to get to Jaime's house, including a quick stop at my mother's house on the way. I parked in the driveway but didn't get out of my Jeep immediately.

The house was completely dark on the outside, no porch light or landscape lighting. Inside, a light from the kitchen appeared to be the only one burning. From a streetlamp at the corner, eerie shadows of power poles and phone lines stretched across the lawn and front porch.

I stepped down and stopped. I had reservations, of course. Driving up, I'd considered everything from the possibility of a cruel joke to a setup. I half expected Jaime and a half dozen of his friends to jump out from the bushes and beat my brains out with baseball bats. Perhaps I was being a little reckless. But the thing I feared more than anything was how the kidnappers might react on Sunday morning upon hearing that the ransom was being cut in half. If anyone could head off that crisis, I figured it was Jaime. I had to put my fears aside and take his offer at face value.

That didn't mean I was an idiot. The stop at my mother's house had been to pick up my father's Smith & Wesson.

I walked slowly across the front lawn in the darkness. With each step, the coarse St. Augustine crabgrass crunched beneath my feet. A car passed at the intersection a half block away, howling-drunk teenagers hanging out the open windows as they ran the stop sign. The noise faded as quickly as it had come, leaving me in what seemed to be an even darker and lonelier silence. At the paved walk I turned and started toward the front door, my shadow from the streetlight reaching far ahead of me. My heels clicked, and then the soles scratched like sandpaper as I climbed the final cement steps. I raised my hand to knock, then stopped. The house seemed too quiet.

I shook it off and knocked three times.

I waited and listened. No lights switched on, I heard no footsteps inside. I knocked again, slightly harder. Again there was no response. Jaime's car was in the driveway, but it was possible that a friend had taken him out for the night. Then I realized why the silence was so troubling.

Not even the dog barked.

The first time I'd visited, Sergeant had practically answered the door herself and nearly eaten me alive on the way out. The second time, she was chained in the yard but barked at my presence. This time, I'd driven up to a perfectly quiet house in a rather noisy Jeep, walked across the lawn, and knocked twice on the front door. It seemed strange that I'd gone unnoticed. Very strange.

I knocked once more, this time with the base of my fist. I pounded hard, and with the third deep thud the door swung open. I stepped back, startled, but no one was there. Evidently it hadn't been completely closed. The mere force of my knock had pushed it open.

I stepped to the open doorway and said, "Jaime?"

I heard nothing. I glanced again at the car in the driveway, thinking it odd that if someone had taken Jaime out on Friday night that they would have taken his dog with them.

I stuck my head inside the dark foyer, just enough to see inside. "Jaime, it's—"

I froze in midsentence. From the other end of the hall, at the entrance to the kitchen, Sergeant was staring me in the face, eyes wide open. She wasn't growling, wasn't blinking. She wasn't even breathing. The dog's body was sprawled across the kitchen floor in a crimson pool of blood.

My instincts told me to run, but I found my feet moving me in the opposite direction, into the house, down the hall, toward the lone light in the kitchen and the grim smell of death. It had been just five hours since Jaime had sent me an e-mail offering to show me where my father had gone. The very sight of his dog lying dead on the floor drew me inside for the answer I feared.

I stopped at the kitchen and gasped.

Jaime was hanging by the neck, twirling slowly round and round at the end of a rope that was fastened to the ceiling fan.

At first I couldn't move, stunned by the ghastly sight of this strangely elongated body. The toes seemed to reach in futility for the floor. The chin pointed toward the ceiling, yanked upward by a rope so taut that his bulging eyes had nearly popped from the sockets. The whole hideous sight just kept turning with the blades of the paddle fan right before my eyes, as if on display.

Murder was my first thought, but then I remembered how Jaime was so afraid of prison that he would have stabbed me to death to avoid ending up like his brother, abused while incarcerated. He was cowardly enough to kill himself. But why would he have killed his dog, too? Then it hit me. This wasn't just an escape. This was Jaime's *exit*, something he'd wanted me to see. The e-mail had said that he knew where my father was. He'd invited me over to show me.

Death was what he'd shown me. Gruesome deaths—a slit throat, strangulation.

I nearly fell against the doorframe, sickened by the perverse and tortured message that I now knew he was sending me.

They're going to kill my father, I realized, almost too weak to stand.

65

An ambulance arrived in minutes. The Miami-Dade police weren't far behind.

I'd told the 911 operator that Jaime was already dead, but apparently she'd thought that paramedics would be better judges. I waited outside as they rushed in, the police just a few steps behind them. The paramedics came out with no body on the gurney, and I presumed correctly that their lifesaving work was over before it had started. In seconds the whole yard was surrounded by yellow police tape. Two more police cars pulled up, one marked, the other unmarked, both with swirling blue lights that gave the dark house the strange glow of the aurora borealis.

A uniformed officer asked to take my statement. I hesitated. I was still concerned about Jaime and the insurance scandal making the newspapers. For all I knew, the kidnappers were Jaime's buddies, and they might take it out on my father if they were to hear that Jaime was dead.

"I'd like to speak to a detective," I said.

The officer seemed to note my reluctance with some suspicion. "Sure. Wait here."

A detective was already on the scene, the guy who'd pulled up in the unmarked car. He was inside with a photographer and videographer. A van from the medical examiner's office arrived, and a few minutes later an entire forensic team was at work. I waited almost twenty minutes before the detective finally came out the front door.

"Mr. Rey?" he said as he crossed the lawn. He walked quickly, a rather athletic stride. The sleeves of his wrinkled white dress shirt were rolled up to the elbows, revealing forearms as hairy and muscular as a grizzly bear's. He wore an open collar with loosened tie, his neck too thick to let him close the top button. I would have bet my father's ransom that he had been a football star at Miami High about twenty-five years earlier.

"I'm Nick Rey."

I was standing at the front gate. A crowd of rubberneckers had already gathered on the street outside the house. Cars slowed as they passed, and a few had stopped for a longer look. This was quickly becoming prime neighborhood entertainment.

He introduced himself as Detective Gutierrez and shook my hand. He seemed concerned about the gathering crowd. "Why don't we go down to the station, where we can talk?"

"Sure. I'll follow you."

"You can ride with me, if you want."

"That's all right. I can follow."

He shrugged as if to say, "Suit yourself."

I got into my Jeep, started the engine, and backed

out of the driveway, dispersing the pack of gawkers that had gathered behind my vehicle. From the street I took one last look at Jaime's house, and that image of him twirling from the ceiling fan popped back into my mind. It stayed there for several moments, till I checked the rearview mirror and saw what, for my father's sake, I had feared most: two news vans with camera crews.

It was only local, but in today's world local could quickly become national, national could turn international. Butterflies churned in my stomach as an image flashed through my mind, the kidnappers sitting around a television or computer screen watching Matthew Rey's son being interviewed about the death of their good buddy, Jaime Ochoa.

I drove away quickly, wanting no part of that.

Detective Gutierrez and I talked in his office, joined by his partner, who simply introduced himself as "Henderson." He was an older detective, skinny, bald-headed, and a man of few words. He was seated on the edge of the lumpy couch cracking pistachio shells, popping the nuts into the air, and catching them in his gaping mouth.

I told them my concerns about Jaime's death, how I feared that media leaks could possibly result in retaliation against my father by the kidnappers. Gutierrez seemed somewhat sympathetic, though it wasn't easy to read the jaded heart of a homicide detective.

"So let me make sure I got this," said Gutierrez. "You went to this guy's house once before. He sicced his dog on you and threw you out."

"Basically."

"You went there again, and you guys got in a friggin' knife fight."

"That's oversimplifying, but yeah."

"You went there a third time, convinced that Jaime's the guy who got your father kidnapped. And Jaime ends up dead."

"He was already dead when I got there."

The skinny guy asked, "Want some nuts?"

"No, thanks."

Gutierrez made a face, seemingly puzzled. "It bothers me that the dog was killed."

"I like dogs, too," I said.

"No, screw the dog. Hate them Dobermans. What I mean is, it doesn't really fit with the suicide."

"What do you mean?"

"Here's one scenario. Jaime slits his dog's throat, then hangs himself. But here's another scenario. Somebody kills Jaime, meets up with his dog on the way out."

I didn't like the way he was looking at me. The skinny guy was staring at me, no longer popping pistachios. "You're a suspicious man, Detective."

"That's my job."

"Are you saying this definitely wasn't a suicide?"

"I'm very interested to hear what the medical examiner has to say." He jotted a note in the file, then looked at me. "Are you planning on leaving Miami-Dade County anytime soon?"

"Why do you ask?"

"Because I don't want you to leave town. And I'd hate to arrest you on suspicion of murder sooner than I have to, just to keep you here."

My mouth fell open. "Hey, I didn't kill this guy."

"All I asked was if you plan on going anywhere."

I paused. The last thing I needed was to have my trip to Colombia screwed up. "I'll be here for a while."

He seemed to look right through me, as if he sensed I was lying. "Can you wait here just one sec?"

"Sure."

He got up and left, leaving his office door open. I watched him through the open blinds as he wound his way through the maze of workstations. Finally he disappeared down a hallway.

"Where's he going?" I asked.

"He'll be right back."

Skinny was back to popping pistachios. I was nervous, starting to sweat. Was I a suspect? What was all this stuff about not leaving town? And where the heck did Gutierrez go?

A chill hit me as I suddenly remembered how police sometimes operated. They might not have sufficient probable cause to make an arrest on the main charge, so they keep you from fleeing the jurisdiction by arresting you on a lesser one. To that end, my shoving Jaime's arm down the disposal would give them plenty of fodder. A case of self-defense could be easily converted to simple battery. Gutierrez was probably on the phone with an assistant state attorney right now.

"Could I have some water, please?"

"Sure."

Skinny got up and went for it. Just as soon as he was out of sight, I made my move.

I popped from my chair, flew out the door, turned

the corner, and broke for the exit. I was out the double doors in a flash, quickly crossing the parking lot to my Jeep. I jumped in, fired the engine, and was back on the road as fast as I could get there without squealing the tires.

Cruising down the expressway, I dialed Alex on my cell phone.

"Where are you?" she asked.

"Headed for the airport."

"What? The flight's not for another twelve hours."

"I'm taking the one at midnight."

"Why?"

"Don't ask."

"What's going on?"

"Pack your bag and stop by my house. The key's under the pot on the porch. My bag's already packed and on the bed. Passport's inside. I'll meet you at the international terminal."

"What's the sudden hurry?"

"Just go, please, or we'll miss our flight. I'll tell you everything in the air."

I hung up and punched the accelerator up to the speed limit, not a mile per hour more. As hurried as I was—and the way my luck was going—this was definitely no time to be stopped for speeding.

66

The door opened and the light switched on. After hours of total darkness, it was like staring into the sun. Matthew shielded his eyes as *Cerdo* came toward him.

It was a ritual that preceded each meal without much regularity. Based upon the hunger pangs and strain on his bladder, Matthew had guessed that visits came anywhere from four to ten hours apart. It seemed longer, naturally, when you were seated in a dark room chained to a bedpost. The boredom was enough to have driven a weaker man mad. He came to appreciate little things, like when *Cerdo* forgot to put the towel under the door. It was supposed to block the sounds and deprive the prisoner of even a crack of light from the hallway. Just that little sliver could make such a difference, some connection to reality. Without it, all he had was the occasional prance of footsteps above him, presumably from a higher floor. At times he could hear water rushing through pipes in the wall. Every now and then he'd hear muffled voices in the hallway. And once—only once—he'd heard a woman scream, the crack of a gunshot, and then silence.

He'd tried to convince himself that he'd dreamt it.

"*Vamos. El baño*," said *Cerdo* as he unlocked the chains.

A bathroom break, and it was surely welcome. Matthew's joints popped as he rose. He'd never thought of himself as particularly arthritic, but those weeks in the cold, damp mountains hadn't done his knees any good.

As his eyes slowly adjusted, he noticed a second teenage guard standing in the doorway. With that baby face, it seemed almost absurd, the way he was aiming an AK-47 at Matthew's chest.

"*Manos arriba*," he said.

Matthew raised his arms. They didn't seem to care if Matthew saw their faces, but they took pains to prevent him from seeing the configuration of the hallways and lay of the building outside his dark room. Each time he ventured to the bathroom, they reapplied the blindfold. This time, however, the kid had done a sloppy job. It was too high across the bridge of his nose, and although the right eye was covered, Matthew still had about half his line of sight from his left.

The gun barrel in his back prodded him forward. He stepped into the hall, then purposely bumped into the wall, so as to mislead his guards into thinking that he couldn't see. *Cerdo* put him back on track, straight down the hallway that led to the bathroom.

Matthew made a mental note of everything they passed. Hallway was three feet wide. Doors on both sides, about thirty feet apart. They were numbered like apartments. At each end of the hall was a table and chair, guard posts.

Cerdo grabbed his shoulder, and Matthew stopped. A blindfolded prisoner passed before him, an old woman, someone he'd never seen before. A man with a pistol led her to room number eleven, opened it, put her inside, and locked her in.

Cerdo gave him another nudge, and Matthew continued down the hall. Some of the doors had slots for food trays, as in prison. He heard whispering as they passed room number fifteen, and *Cerdo* gave a shout.

"*¡Silencio!*"

The whispering ended. Matthew shuddered. He'd walked this way before, blindfolded, never imagining this. It was exactly what *Cerdo* had described in the van, what Emilio had translated. This *was* a hostage hotel.

Cerdo opened the bathroom door and pushed him inside. "*Dos minutos,*" he said.

Two minutes to empty his bladder, before another "guest" would arrive.

67

I never thought I'd be so glad to reach Colombia.
It was four o'clock in the morning when we went through customs. A long line of bleary-eyed passengers proceeded through the airport checkpoints. Unlike the shakedown for travelers leaving the country, inspections for incoming passengers at El Dorado International Airport were random. Visitors pressed a button as they exited. If it came up green, they sailed through; red, their bags were searched. At this hour most of the stations were closed. Alex and I were twentieth in a slow-moving line.

I had nearly fallen asleep standing up when she nudged me. "See that guy over there?" she asked in a voice barely above a whisper.

I followed her eyes toward a man standing near a closed newsstand on the other side of the gate.

"He's a legal attaché," she said.

"A what?"

"An FBI agent. That's what they're called abroad.

That guy's definitely with the bureau's office in Bogotá."

"Are you sure?"

"Positive. I dealt with him six months ago in another kidnapping case."

The line inched forward, and we took a step closer. "What do you think he's here for?"

"You."

"Me?" I said, startled.

"Keep your voice down."

"How would they even know I was here?"

"Same way they knew the last time. The wire transfer."

"You think I'm in for another hassle about the money, like they did at Miami?"

"I think it's one of two things. It could be that the FBI evaluated what you told them and want to help you nail Quality Insurance."

"What's the other possibility?"

She cupped her hand to my ear, making sure no one could possibly overhear. "He's here to execute an arrest warrant. For the murder of Jaime Ochoa."

"Oh, boy."

"That's an understatement."

"What do we do?"

"I don't think he's spotted us yet, so stop acting like you know me. Let me go through first. I'll strike up a conversation with him. As soon as you clear, break for the exit. Don't run, but be quick. Remember where my friend Pablo left his Vega for us last time?"

"I think so."

"It should be in the same spot, or thereabouts. Go straight to it, I'll meet you there."

I stepped out of line and let the two passengers behind us get between me and Alex, creating some distance. One was a guy so big he could have blocked the sun. I stood directly behind him with my head down, trying not to let the legal attaché spot me. Slowly the line worked its way to the checkpoint. Alex went through without a hassle, as did the woman behind her. The big guy hit the button. The light flashed red, and they pulled him aside for a bag inspection. Alex was already on the other side, headed directly for the agent. I hit the button and prayed. It was green. I stepped through, presented my passport, and made a quick left at the gate.

Alex was all grins as she approached the agent, as if they were old friends. He was clearly uncomfortable, but Alex poured it on. I was moving fast through the terminal, bag in tow, my chin to my chest to minimize the chance of being recognized. I felt the urge to run but didn't. Still, with each step my stride widened, and I could feel myself gaining momentum. I sensed I was breaking free. *This was actually going to work!*

"Nick Rey?" someone called.

Instinctively I stopped cold, and we locked eyes. I didn't recognize the man's face, but I had the distinct sense that these legal attachés traveled in pairs.

For an instant neither of us moved. I tried to read his expression, tried to discern whether he'd come to help me or arrest me. I couldn't tell for sure, but he didn't look friendly.

On impulse, I ran for it.

"Stop!"

I ignored him, just kept running at full speed. I glanced back, and he was right on my tail. Just ahead, between me and the exit, were a janitor with a mop and a bucket, and a five-meter stretch of glistening wet floor. I kicked into another gear and leaped across it. Just as I made it to the revolving doors, I heard a shout, a thud, and painful groan behind me. I glanced back to see a disheveled FBI agent sprawling across the floor and showing the world the bottoms of his shoes. Luckily, he wasn't quite the long-jumper I was.

I burst through the door, ran past the taxis that Alex had warned me not to take. I followed the sidewalk to the parking lot, sprinting as fast as I could. A car suddenly cut in front of me and slammed on the brakes. I tried to stop but couldn't. My bag flew, and I ended up on the hood.

"You idiot!" I shouted, then froze.

It was Alex. "Get in!"

"How'd you get the car so fast?"

"You went the long way, dummy. Now, get in!"

I hurried to the passenger side and was barely inside before Alex squealed the tires. We flew past the taxis, past the airport entrance, past a breathless FBI agent who was hobbling toward a bench, holding his aching back.

We took a circuitous route to the apartment, just in case we were being followed. We finally arrived around 6:00 A.M., certain that we'd beaten whatever tail they might have tried.

Before going upstairs, I had Alex stop at a pay

phone. I desperately needed sleep, but first I needed to call home. I'd expected to get my mother, but Jenna answered.

"Nick, where are you?"

"Bogotá."

"Jeez, your mom's a wreck. I've been here with her all night. Why didn't you tell us?"

"I couldn't call till I got here. Just in case somebody asked, I wanted Mom to be able to say she didn't know where I was."

"Well, believe me, they're asking. This Detective Gutierrez won't leave us alone. It's crazy, but I think he has you pegged for murdering Jaime Ochoa."

"Don't worry about that. The guy hanged himself."

"No, he didn't. Somebody killed him."

"What?"

"What I'm hearing from Gutierrez, somebody forced him up on the kitchen chair, probably at gunpoint, and then tied a rope around his neck and hung him from the ceiling fan. Something about ligature marks around his wrists. It looks like his hands were untied after he was dead so it would look like suicide."

That didn't totally shock me, but I hated to think that lawyers I had once respected might have taken the cover-up this far. "This just keeps getting worse."

"It didn't help matters much when your mother told Gutierrez that you stopped by the house to pick up your father's gun on your way over to see Ochoa."

"Oh, my God."

"And now the way you raced out of town, that doesn't look so good either."

"It's not like I want to be here."

"Nick, I know I don't have to ask you, but . . ."

"No! He was dead when I got there."

She paused, as if relieved to hear me say it. "I know you have a lot on your mind. But when you get home, I hope you can prove it."

"I can't believe this."

"I'll find a criminal defense lawyer while you're away. I'll get a good one, I promise."

I lowered my head, closing my eyes in disbelief. "Thanks."

I was about to hang up, then said, "Hey, Jenna?"

"Yes?"

"Get a *really* good one."

68

Even the rain seemed black. Sunday was my third predawn climb to the summit of Monserrate and definitely the darkest, even darker than the fog had made our last visit. It wasn't a downpour, more a steady drizzle that soaked you to the core. The grass and mosses along the way were weighted down, saturated. Stones in the path that normally aided climbers with their footing were slippery and treacherous, shining wet in the beams from our flashlights. The temperature dropped a few degrees with the ascent, but I was sweating beneath a rain poncho that didn't breathe. The good news was that lousy weather lessened our chances of being stopped by bandits. The last thing I needed was to have our radio stolen minutes before the most important communication with the kidnappers.

"Is it the rainy season?" I asked, wiping the raindrops from my chin.

"October and November can be pretty wet in Bogotá," said Alex.

I thought of my poor dad braving the elements,

assuming he was anywhere near Bogotá. Assuming he was in Colombia, for that matter. With all the time that had elapsed, he could have been taken just about anywhere.

It took us longer to climb this time, better than ninety minutes nonstop. The rain was falling harder as we neared the church at the top. Muddy brown water was running downhill in the gutters. The vendor stands that catered to tourists were locked and closed. We chose a table in the picnic grounds behind the church and rigged up an umbrella to keep the radio dry. Alex and I worked in silence. It was becoming a routine, one that I definitely wouldn't miss when this was finally over.

I checked my watch. Sunrise was perhaps minutes away. Alex switched on the radio. I sat in the darkness with my back to it, hearing only the falling rain.

A sudden noise startled me, a lonely cawing sound that soon grew into a chorus. It was a flock of birds near the church.

"Macaws," said Alex.

It was too dark to see them, but I had no trouble conjuring up the image of the big, colorful birds from my visits as a kid to Miami's Parrot Jungle.

"I wonder what startled them."

Their cawing ceased as abruptly as it had started. Alex and I stared into the darkness, trying to listen beyond the patter of raindrops. In the glow of our flashlight I could see the concentration on her face.

"Do you hear something?" she asked.

I wasn't sure if it was the altitude or the simple effects of rainfall, but I was having trouble discerning anything. "Maybe like a shuffling?"

"More like a squish-squish to me."

Alex bristled, listening more closely. Now I could hear it, too. It sounded like footsteps. She reached for her knapsack, where she kept her gun.

"Buenos días."

The voice had come from total darkness. Alex shone her flashlight, revealing a man beneath an umbrella.

"Stop right there," she answered in Spanish.

He stopped about ten meters away. His eyes narrowed, as both Alex and I had our flashlights trained on his face. Shiny drops of rain dripped from the rim of his black umbrella.

"You are the Rey family, I presume?"

She asked, "Who wants to know?"

"Joaquín."

"Who are you?"

"I'm here to pick up the money for Matthew. My name is Father Balto."

I looked at Alex, not quite believing. "A priest?"

Alex slipped her hand inside her bag, grasping her gun. It was obvious that she didn't take anything at face value.

"Come forward, Padre. I have a few questions for you."

"Why don't we go inside the church, where it will be warm and dry?"

"We're waiting for a radio transmission at sunrise."

"There will be no transmission this morning," he said. "They've sent me for the money."

"If it's all the same to you, I think we'll wait here a few minutes to make sure."

He shrugged and said, "I'll wait inside. Please come visit when you're satisfied that I'm speaking the truth."

He turned and walked away, back into the darkness of the falling rain, beyond the reach of our flashlights.

We waited for nearly an hour past sunrise. The rain continued. The sky brightened slightly, but the sun never really came. No message came either. The radio was silent.

We gathered our equipment and headed for the church. The main doors were locked, but we found a side entrance with a bell beside it. I rang it twice. Father Balto answered, clearly having expected us.

"I spoke the truth, no?" he said as he led us to a small room off the vestibule.

Perhaps he had been truthful about the kidnappers, but he'd lied about it being warmer and drier inside. The stone walls were moist with condensation, and with our coats off it actually felt colder and damper in here. We sat around a simple wooden table that had been worn smooth around the edges from decades of human touch. A cluster of three candles burned in the center, a meager enhancement to the glow of one burning bulb in an eight-socket chandelier overhead.

Alex took a few minutes to explain who we were, how my father had been kidnapped, the details of the communications so far. Then it was Father Balto's turn.

"I was contacted on Friday," he said. "They asked me to act as intermediary."

"The Catholic Church allows this?" I said.

"It's fairly common," said Alex.

"We do it for humanitarian reasons. Our only interest is in reuniting families."

"Did they give you any proof that he's alive?"

He shook his head. "My instructions were very limited. Go to the picnic grounds behind the church at sunrise and collect the ransom from the Rey family."

"We don't have the money with us. We were expecting a radio contact, not an exchange."

"No problem. I've dealt with Joaquín before. It's not his practice to come banging on my door for the cash a half hour after pickup. You and I simply need to set up a safe place for delivery. Where's the money now?"

"With all respect, Father, I don't even trust a priest with that information."

"I understand," he said. "You do have it, though, don't you?"

"We spent all day yesterday and a good part of last night converting the funds to dollars. We have everything we intend to pay."

"What does that mean?"

"Simply this: We don't intend to pay the full amount of their demand."

He paused, obviously concerned. "That is a problem."

"I need you to pass a message to Joaquín. As far as we're concerned, we're still negotiating."

"I tell you this for your own good. I believe that Joaquín is through negotiating."

His grave tone chilled me. Alex seemed unfazed.

"Tell him that we will pay one and a half million dollars, not a penny more. That's a good price for a fisherman, even if he is an American."

"I can take your money, but I'll be honest. Joaquín is so set on three million that I'm almost sure you'll be double-dipped."

I asked, "What does that mean?"

Alex said, "It's a common ploy. The family delivers a sum of money to an intermediary, thinking that their loved one will be released. The kidnapper takes the money but doesn't release the prisoner. The message comes back that you've paid only the first of two installments. Then you're stuck delivering another ransom."

"How do you avoid that?" I asked.

"You can't," said Father Balto.

"Only one way," said Alex. "A simultaneous exchange. We hand over the money at the exact same moment that they hand over your father."

"Nobody does simultaneous exchanges," the priest said.

"Father, I've been involved in enough kidnappings in Colombia to know one thing: *Anything* is possible."

"But a simultaneous exchange is very dangerous. So many things can go wrong."

"Are you sure about this, Alex?" I asked.

"If we give Joaquín half the ransom he expects, he'll either kill your father or continue to hold him until we cough up the other half. We have to tell him up front that one point five million is it. And the only way to make sure he doesn't double-dip is to insist on a simultaneous exchange. Unless you can think of a better idea."

I looked away, uneasy. "Father, do you see another option?"

He just looked at me, his eyes filled with pity, as if there were no right answer.

"Then deliver the message," I told him. "Exactly as Alex said it."

He grimaced, obviously uncomfortable. "I'd rather not have that responsibility. I fear the consequences."

"You're our only connection to the kidnappers."

"I don't like to negotiate with Joaquín. He's not like the organized guerrilla groups. He's too . . . volatile."

That gave me pause. We were dealing with a guy who made narco-guerrillas seem stable.

Father Balto seemed to sense my anxiety and said, "This is what I can do. Joaquín is supposed to call me at noon. Stay here, and you can deliver the message yourself."

Alex looked at me, as if for approval.

"Let's do it," I said. "There's no place I need to be."

"I have a suggestion," said Father Balto.

"What?"

"Mass is at ten. Why don't you join us?"

"Thank you," I replied. "I will."

69

B y the time the mass was over, the rain had stopped. We waited outside in the picnic area for the noon telephone call. A South American priest with a cell phone struck me as somehow odd, but I sensed he had it for a very specific reason. Undoubtedly this wasn't his first kidnapping.

The cell phone was resting on the table between us, Alex and me on one side, Father Balto on the other. I watched without interest as a group of tourists snapped photographs on the observation platform behind the church.

The priest seemed to have something on his mind. Alex asked, "What is it, Father?"

His reluctance was evident, but curiosity won out. "Three million dollars is much money for a ransom. Even half that is much, much more than I've ever delivered before."

"This is not your usual case," said Alex.

"Your father must be very wealthy."

"He's very blessed." I preferred to sidestep the

whole insurance nightmare, though I had a sense that he'd know soon enough. If Joaquín would ever call.

It was a few minutes past noon, and I was getting nervous. I checked to make sure the telephone was on. "Father, are you sure Joaquín said noon?"

"He'll call. Don't worry."

"And you're certain he said he'd phone you? He talks to us only by radio."

"That's because a cell phone isn't an option when you're calling from the jungle."

"So this means they're in the city now?"

"Definitely."

I asked Alex, "Do you think they ever were in the jungle, or were they just using the radio to make us think that they were?"

"You never know. A straight criminal element like this, as opposed to one of the Marxist groups, is more often an urban operation. Unless they have some kind of working arrangement with FARC or ELN."

"So this is good," I said. "They're back to where they feel most comfortable."

"I suppose." Her voice was flat, as if she sensed that I was reaching too far for anything positive.

The phone rang, and I nearly jumped. The priest answered and gave me a nod, confirming that it was Joaquín. He spoke in such rapid Spanish that I didn't catch every word, but I detected considerable pleading in his tone. His hand was shaking as he handed the telephone to Alex.

"God be with you," he said.

Alex held the phone just far enough away from her ear so that I could lean close and listen. "Good afternoon," she said amicably.

"Where's the money?" he replied.

"In a very safe place. We have one and a half million dollars for you."

"Congratulations. That's just enough to get him back dead."

That made my stomach flop. Alex said, "Listen to me, Joaquín. This is a good-faith offer."

"I'm tired of this stalling. I don't know if it's you or the insurance company, but either way I've had enough."

"You have no idea what's going on with the insurance."

"I know it's a three-million-dollar policy. That's all I need to know."

"It's blown up in everybody's face. Jaime's dead."

"What?"

"He killed himself. It's over. The family was able to get you one and a half million. It's all you're going to get."

"That's not enough."

"Don't be a pig. It's all yours, all one and a half million. There's no kickbacks, no one you have to split it with. I'm serious. Jaime's dead."

There was silence on the line. Finally he said, "If you're lying to me . . ."

"I'm not lying. Get on the Internet, check yesterday's *Miami Herald*."

Again he paused. I was biting my lip, not sure that Alex had played the right card by dragging Jaime's death into this.

"All right," he said. "Give the money to the priest. If Jaime's really dead, I'll let the prisoner go."

"No."

"No?" he said, his voice rising with anger.

"We're doing a simultaneous exchange."

"Never."

"Then you don't get your money."

"Then I kill the prisoner."

"Then I repeat, you don't get your money."

"This was not the deal, damn you!"

"It's the deal now."

"Then there's no deal!"

"Come on—"

"No, it's over! This guy has been trouble from the beginning. That was my fifteen-year-old cousin that got shot and killed by his Nicaraguan piece-of-trash crewman in Cartagena. I've had to watch him constantly, feed him, clothe him, put up with his disrespect. I couldn't get a fair price from FARC, couldn't get half a fair price from ELN, and now *you* want to shortchange me? Forget it. I'm done. We're done. *He's* done."

"Wait," Alex said, but the line clicked.

I'd heard it all, my ear practically pressed against hers. I pulled away slowly, the sound of dead air from the telephone humming between us.

70

Matthew heard footsteps in the hallway, then shouting outside his closed door. He recognized the voices, the wild tempers. Evidently drugs were as plentiful here as in the mountains. As the lock on the door rattled open, he braced himself for the worst.

"¡*Gringo!*" Joaquín shouted.

The light switched on, but the sudden brightness was an assault on his eyes. He felt snow-blind to his surroundings as he sat up and shaded his eyes with chained hands. His vision was just beginning to return when, seemingly out of nowhere, a calloused hand slapped him across the head and knocked him to the floor.

"Get up!"

Matthew lay motionless. Joaquín grabbed him by the collar and threw him against the wall. Matthew was like a dog on a short leash, his body jerking in midair as the chains went taut.

The fall had hurt his shoulder, and he heard himself groan. He heard laughter, too, and as his sight returned, he saw *Cerdo* and another guard standing in the doorway. It had been the same way in the mountains, when they'd thrown him in the hole. Punishment of the prisoners was the guerrillas' chief source of entertainment. *Cerdo* and his buddy were passing a bottle of rum between the two of them as Joaquín ran the show.

"How much was your policy worth?" shouted Joaquín.

"What policy?"

He kicked him in the groin. Matthew nearly blacked out, then struggled through it.

"Don't lie to me! I know about Quality Insurance Company. How much was it?"

Matthew could barely breathe, let alone answer. But if Joaquín knew the company name, there was no sense in playing totally dumb. "A couple hundred thousand."

Joaquín kicked him again, this time in the kidney. The pain shot in all directions. Another kick like that and Matthew feared it would kill him.

"It's three million!" said Joaquín.

"Whatever you say."

He grabbed Matthew by the hair—long, greasy locks that sorely needed shampoo. "It's not whatever I say. It's three million!"

Matthew didn't answer.

Joaquín seized his prisoner by the jaw, forcing him to look him in the eye. "I should kill you now," he said, snarling.

Matthew stared right back, more than matching the contempt of his captor. Joaquín shoved him down to the floor.

"Unchain him."

On command, *Cerdo* rushed over with the keys. He was staggering, too much to drink. He rested the near-empty bottle of rum on the bed, then knelt down to unlock the cuffs.

Matthew's mind raced, sorting through his limited options. This seemed to be the end of the line. After that speech from *Cerdo* the other day, he was certain that they were going to take him out to some alley, pump a dozen bullets into his face, and dump his body in the street. His fate seemed to be a pauper's grave, an unidentified corpse. He could go peaceably, or he could make good on the promise he'd made to himself when they'd left the mountains, when *Cerdo* had called out to Nisho, taunting the woman he and his buddies had gang-raped, "*Nishooooooo, I love you!*"

Nothing would have been better than to take out *Cerdo and* Joaquín. But this might be his only opportunity. He'd settle for just *Cerdo*.

The moment the chains loosened he shook free and grabbed the bottle of rum. In a blur, he slammed it against *Cerdo*'s skull and burrowed the jagged glass into his neck, pushing down hard, twisting and turning the razor-sharp edges, gouging right at the carotid artery until his hands were covered in red.

Cerdo squirmed and screamed in pain, blood gushing from his neck like a fountain. Joaquín slammed Matthew across the side of the head and knocked him to the floor. *Cerdo* rolled to one side, grabbing his throat, but the bleeding was unstoppable. The blood ran through his fingers and soaked his shirt. A huge crimson puddle covered the floor.

"The blood, stop the blood!" he cried in a panic.

The other guard grabbed a dirty white bedsheet and shoved it against his neck. In seconds it had soaked through, bright red. *Cerdo* got up on one knee, shook his fist weakly at Matthew, then fell to the floor. He lay motionless in his own blood.

No one moved. Matthew stared at the lifeless body, then turned his gaze to Joaquín, certain that he was about to be executed.

Joaquín stepped around the pool of blood to face Matthew directly. He drew his nine-millimeter pistol from his holster and aimed at the prisoner's forehead. Matthew stared down the barrel of the gun, looking straight into the dark, narrow tunnel of death. It hardly seemed a fair trade, his life for trash as worthless as *Cerdo*. But it was the closest thing to justice that a prisoner could hope for.

"Go ahead," he said defiantly. "Shoot me."

The gun was shaking, Joaquín was so angry. His finger tensed on the trigger, but he didn't pull it. "Lock him up!" he shouted.

Cerdo's buddy looked confused and horrified, but Joaquín shouted the order again. "Lock him up!"

This time the guard obeyed, and Matthew didn't resist. When the cuffs were in place, Joaquín came to him, put the gun to Matthew's temple, and said, "I promise, I *will* shoot you. Right before your son's eyes."

71

A lex brought dinner back to the apartment, but I didn't touch the food. As much as she'd assured me that the negotiations weren't really over, that Joaquín would cool down, it was hard not to take his outburst as final. My mind was already at my father's funeral, or perhaps memorial service was a more appropriate term, as I was certain that we'd never recover the body.

We sat at opposite sides of the kitchen table, saying little. Another tearful bolero of lost love was playing on the evening program of Radio Recuerdo. The Holy Infant and Our Lady of Perpetual Help were watching us from framed pictures on the wall. Alex kept apologizing for eating in the face of my total loss of appetite, but I was caught up in my own thoughts.

"Maybe you shouldn't have mentioned Jaime." It was out of the blue, a random comment that had jumped the track in my speeding train of thought.

Alex looked up from her plate of pasta. "Are you going to dissect every word of that phone call?"

"I just remembered catching my heart in my throat when you mentioned Jaime. For all we know, he was Joaquín's uncle or cousin or whatever. Telling him that Jaime was dead might have been the very thing that triggered his anger."

"He was bound to find out sooner or later. Better that I presented it as a suicide, rather than let him leap to the conclusion that you killed him, the same way the police did."

I went to the refrigerator for a bottled water. I was trying to stay focused on my father and deal with one problem at a time. Soon, however, I'd have to clear my own name back home.

"Do you think I killed him?"

She coughed and said, "What?"

"You heard me. Do you think I killed Jaime?"

"Of course not."

"Why not? After all, the guy turned my father over to kidnappers."

"I didn't say you didn't have motive."

"Then how can you answer my question so quickly and say 'Of course not'? Why wouldn't I kill him?"

She was half smiling. "Because you have much more self-restraint than I do."

"Thanks. I think."

Her expression turned serious. "You're not the only one who had motive, you know. Maggie Johans had motive, too. So did a lot of people at Quality Insurance, people who stood to lose plenty if Jaime started to name names. The police will realize that."

"I hope you're right."

"I know I'm right."

I saw no doubt in her eyes, only a reassuring blend of confidence and sincerity. "Thanks."

A knock on the door broke the silence. "Visitors?" I asked, confused.

"Let me check." She rose quickly and went straight to her room. In seconds she was back with gun in hand. It was the first time I'd seen her react so defensively, a sure sign that I wasn't the only one feeling the tension.

Standing to the side of the door, she asked in Spanish, "Who is it?"

"Father Balto."

It sounded like his voice, and he was the only person to whom Alex had given our address. She opened the door cautiously, leaving it chained.

"Are you alone?"

"Yes. May I come in, please?"

She peered into the hallway through the opening, then removed the chain and let him in.

His black raincoat was wet with the early-evening drizzle. Alex took it and left it on the hall tree with his umbrella. He greeted me kindly as we gathered at the kitchen counter.

"I have a message from Joaquín," he said.

I caught my breath. "Good or bad news?"

"Good, I believe. He will take the deal."

"Seriously?"

"One point five million, simultaneous exchange. On one condition," he said, raising a finger to make his point. "The son delivers the ransom."

"No," said Alex.

"How can we say no?"

"I don't like it," she said. "I would have expected

him to make us wait, sweat a few days. That was too fast on the turnaround. Makes me nervous."

"That's Joaquín," said the priest. "I said it before. He's very volatile."

"Which means that we can't keep pushing his buttons," I said. "He's cut the ransom in half. He's giving us a simultaneous exchange. We have to give him something."

"That doesn't mean we should give him *you*," said Alex.

"He said this is his final offer," said the priest.

"Kidnappers always say that."

"Maybe this time he means it," I said.

She hesitated. I could see in her eyes that she didn't want to go out on that limb, telling me that Joaquín *didn't* mean it, only to have my father's death on her own hands.

"If you go," she said, "I'm going with you."

"How about it, Father?" I asked.

He shrugged, struggling. "Technically, he didn't say you had to come alone. He just wants the son to deliver the ransom."

"Then it's settled."

Father Balto placed his cell phone on the counter. "Joaquín asked that I give you this. From here on out, your instructions will be by cell phone."

Alex reached for it, but the priest stopped her. "You can join in the delivery of the ransom, but I think he's expecting to speak directly with the son."

She stepped back warily. "I don't like this, Nick."

"Nobody does, least of all my father." I took the phone and tucked it into my pocket. "But none of us has a choice."

* * *

Father Balto and I shared his umbrella on the short walk down the street to the drugstore. I had no conception of the traceability of long-distance calls from Bogotá to Miami, but I didn't want to learn the hard way. The last thing I needed was to lead the FBI's legal attachés to the apartment. I closed myself in a phone booth in the back of the drugstore and dialed Jenna. I wanted to tell her what had been happening, but she seemed more eager to tell me something.

"I found you a lawyer. A sharp former prosecutor named Jerry Houlihan."

"I've heard good things about him."

"I was hoping you'd approve. Your mom and I authorized him to start working right away. The police executed a search warrant on your Jeep today."

"They what?"

"They found your father's gun under the front seat."

I could have clubbed myself with the phone. "Damn. I put it there when the police got to Jaime's house and ended up going straight to the airport from the police station. Couldn't very well take it on the plane with me."

"Nick?"

"What?"

"Why did you take a gun with you to Jaime's house?"

"Because he invited me there, and I didn't know what to expect. Hell, the last time I went there, he pulled a knife on me. You know all about that."

"I don't know as much as you think. You and Jerry

have to talk soon. He keeps asking me questions that I can't answer."

"I'll try to call him tomorrow."

"Try hard, please. I don't mean to downplay the kidnapping, but this is serious. They could charge you with murder."

"Don't get discouraged, all right? And tell my mom not to worry either. We'll straighten the whole thing out when I get home. Could be soon."

"Is something about to happen with your father?"

"Definitely."

"You think it could finally be over?"

"One way or the other, yes. It could be over."

She paused, as if she didn't like the sound of that. "Be careful, okay?"

"I will."

"This is really scaring me."

"Me, too," I said, my voice fading.

The call came at midnight, the distinctive chirping of a cell phone on the end table. I nearly jackknifed in response, launching my tired body from a comfortable slumber on the couch. Alex came running from the bedroom. I flipped open the receiver, swallowed the lump in my throat, and answered.

"*Hola.*"

He didn't answer right away, but I recognized the voice as soon as he began. "We'll do this in English, but I'll only say it once. So listen good. Understand?"

Alex sat right beside me on the couch, her ear close enough to listen.

"Yes," I answered.

"Five-thirty tomorrow evening. Be at Cementerio Central."

"The cemetery?"

"Don't interrupt! Go to the grave of Gonzalo Jiménez de Quesada. Bring the money and the cell phone. Wait in front of the monument. I'll call you. Don't be late."

"Wait, what grave?"

"I told you I'd say it once." The line clicked.

"Damn it! What grave!" I clutched the phone tightly, shaking it in frustration.

"Don't worry, I got it," said Alex.

"You sure?"

"It's probably the largest monument in the cemetery. He's the founder of Bogotá."

"Why would Joaquín send us there?"

"A quiet, isolated spot in the middle of a city of eight million people. If something goes wrong, he has hundreds of escape routes down surrounding side streets in every direction."

"He could have sent us to the park."

"He could have. But that wouldn't have set your mind to thinking the way a cemetery does, would it?"

"No," I said, trying to keep my mind from going there. "Definitely not."

72

We reached the cemetery right on schedule, just a few minutes before 5:30 P.M. Our arrival was timed perfectly. We didn't want to be standing around any longer than necessary with one and a half million dollars in a knapsack, even if we were both armed.

Alex had insisted that I carry a gun, which made good sense to me. It had taken her only a small portion of that Monday to scrounge up an Austrian-made Glock nine-millimeter pistol.

"This will stop a charging rhinoceros in its tracks," she'd said, placing the gun in my hand. "Use it only if you intend to kill someone."

Her warning had unleashed weeks of pent-up emotions that suddenly bubbled forth to form a conscious thought that chilled me. I'd never laid eyes on this Joaquín, but for all he'd done to my father, my mother, my family, I did indeed want him dead. Trading in human lives had to be the most despicable crime on earth.

The afternoon was overcast, the sun completely

hidden. Less than a half hour of daylight remained. Trees stood leafless against a sad, gray November sky. There was a slight chill in the damp air, no breeze to stir it. Bogotá's notorious smog, the by-product of more than a million vehicles, hovered over the graves like the stench of death itself. The cemetery grounds covered a vast rectangular expanse, surrounded by a city that had grown around it. Many of the magnificent stone memorials were centuries old, discolored and decaying from the elements, the pollution, the vandals. Blaring horns and other rumblings of urban life could be heard in the distance, not loud enough to be disruptive, but enough to make me wonder if anyone here truly rested in peace.

Alex and I followed the footpath to the impressive crypt of Gonzalo Jiménez de Quesada. She hadn't overstated the size of the plot. In the rear was a crypt as large as some churches. Before it was an impressive stone marker in a courtyard setting. The entrance was flanked by two short, decorative iron posts that were linked by a single strand of black chain. It sagged in the middle, like a sad smile.

A man emerged from behind the crypt. I started, then calmed at the familiar sight of Father Balto.

"Joaquín asked me to come," he said. "I'm supposed to go with you from here."

"Go where?"

The question had barely left my lips when the cell phone rang. "Hello," I answered.

"Walk a hundred meters to the statue of the Blessed Virgin. Wait there. Just you and Father Balto."

"We have Alex with us."

"Not Alex. If I see anyone but you and the priest at that statue, your father gets a bullet. Got it?"

He hung up, leaving no room for debate. I switched off the phone and repeated his orders, verbatim, to Alex.

"You can't go without me," she said.

"He said he'd kill my father if you come."

"If I don't come, he'll kill your dad and take you in his place."

"How do you know that?"

"He's a kidnapper and a murderer. Your only hope is if I'm there."

"I'd agree with you, if he'd told me to come alone. But I have Father Balto with me. That has to be a show of good faith."

"Are you crazy? These people would shoot you in front of God Himself. They kidnap people from churches."

"Can I say something?" the priest said.

"Sure."

"I've dealt with Joaquín before. My only wish is to help you get your father back safely, but I'm not going anywhere if we don't follow Joaquín's instructions to the letter."

Alex was about to say something when a sudden noise silenced us, a cry from somewhere beyond the statue. I listened more closely. It came again, this time more clearly.

"Nick!"

It was my father. Just the sound of his voice had my adrenaline pumping. I looked at Alex and said, "Cover us. But stay out of sight."

I checked my gun, slung the money over my

shoulder, and started toward the statue of the Blessed Virgin, just me and Father Balto.

The gag was back in his mouth, fastened tightly behind his head. A fresh cigarette burn smoldered just below his eye in the soft, sensitive skin near the tear duct. Matthew had refused to play a voluntary role in Joaquín's scheme. He'd yielded to the command and shouted his son's name only after the pain had become unbearable.

Joaquín peered out over the top of a huge granite marker. Matthew was even better concealed, kneeling in a half-dug grave behind a pile of fresh dirt. Joaquín's partner, the one who'd watched *Cerdo* bleed to death, kept the prisoner in check at gunpoint. Only now did Matthew finally recognize him as one of the executioners who, along with Joaquín, had taken Will the Canadian for his last walk into the jungle.

The sound of approaching footsteps made Matthew cringe. He knew that his son was coming. Worse, he knew it was an ambush.

Joaquín cocked his pistol and smiled. "Way to go, fisherman. You reeled him in nicely."

73

"That's far enough."

I stopped just a few paces away from the statue of the Blessed Virgin. I recognized the voice as Joaquín's, yet I resisted the impulse to turn and look behind me, fearing the consequences of any sudden movements.

"Look straight ahead, put the money on the ground, and put your hands over your head. Move very slowly."

I did exactly as told, moving almost in slow motion. I slipped the knapsack off my shoulder and lowered it to the ground, then raised my hands.

"Count it, Padre."

Father Balto knelt on the grass and opened the knapsack. His hands shook as he fumbled through the stacks of hundred-dollar bills. I watched for a few seconds, then better used the time to get a lay of the land, though my line of sight was shrinking in the waning daylight. With each passing moment another distant row of stone crosses and headstones slipped into the dark onset of night.

"It all appears to be here," the priest shouted.

Joaquín said, "Take the bag and step over to the statue."

He took it, then retreated in silence to the statue of the Blessed Virgin.

"Turn around, *yanqui*."

I assumed that was me. I turned my head slowly, then my whole body. I visualized myself reaching for my gun, trying to discern how quickly I could get to it, if needed. Not quickly enough, I feared.

The gray skies were nearly black. All around the perimeter of the darkening cemetery, city lights began to twinkle, marking the end of another day. Deep within this vast urban graveyard it was as if we were falling into a black hole. Distant lights were visible, but my immediate surroundings were fading into the shadows. Slowly my eyes began to adjust, and I could almost make out the pained expression on the familiar face that was staring back at me from twenty meters away. The body was slimmer than I'd remembered, but the countenance was the same.

The man with the gun to his head was definitely my father.

My eyes locked on his battered image. Weeks of captivity seemed to have taken a greater toll than a lifetime at sea.

My gaze shifted toward Joaquín. "You have your money. Now let him go."

"Is that what you expect?"

"That was the deal."

"We have a deal, you say? Is that how you think this works? You change it every which way you please, and then finally you announce that we have a deal?"

"We were negotiating."

"There wasn't supposed to be any negotiating. *That* was the deal."

"Your deal with who, Jaime?"

He just scoffed and said, "This was supposed to be an easy one. What a joke."

"It can still be easy. There's a sack full of money right over there. Take it, and give me my father."

He let out a mirthless chuckle. "Just let him go, eh?"

"That's what we agreed."

"Sure, I'll let him go. If you come with me."

It was as if he'd punched me in the chest. "That's not what we talked about."

"I don't care what we talked about."

"You're getting the money, no more."

"What's the matter, don't you love your father? Hasn't he suffered enough? Be a good son. Come with me. Set your old man free."

Father Balto stirred. "Joaquín, please—"

"Shut up! I'm talking to the *yanqui*."

I was out of things to say. I couldn't possibly go with him, but I didn't want to set him off.

"Time's up," said Joaquín.

"Stop playing games."

He shoved the pistol against my father's skull. "You're right. Forget the swap. Why don't I just kill your old man and take you at gunpoint?"

I was a split second away from reaching for my gun.

"Wait!" Alex shouted, gun drawn. She'd given up her hiding spot and was standing in the open—not exactly what I'd had in mind when I'd asked her to cover us. I braced myself for a three-way gunfight, but Joaquín showed restraint.

He tightened his grip on my father and said, "Get out of here, Alex."

She aimed her gun in his direction, but he was using my father as a human shield.

"Give me the prisoner," she said.

"Go to hell."

"Give him to me, and I'll give you the other one and a half million."

My heart was racing. I couldn't possibly stop her, but this seemed like a dangerous bluff.

Inch by inch she was moving closer to Joaquín, talking to him all the way. "Jaime didn't kill himself."

My God, is she going to point the finger at me?

"So he's not dead?" said Joaquín.

"Oh, he's dead, all right. He was about to name names. I couldn't let him do that."

I nearly buckled at the knees. *Is she still bluffing?*

"You scammed me," said Joaquín.

"No. You scammed *me*. Killing the prisoner wasn't part of the deal. Now, hand him over if you want the whole three million."

I could hardly speak, but I forced out the words. "Alex, what the heck is going on?"

She didn't answer.

Joaquín said, "What's the matter, *yanqui*? Did she fool you into thinking that Jaime acted alone? Did you really believe that a little insurance dweeb in Miami has guerrilla friends?"

I looked at Alex, the former FARC girl. "My God, you know him. That's why he agreed to a simultaneous exchange. He knew we wouldn't call the police, because someone on the other side was on *his* side."

"Quiet, Nick."

Joaquín jerked my dad forward. "Everyone, shut up. I'm in control here."

"That's right," said Alex, speaking more like the calm negotiator. "And you can still be the big winner. All three million. No one to split it with."

My eyes darted back and forth from Alex to my father to Joaquín. She may have scammed us at the beginning, but when it came to the money, I knew that she was bluffing Joaquín. *Was she trying to make amends?*

"Whose side are you on, Alex?"

"Stay out of this," she answered.

"I'd like to know that, too," Joaquín snapped. "Whose side *are* you on?"

"Do you want the money or don't you?"

"Does this mean you're not taking your cut?" he asked.

"I said you could have it all."

"But I want to hear you say it to your client. Tell the *yanqui* that you're not taking your cut."

"I was never getting a cut."

"What do you call fifty percent?"

"Every penny of it was Jaime's." She was staring at Joaquín as she spoke, aiming her gun right at him, but I sensed that she was talking for my benefit. "All I wanted was for you and your thugs to leave my family alone." She raised her voice, as if to make sure I heard. "That's all I ever wanted, Nick. Just to buy a little peace for what's left of my family in Bogotá."

"Such a sad story," Joaquín said with sarcasm.

She adjusted her aim. "Someone should have killed you a long time ago."

"A long time ago I should have let you bleed to death on the side of the road with a knife in your back."

"You don't own me just because you pulled me out of a ditch. And you can't make me come back to you by threatening my family."

"But I could make you scam the *yanqui*."

Even in the dim light I could see the anger on her face. One look at my father confirmed that we were sharing the exact same fear: Alex was about to squeeze off a shot at Joaquín, but anything less than perfection would kill the hostage, the human shield.

"Alex!" I shouted, reaching for my gun.

In the same instant my father broke free from Joaquín's grasp. A shot rang out as he rolled to the ground, but it missed and shattered a clay pot. I dived to the ground and fired repeatedly at Joaquín. Alex was shooting, too, as she and Father Balto ran for cover behind the big statue. Joaquín fired back, as did someone else from behind a dirt pile, and the barrage of bullets erupted as if it were a war zone. My father was out of sight, having slid behind a gravestone. Joaquín fired a few more shots in his direction, but Alex and I pinned him down with gunfire. I crouched low behind my marker, bullets whizzing over my head.

Suddenly all was quiet in the darkness.

I sat crouched behind the headstone, breathless from the exchange of gunfire, my back against cold granite. Darkness had completely overtaken us, no moon or stars in the night's overcast sky, just a dim glow from distant city lights. I listened carefully for any movement about me, but I heard only the sounds of my own erratic breathing.

"Brothers, please," shouted a brave Father Balto, but three quick gunshots sent him scampering back into hiding.

That son of a bitch just tried to kill the priest!

My hand shook as I dug the cell phone from my pocket. I dialed the police and tried to speak to a dispatcher in Spanish, but the wireless reception was terrible, and my scattered thoughts produced only fragmented sentences, partly in English.

"*Las pistolas. Los* kidnappers *en el Cementerio Central. ¡Ven acá, por favor!*"

Bullets sailed over my head. In my panic I was making no sense, and my talking was giving away my position to the enemy. The dispatcher hung up on me, and I held little hope that Colombian police would actually come charging into the cemetery at night to stop an ill-described gunfight.

I crouched low to reload my weapon. My first shoot-out, and it was going to be to the death of one of us. But who would fall? And who was on which side? In my mind I quickly replayed the last exchange of gunfire. Alex had fired at Joaquín. That meant she was in my camp, despite anything she'd said. But someone else with Joaquín had been firing what sounded like an automatic weapon. That made it two against two, at best. Father Balto was unarmed, but he was with Alex. The only unprotected player was my father. A sick feeling came over me, as I knew what I had to do. Somewhere in the darkness among all those gravestones, my father was hiding, praying for his life.

I had to find him before Joaquín did.

74

Matthew thanked the Lord for darkness. In the confusion of gunfire, slithering across the grass like a snake on his belly, he'd found his way to an overcrowded collection of tall markers that stood one beside the other, almost on top of one another, a veritable forest of towering stone crosses and statues of patron saints.

His hands were cuffed behind his back, his ankles tied, and his mouth gagged. It was a bit of ironic luck that Joaquín had removed the blindfold to torture his eye. The left one had blistered and swollen shut from the cigarette burn, but the right one gave him the precious advantage of sight.

He lay perfectly still, almost afraid to breathe. The slightest movement could reveal his whereabouts, which would be deadly. He knew that Joaquín had brought him here to avenge the death of *Cerdo*, to execute the prisoner right before his son's eyes. Matthew was ready for that. For weeks he'd been preparing himself for the possibility of his own death.

One thing, however, he hadn't prepared for: the death of his son in a botched rescue effort.

He burrowed into hiding at the base of a huge stone marker, pleading with his Maker to take him and not Nick.

Nothing moved, not anywhere. I was peering out over the top of my marker, some dead stranger's resting place. Somewhere across the grounds, hiding behind one of those countless slabs of stone, were Joaquín and his well-armed buddy. I'd been waiting for one of them to break toward my father, or at least in the direction I'd last seen my father go. Maybe they were being patient. Or maybe they'd already made their move, and I'd missed them. I couldn't risk it. I had to take the offensive. But to where?

Had I been my father, I would have crawled toward the cluster of old monuments beneath the two sprawling oak trees. Compared to the rest of the cemetery, it was like midtown Manhattan, towering granite everywhere, lots of little places to get lost. On hands and knees, keeping low to the ground, I headed in that direction, one monument at a time.

Matthew's heart nearly stopped. He hadn't budged from his hiding spot, hadn't made a sound. Lying in the darkness with hands and feet bound, he felt invisible and vulnerable at the same time. He knew it was only a matter of moments before Joaquín would spot him.

He knew, because he could see Joaquín.

Joaquín was kneeling behind the dirt pile, the

lower half of his body hidden in the half-dug grave. His pistol at the ready, he raised his head just high enough to see over the tops of the gravestones, searching for the enemy.

It would have been an easy shot for Matthew, a steady target at just fifteen meters. The kill shot would have been to the side of Joaquín's head, as Matthew was perpendicular to him on the same row of graves. If only his hands were free, if only he'd had a gun, a knife—anything. So many times he'd thought of giving Joaquín exactly what he'd deserved for the murder of his friends on the boat in Cartagena, for the gang rape of Nisho up in the mountains, for countless other atrocities that he and his buddies had bragged about. Matthew had no regrets for having killed *Cerdo*; it sickened him to think that Joaquín might walk free, a wealthy man.

Joaquín looked in his direction, looked away, and then did a double take. Their eyes met in the darkness. Matthew had been spotted.

Neither man blinked, neither looked away. Matthew refused to cower to his executioner.

Joaquín smiled slightly, then raised his pistol and aimed between the eyes.

I was just a few meters from the forest of monuments when I heard Alex shout from somewhere in the darkness.

"Joaquín, take it!"

The knapsack sailed through the air and landed with a thud. A volley of gunshots erupted, both Joaquín and his accomplice reacting with pointless fire at the sack full of money. It was exactly what

Alex had intended, I presumed, and she'd startled Joaquín into revealing his position. Alex and I fired repeatedly in the direction of the half-dug grave, me from my position at the forest of monuments and Alex from farther away, near the statue of the Blessed Virgin.

Return fire ripped through the night, mostly in my direction, as I was the closer threat, just a few meters away from them. I scampered into the maze of taller monuments for better cover, a trail of bullets rattling off the stones with the beat of a jackhammer. I rolled several times to avoid the spray of gunfire, collided with a large stone pedestal, then froze at the sight of the body two graves away.

Dad!

I crawled as fast as I could to his side. He was facedown in the dirt but raised his head at my touch.

"It's me!" I said in an excited whisper. I yanked the gag from his mouth. "Are you hit?"

"No, no. They're so coked up, they shoot worse than you do."

I hoped that someday we'd laugh at that. "Thanks a lot."

"Untie me."

I unknotted the ropes at his feet, but his hands were in cuffs, which would have to wait.

"There's two of them," he said. "Who's with you?"

"Just the priest and Alex."

"Who's this Alex?"

I thought for a second about all the things she'd just said. "Damned if I know."

We ducked at the explosion of gunfire, but it wasn't

coming our way. They were shooting in the opposite direction at Alex.

"She must be making a move," I said. "If I attack from this flank, we might take them. Stay here."

He nearly tripped me in his zeal to keep me down. "What do you think you're doing?"

I looked him in the eye, hoping that he wouldn't take it the wrong way. But it was something that I'd wanted to say for fifteen years, since that day on the fishing boat that had driven us apart.

"Acting like my father's son," I said.

"You don't have to do this."

"If I don't, neither one of us is getting out alive."

He didn't argue, and there wasn't time for it anyway. Another burst of gunfire erupted on the far side. I glanced up and saw Alex running from the statue of the Blessed Virgin to another monument. She was definitely on the offensive, and she was definitely outgunned.

"This is it," I said, then sprinted forward, zigzagging from monument to monument.

I moved in short bursts to avoid getting hit, but I didn't fire a shot, as the exchange was all in Alex's direction. The noise was deafening, one shot after another without interruption. Alex had come on so strong that both kidnappers had turned their weapons on her. I was just ten meters away, approaching from the side, when Joaquín's sidekick took a bullet from Alex to the forehead. His head snapped back as he tumbled to the ground, his gun silenced.

Joaquín kept firing his pistol, stopping only briefly to reach for his slain friend's AK-47.

"Freeze!" I shouted. I had him from behind.

"*¡Manos arriba!*" shouted Alex. She had him from the side.

He raised his arms, still on his knees behind the pile of earth from the half-dug grave.

"Stand up!" I shouted.

He rose as commanded. The pistol was still in his hand.

"Turn around slowly and drop the gun."

He turned to face me but kept his weapon.

"Drop the gun!"

It was pointed in the air, but he wouldn't let go.

"Drop it right now, or I'll shoot!"

"How many men have you killed before, *yanqui*?" He was clearly mocking me, reminding me that the dead guerrilla at his feet was Alex's work, not mine.

"You'd be a good start," I said.

His hand moved in a blur as he fired off what seemed to be a wild shot. I squeezed the trigger again and again, firing off as many shots as possible. His body jerked with each hit as he fell, landing in a heap in the open grave.

I took a half step forward, close enough to confirm that he looked very dead. The body was twisted, the limbs angled in every direction, like a mangled spider. I'd hit him at least three times, twice in the chest and once in the face. I moved closer and checked for a pulse.

"He's gone," I said, loud enough for my father to hear.

I turned away from the grisly sight. As I rose, out of the corner of my eye I saw Alex stagger and fall to the ground.

"Alex!"

She didn't answer. I ran to her, weaving between monuments, jumping over the last one to find her lying on her side between two gravestones. She was shivering as I rolled her onto her back. Blood had soaked through her sweater at the rib cage, just below the heart. Joaquín's last shot had hit its mark.

"My God, you need an ambulance."

"Don't bother. Nobody survives this. I got what I deserved."

I just shook my head. "So it's true? You killed Jaime."

"I never thought it would get this crazy."

"Damn you. I trusted you. I believed in you."

A trickle of blood oozed from the corner of her mouth, her voice barely a whisper. "Funny, I thought they'd hold some rich guy for a week or two, get the insurance money, and let him go. That was the deal. Get Joaquín a nice chunk of money, and he'd leave me and my family alone forever."

"I can't believe you'd do that."

"Live in fear for fifteen years. You'd be surprised at what you'll do."

"I'd never sell out another human being."

She grimaced from the pain and took my hand. I pulled back, but she squeezed harder and wouldn't let me go. "Please don't hate me."

I was trembling, still shocked. "I just wish this weren't true."

"Then let's just leave it that I was . . . a friend."

She looked at me and tried to smile, the life draining from those dark, mysterious eyes. She started to say something more, but it passed. Her body went limp in my arms. I held her for a moment, my emotions running the gamut. I lowered her head to the ground, then looked up and saw my father standing over us.

"Was she a friend of yours?" he asked sadly.

The question made me think back to the anonymous note that had led me to Jaime's door, the way it had been signed, and the way Alex had just used the same words to say good-bye.

"In a weird way, yes. I guess she was 'A Friend.'"

I rose and embraced my father so tightly that our bodies shook. He was sobbing cathartically into my shoulder as I opened my eyes for one last look at Alex, her beautiful face, the sad expression, the troubled life. If she hadn't told me herself, I would never have believed a word of it.

From her lips it all made perfect, horrible sense.

"Let's go home," my father whispered.

"Yes," I said with a lump in my throat. "Let's."

Epilogue

•

There were no empty seats at our Thanksgiving dinner table. Lindsey, my sister, was home for the first time in two years. Grandma was with us, doing as well as could be expected. My mother was smiling again, finally exuding the fabled glow that kicked in around the fifth month of pregnancy. In less than two weeks Dad was already looking better and slowly gaining some needed weight. The mountain of mashed potatoes and dressing on his plate would surely help the cause.

"Do we have any sushi?" asked Lindsey.

"It's Thanksgiving, dear," my mother said reprovingly.

She rolled her eyes and put a sliver of turkey on her plate. I just smiled to myself. For all the family had been through, thankfully we hadn't changed completely.

Naturally, some things would never be the same. My days at Cool Cash were over. That was just as well, since the Miami office surely wouldn't survive the firestorm anyway. Before his murder, Jaime

Ochoa had given a sealed letter to his mother with instructions to hand it over to the state's attorney if anything untoward should happen to him. It spelled out the entire scheme. Maggie Johans was named prominently in the cover-up, and she'd spent the last two weeks trying to save her own criminal skin by insisting that she'd acted on the advice of Duncan Fitz. From what I'd read in the newspapers, it wouldn't be long before they both came crashing down, taking a huge chunk of the firm's pristine reputation with them.

The saddest part of Jaime's letter was what he'd written about Alex, detailing the way she'd linked his stolen information about the insurance policy to the kidnappers who capitalized on it. I imagined she'd regretted it from the beginning, which was why she'd stayed on to help negotiate Joaquín down even after the insurance company had fired her and denied my father's claim. A bigger part of me, however, felt only anger, betrayal—and increasing confusion over that speech she'd delivered before dying. I wondered if she'd *really* believed that serving up an American would buy her own family a lifetime of safety from Joaquín and his band of killers. Or had she made the whole thing up, one last deception? The more I thought about it, the more it seemed that even if her motive hadn't been greed, perhaps she and Jaime both had gotten what they'd deserved. My sense that justice had been done only intensified when I learned that a certain Japanese couple, Nisho and her husband, were also K&R policyholders with Quality Insurance Company. Fortunately, the scam was uncovered before any other names were sold to kidnappers. From what my father had told me, I was certain that when Nisho was finally released, it would take a lot more than a million and a half dollars to settle her claims against Quality Insurance.

As for my own legal woes, Jaime's letter was a godsend. His own written words had taken me off the list of murder suspects, as did the forensic evidence. Before its throat was slit, Jaime's dog had clawed the skin of the real murderer, and the DNA test of the scrapings from under the nails didn't match me. They matched Alex. That, plus the sworn affidavit of the Colombian priest who had overheard Alex's confession, pretty much guaranteed that my next role would be not as a defendant in a murder trial but as a grand jury witness in the imminent criminal prosecution against Quality Insurance Company and the lawyers who'd orchestrated the cover-up. It was one more thing to be thankful for on this holiday.

"Everything's delicious, honey," my father said.

"Best ever," I added.

My father smiled at me as he reached for another slice of my mother's famous cornbread. "Nick, I was thinking about taking the Bertram out tomorrow. Sailfish are running. It's catch and release, pure sport."

"Who's going?"

"Just me, so far. I was hoping you might want to come along."

It might have been a small thing in other families, but with our past this was huge. "I'd like that a lot."

"Good. Set your alarm for four-fifteen."

I coughed on my ice water. Lindsey snickered and said, "Be careful what you wish for."

The phone rang, and my mother dropped the gravy ladle. The kidnapping was over, but some of the reflexes remained. The ringing continued, two, three times. With my mother's reaction, no one moved. It was strangely cathartic, allowing the phone to beckon until it stopped, no compelling need to answer it.

Dad broke the silence. "This seems like a good opportunity to settle some family business. Your mother and I have been talking about what to do with the money."

He meant the million and a half, of course. Though technically it was supposed to have been used for payment of his ransom, it was ours now, the proceeds of my lump-sum settlement with Quality Insurance. My father could do with it as he wished.

"After Nick gets back his out-of-pocket losses, I want to buy out Guillermo and take over the business myself. The way the company's been losing money, it shouldn't take much. I'm sure I can turn it around with him out of my hair."

I nodded. Even though the drug allegations appeared to have been manufactured by Guillermo's ex-wife, Dad was still better off without him. "You'd do well to distance yourself from him anyway," I said.

"I want Grandma to get the best care available. And of course we'd like to set something aside for our three children—the two of you and your future little brother or sister," he added, smiling as he laid his hand on my mother's belly.

"Sounds good to me," said Lindsey.

His expression turned more serious. "Beyond that, there are a couple people outside the family I want to take care of. Hector's widow, for one. She lost a husband and a son in that shoot-out in Cartagena."

"That's the right thing to do," I said.

"And there's Jenna. She put a lot of time into this for no pay."

"She definitely came through when no one else would," I said.

"I thought fifty thousand would be fair."

I totally agreed with him, but I was slightly uncomfortable with the concept, or at least the timing. "You think it'll look like I'm trying to buy her back?"

"It might," said Lindsey. "Especially now."

"What do you mean?"

She seemed reluctant to speak up, not quite looking me in the eye. "I wasn't going to say anything on the holiday, but my jogging route took me past Jenna's place this morning. There's a 'Sold' sign out on the front lawn."

It hit me hard, though I tried not to show it, hoping to keep our Thanksgiving upbeat. The way I felt about Jenna, however, was no secret in our house.

Lindsey lowered her eyes, as did my mother.

"I'm sorry, Nick," my father said.

"Me too," I said as I poked at my cranberry sauce.

I went to see Jenna that night. Sure enough, dangling from the real estate agency's sign in her front yard was another little sign that said SOLD.

Jenna had lain low since my father's return, insisting that it was best for the family to heal on its own for a while. I'd felt as if there were things left unsaid. Seeing the "Sold" sign with my own eyes had only reinforced the feeling. I walked up the old Chicago brick walkway and knocked on the front door. Her car was in the driveway, so I knew she was home.

The door opened, and she smiled faintly. "Hi."

I suddenly didn't know what to say. "Wasn't sure you'd be in town."

"This year the family was doing Thanksgiving with my brother and his kids in Seattle. I made an excuse. Just didn't feel like flying across the country."

"Can I come in?"

"Sure."

I stepped inside, closed the door behind me, and followed her into the living room. It seemed strange the way our relationship had changed, yet everything in this room had remained exactly the way I remembered it. Even the big cushy reading chair was in the same place, covering that ugly brown paint stain on the old Persian rug we'd purchased at an antique store for next to nothing. The chair was a recliner, but it had been out of commission ever since that night I was studying for the bar exam, when Jenna had climbed in with me, tossed my outlines aside, and nearly set the thing on fire, figuratively speaking.

"Have a seat," she said.

I started toward the memory chair, then thought better of it and took a seat on the couch.

"Want a soda? Beer?"

"No, thanks. I just wanted to talk."

She took a seat on the ottoman, on the other side of the cocktail table. "How's your job hunting coming?"

"I've narrowed it down to two medium-sized firms in the Gables. Both good groups of people. And they all seem to have a life outside the law firm. Imagine that, huh?"

"That would be a good move for you."

I nodded. "I saw the 'Sold' sign out front."

She blinked and said, "Oh, that."

"Yeah, that."

"The deal's not even inked yet, and my agent put that out. She's fed up with me. Said that if I kill the deal this time, she's quitting."

"Kill the deal?"

"This is actually the third full-price offer I've received this month. I've managed to wiggle out each time."

"Sounds like you're not really sure about this move," I said, hopeful.

She looked away, then back. "I'm all over the map, literally. When I think about the low times, I feel like packing. Then I'll find something while I'm going through my stuff. A piece of jewelry or one of those mushy cards you used to write me in your own words. I'm totally confused."

My throat tightened. I had plenty to tell her, but I didn't want to say the wrong thing. "I don't want you to go."

"Is that what you came here to tell me?"

"That, and a lot of things."

"Like what?"

"I—I didn't prepare a speech. I was kind of hoping you'd get all *Jerry Maguire* on me and tell me I had you at hello."

That got a smile, then a little laughter. We'd seen

the movie a few years earlier on one of our first dates, and she'd clearly remembered it as well as I had. "Every now and then, you get me right in the funny bone, you know that?"

Her smile faded, and our eyes met. "What are you thinking?" she asked.

"That I always want to make you laugh. That I wish you'd give us a second chance. That if you insist on trying to sell this place, I'm going to put a full-page ad in the paper saying it's haunted."

"Funny. That's exactly what I told the last buyer to get myself out of the deal."

"What do you say we go out and talk about this over a couple of drinks?"

"What do you have in mind?"

"Anything but a Dark 'n' Stormy."

"Mojitos?"

"Now you're talking."

She grabbed her sweater, and we started for the door. "I know a new place over on South Beach. Best Mojito you ever had," she said.

"Really?"

"I guarantee it."

She locked the front door, and we walked toward my Jeep. "That wouldn't be a lifetime guarantee, would it?" I asked.

She climbed into her seat, shooting me a playful look. "One step at a time, bozo."

"Sure," I said as I turned the ignition. "Sounds good to me. Really good."

Acknowledgments

•

I'm grateful to so many people who contributed to this novel.

My editor, Carolyn Marino, and my agents, Richard and Artie Pine, helped to shape a timely story, and from my vantage point, worked miracles to get it to press in timely fashion. Erica Johanson added keen editorial insights. As always, thanks to my team of readers who turned the manuscript around in short order: Terri Gavulic, Eleanor Rayner, and Carlos Sires.

I owe a huge thanks to Cauley Dennis for a crash course on the Latin American fishing industry and a personally guided tour of Nicaragua. It didn't all make it into the book, but it's a trip I'll never forget. Also in Nicaragua, *muchas gracias* to Alfonso and Gustavo.

That other world of kidnapping negotiators and K&R insurance was brought to life by Richard Fenning and Armando Lara at Control Risks Group. Janet Crist shared her past experiences at the U.S. embassy in Bogotá. Information from the *Fundación*

País Libre in Bogotá was invaluable to my understanding of the scope of the kidnapping crisis in Colombia. (In the time it would take to read this novel
in one sitting, four more people will be kidnapped
for ransom in Colombia.) Juan Camilo Nariño at the
*Centro de Información Sobre el Desarrollo de la Demo-
cracia en Colombia (CIDEC)* in Bogotá was particularly accommodating.

Many others wish to remain anonymous, some of
whom have suffered firsthand through the horror of
kidnapping in Colombia—some of them more than
once. I can't thank you enough.

Finally, to Tiffany, I love you and couldn't have
done it without you. Thanks especially for braving a
Miami hurricane and keeping the house dry while
Cauley and I were off "doing research" in Nicaragua.
It *really was* a research trip.

Turn the page for an excerpt from

James Grippando's

NEED YOU NOW

It was too good to be true: A Wall Street whiz whose performance was the statistical equivalent of a baseball player with a career batting average of .962. For years, critics had voiced their skepticism. Whistleblowers had laid out dozens of red flags for the Securities Exchange Commission. Yet no one would listen. The entire law-enforcement arm of the U.S. government—tireless teams of federal agents and prosecutors who had dedicated their careers to fighting sophisticated financial crimes—was just a bunch of incompetent, bumbling fools who couldn't spot a massive Ponzi scheme that had unfolded right under their regulatory nose for more than a decade. It was the Wall Street version of the Keystone cops.

Or so the world was led to believe.

I sure bought into it, hook, line, and sinker. Perhaps a financial advisor—even a relative newbie in his twenties—should have been more skeptical.

I worked in private wealth management at the midtown Manhattan office of the International Bank of Switzerland—that's "BOS," mind you, as the German-speaking founders of this century-old juggernaut were quick to appreciate the unfortunate English-language connotation of bankers with business cards that read "I.B.S." Over the decades, bright minds and bank secrecy had swelled the bank's total invested assets to two trillion dollars. I was the junior member on a team of high-net-worth specialists that managed a nine-figure piece of that pie. Clients counted on us to know fraud from legit. I never steered a dime of their money toward Cushman, but it wasn't because I *knew* anything. My reaction to Cushman's scheme was like everyone else's. I was stunned as the estimated losses climbed ever higher—thirty-billion, forty-billion, sixty-billion dollars. I felt sorry for the innocent victims. I wondered if I knew any of them. I wondered who else was a crook. I joined in speculation around the water cooler as to where in the world all that money had gone. And then I went home at night, switched on cable news, and nodded off as politicians debated whether Wall Street needed tighter regulation. I was convinced that nothing would really change—until somebody did something from the inside. So I did something. Something a little crazy. I'm still not sure I learned the truth. But I did learn something *about* the truth, especially where unimaginable sums of money were involved. The truth can get you killed. Or worse.

The epiphany came right after my return from Singapore.

I'd been away from New York longer than planned—months longer. Asia was a BOS stronghold, even stronger than Europe. Our weakness was in the

United States, where the bank was generally regarded as a mere shadow of itself. "Uncertainty" had been the market watchword before my gig in Singapore. A new management team was about to change all that, if the BOS press releases were to be believed. Wall Street wasn't exactly whistling with optimism on the day of my return, but the fact that the bank's managing director wanted to meet with me—a junior financial advisor—put a spring in my step. I rode the elevator to the executive suite, breezed into a lobby that showcased museum-quality art—*Is that a Van Gogh?*—and announced my arrival to the receptionist.

"I'm here for a meeting with Ms. Decker," I said.

The young woman at the desk smiled pleasantly. "And you are?"

"Patrick Lloyd. I'm an FA here in New York."

"Oh, my. You're in the wrong place. The meeting for financial advisors is in the Paradeplatz conference room."

Paradeplatz was one of Switzerland's famous squares, near the end of the Bahnhofstrasse and Lake Zurich, home to BOS headquarters. BOS/America was filled with such reminders of who we answered to.

"But the message said to meet Ms. Decker in her—"

"You need to hurry," she said. "You don't want to be late."

Apparently, my one-on-one meeting with the managing director was a group session. The message from Decker's assistant had made it sound more personal, and I had spent half the night pondering what it could be about. A promotion? The recognition of "rising stars" in the new world of BOS/America wealth management? It had been silly to let my imagination run wild. I picked my ego up off the carpet and rode the elevator down to the seventeenth floor.

It was straight up on ten o'clock, and the last of the latecomers were filing into the Paradeplatz conference room at the end of the hall. I caught up as the carved mahogany doors were closing. It was packed inside. The room could comfortably seat about fifty, but the headcount was easily double that number. The meeting was about to begin, and all chatter had ceased—which meant that the door closed with an intrusive thud behind me. Like a reflex, heads turned toward me, the only guy still looking for a seat.

A distinct uneasiness gripped me as my gaze swept the room. It was my first time in the Paradeplatz, and under different circumstances I might have been taken with the rich maroon carpeting and burnished walnut paneling. Adorning the longest mahogany table I'd ever seen was the emblazoned gold insignia of BOS: three golden cherubs that symbolized the bank's core principles of discretion, security, and confidentiality. What I noticed most, however, was all the gray hair around that table. A second row of chairs lined the walls, like the back benches of Parliament—less gray hair, but plenty of salt and pepper. The financial advisors in this room were not like me. These were senior advisors, some from New York, and others I recognized only from press coverage of their accomplishments.

"Patrick?"

The voice was little more than a whisper, but I recognized the gravel in my team leader's delivery. Jay Sussman was one of the salt-and-pepper advisors in the second row. I skulked my way over, like a theatergoer arriving halfway through the first act, and took the empty chair beside him.

"What are you doing here?" he asked under his breath.

A door opened on the opposite side of the conference room. In walked the managing director of BOS/America, Angela Decker, with whom I was scheduled to meet. Or so I'd thought. With her—and my quick double take confirmed it—was the chief executive of the International Bank of Switzerland, Gerhardt Klaus.

"Is this the meeting for FAs?" I asked through my teeth.

"Yeah, the *top one-hundred-producing* FAs."

BOS had over eight-thousand financial advisors in the United States. My invitation from Decker's office had obviously come by mistake. "Should I leave?"

"Stay," he said, smiling with his eyes. "Watching you squirm will keep me awake."

The chief executive walked to the head of the table and remained standing as the managing director took a seat at his side. I'd never met Klaus, of course, but it was well known that he never allowed anyone to introduce him at internal bank gatherings. A vice president had sucked up so badly in Zurich last year that Klaus had forever banned all "*welkommen*" speeches.

"*Guten morgen*," he said. "And thank you for

coming, especially those of you who are visiting from out of town."

Klaus had a booming voice that required no microphone. Disciplined living and cross-country skiing kept him fit and looking younger than his years. He'd been born into a family of Zurich bankers at the height of the Second World War, at a time when his country couldn't decide which side it was on. It has been said that certain Swiss banks had suffered no such indecision.

"Each of you was invited to this meeting because we wanted you to be the first to hear a major announcement, one that is vital to the future of the worldwide operations of BOS. Without further ado, I'm pleased to tell you that a final settlement agreement has been reached between the International Bank of Switzerland and the U.S. Department of Justice."

A chorus of murmurs coursed the room like the breeze through a wheat field, followed by sparse and nervous applause. Then silence.

"As you all know," Klaus continued, "both the Swiss government and BOS officials have been engaged in discussions for several months with U.S. authorities. These discussions . . ."

Discussions. Talk about a fudge word. Justice had BOS by the short hairs. The same excesses and mismanagement that had rocked the largest Wall Street investment banks had forced BOS to write down fifty-billion dollars in subprime losses in the fall of 2008. The market was in freefall, the world economy was in shambles, and investors from New York to Hong Kong were in a state of panic. The oldest and largest Swiss bank was on the verge of collapse when the government had come to the rescue with a bail out. At that precise moment, the Justice Department swooped in. With the Treasury Secretary and the New York Fed warning that the collapse of institutions "too big to fail" could unleash another Great Depression, someone at Justice had the presence of mind—nay, the stroke of genius—to realize that the time was ripe to make Swiss cheese of the secret Swiss banks. The DOJ officially demanded the names of "serious tax evaders." When BOS balked, they arrested a top financial advisor who was silly enough to state publicly that he'd smuggled a diamond in a tube of toothpaste for a client. When BOS stalled again, they indicted the bank's head of private wealth management. They threatened to indict the chairman, himself. They demanded a "collateral consequences" report from BOS lawyers, which is typically the final step before the indictment of an entire company. Finally, BOS—still in a weakened state, despite the multi-billion-dollar bail out—blinked. It turned over the names of 280 of the most serious tax avoiders. *Poof.* A century of Swiss bank secrecy went up in smoke, just like that. Justice had been hammering away for more names ever since.

Apparently not everyone who worked for the U.S. government was a dumbass. Yet, Abe Cushman had gone unnoticed by law enforcement. Those Ponzi schemes sure are hard to sniff out, especially the ones that last for only two decades and involve a measly sixty-billion dollars.

Hmmm.

"As part of this settlement," the chief executive continued, "we have agreed to release the names of four thousand additional clients over the coming year."

"*Four thousand?*" my team leader whispered. "This is *good* news?"

I leaned closer. "Actually, the good news is that the bank is offering a free box of *Depend* to each of our clients."

My boss snorted with laughter, a reflex. The chief executive stopped, clearly annoyed. His steely-blue-eyed glare silenced the room—and it nearly sent me running for my own box of adult diapers.

Klaus leaned forward, his palms resting on the polished wood tabletop as he spoke. "I want to underscore that the only names on this list are clients of our cross-border business. This settlement agreement respects the fact that the cross-border business of BOS consists only of wealth management services offered to American residents outside the United States, that it operates entirely out of Switzerland, and that it is completely separate from the BOS/America wealth management business. In other words, this settlement affects less than one percent of the bank's total invested assets. To put an even finer point on it, the settlement does not affect our U.S.-based private wealth management clients."

Yet, I wanted to say.

"Which brings me to even more important news," said Klaus, "and to the real purpose of this meeting. With the DOJ settlement behind us, it's time to look forward. Ladies and gentlemen, I am pleased to introduce the new head of private wealth management for BOS/America, a man who truly needs no introduction, Joe McGriff."

My supervisor and I exchanged glances. His expression matched my unspoken sentiment: *Joe McGriff? You must be joking.*

Advisors and their clients had been walking away from BOS since the fifty-billion-dollar write down of subprime losses. The recent threat of a criminal indictment over bank secrecy had pushed the total loss of assets for the year to over two-hundred billion Swiss francs. BOS was on the fast track to No. 2—not in the world, but in *Switzerland*. The much-anticipated announcement of a new head of private wealth for the U.S. was supposed to restore faith and calm everyone's concerns. The chosen one, however, was from Saxton Silvers.

McGriff entered the room, the picture of Wall Street confidence as a photographer captured him and the chief executive smiling and shaking hands.

It was Bear Stearns, Lehman Brothers, and Saxton Silvers—in that order—on the list of Wall Street investment banks that had gone the way of the T. Rex and the Dodo bird, swept away by the financial tsunami of subprime lending and mortgage-backed securities. McGriff had sewn the seeds of disaster at Saxton Silvers before accepting a presidential appointment as Deputy Secretary of the Treasury, the department's number two post. Government service required him to liquidate his holdings, which meant that he had cashed out at the height of the market. He took twenty-eight million dollars out of Wall Street, and a year later he orchestrated a government bail out that pumped billions of taxpayer dollars back into the disaster that he and others like him had created. It still wasn't clear what indictments might come out of the Saxton Silvers collapse. But there he stood, handpicked by the top executive in the world of bank secrecy: Joe McGriff, our new leader, the power-drunk pilot who had put Wall Street on autopilot, headed straight for the side of a mountain, only to watch the crash from Treasury's ivory tower.

"Gee, I feel better already," my boss muttered.

"Me too," I said, joining in the lukewarm applause.

I left the conference room quickly, as soon as the meeting broke, before anyone could ask what the heck I was doing there.

My palms were sweating as I hurried down the hall to the elevator, but I tried to keep things in perspective. I wasn't the first junior advisor in BOS history to end up in the wrong place at the wrong time. Any number of my predecessors had surely crashed a meeting of top producers. In the hallowed Paradeplatz conference room. With the Chief Executive from Zurich, the managing director of U.S. operations, and the new head of private wealth management in attendance.

Good God, what was I thinking?

The chrome elevator doors parted, and a man wearing a black suit was inside. I entered and pressed a button, but the man froze the control panel with the turn of his passkey.

"Patrick Lloyd?" he said.

"Yes."

He looked like a secret service agent, and my impression wasn't far from the mark. "BOS Corporate Security," he said as he punched the button for the executive suite. "I need you to come with me."

My jaw dropped. I expected some good-natured ribbing from colleagues about the mix up, perhaps even a brief reprimand from a divisional manager. But calling in security was over the top.

"It was a mistake," I started to say, but he wasn't interested. We rode up to the executive suite, and he escorted me into the lobby. I was hoping the receptionist would recount our earlier conversation and clear things up, but she was away from her desk. My escort from corporate security directed me to a leather couch by the window, and he sat in the armchair facing me, as if keeping guard. The expression on his face was deadpan even by Swiss banking standards. Had I still been in Singapore, I would have thought I was in line for a public caning.

I surveyed the lobby. A Jasper Johns original oil painting hung on the wall opposite the Van Gogh. Fresh-cut flowers were placed tastefully around the room in crystal vases. A table by the window displayed a small vase so priceless that there was actually a plaque to identify it as being from the Ming Dynasty. A row of Swiss clocks on the wall caught my attention, each set to the time zone of a different trading market. New York. London. Frankfurt. Tokyo. Hong Kong. Singapore.

Singapore. I thought of Lilly. She worked with BOS/Asia. Our relationship had been purely business at first, but we ended up dating for six months. Arguably the best six months of my life.

I looked away, then checked the clock again, and a song popped into my head. In Singapore, it was a quarter after one, and I had a sudden vision of Lilly, all alone, and listening to that mega-hit by Lady Antebellum that seemed to be playing nonstop on the radio since our break up.

I'm a little drunk and I need you now.

Yeah, right.

It was four weeks, exactly, since Lilly had texted me and said that I should meet her for a walk on Changi Beach, that she had something important to say to me, and that it couldn't wait. Any dolt could have seen what was coming, but I was so smitten that I'd actually shown up with a blanket and a bottle of wine. This was going to be one of those "talks" that was really just a speech with a few permissible interruptions. It was so over-rehearsed that Lilly had lost all sense that it would hit me like a brick between the eyes. The way she looked on that day would never leave my memory—the sad smile, her chestnut hair blowing in the gentle breeze, those big eyes that sparkled even in the most dismal of circumstances. I was speechless, just like the first time I'd ever laid eyes on her, only this time for far less enchanting reasons. The silence was insufferable once she'd finished, both of us waiting for me to move my lips and say something. Nothing came, and then it started to rain. At least I'd thought it was raining. I felt a drop on my head, and Lilly promptly lost it right before my eyes. She was embarrassed to be laughing, laughing not at me but at the absurdity of the situation, but laughing nonetheless. It was then that I heard the shrill screech in the sky, saw the

winged culprit swooping down from above the coconut palms to mock me. A seagull had shit squarely
on my head.

This I took as an omen. I put in for an immediate
transfer back to New York, and Lilly and I said
goodbye for life.

Angela Decker's assistant entered the waiting
area. "Ms. Decker will see you now."

Great. More shit to fall from the sky.

I still couldn't believe the big deal this had become. The assistant showed me into the office, and
it wasn't just the managing director inside. Joe Mc-
Griff, who'd been head of private wealth management for all of one hour, was with her. So was the
general counsel. Executives at this level traveled like
international diplomats, and it was rare indeed for
three of them to actually be in New York at the
same time. For the holy trinity of BOS/America to
be in a meeting with a junior FA was preposterous.

"There is a perfectly benign explanation for what
happened," I said.

"Sit down, Mr. Lloyd," said Decker.

The managing director returned to the leather
armchair between McGriff and the general counsel, neither of whom rose to greet me. This had the
feel of an inquisition, not a meeting. I took the hot
seat opposite them.

"This has nothing to do with this morning's meeting in the Paradeplatz," said Decker. "I told my assistant that I wanted to see you this morning, and
she put you on the list of FA's for the ten o'clock
meeting. An honest mistake on her part."

I breathed a sigh of relief, but it didn't last. The

purpose of *this* meeting clearly wasn't to show me the BOS secret handshake.

"Is there some kind of trouble?" I asked.

The general counsel spoke. "As I'm sure you're aware, Lilly Scanlon's employment at BOS/Singapore has been terminated."

I caught my breath. "No, I was not aware of that. When did that happen?"

"Ten days ago."

"I haven't spoken to Lilly in—I don't know, exactly. Longer than ten days. Can you tell me what happened?"

"To the extent that it pertains to you, yes. Broadly speaking, it has to do with the Abe Cushman Ponzi scheme."

"Cushman?" I said. "I can't believe Lilly would have anything to do with that. I can assure you that I didn't."

McGriff took over. "Mr. Lloyd, why did you go to Singapore?"

His body language made the question anything but innocuous. I tried not to become defensive.

"It seemed like a good career move," I said. "I saw the writing on the wall for Swiss banks. It's no secret that the BOS strategy is to shift to super-high net worth and Asia."

"Why not Hong Kong or Tokyo?" asked McGriff.

I could have recounted my decision-making process; instead, I took the offensive. "Is that what this is about? You think my transfer to BOS/Singapore has something to do with Cushman?"

McGriff ignored my question. "How well did you know Lilly Scanlon?"

"I didn't know her at all before leaving New York. We met in the Singapore office. She was an FA, just like me."

"This is my first official day," said McGriff, "but I've been fully briefed. Don't waste our time trying to pretend that your relationship was purely professional."

Obviously they already knew the answers to most of the questions on their list. This was a test of my truthfulness, not a search for information—so far, at least.

"We dated," I said. "It ended before I left. I've had zero contact since."

"Tell us about her," said McGriff.

I didn't know how to respond. "What do you want to know?"

"We're asking the questions here," said the general counsel.

"I'm just trying to get some color."

"Color" was synonymous with "background" in the BOS lexicon—"*call Goldman for color on the Tesla Motors IPO*"—but from the look on McGriff's face, the operative color here was red. His temper was legendary.

"Listen to me, asshole," McGriff said.

"Joe, please," said the general counsel.

"I'm sorry, but this needs to be said. I spent the last twenty-six years of my career in one of two places—in Washington in public service or on Wall Street with Saxton Silvers. It pained me to watch that firm go down. I've seen the kind of arrogance that can breed disaster for a bank, and it starts in puppies like you. I'm not going to put up with it. Are we clear on that?"

"Crystal."

"I could have gone anywhere when I decided to leave Treasury. I chose BOS/America. And the first thing on my plate is an internal investigation into a junior FA's possible involvement—*criminal* involvement—with Abe Cushman. If you haven't figured it out yet, let me spell it out for you: I intend to put out this fire immediately. I will not allow it to snowball and sidetrack my plans to make BOS number one in private wealth management. Again, are we clear?"

"All I can say is that I had absolutely nothing to do with Cushman."

"Did you and Ms. Scanlon ever talk about Gerry Collins?" McGriff asked.

Of course I knew the name, especially in the context of Abe Cushman. Collins' gruesome murder had been front-page news everywhere from the *Wall Street Journal* to *People* magazine.

"Talk about him in what way?" I asked.

"Don't be cute," said McGriff.

"I'm trying to understand your question. Are you asking me if we talked about him as a person in the news?"

"No, as one of Ms. Scanlon's biggest clients."

It was the bomb, and all three executives measured my reaction when it dropped. I tried not to squirm, but my voice tightened. "Lilly never told me about that."

"You worked in the same office and slept in the same bed, but she never mentioned Gerry Collins?"

Asking how he knew I'd occasionally spent the night at Lilly's wasn't going to get me anywhere. "If you're telling me that Lilly had a business relationship with one of Cushman's front men, that never came up. Never."

McGriff glanced toward the general counsel. Then his gaze returned to me. "I'd like to believe you, Mr. Lloyd."

"Did you ask Lilly? I'm sure she would tell you the same thing."

"Ms. Scanlon was fired after she was caught redhanded trying to access confidential information about BOS numbered accounts. She refused to discuss it. I suggest you start talking, unless you'd like to join her in the ranks of the unemployed."

I couldn't believe what I was hearing about Lilly, but if it was true, she was in serious trouble. "I have nothing to hide."

"Good," he said. "Tell us about Ms. Scanlon."

Again, I wasn't sure how to respond. "What do you want to know?"

"Everything," said McGriff, his tone deadly serious. "Absolutely everything there is to know about that woman."

NEW YORK TIMES **BESTSELLING AUTHOR**

JAMES GRIPPANDO

MONEY TO BURN

978-0-06-155631-9

Michael Cantella is a rising star on Wall Street when his new wife, Ivy Layton, vanishes on their honeymoon in the Bahamas. Four years later—with a beautiful new wife and his career back on track—Michael discovers his finances have been wiped out. All the money is gone. And there's an e-mail message: *Just as planned. xo xo.*

INTENT TO KILL

978-0-06-162869-6

Ryan James' promising baseball career was derailed before it even got started—when a hit-and-run driver killed his wife, Chelsea, leaving Ryan alone to care for their beautiful little girl. Three years later, on the anniversary of Chelsea's death, Ryan receives a chilling message from an anonymous tipster: *"I know who did it."*

Coming soon in paperback

AFRAID OF THE DARK

The ninth exciting book in the popular Jack Swyteck series
978-0-06-184029-6

JGA 0811

Visit www.AuthorTracker.com for exclusive information on your favorite HarperCollins authors.

Available wherever books are sold or please call 1-800-331-3761 to order.